The Best She
Ever Had

Also by Shelly Ellis

Gibbons Gold Digger series

Can't Stand the Heat
The Player & the Game
Another Woman's Man

Chesterton Scandal series

Best Kept Secrets
Bed of Lies

Published by Dafina Books

The Best She Ever Had

SHELLY ELLIS

Kensington Publishing Corp.
http://www.kensingtonbooks.com

DAFINA BOOKS are published by

Kensington Publishing Corp.
119 West 40th Street
New York, NY 10018

All Kensington Titles, Imprints, and Distributed Lines are available at special quantity discounts for bulk purchases for sales promotions, premiums, fund-raising, and educational or institutional use. Special book excerpts or customized printings can also be created to fit specific needs. For details, write or phone the office of the Kensington special sales manager: Kensington Publishing Corp., 119 West 40th Street, New York, NY 10018, attn: Special Sales Department, Phone: 1-800-221-2647.

Dafina and the Dafina logo Reg. U.S. Pat. & TM Off.

ISBN-13: 978-1-61773-397-0
ISBN-10: 1-61773-397-0
First Kensington Trade Edition: January 2015
First Kensington Mass Market Edition: October 2016

eISBN-13: 978-1-61773-396-3
eISBN-10: 1-61773-396-2

10 9 8 7 6 5 4 3 2 1

Printed in the United States of America

To Rachel Barr:
You were a sassy heroine worthy of your own novel.
I will always remember you. Thank you for loving
and believing in me.

Acknowledgments

After you've written a few novels, it's easy to forget what it was like to be an unpublished writer who was just eager to see your work on the bookstore shelves. As an author, you get lost in the maze of deadlines, of nitpicking over contracts and promotional material. You forget what it was like to receive a rejection from the publisher or agent you had set your heart on, to try to work up the courage to write another book and still believe in your talent even though your ego is bruised and you're feeling a little broken. I still can't believe that I was in that place only three years ago—eagerly checking my email and hoping desperately for someone to say "yes." Now that I've finished my last Gibbons novel—the series that started it all for me—I am still grateful to those who gave me my big chance and to those who stuck by me along the way.

As always, I'd like to thank my husband, Andrew. Your role has definitely evolved in the course of my writing journey. In the beginning you were my cheerleader and the coach who talked me through the sad moments, now you're the guy who makes my writing books possible. If it wasn't for you taking over household tasks and watching our rambunctious little girl, I would never have time to write a letter, let alone a novel! My writing career is definitely a joint collaboration.

Thanks to Mom and Dad who are also part of the Ellis collaboration. They say family members make bad beta readers, but Mom you've been my first pair of critical eyes from the beginning of my writing career, meaning since I was twelve years old. Thanks for your honesty and your love of my work.

Thanks to my editor, Mercedes Fernandez, for your belief in my talent, and to the Kensington family for all that you do.

Thanks to the blerds at Black Girl Nerds and to the founder, Jamie Broadnax. Thanks to my Twitter gal pals in the literary sisterhood who are into the double digits now. I'd need a bulleted list to name you all. You guys offer advice on not only the written word, but also how to find decent hair care products and a good movie. I hope to meet you all in person one day!

Thanks to Mala Bhattacharjee at *RT Book Reviews* (and your alter ego, Suleikha Snyder) for waving the flag for diversity in the writing community and helping our platform in the romance writing community. Thanks to DJ Kimberly Kaye for your continual support and hosting me on the radio at KIX 96 FM.

Thanks to Romance Novels in Color, Romance in Color, and other reviewers for your glowing but honest reviews. Thanks to Black Expressions for selecting my books to sell to your readers.

Thanks to the readers who have signed up for my newsletter and those who took the extra step to tell me they liked my books.

Finally, as always, thanks to the family members and friends who I didn't mention by name but who have supported me and my writing.

Chapter 1

(Unwritten) Rule No. 9 of the Gibbons Family Handbook: *Learn from past mistakes or history is doomed to repeat itself.*

"Well, hel-*lo!*" Cynthia Gibbons uttered slowly. A smile crossed her glossy pink lips.

She spotted him instantly: the six-foot-tall dark Adonis in the dark suit with the iPhone at his ear and a gourmet coffee in his hand. She had been loading grocery bags into her black Lexus SUV when she saw him striding confidently across the shopping center parking lot.

Decades of man-hunting had taught Cynthia to scan potential prey quickly and assess in thirty seconds or less whether they were worthy of the chase. Cynthia noticed that his suit was well tailored and looked fairly expensive. Maybe it was even an Armani, though she couldn't tell for sure from this far away. She also noticed his gold watch and the lack of a wedding ring—though a ring wouldn't have been that much of a deterrent for her. Cynthia didn't care if a man was married or not; if he was, it just meant she had to change her approach, that's all.

She watched as he finished his phone conversation and pulled his car remote from his pocket. She then stood on the balls of her feet to get a better view of him as he walked between a row of cars. She waited to see what car he would unlock. If it was the Honda Civic four spaces away or the Town and Country van next to it, he probably wasn't worth her time. Instead, he unlocked, with two quick beeps, a glistening two-door Porsche roadster.

Bingo, Cynthia thought as she watched him swing open the car door and climb inside.

Cynthia could smell blood in the water, and like a circling shark she went in for the kill. She watched as he drove out of his parking space. Seconds later, she scrambled inside her car, tossed her purse into the passenger seat, and followed him. It didn't take long to maneuver in traffic so that she was in the lead. Now he was on his cell phone again, driving distractedly as he trailed behind her.

"That's right, handsome," Cynthia whispered as she adjusted her rearview mirror and gazed at him. "Almost there."

Cynthia had a plan in mind, but she had to be careful. She didn't want to hurt anyone, cause any serious damage to either of their vehicles, or—heaven forbid—cause a roadway pileup! She drove slowly for several minutes, stealthily glancing in her rearview mirror to make sure he was still behind her. Then when they drew near a stoplight, she slammed on her brakes. His Porsche came to a screeching halt behind her, but not before Cynthia heard the telltale *thump*. He had rear-ended her, which was all part of the plan.

Cynthia fought back a smile, undid two buttons on

her silk blouse, and pulled open her collar. She glanced at her reflection one last time to make sure her cleavage was on full display and her makeup was perfect. She then furrowed her brows and cringed, feigning horror and disbelief. She threw open her car door.

"Oh, my God!" she cried, rushing to her rear bumper. Horns blared behind them as the light turned green again. "What happened?"

The handsome driver rushed out of his Porsche. "I don't know. I was . . . I was on the phone." He gestured to the iPhone in his hand, then tossed it onto his car seat. "I'm so sorry. Are you all right?"

She gazed at him with wide hazel eyes, nodded, and brought a hand to her breasts. "I . . . I think so."

"We should exchange insurance information." He reached for his wallet and flipped it open. He then began to dig through several credit cards. Cynthia inwardly jumped for joy when she noticed a black card in the group. He handed an insurance card to her.

"Derrick Winters?" she said, scanning the name on the paper card.

"Yeah, that's me." He pointed down at the text. "And if you call that number, they should—"

"Derrick," she interrupted, smiling ever so sweetly, "do we *really* have to get insurance companies involved in this?"

"What do you mean?"

"Well, it was an honest accident." She took another step toward him and bit down on her bottom lip. "I'd hate for this to appear on either of our insurance records. I'm willing to not let some stuffy old insurance agent get involved in this . . . if you're willing."

"So you . . . you want to do this under the table?"

She laughed and batted her lashes. "Well, that's an interesting way to put it."

"So you want me to pay for the damage in cash?" he asked, eying her suspiciously.

"Well, it's just a little old dent, isn't it?"

Cynthia swept her blond locks out of her face and leaned down to peer at her bumper. She inwardly moaned. It wasn't exactly a "little old dent." Dark Adonis had left quite a gash on her bumper, depositing a great deal of silver mica glossy paint while he was at it.

"But sacrifices have to be made," Cynthia could hear her mother Yolanda's voice say in her head. "You have to take some risks to land a big fish, honey!"

Cynthia stood upright. "Yes, it's just . . . a . . . a little old bitty thing." She breezily waved her hand. "It shouldn't cost much."

He frowned, still contemplating her offer. After some time, he nodded. "I appreciate you doing this, Mrs.—"

"Miss . . . It's *Miss* Cynthia Gibbons." She handed him back his insurance card. "But you can call me Cynthia."

"Well, I appreciate you doing this, Cynthia." He finally smiled, brightening his handsome face. "Look, why don't we move our cars out of the way of traffic. If you don't mind, I'll give a friend of mine a quick call. He does auto body work for me occasionally."

"*Occasionally?* Do you have these kinds of accidents often, Mr. Winters?" she joked.

He chuckled and shook his head. "Please, call me Derrick, and, no, I just have a few vintage cars that I'm working on. I like to restore them and my friend helps me. It's my little indulgence. I've got a 1958 Chevrolet Corvette and a 1960 Jag XK 150—both set me back a pretty penny. When you're dealing with one-hundred-thousand-dollar cars, you don't trust them to just anybody. My friend does good work."

Expensive vintage cars? Jackpot! Cynthia grinned. Oh, Derrick had *definitely* been worthy of the chase.

"My friend can make a quick drive here and give me an estimate on the damage to your Lexus. Then I can have him take care of it for you. It shouldn't take long."

"Oh, I'm not in a hurry." She glanced at her watch. "I don't have an appointment for another few hours."

"It'll only take forty-five minutes, tops. He isn't far from here."

Cynthia didn't care if Derrick's mechanically inclined friend took until doomsday. The ice cream she had bought at the grocery store that was now sitting in her trunk would just have to melt. She had an excuse to talk to Derrick even longer and even more time to reel him in!

They pulled over to the side of Main Street and stood on the curb together, waiting for his friend to arrive.

It was a slow weekend afternoon in Chesterton, her hometown in northern Virginia. The one-mile stretch of roadway was designed to look like an old-fashioned, small-town Main Street, with scrolled Victorian street lamps and striped awnings over two-story brick storefronts. It was summertime, so the oversized ceramic flowerpots lining the sidewalks were filled with newly bloomed lilies and geraniums. The flowers alternated with each season.

Two doors down was an old favorite in Chesterton, Mimi's Coffee Shop, which was known for its freshly brewed coffee and the cinnamon buns Miss Mimi baked every morning. You knew you were near it because you could smell the delicious aroma wafting out her front door for blocks around. At the end of the block was the bridal shop where Cynthia had purchased her first wedding dress. At the other end of the block was the savings and loan bank, with a clock tower that marked the twelve o'clock hour. Its chime could be heard throughout Chesterton.

Derrick leaned against an old-fashioned mailbox while they talked and laughed for a good half hour. Cynthia could feel she was making headway with him. She was just about to venture the topic of cooking him a meal at her home as thanks for fixing her car when he suddenly looked up and over her shoulder.

"Looks like my friend's here," Derrick said.

Cynthia turned to follow his gaze. She spotted a tow truck gliding toward them with its engine chugging loudly, drowning out the other roadway noise.

The truck was haloed by the afternoon sun. Cynthia raised her hand to her brow to block out the blinding light. She squinted. When she recognized the man in the driver's seat, her bright smile faded. Her mouth fell open, aghast.

"*That's* your friend?" she squeaked.

"Yeah, that's Korey." Derrick noticed the change in her facial expression. "Why? What's wrong?"

Cynthia glanced nervously at Derrick as the truck came to a stop not far from where they stood. Her pulse started to race. Her throat went dry. Sweat instantly formed on her brow and underneath her arms. She felt cornered, like a bank robber who had flubbed a getaway after a robbery, had hit a dead end, and now saw red and white flashing lights swirling behind her.

"Are you okay?" Derrick asked, touching her shoulder. "You look flushed."

"I'm fine," she lied, clearing her throat. She shrugged off his hand. "I'm fine . . . really. I'm just a little h-hot . . . th-that's all."

Derrick stared at her warily.

The driver of the tow truck killed the engine and

threw open his car door. Cynthia fought the urge to
bolt. Her car wasn't that far away. She could make it
before he even reached them. Instead, she forced herself to stay put and watched as he climbed out of the
truck and stepped onto the asphalt. After slamming the
door shut, he casually strolled toward them.

God, he hasn't changed! Even after all these years,
Cynthia thought.

Korey Walker still looked the same way he had
looked almost twenty years ago when they were in
high school together, except now he had a few sprin-
kles of gray hair on his head and in the beard stubble
on his russet-brown cheeks. But he was still tall, still
muscular, and still handsome as the devil, which was
one reason why she had avoided going anywhere near
his auto body and repair shop in Chesterton since he
had opened it a little more than a year ago.

Back when they were younger, Korey had been the
kryptonite to her Superman, and she had been powerless under his spell. Though decades had passed since
those days, Cynthia feared she would be powerless
again if she got near him—and she didn't need the
confusion he could bring to her life. Korey was not the
right man for her now, just as he hadn't been the right
man for her back then. But there was no avoiding him
today.

"Thanks for coming, man," Derrick said, stepping
forward. He and Korey shook hands, then embraced
and slapped each other's backs.

They were quite the contrast: Derrick in his chic,
immaculate suit, and Korey in his oil- and greased-
stained navy blue shirt and pants, with grime on his
hands and dirt under his nails. But even in his shoddy
attire, Korey was by far the sexier of the two.

Hands down, she thought.

"Looks like I've got myself in a real fix, Korey," Derrick said. "I accidentally rear-ended this beautiful lady right here." He gestured to Cynthia.

Korey turned and looked at her. His dark eyes regarded her coolly and then shifted downward by several inches. She followed the path of his gaze, instantly getting an eyeful of her own cleavage. She was spilling out of her top. No wonder he was staring! Now self-conscious, Cynthia quickly raised her hand to cover her breasts.

"Are you sure it was an accident?" Korey asked softly in a heavy baritone she remembered all too well. He was looking at her, not Derrick, as if he was posing the question to her, not his friend.

She looked away, choosing to focus instead on the flower shop across the street.

"What? Are you trying to say I hit her *on purpose?*" Derrick asked with a chuckle.

"No, nothin' like that, man." Korey shook his head, still gazing at her. "Nothin' like that."

Damn it, stop staring at me!

She knew Korey was judging her, as he always had and always would. She could read his mind even now, after all these years.

Still playing the same ol' tricks, Cindy? Still runnin' the same ol' game? Aren't you getting a little old for this? Isn't this getting a little bit tired?

Well, to hell with you, Korey, she thought, raising her chin defiantly and meeting his gaze. She had nothing to be ashamed of. She was a grown woman who lived her life on her own terms! His judgment meant nothing to her. He wasn't going to make her question herself like he had two decades ago. She wasn't that girl anymore.

"So," Korey said, finally returning his attention to Derrick, "let's take a look at the damage." He strode toward her Lexus. "Where'd you hit her?"

"Back bumper," Derrick said, pointing at her SUV. "I left quite a scratch too."

Cynthia watched as the two men leaned down to examine her car. She crossed her arms over her chest and tapped her foot restlessly as they consulted each other, ignoring her. She wondered why Korey didn't acknowledge that he knew her.

So be it, she thought. She wasn't going to acknowledge him either. She could pretend they were total strangers if that's what he wanted.

Korey dropped to one knee and traced his finger along the gash in her bumper, giving Cynthia plenty of opportunity to further examine him in profile: his long dark eyelashes, high cheekbones, and full lips. The diamond stud he used to wear in his left earlobe was gone. She could remember sucking on that earlobe when they parked in the deserted lot behind an old drive-in movie theater outside of Chesterton. And she could remember eighteen-year-old Korey sucking on a lot more than that while they made love in the backseat of his mother's 1987 Chevy Cavalier. Those passionate moments they shared were not only hot and heavy, but done in secret. Not even her sisters knew about him because Cynthia worried the information eventually would find its way back to their mother. Yolanda Gibbons would have killed her if she knew Cynthia was fogging up the car windows with the likes of Korey Walker.

Cynthia thought back wistfully to those clandestine nights. Just the memory of Korey's hands and mouth on her skin made her shiver. And another appendage besides his hands had been just as memorable. One night, she had playfully nicknamed it "Big Korey."

From then on, the nickname stuck, and all she had to do was whisper it in his ear to get his engine going.

She watched as he now stood up. "Yeah, that's a pretty bad dent, but . . ." He winked at Derrick. "I can fix her. It's no problem, and you won't even be able to tell the difference."

"Good! And I get the friend discount, right?"

Korey laughed and nodded. "Yeah, man, you get the friend discount. Though with all the money you make, I should charge your ass extra, not less."

Korey suddenly turned to look at Cynthia, and she felt her body temperature rise again under his warm gaze. He walked toward her, reached into one of the pockets of his stained blue short-sleeved shirt, and pulled out a business card. He offered it to her.

"You can bring it in anytime next week," he said. "I'll take care of it personally."

"Thank you." She took his card and quickly tucked it into her purse.

"We're the auto repair and body shop that's not far from Stan's Bakery. We're on the corner of—"

"I *know* where you are," she said then grimaced. She hadn't meant to admit that.

"Oh, you do?" He inclined his head. "I'm surprised to hear that . . . considering that you haven't paid me a visit the whole time my shop's been here, Cindy."

Derrick furrowed his brows. "Wait! You two know each other?"

"I haven't had a reason to visit you," she said breezily, tossing her hair over her shoulder and ignoring Derrick's question. "Why would I?"

"Oh, I could think of *plenty* of reasons." Korey took another step closer to her. She saw a shadow of an impish smile tug at his lips and the heat in his dark eyes intensify. "You and I have a lot of history."

She gritted her teeth at those words.

Cynthia had pushed that "history" out of her mind years ago when she found out that Korey was engaged to Vivian Brady, Cynthia's old arch nemesis in high school. Vivian had been the ring leader of the pack of girls who had ridiculed Cynthia endlessly about her mother, Yolanda—"the biggest gold-digging ho in Chesterton," as Vivian and her girlfriends liked to call Yolanda back then. Korey marrying a girl like Vivian had felt like the ultimate betrayal to Cynthia, especially when she figured out later that he had been cheating on her with Vivian while they were together. It definitely made her feel less regretful about dumping him and getting engaged to her first husband, Bill, a millionaire who was fifteen years her senior. She had chosen Bill instead of Korey because he was handpicked by her mother.

"Bill is the *right* kind of man for a responsible woman who wants to ensure her future," her mother had said at the time.

Cynthia had since heard that Korey and Vivian were divorced, just like she and Bill, but that didn't change her feelings about Korey's betrayal. He had hurt her indescribably. She would never forgive him.

"I'll bring my car in on Wednesday," she said curtly. She then strode toward her SUV, forgetting Derrick, her big catch, and Korey, the first and last man to ever break her heart. Seconds later, she put her key in the ignition and pulled away, leaving the two men standing on the sidewalk, looking dumbfounded.

Chapter 2

Cynthia let out a deep breath as she opened her maroon front door, balancing her grocery bags in her arms and on her hips.

She still felt shaky, but at least her stomach had stopped doing flip-flops during the drive home. She guessed it was inevitable that she would run into Korey. She had gone to great lengths to avoid him or hear any news about him, but he owned a business in town, after all. She just hated that she hadn't been more prepared when she saw him again. Worse, she had thrown back a big fish like Derrick because Korey had distracted her with his "Ghost of Christmas Past" act. No doubt, after she left, Korey had filled in Derrick on their mutual "history." She'd have absolutely no chance of winning Derrick over now!

"Let it go," a voice inside her head urged. "Another rich man will come along. They always do."

Cynthia nodded in agreement. Today she had been off her game, but she would get back on it—quickly. She could sense that her next husband was just around the corner, and she would have a ring on her finger again in no time. She just had to keep her eyes open and stay focused. Maybe this husband would finally be her last.

I certainly hope so, she thought with a sigh.

Cynthia knew she was starting to get up there in age, making it harder to "peddle her wares." To mask her increasing number of gray hairs and to add a little *va va voom,* she had gone blond that spring.

Her sisters had given up their gold-digging ways for good, and she had to admit, even she was starting to grow tired of the hustle. But she wouldn't settle for second-best like some of her sisters had. She still wanted her big fish—her great white shark—before she finally retired from the game. She wouldn't settle for anything less than a man who made seven figures or who had enough overall wealth to buy a small island.

With that, she kicked the front door closed behind her, bringing an end to her bad mood. Cynthia dropped her keys into the glass bowl on her mahogany foyer table. Her high heels clicked over the ceramic tiles as she strolled toward her eat in kitchen.

She had purchased the colonial soon after her divorce from her second husband, Richard. The sweeping, three-story house, with its charming rose garden and enclosed pool, seemed like a suitable payoff for enduring five years of marriage with that old windbag. She shared it with her only daughter, Clarissa. But now that Clarissa was spending most of her time away from home with friends or on her college campus during the school year, the expansive house felt a bit empty. The rooms echoed at night, and the hallways felt hollow with just one person walking around them during the day. Cynthia wondered if after Clarissa graduated, maybe she should put the house on the market. Her younger sister, Stephanie, was a Realtor. She could sell it for Cynthia. Maybe Cynthia could take the proceeds of the sale and buy a smaller condo. But Clarissa wouldn't graduate for another two years. Cynthia still had some time to come up with a plan. Until then, she would keep the house the way it was.

"Clarissa, baby!" she called out as she walked into her brightly lit kitchen.

Most visitors to her home would be shocked to discover that the Ice Queen (as she was called by some people in town) had a home that was filled with warmth and decorated in a French country style that encouraged anyone to kick off their shoes, grab a glass of lemonade, and relax. The kitchen was painted a soft yellow, and the cabinets were off-white and distressed to give the illusion of age. A bouquet of sunflowers, calla lilies, and tulips sat in the center of the butcher-block kitchen island. A thirteen-inch-tall porcelain rooster sat next to the flowers. Cynthia sat her bags on the granite countertop near the stove and opened her stainless steel refrigerator door.

"I saw your car in the driveway, Clarissa! Honey, are you home?"

"I'm here," Clarissa said. She casually strolled into the kitchen barefoot while flipping the pages of a magazine.

Cynthia paused from shelving a head of lettuce, turned, and smiled at her daughter. "Well, to what do I owe this honor? I thought you had classes all day today. I didn't expect you to be home until tonight."

Clarissa pulled out a wooden stool at the kitchen island. She sat down and started flipping pages again. "My only class today was canceled for summer vacation," she answered, not lifting her gaze from the magazine. "The teacher's aid was in a hurry to get to the beach, I guess." She sat hunched over with her elbows on the counter, reading an article.

Cynthia stopped unloading her groceries and eyed her daughter. "Honey, don't slouch like that. It's not—"

"Ma!" Clarissa grumbled. "You said you would stop lecturing me."

"I'm not lecturing you."

Clarissa looked up from the magazine and smirked.

"Okay, I'm lecturing." Cynthia pursed her lips. "But I only promised that I would *try* to stop lecturing."

Cynthia had agreed to work on her berating after Clarissa had attempted to run away when she was seventeen. Luckily, she hadn't gone far. She went straight to Cynthia's baby sister Lauren's apartment. After that, Cynthia agreed to go a little easier on her daughter.

"I don't remember promising to stop lecturing completely. Besides, I can't." She wiggled her eyebrows. "I'm your mama. It's in my contract."

Clarissa shook her head and chuckled, while Cynthia admired her daughter despite the slouched shoulders.

It was hard to believe this was the same little girl who had been toddling behind her in pull-ups, who had worn crinoline skirts and patent-leather shoes with buckles on the ankles. Now Clarissa was a beautiful young woman. The nineteen-year-old was tall and curvy like her mother, though with a slightly darker skin tone and darker eyes. She also shared Cynthia's stubborn streak. Cynthia had been trying for the past three years to teach Clarissa the Gibbons family rules of gold digging. They had been passed down for generations, starting with the family matriarch, Althea Gibbons, who had used her feminine wiles to go from being a poor sharecropper's daughter to a millionaire's wife. But so far Clarissa wanted no part of her family legacy.

Pity, Cynthia thought, eying her daughter again. Clarissa was a natural beauty and graceful. Many a man would jump at the chance to be with her once she learned how to use the natural gifts God had given her. She could probably go far in gold digging if she gave it a chance.

"Give it time, Cindy," Yolanda had assured her when Cynthia expressed dismay that Clarissa didn't want to follow in the family footsteps. "She'll fall into the fold just like all of you did. Just be patient and give her time."

"Aunt Dawn called while you were out," Clarissa said casually, pulling her mother from her thoughts. The young woman pushed her magazine aside, stood from her stool, and reached for one of the grocery bags. "She said you still haven't returned the RSVP for Aunt Stephanie's engagement party."

Cynthia groaned as she opened one of her oak cabinets. She put a box of crackers in the open space on one of the shelves.

Clarissa frowned. "You don't want to go to the party?"

"It's not that I don't want to go, sweetheart. It's just . . . It's just that I don't understand how your Aunt Steph could marry a man like that."

Clarissa opened a grocery bag and took out a carton of milk. Her frown deepened. "A man like what? What's wrong with Keith? He seems nice to me!" She opened the fridge and put the carton on one of the shelves.

"Yes, he's nice, but nice doesn't cut it. He's just not the caliber of man I thought someone like Steph would go after."

"Umm, Ma, it's not like she's marrying a homeless guy."

"He's a *private detective!* Do you know how much he makes doing that?" Cynthia snorted. "I bet not enough to buy Stephanie all those designer shoes and purses she likes! Married to him, she might as well start getting used to shopping at Payless and Walmart!"

Clarissa sighed as she placed bananas on the granite counter near their toaster. "It's not always about money."

"Spoken like a girl who's always had it," she replied, making Clarissa roll her eyes in exasperation. "Your Aunt Dawn isn't much better. She's lucky she has that inheritance from her father coming to her! It was her bad luck to hook up with a corporate lawyer who up and decided to quit his job as soon as they got together. Now he works full-time at a broke-down community center. He probably makes half of what she does—if that! She'll be the one taking care of *him* financially!" Cynthia shook her head in disgust as she balled up an empty grocery bag and tossed it into a nearby recycling bin. "It's like Dawn and Stephanie forgot all the fundamentals that we've learned since childhood. They just threw away the family rule book!"

"Please," Clarissa muttered under her breath as she emptied a bag of oranges into one of the refrigerator's plastic storage trays, "not the family rule book again."

"Now Stephanie is pregnant again! That's the *real* reason why they're getting married! I swear that man cannot keep it in his pants!"

"Ewww! Ma!"

"Another baby on the way. . . . How in the hell are they supposed to—"

"But they're *in love!*" Clarissa argued, gazing into

her mother's eyes. "They're in love and they're happy. *That's* what's important . . . not how much money Keith makes."

"Aww, honey." Cynthia raised a hand to her daughter's cheek and rubbed it lovingly. "You are so sweet and so damn gullible, it's almost charming!"

"I am *not* gullible." Clarissa shoved her mother's hand away and crossed her arms over her chest. "I may be young, but that doesn't mean I don't know anything about relationships or love."

Cynthia paused. She closed the open cabinet door and narrowed her eyes at her daughter. "And just how much *do* you know?"

"Oh, Ma, please!" Clarissa turned away.

"Don't 'Ma, please!' me. Look at me." Cynthia gently but firmly turned her daughter around to face her. She examined her daughter's features, trying to see if any of Clarissa's secrets would be revealed on her delicate face. "Just how much practice have you had with 'relationships and love' on that little campus of yours?"

Clarissa no longer met her mother's eyes. The young woman looked over Cynthia's shoulder and stared at the freshly cut lawn outside the kitchen's bay window. "I've gone on a few dates."

"A few dates?"

"Yes, just a few dates." Clarissa hesitated. "And maybe I let one or two guys kiss me . . . on the cheek," she quickly clarified, "but that's all. Really, I swear!"

Cynthia continued to gaze at her daughter suspiciously. She didn't believe for one second that Clarissa's romantic experiences consisted of only a few dates and chaste kisses on the cheek.

I remember what it was like to be nineteen, she thought.

The memory of Korey Walker, his Chevy sedan, and his teasing licks and kisses came rushing back again, but Cynthia quickly shoved it aside. Damn Korey and that warm mouth of his! He used to leave her begging him never to stop kissing her and touching her! She didn't want to think about that right now!

Cynthia focused again on her daughter. She wouldn't force Clarissa to divulge more details about her budding romantic life, but Cynthia resolved she would have to keep a closer eye on Clarissa from now on. She didn't want Clarissa to get sidetracked by a boy who wasn't worthy of her.

"Just like your mama didn't want you sidetracked by Korey?" a voice in Cynthia's head mocked.

"Let's change the subject," Cynthia said, clearing her throat. She waved her hand dismissively. "Enough of this romance and love talk. I hear enough of that drivel from my sisters. I want to talk about tonight's dinner." She smiled, opened the fridge, and pulled out a plastic container of lean ground beef. "Since you're home, I'm making your favorite, honey. Meat loaf with the smoothest mashed potatoes you've ever—"

"Sorry, Ma. I'd love to stay for dinner, but I already have plans."

Cynthia's smile disappeared. She looked crestfallen. "How can you have dinner plans? You just got home!"

"I told Kayla that I'd meet her at the mall." Clarissa grabbed her magazine off the kitchen island. "We're supposed to go to a movie and get dinner afterward."

"But I hardly ever get to see you!" Cynthia cried. She knew she was whining, but she couldn't help herself. "You're either away at school or . . . or out with your friends or—"

"We'll hang out. I swear." Clarissa leaned forward

and kissed her mother's rouged cheek. "We just can't do it tonight. Okay?"

"All right. I guess I'll . . . I'll take a rain check then."

"Thanks, Ma."

Cynthia watched as Clarissa started to back out of the kitchen.

"Look, I'm supposed to meet Kayla in an hour, so I should probably head upstairs and start getting ready."

"Okay, you guys have fun. Tell Kayla I said hi," Cynthia called as her daughter disappeared through the kitchen entryway. "And be careful!"

"Yes, Ma!" Clarissa shouted back. Her footfalls echoed off the walls as she raced up the stairs to the second floor. Her bedroom door slammed less than a minute later.

Cynthia stood alone in her kitchen, drumming her red fingernails on the butcher block. She blew air out of the side of her mouth, causing her side-swept bangs to flutter.

"Well, I guess it's just me tonight." She turned and placed the Styrofoam container of beef back in the freezer. "Good-bye, meatloaf. Hello, pizza," she said, as she took out a microwavable dinner box of frozen French bread pizza.

Chapter 3

"Jared?"

Korey pounded on the bathroom door with his closed fist. He then tried to turn the brass doorknob, but to no avail. The door was locked.

"Jared?"

There was no answer, only the sound of Korey's precious water going down the drain as his son, Jared, showered. Jared had been showering for more than half an hour now.

He better not be playing with himself in there, Korey thought. He pounded on the door again. "Boy, are you done yet?"

"Almost finished, Pops!" Jared yelled through the closed bathroom door. "Just a sec!"

Korey dropped his hands to his hips and silently fumed.

It had been a long, tiring day. In addition to the usual oil changes and switching out of air filters, Korey had to do the normal office work and management stuff that came with being a business owner. He had fielded calls from two angry customers who swore one of his mechanics had overcharged them for shoddy work. Korey had promised them that they could bring their cars back and get them serviced again, free of charge. He then had made a mental note to talk to the mechanic in question when the guy got back from vacation later that week. He had been on the phone for an hour with his accountant, who droned on and on about some change in the tax code for high earners that still left Korey confused. Korey just assumed that it meant he would have to pay more taxes. And finally, he had answered a call from a good friend and valued customer, Derrick Winters, who had gotten himself into a bind by rear-ending some woman in the middle of Main Street.

Korey hadn't expected that woman to be Cynthia Gibbons—his old flame. The instant he climbed out of his truck and saw her, he felt like he had been given a kick to the chest.

He had thought it odd that he and Cynthia hadn't run into one another in the whole year and a half that he had had his shop downtown. (Chesterton wasn't *that* big.) He had suspected she had been avoiding him. Now he knew for sure that she was purposely steering clear of him this whole time.

"She should after what she did to you," a voice in his head argued.

Cynthia had dumped him. She had decimated his heart almost twenty years ago to marry some older guy who could buy her diamonds and furs. It had taken him a few years to get over her rejection. Even when he married his now ex-wife, Vivian, Korey still had been dragging around a broken heart from his breakup with Cynthia, angering Vivian.

"I can't believe you still have a thing for her, Korey!

Can't you get it through your thick head that she doesn't want your ass anymore?" Vivian had said once during one of their fights.

Seeing Cynthia today had brought back all those old feelings—a tangled mass of longing, sadness, frustration, and hurt. If he had felt tired before he saw her, now he was damn near exhausted. He was even skipping going to the gym tonight.

All Korey wanted to do was take a shower, put on clothes that didn't smell like gasoline or transmission fluid, drink a cold beer, and veg out in front of the television for a few hours. Maybe he could even catch a Nats game. But instead of lounging on his vibrating leather recliner, remote control in hand, he was standing in his hallway still filthy and still exhausted while his unemployed son, who wouldn't know a water bill if it was engraved in gold, monopolized the one shower in the entire house.

Korey slumped against the doorframe. He supposed he should be happy that Jared was at least here. Usually Jared would be at Vivian's house. They had arranged since the divorce that Jared spend the week with his mother and his stepfather, and spend his weekends with Korey. Korey had made sure to rent a 1950s bungalow in Chesterton with a spare bedroom so Jared would always feel at home when he was in town. Jared had since decorated the room with the football and basketball jerseys of his favorite teams (the New England Patriots and the Lakers, to his father's great disappointment), posters of busty bikini models, and a few posters of tattooed rappers. But now that Jared had just turned nineteen, the shared parenting arrangement had officially ended. Jared could spend his time however he wished. Korey, who always felt his relationship with his son was tenuous thanks to his ex-wife's manipulations, expected that he would see less of Jared. But to his surprise, for the past several months, he had seen even more of his son. When Jared wasn't away at school, he was staying in Chesterton. But Korey soon figured out why. It wasn't that Jared was eager to spend more time with his old man. He was eager to spend time with a girl he had fallen madly in love with.

Korey still hadn't met her yet, but he didn't have to meet her to know Jared was head over heels in love with her. He could hear their whispered late-night conversations on the phone. Jared would monopolize Korey's landline *for hours* talking to that girl. Jared no longer boasted about all the phone numbers he got from girls he met at the mall or around town. His girlfriend was the only one he had eyes for. And while returning clean laundry to Jared's sock drawer a week ago, Korey noticed the box of condoms he had given Jared a year ago. He had purchased Jared that twelve-dollar gift after making the boy sit through a lecture about safe sex. That sad little box had sat full for months. Now, more than half of the condom packets were gone.

Well, look at that, Korey had thought as he gazed at the half-empty box. *So Little Jared is getting more ass than his Pops!*

Yes, things between Jared and the mystery girl were definitely serious. He bet this was Jared's first love, and Korey was happy for his son. Maybe Jared's first serious romance would work out better than Korey's had. Korey certainly hoped it would.

Korey perked up when he finally heard the squeak of a faucet handle. The sound of running water ceased. Seconds later, Jared opened the bathroom door, sending out a billowing cloud of steam that slowly rolled into the hallway. The steam departed, revealing Korey's blue-tiled bathroom.

"Hey, Pops!" The young man wiped at the fogged-up bathroom mirror. He stood on the fuzzy navy blue bath mat with one tan towel wrapped around his trim waist and another dangling around his damp shoulders. He turned to his father and gave a dimpled smile. "Are you just getting in?"

"No, I'm not just getting in," Korey answered testily. "I've been home for an hour now . . . and waiting in the damn hallway for half of it!"

Jared laughed, ignoring his father's irritation. He grabbed a can of body spray and began to spray it around himself, making Korey cough into his fist. Jared then turned on the hot water in the sink and sprayed shaving cream into the palm of his hand.

"Don't tell me you're still grooming!" Korey closed his eyes. "Jared, when will I get to use my own damn bathroom?"

"But, Pops, I gotta shave! I'm supposed to go out with my girl tonight." He rubbed the invisible stubble on his dark brown cheeks. "You don't want me to look grubby, do you?" He wagged his finger at Korey playfully. "You know, that's not a good look. Women like a sharp dude."

Korey sighed, opened his eyes, and smiled. He could never stay mad at Jared for long. He watched as his son lathered his cheeks, opened a cabinet door, and pulled out a clean razor from underneath the bathroom sink.

"So when do I finally get to meet this girl? I don't even know her name."

The razor froze in midair. Jared glanced at Korey out of the corner of his eye. "Why do you want to meet her?" The young man then began to shave.

"Because you've been with her for four months now! I think you've officially set a record. You've definitely been with her longer than the last one. You know the one"—Korey snapped his fingers, trying to remember her name—"the girl who sounded like she sucked on helium."

Jared laughed. "Michelle did not sound like she sucked on helium, Pops! Her voice was a just little high, that's all."

"*And* I want to meet this one because I'm your father, Jared. I changed your dirty diapers. I taught you how to ride a bike without training wheels. I taught you how to aim in a toilet. Remember?" He raised his thick brows. "It only seems right that I meet the girl you're serious about."

Jared shrugged. "I don't know, Pops . . . maybe."

"*Maybe?* Has your mother met her?"

Jared rinsed his razor in the pool of water in the sink. "No! Are you crazy? Ma would scare her off!"

Korey nodded. In Viv's eyes, no girl would ever be good enough for Jared, "her little baby." She had frightened many girls away with her heavy line of questioning and her insinuations, driving a few almost to tears. She acted as though every date was a potential wife for Jared, and she'd put the girls through the third degree before she would ever accept them into her family.

Jared wiped at his newly shaven face with his towel, removing the last traces of his Martian-green shaving cream. He admired his reflection in the mirror, then suddenly paused. "Hey, what time is it?"

Korey raised his wrist and looked down at his watch. "It is twenty minutes after six. Why?"

Jared's eyes widened to the size of quarters. He tossed his towel aside and it landed on the tiled floor. "Damn, I'm late!" He rushed past his father and ran into his bedroom at the end of the hall, sliding on the hardwood floors.

"What time are you supposed to meet her?" Korey called over his shoulder as he grabbed the discarded, dirty towel and tossed it into the bathroom hamper.

"At six o'clock!" Jared madly dug through his dresser drawers, looking for clothes to wear. "I'm late, Pops! I'm late!"

Teenagers, Korey thought wryly. He shook his head in exasperation and strolled down the hall with his hands in his pockets. He stood in the doorway of his son's bedroom while Jared hopped on one foot in his gray boxer briefs, shoving his leg into a pair of jeans.

"Just chill out and take a deep breath, son."

"I can't chill out!" Jared shouted. His jeans were still around his ankles. A white T-shirt dangled around his neck. "I'm late, Pops! I was supposed to meet her at—"

"Yeah, I heard you the first time. So just call her and apologize. Tell her the time got away from you. No big deal."

Jared eagerly nodded as if that was the most original suggestion in the world. "You're right. You're right! Why didn't I think of that?" He rushed across the room to his dresser, raising his jeans to his waist. He dug through a pile of papers, baseball caps, and loose change before finally finding his cell phone. He swept his finger over the phone's touch screen. "I'll give her a call and tell her that—*Oh, no!*"

"What now?"

Jared lowered his phone. He gulped. "She texted me. I wasn't answering her calls, so she wondered if something was wrong. She's on her way here!"

Korey grinned. So he would finally get to meet the mystery girl. "And what's so bad about that?"

The doorbell rang. Both men turned and gazed down the hallway at the bungalow's front door.

Jared cringed. "That's probably her."

"Probably." Korey walked out of his son's bedroom and down the hall. He'd prefer to meet Jared's girlfriend wearing something nicer than an oil-stained shirt and pants, but his current outfit would have to do on such short notice.

Jared raced after him and grabbed his arm, clenching it in a death grip. Jared looked frantic.

"Pops, I really like this girl. *Please,* don't embarrass me!"

"Embarrass you?" Korey slowly pulled his arm out of his son's grasp as the doorbell rang again. "Son, I'm not the one standing in the hallway in my underwear."

Jared looked down at himself. His pants had fallen to his ankles again. He hopped back to his bedroom and resumed dressing for his date.

Seconds later, Korey unlocked the front door and swung it open.

She was a tall girl. She almost reached Korey's chin and he was six-foot-two. She had a sweet face: big brown eyes, a slightly pointed nose, and a pouty lower lip. Her long dark hair was held back with a simple black headband. She wore a peach halter top that showed just a hint of cleavage and snug-fitting jeans that showed off her curvy figure. She fidgeted nervously on Korey's welcome mat.

You done good, son, Korey thought as he looked at her. *She's a cutie.*

"Hey," Korey said, extending his hand to her. "I'm Korey, Jared's dad."

"Hi, I'm Clarissa! Pleased to meet you, sir." She smiled and shook his hand. "Is . . . is Jared home? Is he ready to go?"

"Almost." He ushered her inside. "And Jared apologizes for being late."

She stepped past him into the small living room. "That's okay. I just wanted to make sure our plan of where and when to meet didn't change or anything." She looked around her, biting down on her pouty bottom lip. "You, uh, you . . . you have a nice home, Mr. Walker."

"Thank you for saying so."

She was polite too. That was a plus. He'd challenge Viv to find fault with this one.

"Jared should only be a few more minutes. Would you like something to drink?" he asked as he walked into the adjoining kitchenette. "I could get you some water or maybe some—"

"No, that's okay, Mr. Walker." She anxiously fingered the zipper on her purse. She still stood in the center of the living room. "I'm not thirsty, but thanks."

Korey nodded and opened the refrigerator door. He pulled out a beer from one of the shelves and popped off the cap. As he drank, the room fell into awkward silence.

"So . . . ," he said, trying desperately to think of something to talk about while they waited. "Do you and your family live near here, Clarissa?"

She nodded eagerly, sending her long hair flying. "We do. We live about fifteen minutes from here . . . on Pembroke Lane."

Korey raised his eyebrows in surprise. That was a pretty nice neighborhood with fairly expensive houses. The people who lived there were well above the income bracket of Korey's neighborhood. Everyone in Chesterton referred to it as Millionaire Row.

So Jared was dating a *rich* girl too.

Korey leaned against the cracked laminate of his

kitchen counter before taking another drink. "Your dad must have a pretty nice job to live there."

"He does . . . but he doesn't live there with us. He lives in Chicago with his other family. My parents are divorced. It's just me and my mother."

"Oh, I'm sorry to hear that."

She shrugged. "It's okay. They divorced a long time ago when I was little. I barely remember them being together."

"So you moved here from Chicago?"

"No, Mom and I lived in D.C. for a while when she got remarried, but then after she divorced my stepfather, we moved back here. She's lived in Chesterton her whole life. All her sisters are here. So is my grandmother. Mom said it only seemed right to buy a house in Chesterton."

"She's lived here her whole life, huh?" Korey tilted his head. "You know, I grew up in Chesterton too. I wonder if I know her."

"You might. I wouldn't be surprised if you did." She laughed. "I think everybody in Chesterton knows who Cynthia Gibbons is!"

At mention of Cynthia's name, Korey almost spit out his beer. He caught himself just before he did, but then his beer lodged in this throat and he started to choke. He set his bottle on the countertop and pounded at his chest.

Clarissa's face contorted in a look of horror as she rushed toward him. "Mr. Walker, are you okay?" She placed a hand on his shoulder. "Do you need help? I know the Heimlich!"

"Pops?" Jared asked as he finally opened his bedroom door. He raced down the hallway to the kitchenette. "Pops, what's going on?"

"I think your dad's choking, Jared!"

"What?" He then ran to his father's side.

Korey held up his hand. He gave one last cough and finally cleared his throat. "I'm not . . . I'm not choking"—he said between gasps—"anymore."

He grabbed the edge of the counter, took several deep breaths, and blinked his reddened eyes. He then stared at Clarissa. "Your mother is *Cynthia Gibbons?*"

She slowly nodded, looking confused.

Cindy's her mother!

How the hell was this possible? What was the likelihood that out of all the girls in the world that Jared had to choose from, he had fallen in love with the *one* girl who was the daughter of the *one* woman who had haunted Korey for the past twenty years? What kind of prank was the universe trying to play on him? Whatever prank it was, it sure as hell wasn't funny!

Korey turned to look at his son. "Did you know Cynthia was her mother?" he asked accusingly.

"Yeah, I knew." Jared shrugged, taken aback by his father's tone. "Why? What does it matter?"

Clarissa nervously twisted the straps of her leather purse in her hands. "Mr. Walker, I . . . I know the reputation my mom and my . . . my family has around town. B-but we're not that bad . . . really. And I'm . . . I'm nothing like my mom! I don't even want to marry a rich guy! I'm okay with being poor!"

Korey gazed at her. He could see it now in her face, those traces of Cynthia: the narrow nose, the stubborn set of her chin, and the arch of her brows. Yes, this was definitely Cindy's daughter.

"Does your mom know that you and Jared are together, Clarissa?"

Clarissa hesitated. She looked up at Jared.

"Tell me truth," Korey ordered.

Clarissa's eyes shifted to the stained linoleum tiles

underfoot. "She wouldn't understand, Mr. Walker," she said quietly, gnawing on her lower lip again. "I know Jared's great, but my mother has different ideas of who would be the right guy for me. She wouldn't accept us."

That sounded familiar. Korey could remember Cynthia using those very words the night she broke up with him almost two decades ago.

"I love you, Korey. I really do," she had said. "But mama doesn't think you're the right guy for me. She just wouldn't accept us. It'd never work out!"

"You're not going to tell her mom, are you?" Jared asked, sounding desperate. "She'd make us break up, Pops. Please don't tell her!"

Korey shook his head. "I won't tell her. It doesn't feel like it's my place to tell her anyway. Besides, Cynthia and I aren't on the best of terms," he said, remembering his encounter with her earlier that day. She acted like she couldn't get away from him fast enough. "I doubt she'd want to talk to me."

Clarissa looked up at him with puzzlement. "What do you mean?"

"It's a long story, honey, and an old story, at that. Trust me. You don't want me to get into it." His gaze shifted from Clarissa to Jared and back again. "Just know that your secret is safe with me, but . . ." He held up his index finger. "At some point, you guys will have to tell her. You two can't keep sneaking around like this. Cynthia is going to find out, and when she does, knowing her, she's going to be royally pissed off."

Jared protectively wrapped an arm around Clarissa's shoulder. "We will, Pops. We will. We're just . . . you know . . . waiting for the right time."

"Uh-huh?" Korey said, cocking an eyebrow. "Just make sure you don't wait too much longer."

"We won't," Clarissa whispered.

Korey nodded. "All right, I've said what I had to say. Enough preaching. You guys head out now before you miss your movie. Enjoy your date and be safe. And, uh . . . Jared, I expect you back by midnight."

Jared squinted. "Midnight?"

"Yes, *midnight,*" Korey said with a firm nod.

The kids left a few minutes later. When they did, Korey slumped against the kitchen counter again.

How had this happened? How had the past repeated itself?

He had hoped that Jared's first love would turn out better than his had turned out twenty years ago, but it didn't look like that was going to be the case. Korey could see it now. If his son's relationship was anything like Korey and Cynthia's, Jared was in for a world of heartbreak.

Chapter 4

"Cynthia? Cynthia? Can you pass the croissants?"

Cynthia grabbed the basket in front of her and held it to her right. Someone took it out of her hand, though she didn't know who. She was too distracted to pay attention.

Today was Saturday brunch at her mother's mansion, a family tradition that had lasted as long as Cynthia could remember. Everyone had been invited. Cynthia's sisters—Lauren, Dawn, and Stephanie—had brought along their families and significant others. Cynthia had planned to do the same, but Clarissa said she already had plans.

Clarissa's refusal to come today had started Cynthia on a sour mood that she hadn't been able to shake all morning. That bad mood was still firmly in place now.

She gazed with contempt at Crisanto, her brother-in-law; Keith, her sister Stephanie's fiancé; and her sister Dawn's man, Xavier. The men's wide shoulders took up more than their share of space at the table, nudging aside everyone around them. Their deep voices boomed louder than everyone else's in the sunroom as they laughed and joked. The smell of their colognes and aftershaves made her nose burn.

Interlopers, Cynthia thought as she chewed her toast. *Judases,* she thought when her eyes shifted to her sisters.

Lauren sat with her baby, Crisanto Jr., on her lap, trying to convince him to "be a big boy like your daddy" and eat a spoonful of applesauce.

Stephanie sat to Cynthia's right and was playing with her daughter Zoe, whom her fiancé, Keith, held in his lap. She'd tickle the infant's chin or make funny faces, causing Zoe's nut-brown face to light up with delight at her mother's games.

Dawn sat to Cynthia's left, holding hands underneath the table with Xavier. They stared into each other's eyes, whispering some conversation no one else at the table could hear. He slowly lowered his mouth to hers and they shared a passionate kiss.

Oh, please, Cynthia thought. *Get a damn room!*

Cynthia shoved her scrambled eggs around her plate with her fork, having officially lost her appetite. All this "love and happiness" crap was making her ill. She couldn't get away from it! She wanted to tell her sisters and her mother about her run-in with the six-foot looker a few days ago, but she couldn't do that with Cris, Keith, and Xavier sitting at the table. She could never have a conversation like that in front of bunch of men. So instead she stewed silently.

She just wished things would go back to the way they were, back to when it was just her, her sisters, and her mother. They could enjoy Saturday brunch—no male interlopers included. They'd gossip about the rich men they were dating and planning to marry. It would be their own little Eden, with Yolanda's lush garden in the background and the sun shining through the floor-to-ceiling windows.

But it wasn't a gold-digging Eden anymore. The Gibbons girls were no longer plotting about men. With the exception of Cynthia, they were all happily in serious relationships. She wished she could wave a magic wand and make the three men disappear. She was so much more content when they weren't around.

"Excuse me! Excuse me, folks!" Lauren said as she pushed back her chair and rose to her feet. "We have an announcement to make!"

Dawn groaned. "Oh, Lord! *Please* don't tell us you're pregnant again too!" She then made a big production of pushing her glass away from her, sliding it across the chenille tablecloth. "I'm starting to think there is something in the water around here."

Her boyfriend, Xavier, grinned as he slid the glass back in front her. "Then you, sweetheart, need to drink more water."

Dawn made a face before slapping his thigh. He leaned over and kissed the nape of her neck, causing Cynthia to resist the urge to roll her eyes heavenward.

Though Dawn was thirty-eight years old and had expressed no serious interest in having children, that didn't stop her younger lover from constantly hinting that they would make great parents together. Cynthia gave it until next year before Dawn finally caved and ended up pregnant like the rest of them. Dawn, who had once been as much an anti-love stalwart as Cynthia, now seemed to cave to whatever her man wanted.

"No, I'm not pregnant!" Lauren said, followed by the eruption of more laughter at the table. The petite woman clapped her hands. "I wanted to announce that my wonderful, handsome husband is running for mayor of Chesterton!"

Cris waved as several of the brunch guests broke into applause.

While everyone else offered their congratulations and encouragement, literally patting Cris on the back, Cynthia stayed silent. He was running for office . . . *in Chesterton?* Sure, Cris was "Mr. Popular" in their fair little hamlet. At local events, people tripped over themselves to shake the hand of the former NFL star whose face had been plastered on cereal boxes and magazine shoe ads years ago. But Cris was married to Lauren, a *Gibbons girl!* Lauren and the rest of the family had a notorious reputation around Chesterton. Hell, they had kept tongues wagging about their gold-digging exploits for decades! Most of the women in town barely tolerated them. Cynthia doubted that many people would be happy with the idea that one of the hated Gibbons sisters could end up being the mayor's wife. She wondered if Cris realistically considered that before running for office.

"What's wrong, Cindy?" Yolanda asked, narrowing her dark eyes with concern as she pushed her chair back from the table. "You didn't eat a thing, honey? Is everything all right?"

Cynthia looked up from her plate. She hadn't noticed everyone rising from the table. Their chairs scraped on the ceramic tile as they stood. She guessed Saturday brunch was officially over for the day. What a bust!

"I wasn't very hungry." Cynthia tossed her napkin aside and stood. She watched as the men strolled toward the sunroom's entrance. They huddled near the doorway, talking about the mayoral election.

"Yeah, what's been up with you?" Lauren asked. "You've been kind of a sourpuss lately."

"Since when did you start using cheesy-ass words like 'sourpuss'?" Cynthia asked.

Lauren glanced at her son, who was being held by his father. "Since I figured out little ears are like tape recorders. Cris Jr. is starting to babble, and we don't want his first few words to be of the four-letter variety, so the only thing that'll come out of my mouth these days are words like 'poopie,' 'darn,' and 'sourpuss'."

"I know what'll cheer you up, Cindy! Hold her, please!" Stephanie handed Zoe to Cynthia, who scooped her infant niece into her arms. The taffeta of Zoe's pink dress lifted, revealing her lace-covered bloomers underneath. Zoe's big brown eyes widened. She reached up and grabbed a blond lock of Cynthia's hair, making her aunt grimace.

"I got pictures from my first sonogram a few days ago," Stephanie said with a grin. She dug through her leather hobo bag, pulling out her wallet, a bottle of styling spritz, a pacifier, and a baby brush. "Damn it, I know it's in here somewhere!"

"I still can't believe you're pregnant again, girl," Dawn said. "You just had a baby three months ago! Who knew you'd be so fertile?"

"It's not her; it's *him,*" Cynthia said with a curl in her lip as she pushed her hair over her shoulder and out of the reach of Zoe's little fingers. "Don't you know the rule, Dawn? The less money a man makes, the more children he'll have."

Stephanie paused from digging through her purse. She stared at Cynthia. "What does that mean?"

"What do you think it means? By marrying a guy who makes a pittance, you've basically doomed yourself to being forever broke, barefoot, and pregnant," Cynthia snarled.

Stephanie's hands went to her hips. "First of all, we're not broke! Keith doesn't make a 'pittance'! No, he's not a millionaire, but he earns a decent living doing private investigative work. Second, I would never, *ever* walk around barefoot. I am and always will be a stilettos girl." To demonstrate that fact, she pointed down proudly to her Louboutin shoes.

"Please, sweetheart." Cynthia snorted. "It's a slow slide downhill. Just give it time. It's already started. You promised that you would never be bigger than a size six. *Now* look at you!"

All the women breathed in audibly in shock at Cynthia's words.

"Oh, no, *she didn't!*" Dawn exclaimed.

Stephanie's chin shook and her eyes watered. "Give me back my child!" she shouted, yanking Zoe out of Cynthia's arms. "You don't deserve to hold her, you . . . you evil . . . man-hating . . . bitch!"

"Now, girls," Yolanda said slowly, "there's no need for this. We had a lovely brunch. Please don't fight."

"No, I can't fit into a size six anymore!" Stephanie continued to shout. Tears spilled from her blazing eyes. "But that's because I . . . I haven't lost the baby weight yet! I had just started the Mediterranean Diet and my pole-dancing classes when I found out I was pregnant again! You . . . you think I enjoy being this big?" she asked, pointing down at her wide hips and large breasts as she wept. Zoe was crying too now. "You think I like having a butt that jiggles like Jell-O? You don't think I feel bigger than the Love Boat?"

"What the hell is going on here?" Keith asked as he walked toward them. The handsome, mahogany-hued man gazed at his fiancée with worry. "Baby, what happened? Why are you crying?"

"Let's go home," she muttered, wiping away her tears with the back of her hand. "I don't wanna be here anymore."

"Steph," Lauren said, reaching for her sister, "please don't go. Cynthia didn't mean it."

"Oh, yes, she did!" Stephanie waved Lauren away and stomped toward the sunroom's entrance with her weeping baby in tow. "The next time you call me, Cynthia Gibbons, it better be with a damn apology!"

Keith looked around the room and waved. "It was, uh . . . nice seeing . . . umm, everybody again." He then turned and followed his fiancée.

"Nice going, big sis," Lauren muttered.

Cynthia crossed her arms over her chest and gritted her teeth.

Great, once again she was the bad guy for stating the obvious. Stephanie *had* gotten fatter—by more than thirty pounds. Cynthia didn't feel bad for pointing out the reason Stephanie had gained so much weight: namely, the baby-maker known as Keith Hendricks. Okay, maybe she felt just a *little* bit guilty. She bit down on her lower lip, recalling Stephanie's tear-filled tirade.

Fine, Cynthia thought. She would give Stephanie a call later today and apologize.

The rest of the family went home soon after that. Lauren left with Cris and Cris Jr. in tow. Dawn left fifteen minutes later with Xavier. From the steamy gazes they were giving each other, Cynthia figured they would return to Dawn's apartment and finish doing what they couldn't do at the brunch table.

Cynthia stood on the steps of her mother's mansion, watching as Dawn's Mercedes-Benz convertible pulled out of the driveway and disappeared around the bend.

"Need to talk?" Yolanda asked.

Cynthia turned to find her mother standing in the doorway. The older woman raised a finely arched brow and tilted her perfectly coifed head. She was wearing one of her Chanel ensembles today. She always looked so regal, so self-possessed. Cynthia had always wanted to be like her mother.

"I figured something was on your mind," Yolanda said, waving her back inside. "Something has to be bothering you to explain your behavior today."

Cynthia walked up the brick steps and through the French doors. Her mother shut them behind her and wrapped an arm around Cynthia's shoulders.

"I just don't understand why everything has changed so much, Mama," she said as they slowly strolled through the foyer and into one of her mother's sitting rooms. Cynthia sat on the Queen Anne sofa. She gazed at the fireplace mantel.

"It used to be just us—the Gibbons girls—and now *men* have come into the picture." She sneered. "Don't they realize it's just a mistake to depend on those guys? Depending on a man for happiness will just bring about your ruin. Falling in love with a man gives him the ultimate power. You always taught us that!"

Yolanda nodded thoughtfully as she sat down on her settee. She crossed her legs and adjusted her skirt over her knees. "Yes, I did."

"So how did they forget? Why are they setting themselves up for so much disappointment?"

"I have no idea, sweetheart. I tried my best to teach you girls. I felt it was my responsibility to show you the way, as my mother showed me. But now that you're grown women, I acknowledge that it's your own lives. You have to make these decisions yourselves. Your sisters have chosen to follow their own path." She gravely shook her head. "And there's nothing you or I can do about it."

Cynthia dropped her head into her hands. She sat

silently for several seconds. "I just . . . I just wish I could save them like you saved me."

Yolanda frowned. "What do you mean, honey?"

Cynthia removed her hands from her face. She gazed at her mother. "Remember Korey Walker?"

"Ah, yes. *Korey!*" Yolanda laughed ruefully. "Now *that* is a name I haven't heard in quite a while. He was the young man you were in love with, right?"

Cynthia nodded. "I was madly in love with him and ready to run away with him. I wanted to be with him forever and you talked me out of it . . . and I'm glad you did. I would have walked away from the chance to marry Bill, probably ended up marrying Korey, and found out that he had cheated on me and was having a baby with some other girl."

"Darling, why are we talking about Korey now? What brought this on?"

Cynthia stared at the Persian rug beneath her feet. "I ran into him a few days ago."

"Oh, dear! And how did that go?"

"All right . . . I guess. But it brought back lots of memories, both good and bad."

"Looking backward can be *very* dangerous, baby. That's why I always look forward."

Cynthia sighed. "But what if he hadn't cheated on me, Mama? What if he hadn't married Vivian Brady? Would he and I still be together? Instead of raising a kid with Vivian, would we be raising *our* child together and—"

"You can always imagine multiple realities, Cindy . . . see hundreds of ways life could be different. But the only reality that matters is the here and now. You made the right choice."

Cynthia took a deep breath. "You're right. You're right, Mama."

Yolanda smiled. "Of course, I'm right." She rose to her feet and walked toward her daughter. "Now don't forget when you arrive home to call your sister Stephanie and apologize to her. I'm sure she's crying her eyes out right now, stuffing her face with a gallon of fudge ripple ice cream."

Cynthia stood. "I won't forget, Mama."

Yolanda walked Cynthia to her car. She stood near the driveway as Cynthia climbed inside her Lexus.

"Now remember," Yolanda called as she stood on the brick steps and waved, "always look forward, not backward, honey!"

Cynthia nodded. She put on her designer sunglasses, shifted the car into drive, and pulled off.

Chapter 5

"Lookie here. Lookie here. *Lookie here!*"

Korey frowned. "Huh?"

He was in the middle of removing a dead spark plug from a 2002 Cadillac Escalade when he heard the shout behind him.

"Ray, what the hell are you talking about?" Korey said over his shoulder. "Don't you have something to do?"

Ray was one of the mechanics in his shop. He was a good guy, but unfortunately he spent most of his time shooting the breeze and talking about last night's heavyweight fight than he did actually working.

"Oh, no, partna! I can't describe this one to you." He thumped Korey on his back. "You gotta see this one for yourself."

Korey set the spark plug aside and leaned back from the car's engine. He peered around the raised hood, expecting to see the most beautiful automobile Detroit had ever created. Instead he saw a woman standing at the garage entrance.

She slammed the door of her SUV shut, took off her sunglasses, and tucked her snakeskin purse underneath her arm. She was wearing a tight-fitting purple dress that dipped low in the front and hugged her hips. A black patent-leather belt showed off her svelte waist. She wore matching black stilettos that clicked on the cement floor as she strode toward them. Her blond hair was swept up today, revealing her long, delicate neck. Silver teardrop earrings dangled from her earlobes.

He had to hand it to her; Cynthia Gibbons certainly knew how to make an entrance. Ray and about half of the other men in the garage were almost salivating over her as she walked across the room. The conversation and chaotic clamor in the garage died down to a near whisper as they stared.

"Oh, I gotta get me a piece of that," Ray said, elbowing Korey. His smile widened into a grin as he watched her hips sway as she walked. He let out a low whistle.

"Trust me." Korey gave a consolatory pat on Ray's shoulder. "You couldn't afford a piece of that, so put your tongue back in your mouth and get back to work." He grabbed a nearby cloth and wiped as much grease as he could from his hands. He gestured toward the Escalade. "Finish this, will you?"

Ray nodded, though he still kept his eyes on Cynthia as he began to fiddle with the SUV's engine.

"Can I help you, baby?" one of the younger guys asked, rushing forward.

With him now blocking her path, Cynthia came to a stop. She narrowed her eyes.

The young man licked his lips, ran his fingers over his mustache, and looked her up and down. "Anything you need, you only have to ask. Trey can take care of it for you."

Korey shook his head. "That's all right, Trey. I've got this one."

Trey's shoulders slumped. He looked disappointed. The young man nodded and slowly turned around, returning his attention to the Chevy he was working on. A few guys in the garage laughed.

Korey strolled toward her. "Hey, Cindy."

"Hello, Korey," she answered flatly, then extended her keys to him. "I'm here to drop off my car."

He glanced at the dangling car keys.

Korey had been thinking about Cynthia a lot lately, especially since he found out that Jared and her daughter were dating. Frankly, there wasn't a day that went by when he didn't recall at odd times a moment he had spent with Cynthia Gibbons: those afternoons driving to secluded spots to catch a few quick kisses, those nights they had spent making love underneath the stars. Of course, he knew he was being nostalgic. Their past had been far from perfect; they had argued just as they had loved. Still, they had had some good times. It was a shame things had ended so badly between them.

But we're grown-ups now, he reminded himself. Almost twenty years had passed. Maybe he could finally put the heartache behind him and they could at least be cordial to one another. Cynthia couldn't be that bad if she managed to raise a sweet girl like Clarissa.

"You mind if we talk for a bit?" he asked, leaning his head toward the garage entrance.

Her lips tightened. "Why?"

"No reason." He shrugged. "I just wanted to catch up. We didn't really get to talk the last time I saw you."

She stared at him for several seconds, not saying a word. Finally, she nodded. "Fine . . . but I can't stay long." They walked across the garage. "I have a very important appointment after this and I will not be late."

Hey, don't do me any favors, Korey thought irritably, but he bit back those words. It was obvious she was angry at him for some reason, though he couldn't understand why. He was the one who got dumped!

The other mechanics' eyes followed them as they walked together. Korey caught two of the men giving him the thumbs-up and grinning like hyenas.

If only they knew, he thought.

"So how have you been, Cindy?" he asked when they reached the sidewalk. He glanced at the busy roadway near the shop. "How's life been treatin' you?"

"Okay, I guess." She glanced down at her wristwatch, making it obvious that their conversation was on the clock. "I can't complain. And you?"

"I guess I can't complain either." He smiled despite her rudeness. "I've got my own business now and a roof over my head. Though I heard my roof isn't quite as nice as yours."

"What do you mean?"

"I heard you've been doing pretty well for yourself. A nice home on Pembroke Lane." He glanced at her dress. His eyes lingered on the delectable swell of her cleavage near the V-neck of her top. "Nice clothes."

She dropped a hand to her hip. "And just what is wrong with having a nice home and nice clothes?"

"Nothing." He shoved his hands into his pockets. His gaze leapt back to her face, where she was now scowling at him. "I just know that's what you always wanted. I'm glad you got it."

"What I always wanted. . . . Is that supposed to be some kind of a jibe?"

Despite his efforts to keep the conversation light, Korey could tell he was saying the wrong thing. He only seemed to be angering her more. "No, not at all."

"Well, that's exactly what it sounded like to me!"

"If that's how it sounded, that wasn't what I meant. I just—"

"You said that's what I always wanted. I always wanted a nice home and nice clothes . . . like I'm materialistic. That *is* what you meant, right?"

"Well . . ." He shrugged. "You *are* materialistic. You always have been. That's no secret."

Her mouth fell open. She sputtered for several seconds. "To . . . to hell with you, Korey Walker!" she shouted, hurling her keys at him.

He caught them just before they hit his face.

"Just fix my damn car like you were paid to do! Call me when it's ready!" She then turned on her heel and stomped down the sidewalk.

Now he was just as furious as she was.

"Can't stand to hear the truth, huh, Cindy? Can't stand to hear that all you care about is money? Wasn't money the reason you married Bill?"

She halted.

"You left me and married him because he could buy you everything you wanted!" he yelled. "Admit it!"

She turned to face him again. "You're right, Korey. That's *exactly* why I married Bill. I like nice things, nice clothes. I always have, but it's still better than being a romantic like you."

"I'm a romantic?"

And even if he was, what was wrong with that?

"Of course, you are! That would explain how you've always been able to fall in love so quickly. One moment you were in love with me. Then"—she snapped her fingers—"the next moment you were in love and having a baby with someone else. It was amazing how quickly it happened, how easily you just shifted gears like that. It's like what we had didn't even matter." She inclined her head. "But then again, maybe what we had *didn't* matter to you."

She then turned again and walked off. He watched her retreating back, and he seethed.

That was so typical of her. She was the one who wronged him and yet she acted like some martyr.

Fine, he thought as he angrily strode back to the garage. If she wanted to pretend to be the wronged party, so be it. This would be the last attempt he would make to be civil with Cynthia Gibbons.

Chapter 6

Cynthia shifted uncomfortably on the plush leather cushions in the restaurant booth, trying yet again to delicately fend off another kiss. Lyle wasn't taking the hint, though. He'd had enough champagne and oysters that his libido was on overdrive. If his mouth wasn't on her, then his hands were. One of his hands was currently sliding up her knee and inner thigh. He had started to roam higher underneath her skirt when she swatted the offending hand away.

"What do you say we go back to my place afterward? Huh?" he whispered hotly against her ear. Cynthia had to fight back a cringe. "We can put on some jazz music, turn the lights down low, and you can wear nothing but high heels and that beautiful smile of yours."

"Not tonight, Lyle." She motioned to get the waiter's attention as he passed their table. "I'm a little tired."

The young waiter quickly nodded and walked off in search of their dinner bill.

"Tired?" Lyle sat back. "It's only eight thirty."

"I'm aware of what time it is," she snapped.

When Lyle glowered at her, looking offended, she backtracked a little.

"I've just had a hard few days, sweetheart." She patted his arm.

The truth was that her mind was still focused on the last time she had spoken with Korey. She couldn't believe he still had such an unnerving effect on her, but he did. She kept replaying her argument with him, remembering his jibe about how all she cared about was money. Frankly, it wasn't something she hadn't heard before. Usually she could dismiss it with a smile or a laugh, but she couldn't this time.

Worst, Korey had the gall to act as if she had hurt him by her leaving him and marrying Bill instead, which was just a load of bull! If he was hurt by her leaving him, he certainly had an odd way of showing it. It didn't take him long to hook up with Vivian, the girl who had hung on his shoulder whenever Cynthia wasn't around. Cynthia knew Vivian had been waiting to steal Korey from her. She just didn't know that Korey had been sneaking around with Vivian that whole time.

"I'll tell you what can cure a hard few days," Lyle said, leaning toward her ear again. He draped an arm around her shoulder. "A nice massage with some warm baby oil. I could lather you up and . . ."

Jesus, this man will not give up, she thought as he prattled on. She finished the last of her wine and told herself to focus on the sports car he had driven to their date, on his Caribbean vacation home, on the stock portfolio he had boasted about earlier, but she couldn't. It was true that she was shallow, but even her shallowness had limits. She had to get away from this guy.

"Here's your check," the young waiter said as he walked back toward their table. He set the leather case in front of Lyle. "I'll take it whenever you're ready."

"We're ready *now*." Cynthia opened her purse, took out her wallet, and slapped her credit card on the table-cloth. She rarely, if ever, paid for her own meals, but this time she would make an exception.

They left the restaurant five minutes later. Lyle had shifted from selling the benefits of a massage with baby oil to how a warm bubble bath in his oversized, jetted hot tub would make her feel better. It was funny how his suggestions for her feeling better always required her to get naked. He opened the car door to his Corvette and she climbed inside. When he shut the door behind her, she gazed out the passenger window at Main Street, trying her best to ignore him.

A few people strolled past the storefronts, though much of the foot traffic had winnowed down for the day. Cynthia noticed an elderly man walking his cocker spaniel. She saw an evening jogger pausing at the intersection to let a car pass before the jogger made a mad dash for the next sidewalk. Cynthia also noticed a teenaged couple strolling in front of an antiques shop. They walked hand in hand, the girl leaning her head against the boy's shoulder. The light from the overhead lamp silhouetted them.

As Lyle put his key in the ignition, Cynthia got a pang of wistfulness. The teenaged couple reminded her of herself and Korey. How many moonlit strolls had they taken together back in the day? How many kisses had they stolen under the Victorian street lamps on Main Street?

Lyle pulled out of the restaurant parking lot, passing the young couple. Cynthia could see them more clearly now. She smiled at them, but her smile abruptly disappeared as the car drew closer. She recognized the young beauty holding the handsome boy's hand.

Clarissa?

Clarissa was supposed to be at the movies with her best friend, Kayla! Why was she here, and who the hell was this boy?

Cynthia watched in horror as Clarissa stood on her toes, linked her arms around the boy's neck, and gave him a kiss. And it wasn't just any virginal kiss. It was long, heated, and wet. Cynthia could swear she saw tongue!

"Honey, you all right?" Lyle asked as he drove. He glanced worriedly at her.

Cynthia couldn't speak. She couldn't breathe! She had just seen her worst nightmare come to life, and she was still reeling. She closed her eyes, took a calming breath, and opened her eyes again. She gave one last glance in the rearview mirror and slouched lower in her seat so that the young couple couldn't see her.

Lyle looked to his right, saw her almost sitting on the Corvette's floor, and did a double take. "Wh-what are you doing?"

"Shssssh!" she snapped. "Just keep driving!"

Lyle grumbled but did as he was told.

In the rearview mirror, Cynthia could still see Clarissa. The boy's arm was now draped around her waist. He opened the door to an ice cream parlor, and he and Clarissa walked inside, gazing into each other's eyes.

Cynthia's hands tightened into fists. Her thin nostrils flared. *This won't do. I won't have it!*

She would have a talk with Clarissa about this one and nip it in the bud faster than you could say "young dumb love."

Cynthia was sitting on the sofa in the living room, still wearing her clothes from her date and fighting a raging headache, when Clarissa walked through the front door. She watched as her daughter locked the door behind her and twirled toward the stairs at the end of the foyer. A sparkle was in Clarissa's eyes that made Cynthia nauseated.

Cynthia had a sense of déjà vu as she watched Clarissa, except it was herself she recalled wandering into the house late at night almost twenty years ago and her mother quietly waiting for her to come home. Three and half weeks after a tear-filled argument with her mother, Cynthia saw Korey one last time, then broke up with him.

"Clarissa," Cynthia called out, fighting to keep her voice even, fighting to hold back her anger. She could feel it threatening to boil over though.

Screw déjà vu, she thought. Clarissa had lied to her and probably had been lying for a while now. Cynthia could tell from the kiss she'd witnessed between Clarissa and that boy that they weren't on a first date. Her daughter had probably been sneaking around with him and lying to her over and over again.

At the sound of Cynthia's voice, Clarissa stopped on the second riser. She turned and looked at the darkened living room. She squinted and finally saw her mother sitting on the sofa.

"Hey, Ma," she said, stepping back down to the hardwood floor. She walked into the room. "You're back from your date already?" She tugged her purse strap over her head and set her purse on one of the wooden end tables. "Why are you sitting in the dark?"

"How was the movie?" Cynthia asked, gazing into her daughter's eyes.

Clarissa shrugged. "Umm, okay, I guess. I'm not a big fan of action movies, though. That's more Kayla's thing."

Another lie—and she does it so easily.

"You two have been seeing a lot of movies lately."

"Yeah, I guess. It isn't like there's much else to do around Chesterton. You know how it is." Clarissa paused and looked at her mother more carefully. "Ma, are you all right? You don't look so well."

Cynthia clenched her hands in her lap. "Have a seat, Clarissa."

The young woman hesitated before lowering herself into a leather wingback chair facing the sofa.

Cynthia scanned Clarissa's face, wondering how her daughter could look so innocent.

"Ma, what's wrong?" Clarissa laughed nervously. "You're starting to freak me out a little."

"I saw you tonight. I saw you on Main Street—and you weren't with Kayla."

Clarissa's eyes widened.

"You were with a boy, and you were kissing him. Who is he?"

Clarissa loudly swallowed. "Ma, I-I didn't . . ."

"If you're about to lie to me again, don't do it. Because I'm ten seconds away from slapping you right across the face! I'm twenty seconds away from opening that front door and telling you to get the hell out of my house!" She closed her eyes and took a deep breath, fighting to regain control. She promised herself that she wouldn't show how furious she was, and she was failing miserably at hiding it. "Now who is he?"

Clarissa's eyes began to water. She bit down hard on her lower lip and sniffed. "His name is Jared and . . . and . . . we're in love."

"In love?" Cynthia gave a cold laugh. "Is that so?"

"Yes, Ma, that is so! Jared and I are in love and . . .

and we want to get married . . . one day, maybe after we both graduate from college. Jared said he—"

"I don't think so." Cynthia slowly stood from the sofa and shook her head. "You're not getting married to this boy. I don't care how in love you *think* you are. I'm not going to let you be so stupid and just throw your life away like that! You're not seeing him anymore either." She whipped around and pointed toward the stairwell. "Now what you *will* do is—"

"Yes, I am," Clarissa said softly with her eyes downcast.

Cynthia stilled and stared at her daughter. "What did you say?"

"I said I'm still going to see Jared and you can't stop me. I'm not a little baby, Ma!" she shouted as she shot to her feet. Tears were streaming down her face now. "Stop treating me like I am!"

Who is this person standing in my living room? Where was her meek little girl?

"I'm . . . I'm a woman! You were pregnant with me and engaged when you were my age! I should be able to make my own decisions! I want to be with Jared!"

"Not while you live under my roof." Cynthia took a step toward her so that they were almost nose to nose. "When you live under *my* roof and *I* pay for the clothes on your back and the car in the driveway, you will do what *I* say. When it's my money that—"

"That's all you care about is money," Clarissa hissed, pulling back her lips. "That's why you don't like him! You don't even know him and you say I can't see him anymore! Why? Because you want me to end up with some old fart with money, some old guy just like dad! But I don't want your life, Ma!" she yelled into her mother's face. "I don't want to be rich and divorced and alone and pissed off all the time like you! I want to be in love and happy and—"

"There is no such thing," Cynthia said. "And the fact that you believe that being in love with a man will bring you anything but grief in the end shows me just how damn naïve you are and why I have to save you from yourself."

"That's not true!"

"No, money doesn't buy you happiness, but it does buy you independence. It's one of the oldest family rules, and it's a lesson you've obviously ignored. You shackle yourself to deadweight and he'll bring you down your whole life. That's not freedom. That's servitude to your heart—and sheer stupidity! So I'm cutting the chain *now*. You're breaking up with this boy, and that's that." She pointed to the stairwell again. "Now go to your room!"

"But I don't—"

"I said 'go,' Clarissa! Go upstairs or you can leave this house!"

The young woman balled her fists at her sides. She clenched her teeth. Again, Cynthia saw herself reflected in her daughter's face. Based on the fury she saw in Clarissa's eyes, she wasn't sure if Clarissa was going to do what she had not done all those years ago: march to the front door and walk out. Cynthia held her breath, wondering if she had played the wrong hand and if she was about to lose her daughter forever.

But suddenly Clarissa relaxed her fists. Her eyes went flat and cold. She slowly walked toward the stairs and Cynthia released a breath.

She watched as Clarissa marched up the stairs, taking two at a time. Seconds later, Clarissa's bedroom door slammed.

Cynthia's heart felt heavy in her chest, and her pounding headache only got worse.

But I did it, she thought. She had stuck to her guns in order to save Clarissa. *She hates me now, but she won't in the future. She'll see I was right.*

Cynthia leaned against the newel post on the stairs, hoping that would prove to be true.

Chapter 7

Cynthia woke up the next morning feeling as if she had endured a twelve-round bout with a champion heavyweight. She had barely slept last night because of her fight with Clarissa, tossing and turning in her king-size bed for hours. She finally gave up at around five a.m., threw on her robe, and slunk downstairs to the kitchen to drink a cup of coffee and watch the sunrise from her kitchen's bay window. She had expected to be emotionally drained, but she had no idea she would feel physically exhausted too. Her head still ached. Her body was sore. Her eyes felt swollen, as if they were filled with sand. She knew her daughter was hurting too. She just wished Clarissa would understand that this was for the best.

Cynthia stood up from her kitchen stool a little after eight a.m. and decided to make breakfast. The house was eerily quiet, save for the sound of bacon sizzling on the griddle. When the toast and eggs were done, she opened the kitchen cabinets to retrieve glasses and ceramic plates.

"Clarissa!" she called out, opening the fridge to grab a bottle of OJ. "Clarissa, I made breakfast!"

She placed the plates, glasses, and orange juice on the kitchen island and waited a beat. She didn't hear her daughter rouse upstairs.

She walked out of the kitchen, stood at the foot of the staircase, and stared at the floor above. "Clarissa?"

There was still no answer. Clarissa's bedroom door didn't even open. So it looked like she was getting the silent treatment. She should have expected as much.

She took a deep breath and slowly climbed the steps. She walked down the hall and gently knocked on Clarissa's bedroom door.

"Clarissa, I made breakfast."

She dropped her hands to her hips and tilted her head. Still getting no response, Cynthia tried the door handle. At least the door wasn't locked. She pushed it open and the door slowly swung on its hinges with a loud creak.

The curtains on Clarissa's two windows were drawn, so the room was dark. Cynthia could see the outline of Clarissa's body on the bed. The young woman was buried under a mound of blankets with her lavender sheets pulled over her head. Her teddy bear sat on the pillow beside her.

Cynthia stepped into the room, feeling an enormous weight on her shoulders. She hated having Clarissa angry at her. She just wanted her daughter to be happy, and in the long run hooking up with some boy with barely a dollar to his name wasn't going to do that. It wasn't easy being the bad guy.

I wonder if Mama felt like this twenty years ago, Cynthia thought as she crept across the room to Clarissa's bed. Her footsteps were drowned out by the plush gray carpet.

Cynthia could remember the morning after she had broken up with Korey, and how much she had hated her mother for making her do it. She also remembered the conversation she had had with her mother and how the older woman had explained herself and made Cynthia feel that leaving Korey and moving on with Bill was the best choice. A couple months later, when Cynthia discovered that Korey had been cheating on her all along with Vivian, she'd realized that her mother had been right after all. Cynthia struggled now to remember exactly what her mother had said that day. She could use those words of wisdom right now.

"Clarissa, sweetheart," Cynthia said, sitting on the edge of the bed, "look, I know you're angry. I know how you feel, honey. Really I do."

She faced Clarissa's cracked closet door and saw that clothes were spilled onto the floor. She would lecture Clarissa about cleaning up her closet later, but for now, she'd focus on the issue at hand.

"I'm going to tell you something . . . something that not any of my sisters know." Cynthia cleared her throat. "They all act like they invented breaking the rules, like they're the only ones who've fallen in love with guys that no one suspected they would, but it's not true. I-I . . . ." She pushed back her shoulders. "I did it too, honey, before I married your father. I fell in love with a guy who probably would have been a mistake. He loved me too . . . or at least I thought he did. It made it even harder to walk away from him. But your grandmother explained it to me logically. And she made a lot of sense, baby. She said, 'Cindy, a woman doesn't have the luxury of thinking with her heart. She has to think with her head. She doesn't have just the responsibility of herself to worry about. She has to think about the children she'll have in the future. Will the man be a provider? Will she have to hold him up? Love will come and go—that's just a fact of life—but money and a roof over your head can be a shelter against many storms.'"

Cynthia paused, hoping she was getting through to her daughter. She anxiously fingered the belt of her silk robe as she spoke.

"It still hurt, Clarissa, and . . . I'll tell you the truth. In some ways, after all these years, the pain of walking away from him has never gone away. But I-I still think it was the right decision. I made a good life for you—for *us*. You've never wanted for anything. You've always been taken care of. I hope you can make the same sacrifice, honey." She turned to look at her daughter. Cynthia reached for her. "So if you would just—"

She halted when she placed her hand on her daughter's shoulder. Instead of feeling solid bone underneath her fingertips, she felt the soft give of a pillow. Cynthia hesitantly pulled back the sheets and saw that it *was* a pillow. She stood and yanked back the sheets even farther and saw that in addition to the pillow, an oversized stuffed giraffe—a keepsake Clarissa had won years ago at a carnival—was also underneath the sheets, but Clarissa wasn't there. She wasn't in her bed.

"Clarissa? *Clarissa?*" Cynthia shouted. She looked around her daughter's bedroom frantically. "Oh, my God!"

She ran toward the walk-in closet and threw open the French doors. Not only were clothes strewn around the floor, but several hangers were empty. Cynthia's eyes darted to the closet shelves. Two pieces of Clarissa's Louis Vuitton luggage were missing too.

"Oh, God, please don't do this to me! Please don't

tell me this is happening! Not again!" Cynthia's eyes glistened with tears.

How had she not heard Clarissa packing? Why didn't she hear her leave? Did Clarissa sneak out of the bedroom window again?

Cynthia grabbed the frame of the door to steady herself. She felt faint.

She turned and stumbled out of the closet, intending to run into the hallway to call her sister Lauren. Maybe Clarissa had gone running to her again. Cynthia dashed toward the bedroom doorway, then paused when she caught something out of the corner of her eye. It was a note on Clarissa's dresser. Cynthia spotted her daughter's distinctive bubbled cursive script. She grabbed the pink sheet of paper and read it.

> *Mama,*
> *I wish I could make you understand how I feel. All my life you've tried to teach me about the 'family rule book,' but I don't know how many times I have to tell you: <u>I don't care about those rules.</u> I don't care about money either. I'm in love with Jared, and we want to be together. We're going away for a while. When I come back, I'll be Mrs. Jared Walker. If you love me, you'll accept him!*
> *Love,*
> *Clarissa*

Cynthia brought a hand to her mouth. Warm tears spilled onto her cheeks. She'd never felt so powerless in her life. Her baby had run off to God knows where, was getting married, and there was no way she could stop it.

Chapter 8

"Honey, just take a deep breath," Lauren said, rubbing Cynthia's back. "We're going to find her. Don't worry."

Cynthia sat on her living room sofa between her sisters Lauren and Dawn. She was still wearing her robe, nightgown, and fluffy bedroom slippers. She was too distraught to change into real clothes. She sobbed uncontrollably onto Lauren's shoulder, clutching Clarissa's teddy bear against her chest. She hiccupped.

When she had called Lauren to tell her that Clarissa had run away, the Gibbons emergency network instantly mobilized. Lauren called Dawn and left Cristanto Jr. in the care of his father before rushing to Cynthia's side.

Dawn, who had been enjoying a bit of Sunday morning nookie with Xavier, immediately stopped mid-coitus (to her man's great consternation), threw on some clothes, and sped to Cynthia's colonial soon after. Dawn called Stephanie during her high-speed drive to Cynthia's house.

Stephanie left a message with their mother, who was on vacation in Nantucket.

Now Cynthia, Lauren, and Dawn were putting their heads together while they waited for Stephanie to arrive. They thought of ways to track down Clarissa. Well, Lauren and Dawn did the thinking. Cynthia was too busy crying her eyes out to form a plan.

Dawn held Clarissa's letter in her hands. She read it for the umpteenth time and slowly shook her bobbed head. "I wish she'd said where she went." She gazed at Cynthia. "Do you have *any* idea where she might have gone?"

"No! She didn't tell me anything! She just snuck out of the house in the middle of the night, and it's all my fault!" Cynthia cried. She wiped her runny nose with the back of her hand. "I drove her away! Now she's going to marry some boy I don't even know! She's ruining her life just to get back at me!"

Lauren pursed her lips. "I don't think she's trying to get back at you, Cindy. I read the letter too. It sounds like she really thinks this is what's best for her."

"Oh, what does she know?" Cynthia spat. "She's nineteen years old! She's still a baby! And no one will help me get my baby back! Not even the police would help!"

"When did you call the police?" Dawn asked, lowering the letter back to her lap.

"As soon as I found her note! I tried calling Clarissa about a half dozen times. She wouldn't answer, so I called the police instead. I told them she'd run away and she wasn't returning my phone calls. They said because she's not a minor, legally she's old enough to leave the house if she wants. She doesn't have to answer the phone either. And she can get married if she wants to!"

Cynthia closed her eyes and flopped back onto the couch cushions. She held the teddy bear over her face. Her sisters watched helplessly as she sobbed. Of all the Gibbons sisters, usually Cynthia was the least likely to become an emotional wreck, but Cynthia couldn't turn off the waterworks now. Thank God Chesterton wasn't near any cliffs! She probably would have hurled herself off of one by now.

The doorbell rang and Cynthia instantly sat bolt upright. She sniffed. For a split second, she hoped it might be Clarissa returning home. But then she remembered that Clarissa had a key. She would never ring the doorbell to her own home.

"It's probably Steph," Lauren muttered softly. "She said she was on her way over. I'll let her in."

Cynthia slowly nodded and continued her weeping. She reached for a box of tissues on her coffee table. At least the sobs weren't as loud anymore. She didn't know it was possible, but she was running out of tears.

"I'm here!" Stephanie shouted, sprinting into the living room in her stilettos. She wore a baby carrier on her chest, where little Zoe dangled in cow-print baby pajamas with her slobbery fist in her mouth. "I came as soon as I could!" She pointed down at the little one. "Sorry, I had to feed Zoe first."

Zoe gurgled and smiled.

Keith trailed in after them, carrying a diaper bag on his shoulder and a stuffed frog in his hand. He shut the front door behind him.

"What the hell is he doing here?" Cynthia asked, narrowing her hazel eyes at Keith.

"Cindy!" Lauren cried.

"Don't 'Cindy' me!" She glared at Lauren, then snapped her head around to glare up at Keith, the one male in the room. She looked him up and down with contempt.

Men, she thought. It was a man who probably put the thought into Clarissa's head to run away. It was men—namely Crisanto, Xavier, and Keith—who had pulled her sisters away from her with their talk of love until death do us part and romance and all that crap! She'd be damned if she let a man intrude on this too!

"This is a family problem!" she shouted at Keith, making him take a hesitant step back. "*Our* family! So if your last name isn't Gibbons, then I suggest you get the hell—"

"How dare you talk to Keith that way," Stephanie said firmly. She bounced the baby, who was now crying. Zoe was never one for shouting. "He *is* family, Cindy, whether you like it or not! He's the father of my child, my soon-to-be husband, and your future *brother-in-law.* So stop treating him like he's some outsider! You're not going to disrespect him anymore! I'm not putting up with it!"

"Look, ladies," Keith said softly, holding up his hand and the smiling frog. "I'm not trying to start a fight here. I just came to help."

Dawn's expression brightened. She slowly stood from the sofa. "You . . . you think you can help us, Keith?"

Stephanie took her daughter out of her carrier, cooed to her, and rocked her back and forth, while shooting daggers with her eyes at her eldest sister, Cynthia. Zoe's cries died down to a few soft murmurs.

Keith nodded. "Sure. I track people down for a living. I don't see why I can't track down Clarissa too." He walked toward Cynthia and sat down in the wing-back armchair facing her. He opened a side pocket in the diaper bag and pulled out a pen and a notepad.

"Tell me about Clarissa's boyfriend. What's the kid's name?"

Cynthia hesitated. He wasn't family. She didn't care what Stephanie said.

"His name is Jared Walker," Lauren answered for her.

Cynthia angrily cut her eyes at Lauren. Lauren raised her chin, ignoring her. They watched as Keith scribbled the name on his notepad.

"Do we know where this Jared lives?" he asked.

Lauren nudged Cynthia's shoulder, urging her to answer this time.

Cynthia sighed. "I didn't even know the boy existed until yesterday."

Keith looked up from his notepad. "So I guess that's a 'no' then?"

She shook her head.

"Well, I'll run the name through a few databases and see if I get any hits. Maybe I can find an address that way. If I do, we should talk to his parents and see if maybe they have an idea where the kids might have gone." He flipped his notepad closed. "In the meantime, I'm going to need you to pull any copies of Clarissa's cell phone bills you may have. If you can go online and see what recent calls she's made, that would help a lot too. We could try to create a timeline that way." He leaned forward. "Does she have any credit cards or debit cards she likes to use that we can trace?"

Cynthia frowned. "She has a gas card with a $200 limit, but that's about it. If she wants to buy anything more than that, she uses my credit cards, but only with my permission. She hasn't borrowed any lately."

"Well, you may want to check your wallet to see if any of your cards are missing."

"You think she took my credit cards?" She quickly shook her head. "No! No, that's impossible! Clarissa would *never* steal from me!"

"Uh-huh." He didn't look convinced. "But why don't you go check?"

When she didn't budge, he inclined his head.

"Humor me," he said with a wink. "It's just a hunch."

Cynthia slowly stood from the sofa. While her sisters and Keith waited in the living room, she walked upstairs and looked for her purse, though she knew it was a waste of time. Clarissa had never taken anything from Cynthia without permission in her entire life. Cynthia rifled through her Hermès wallet. She checked each slot, counting her credit cards. She returned to the living room seconds later.

"She stole from me!" Cynthia shouted, waving her wallet around in the air. "She stole from her own mother!"

"What's missing?" Lauren asked.

"My Discover *and* my Visa! I can't believe she stole from me!"

"Well, in this case, her stealing is a good thing," Keith said. "It makes it easier to track her down. We can monitor all her purchases and maybe see where she's headed."

"See!" Stephanie beamed as she plopped on the arm of the chair where Keith sat. Zoe slumbered in her arms. She leaned over and kissed Keith on the cheek. "I knew my baby could help! Isn't he a genius?"

"Not quite," Keith said. "I'm just someone with a lot of detective experience. I'll try my best to help you guys find Clarissa. And I'll do it as quick as I can. I heard time is of the essence here, so I will need you guys to help out on this one."

They nodded, including Cynthia. Maybe she had been

wrong about Keith. She still considered men to be something of another species, but for now, she was willing to make a few exceptions.

The family attacked their tasks simultaneously. Dawn and Lauren went online and checked for any recent purchases Clarissa may have made with Cynthia's credit cards. Cynthia went through Clarissa's old cell phone bills, noting anything that looked out of the ordinary. Keith pulled out his laptop and went through his databases, including criminal and DMV records, looking for the name Jared Walker. Meanwhile, Stephanie stayed in the kitchen, making sandwiches and tomato soup for lunch to help fortify everyone. She only paused from her culinary tasks to breast-feed Zoe again.

Half an hour later, they all met in the kitchen to share the information they had found. They commiserated between bites of sandwiches and spoonfuls of tomato soup.

"I saw the same number five times yesterday!" Cynthia shouted, slapping down the computer printouts on the kitchen island's butcher block. "And it had a Chesterton area code. One of the phone calls lasted for almost an hour! You can't tell me that wasn't the number of the little jerk Clarissa ran off with!"

Keith stared at Lauren and Dawn, who sat on stools on the opposite side of the kitchen island. "What did you guys find out?"

"She withdrew a cash advance of three hundred dollars at an ATM in Great Falls last night," Dawn said. She shrugged. "Nothing else after that. Sorry, I don't have more."

"That's okay," Keith assured. "We'll pick up the trail somewhere else."

"I think I found something," Lauren ventured quietly. "I saw a purchase for two plane tickets for Delta Airlines dated last night."

Cynthia grabbed her chest. She gulped for air. "*Plane tickets?* You mean . . . you mean they're flying somewhere?"

Lauren nodded. "Another purchase was for a hotel in Las Vegas."

Cynthia slowly lowered her forehead to the wooden surface. "Oh, my God! So she *is* going through with it! My only daughter is going to get married at some tacky drive-thru chapel on the Las Vegas Strip!" She closed her eyes. "Why is this happening to me? *Why is this happening?*"

"Calm down, Cynthia," Keith said. "At least we know where she's going . . . and we may be able to stop her before she goes through with it."

"*How?*" Cynthia shouted, raising her head and glaring at him. "Clarissa won't even answer my phone calls! She knows I'm going to tell her to come home. I'd probably have to physically stop her from putting a ring on her finger, and how the hell am I supposed to do that? I won't make it to Vegas in time!"

"Well, maybe the boy's parents can stop them," Keith insisted. "Maybe they can talk *him* out of it."

All the sisters fell silent.

"What do you mean, baby?" Stephanie asked as she finished the last of her sandwich.

"I got a hit on the name Jared Walker," Keith explained. "He got a speeding ticket in Chesterton three months ago. It listed his name, but it also listed the name of the person who owned the car. It had the car's registration. It was a Ford Taurus registered to Korey Walker of Langley Court. I bet one hundred bucks he's the boy's father."

Cynthia blinked. She gazed at Keith, dumbfounded. "What name did you say?"

"Korey Walker." Keith paused. "Why? Does the name sound familiar?"

Cynthia's lips tightened and so did her fists. Her puffy eyes narrowed into thin slits. It was such a common last name, she hadn't even considered the possibility that this boy could be Korey's son, but it seemed that was the case.

"Yes. Yes, the name sounds *very* familiar. Give me the address on that registration. I need to pay someone a visit."

Chapter 9

Korey raised his gaze from the PVC pipe. The wrench in his hand hovered in midair.

"Who the hell is that?" he murmured as he slowly climbed to his feet.

Someone was ringing his doorbell over and over again and pounding on the front door, making the frame rattle.

He set the wrench on the laminate countertop and wiped his wet hands on a dish towel.

His bathroom sink had been clogged for the past two days, and no amount of Drano or snaking seemed to do the trick. He had finally decided to break out his toolbox and had just started a bit of DIY plumbing when he heard the sound of screeching tires in his driveway. Now it sounded like the police were at his door with a battering ram.

He ran down the hall and looked through the front door's peephole. His eyes widened in shock. Cynthia Gibbons stood on his welcome mat, screaming like a crazy woman.

"Open up, damn it!" she yelled. "Korey, I know you're in there! Open up the door!"

He quickly undid the locks and swung his door open. "What the hell . . . Damn, woman, where's the fire?"

She looked like she had just stumbled out of bed. Her hair was pulled back into an askew ponytail, and she wasn't wearing any jewelry or her usual heart-stopping attire, only a blue blouse that was buttoned the wrong way and wrinkled jeans. This was the first time in his life that he had seen her without makeup. The freckles on her nose and cheeks stood out even more, and so did the gold flecks in her eyes. Not surprisingly, Cynthia Gibbons was a natural beauty, even though she looked like she had been through hell and back.

"Did you know about this?" she asked, shoving her way inside his home and barging into his living room. "Did you know about Clarissa and Jared?"

Korey's shoulders slumped. So Cynthia had finally found out. He figured she would be angry when she did. He probably should have assumed she'd be angry at him too.

Korey shut the door behind her. He turned and nodded.

"Yes, I knew."

"Well, why the hell didn't you tell me, Korey?" she screamed, throwing up her hands. "You didn't think I had the right to know? She's my daughter, damn it!"

"I know she's your daughter, but—"

"*How could you?* How could you let this happen? What on earth were thinking?"

Korey took a deep breath. "Cindy, I didn't *let* anything happen. I had no control over this. You know how these things are. A boy and girl meet and . . . it evolves all by itself."

She balled her fists at her sides. Her lips tightened. She looked on the verge of a Mount Vesuvius–worthy volcanic explosion.

"Look, Jared, Clarissa, and I knew you would be upset by this. That's why they kept it a secret and asked me to keep it a secret too. I know you're pissed off now, but just give it some time to let it sink in, okay? Don't make any rash judgments right now."

He reached out and touched her shoulders. Her warmth made his fingers tingle. He hadn't touched her like this in such a long time. It felt good to do it again.

"They're smart kids, Cindy, and they know their own hearts."

Just like I thought we did back then, Korey thought, but he didn't say those words aloud.

"If you just give it a chance, you might—"

"I will *never* 'give it a chance,' Korey Walker," Cynthia said with a deadly calm, shoving him away from her. "I'm putting the brakes on this right god-damn now! Do you understand me? Your son and my daughter are getting married over my dead body!"

"Getting married?" Now he was confused. His hands fell to his sides. "Who the hell said anything about them getting married?"

"What do you mean who the hell said anything about them getting married?" she shouted. The tendons were almost bulging out of her neck. "You told me that you knew! You knew they were headed to Vegas to get married! Don't act stupid!"

"What?" Korey shook his head. "Jared's not headed to Vegas! He's going on a three-day trip to Virginia Beach with his . . . with his boys . . . you know, his friends from college."

Cynthia went silent. She furrowed her brows and

crossed her arms over her chest. She looked at Korey as if he was the most gullible man in the world. "Oh, is that what he told you? And when did your son leave for this three-day trip to Virginia Beach?"

"Uh . . ." Korey struggled to remember. He ran a hand over his head. "Sometime last night, I guess. He got a call from his friend. He asked Jared to pick him up, and they were supposed to stay at another guy's house until—"

"Clarissa and I had a big fight last night about your son, Korey," Cynthia said, cutting him off. "She took some clothes and her luggage and snuck out of the house in the middle of the night. Her car is still in my driveway, so someone had to pick her up. I know it was Jared who did it! And how do I know? Because she left a note saying she was running away with *your* son, and when she came back, she would be Mrs. Jared Walker."

Korey felt the blood drain from his head. *No,* he thought. *No, that's not possible!*

The kids wouldn't do anything that stupid! He knew young people could be passionate and impulsive, but there was no way Jared would agree to run away to Las Vegas to get married to a girl he had only known for a few months!

"There's a quick way to settle this," Korey muttered. He walked toward the cordless phone hanging on the kitchen wall by the fridge. "I'll call Jared to see where he is."

Cynthia sucked her teeth. "He probably won't answer your call. Clarissa didn't answer any of mine."

Korey bit back the remark, *If you were my mother, I probably wouldn't have answered either.* Instead he said, "Well, it wouldn't hurt to try, Cindy, now would it? What have we got to lose?"

Cynthia hovered at his side, watching him as he dialed Jared's cell phone number on the punch pad.

"Maybe she just lied to scare you," Korey said as Jared's phone began to ring in his ear. "She wanted to get back at you for freaking out. I bet she's hiding out at a girlfriend's house somewhere, safe and sound. Or maybe she's in Virginia Beach partying it up with Jared, but they're not—"

"Hey, Pops, what's up?" Jared casually answered.

Korey breathed a sigh of relief, elated to hear his son's voice. "Hey, Jared."

Cynthia's mouth fell open. She grabbed Korey's back, digging her long nails into his shoulder blades. "Find out where they are!" she whispered frantically.

Korey nodded, then returned his attention to the phone call. "Just wanted to check in with you, son. Are you guys on the road yet? Still headed to Virginia Beach?"

"Yeah, Pops," Jared answered distractedly, "we just hit I-95. We're going to stop at a rest stop in an hour or so. Then it'll be my turn to drive."

"Oh, okay, well you . . . you guys stay safe."

"Sure, Pops."

Cynthia slapped Korey's shoulder. "Ask about Clarissa!" she mouthed. "Ask him!"

He nodded again, getting tired of her physical abuse. "Hey, Jared?"

"Yeah? Look, I should probably get off the phone now, Pops. I'm supposed to—"

"Have you heard from Clarissa?" Korey glanced at Cynthia, who was nodding so hard her eyes were rolling. "Her mom stopped by today. She said she had a fight with her last night and Clarissa ran away. She's really worried about her. She wondered if maybe you had spoken to her."

"Oh," Jared said. "Umm, n-no, I haven't heard from Clarissa. I haven't talked to her since yesterday. Sorry, I can't help you."

Korey squinted. That wasn't the reaction he expected from a guy who had just found out that his girlfriend had run away from home. Jared didn't sound vaguely concerned.

"Jared," Korey said, "don't lie to me. Are you with Clarissa?"

"Pops, I told you. I don't know where she is! I haven't . . . I haven't spoken to her."

His voice was high. Jared's voice always went an octave higher when he lied.

"I've gotta get off the phone, Pops. All right?"

Korey suddenly heard a dinging sound in the background. Then a muffled voice came over a loudspeaker.

"Now boarding Flight 557 to Las Vegas, Nevada," a woman's syrupy voice boomed. "First-class passengers and passengers with small children—"

"Jared?" Korey shouted. His throat felt tight. His heart started to pound in his chest at a breakneck speed. He gripped the cordless so hard in his hand, he felt as if he would crush it. "Jared, don't you dare get on that plane! Boy, I will—"

"I'll talk to you later, Pops," Jared said hastily. Then the phone line went dead.

Korey tried to call Jared's cell phone again, but each time the call went to Jared's voicemail. He finally lowered the phone back into its cradle, feeling dazed.

"So they took the flight then?" Cynthia asked.

Korey jumped. He turned and found her gazing up at him expectantly. He had forgotten she was standing there. He gradually nodded. "Yeah, and it sounds like they're definitely headed to Vegas."

"I have to stop this, Korey! I *can't* let this happen. I know the hotel where they're staying. Clarissa used my credit card for the reservations." She turned around and headed to his front door. "I'm booking a flight. When I arrive in Vegas, I'll—"

"I'm booking a flight too."

Cynthia paused with her hand on the doorknob. She slowly turned to stare at him. "Huh?"

"Clarissa may be your daughter, but Jared is *my* son," he said, pointing at his chest. "I could accept them dating, but this marriage stuff is crazy! They're way too young! They've only been together four months! Not to mention the fact that Viv would kill me if she found out I let this happen! I wouldn't hear the end of it." He nodded firmly. "So I'm going there too."

"You . . . you want us to go to Vegas . . . *together?*"

He smirked. "What? Scared to be alone with me for a couple of days?"

She licked her pouty lower lip. "Well, n-no."

Korey strolled toward her. His smile widened. He could swear he saw nervousness flicker across her honey-colored face. "You don't have to be scared, Cindy," he said softly as he stood in front of her. He gazed into her eyes. "I'm not going to try anything."

She straightened her shoulders and raised her chin. "I told you that I'm not scared," she bluffed bravely, putting on the Ice Queen act again. "Why would I be? It takes two to tango, and frankly, I'm not interested."

He reached out and trailed a finger along her soft cheek. Her eyes fluttered closed. He felt her tremble beneath his fingertip. "Are you sure about that?" he whispered.

He wondered if she still sighed before she kissed. Did she still moan and do those high-pitched whines when she made love? She had a symphony of sounds back when they were younger. What new moans and cries had she added to the mix?

As if reading his thoughts, her eyes flashed open. She stiffened.

"I'll see if I can book us both a flight for later today," she said, pushing away his hand. "You can pay me back later. Just be ready to leave this afternoon."

She then turned and opened his front door, slamming it shut behind her.

Chapter 10

Cynthia took a deep breath, then released it.

Inhale, exhale, she thought. *Inhale, exhale.*

But the deep-breathing exercises weren't working. She still had a death grip on the armrests of her airplane seat. She was gritting her teeth so much, her gums hurt. Oh, once she got her hands on Clarissa, she was going to strangle that little girl! Not only had Clarissa run away from home, was well on her way to getting married, and had stolen Cynthia's credit cards to pull off the whole debacle, she was now forcing her mother to ride on an airplane. Flying was one of Cynthia's worst fears—just below being broke and living in a hovel.

Inhale, exhale. Inhale, exhale.

These things were death traps! The people were packed in so tightly they all would probably catch tuberculosis from the fat old man with glasses who was coughing over and over again into his fist two seats in front of her. And if the plane went down, she knew they didn't stand a chance of survival. The flotation devices under the seats were a joke, and what if they didn't land in water, but on the ground? It wasn't like they had any parachutes. No, they would all go hurtling to the earth in a flaming fireball. Her only hope would be to lose consciousness before impact.

Inhale, exhale. Inhale, exhale.

Damn it, why hadn't the Xanax Dawn lent her kicked in yet? What was taking it so long?

"These are nice seats," Korey said.

Cynthia cracked one eye open to look at him.

"I've never flown first-class before because I thought it was a waste of money." He shifted in the padded leather seat beside her and stretched. "But I should do this more often. You get plenty of leg room."

She didn't respond.

He turned to her and frowned. "Are you okay?"

"I'm fine," she said through clenched teeth.

She heard a thudding sound and turned, wild-eyed and panicked. She looked out of her seat window. It was only the sound of two guys on the tarmac, loading suitcases onto the plane.

"You don't look fine," Korey said, still eying her. "You look like you're about to rip the metal off that armrest."

"I told you, I'm all right. I'm just not . . . I'm just not a fan of flying, that's all."

"*Ooooh!* I didn't know that."

She sighed. "Well, now you do."

Cynthia glanced out of the window and saw that the two men were loading the last of the baggage onto the plane. That meant they would be taking off soon. She inwardly moaned.

"You don't have to worry," Korey assured her, leaning toward her. His dark eyes twinkled. "You know, I used to be afraid to fly too. I'm a lot better now, though.

In the old days, every time I sat on a plane I felt like I was stuck in jet-sized coffin."

Was this conversation supposed to make her feel better?

"And the turbulence can be the worst. I was on a flight to Chicago once where it felt like the whole plane was rattling." He shook his arms to demonstrate. "It felt like we could drop out of the sky at any moment."

"Korey, is this your version of a pep talk?" she asked, glaring at him. "If it is, you *suck* at it!"

He chuckled. "Look, I'm just saying that it's possible to get past the fear. Besides, statistically you're more likely to die in a car crash than a plane crash, right? So odds are that both of us will survive this flight. Don't worry."

She'd like to see those odds.

Suddenly, a voice came over the plane's PA system. It was the captain announcing that all passengers should buckle their seat belts because they were headed to the runway.

Cynthia closed her eyes again. "Inhale, exhale. Inhale, exhale," she chanted aloud.

Korey chuckled again and patted the hand that was still gripping the armrest. "You'll be fine. Just focus on something else."

"Like what?" she cried hysterically, opening her eyes. The flight attendants were demonstrating where the exit doors were on the plane. "What the hell else am I supposed to focus on when I'm surrounded by an airplane on all sides?"

Cynthia could hear something mechanical happening over her shoulder. She snapped her head and turned to look out the window again. The pilot was adjusting the flaps on the wings. She flapped her hands wildly in front of her face. She wanted to unbuckle her seat belt, race to the plane doors, and scream to be let out.

Oh, my God, I'm having a panic attack!

"Focus on our kids, for one," Korey said. He casually adjusted his seat belt and grabbed the in-flight magazine in the seat pocket in front of him and began to flip its pages. "Think about how the hell we're supposed to find them once we get to Las Vegas."

She stopped flapping her hands. "What do you mean how are we supposed to find them? We already know the hotel where they're staying."

"Cindy, haven't you ever been to Vegas? Those hotels are huge! Some have multiple buildings. We may know where they're staying, but we don't know their room number."

"So we ask the reservation desk!"

"But the reservation desk doesn't have to give it to us just because we ask nicely."

"I'm not going to 'ask nicely'!"

Korey was right. She was starting to forget she was in a jet-sized coffin. She was more pissed about him pointing out an obvious obstacle to her plan for finding Clarissa.

"I'm going to tell them to give me the damn room number because she's *my* daughter and she used *my* credit card to get that hotel room!"

Korey snorted and turned another magazine page. "And I'm sure that'll go over well."

"So what do you suggest?" she shouted over the noise of the plane as it raced down the runway. "What's your brilliant idea on how to find the kids?"

"Well, I say when we get there, we be honest with them: We explain the situation. They're two young people who ran off and now are about to do something really stupid. And if that doesn't work—we slip the guy at the desk a hundred bucks and ask again."

"And if *that* doesn't work?" she yelled as they were suddenly thrown back in their seats. Cynthia closed her eyes and slapped a hand against her chest as the plane tilted to a forty-five-degree angle. She was going to have a heart attack. She was sure of it! The pressure against her chest and in her ears increased as the plane flew into the air.

Korey thought for a minute or two. "I guess the only other alternative we have is that we get a room at the hotel, hunker down in the lobby, and try to track them down that way."

Her eyes flew open. "*We?* What do you mean *we'll* get a room?"

"I meant separate rooms, of course. Damn, woman!" He shoved the magazine into the seat pocket in front of him, looking offended.

The plane finally started to level out. Her heart rate decreased a little. She took a deep breath.

"Look, I told you that I wasn't going to try anything on this trip," Korey said. "Why are you so convinced I'm trying to get into your pants?"

"*Honestly?* Because you always tried in the past. There wasn't a single date we had, Korey, when you weren't reaching for—"

"Well, that's in the past," he said steadfastly, glaring at her. "I'm a grown man now. I know how to control myself. My son's the one who seems to be going at it like there's no tomorrow. Trust me! He's getting a lot more ass than me nowadays."

Cynthia went stock-still. Her heart started to race again, this time for a very different reason.

"What . . . what do you mean? You're not . . . you're

not suggesting that he's having sex with Clarissa, are you?"

Korey started to laugh. "You're joking, right?"

"No, I'm not joking!"

The orange seat belt sign went off. Over the PA system, the captain said that they were free to move about the cabin and that flight attendants would soon be going around with drinks and snacks.

"Cindy, I think it's pretty safe to assume that those two are having sex—*a lot*."

"You don't know that for a fact! They could just be . . . they could just be kissing on occasion, or making out . . . lots of kissing and rubbing! Kids like to do that. I thought . . . I thought that's what this whole marriage business was about. Clarissa wouldn't have sex until they got married, so that's why they're rushing to Vegas!"

Korey was laughing even harder now, absolutely infuriating her. For the first time, Cynthia noticed a white-haired old woman sitting in the first-class seat across the aisle. She was staring at them over the top of her romance paperback with a bare-chested hunk on the cover. She was avidly listening to their conversation.

"Mind your own damn business!" Cynthia shouted at her. "Read your book!"

The woman's eyes snapped back to her book's pages.

"Cindy, calm down!" Korey said

"I can't calm down when you're insinuating that my daughter is having sex with your son!"

"I'm not insinuating. I'm about ninety-nine percent sure the kids are having sex."

"Why ninety-nine percent?"

"Because I have evidence, sweetheart."

"What *evidence?*"

He glanced at the old woman, who was back to listening again but making a poor attempt to mask it. He motioned Cynthia to lean toward him. She did. Then he whispered in her ear, "I gave Jared a box of condoms last year that he didn't touch for months. I saw the box a few weeks ago and now half of it is empty."

She leaned back and stared at him.

"Hey, don't look at me like that! Just be happy they're using condoms." His brows knitted together as he grimaced. "I just hope she isn't pregnant."

"You better shut your mouth, Korey Walker!"

"It's not that crazy of an idea. That would definitely explain that whole eloping thing."

This can't be happening, she thought as he spoke. Things were spiraling out of control and she couldn't stop them. She had to get to Clarissa! She had to talk to her before this thing went beyond the point of no return!

"It already has if Korey's right," a dire voice in her head warned. "If he's right, we've got a major catastrophe on our hands."

"I need a drink," Cynthia muttered. "I need a drink right goddamn *now!*"

When the flight attendant came by with her rolling cart, Cynthia ordered a gin and tonic. Korey ordered a rum and coke. He sipped his drink. She finished hers in one gulp. Of course, it was just her luck that after she had her gin and tonic, the Xanax finally started to kick in. Instead of feeling as if she had had one drink to soothe her nerves, she felt as if she had just downed *five* of them!

After an hour, Cynthia took off her seat belt and then her sweater.

God, it's hot in here, she thought.

She flopped back into her seat and stared out the

airplane window at the view. They were somewhere over the Midwest but so high up in the air that she couldn't see buildings anymore.

All the fluffy clouds. Look at all the pretty fluffy clouds.

The Xanax and alcohol had done the trick. Instead of thinking about crashing to the earth, she wanted to put on a bathing suit and dog-paddle in the clouds outside her window.

Cynthia turned and looked at Korey. He had his headphones on and was staring at the screen in the headrest in front of him, watching the in-flight movie. She gazed at his face in profile. He was definitely a handsome man and sexy as all hell.

The bastard, she thought.

She wondered if he was still a good kisser. God had given him a mouth to bring a woman infinite pleasures. She reached out and ran her index finger over his full lips, making him jump in surprise. He yanked off his headphones and frowned down at her.

"What are you doing?"

Cynthia smiled dreamily and turned sideways in her seat to face him. She pulled up the armrest and leaned toward him. She was almost in his lap. "Do you . . . do you remember that time senior year when we went down to the lake to go tubing?" she said in a breathy whisper. "Remember? It was a class trip, but we walked off by ourselves."

"Cindy, are you drunk?"

"We walked to this deserted spot, and you dared me to take off all my clothes and jump in the water with you."

He hesitated. "Yeah, I remember. I thought I was being spontaneous. I had to get naked first for you to even do it . . . and it was freezing in there." He shook his head. "It was nothing like the movies. That's for damn sure."

"We swam around for a half an hour and then when we came back to shore, you laid down your T-shirt in the grass, in the spot hidden behind a thicket of bushes, and we made love right there, Korey." She closed her eyes and laid her head against his shoulder, thinking back to the memory. "I think I came three times that day! Gah, you had a mouth on you . . . and you used to do that thing with your tongue! What was that thing?"

Korey glanced at the old woman who sat across the aisle from them. She was staring at them again, totally riveted.

"And those hands. I loved your fingers, Korey! You could make me come that way too." She smirked. "But it was nothing . . . and I mean *nothing* compared to that big d—"

"Cindy, why are we talking about this?" he asked, cutting her off.

"Because I was thinking about the fact that I haven't had sex that good since I was eighteen." She lazily stroked his arm. "Bill tried in the beginning. Really, he did. But it just wasn't the same. And Richard couldn't find a G-spot if it had a siren and flashing lights." She opened her eyes again and gazed up at him. "That's just pitiful, Korey. I'm almost forty and I still think about sex that I had on a lake almost twenty years ago."

He didn't respond.

"Do you still think about it too?" she whispered, staring at his lips.

"Do I"—he tugged his arm out of her grasp and stared at the screen in the headrest—"do I, uh, still think about what?"

"Do you think about what it was like to touch me, Korey?"

He looked down at her.

"To kiss me . . ."

Now he was staring at her lips too.

"To be inside me?"

She abruptly raised her mouth to his. All the heat she had fought to keep at bay for the past several days now came hurtling forward. She teased his lips with her teeth and tongue and opened her mouth. He accepted her ready invitation and kissed her back just as hungrily, delving his tongue inside her mouth too.

The woman sitting across the aisle had lowered her steamy romance novel to her lap. Her eyes were almost popping out of her head now as she watched them. Why read about it when you had the real thing happening eighteen inches away from you?

Cynthia wrapped her arms around Korey's neck and let out a soft moan. Oh, she loved this! The kisses were still the same. She knew they would be! They weren't inflated memories from her teenaged years. His kisses were hot and ravenous . . . and *delicious*. She pressed herself against him, rubbing her breasts against his chest. He started to wrap his arms around her. Then, abruptly, he reached up and tugged her hands away. He shoved her away from him, catching her by surprise.

"What I remember is you dumping me for Bill," he said between labored breaths. He adjusted in his seat and tugged at the front of his jeans, where there was now a conspicuous bulge. "*That's* what I remember."

She stared at him as he put his headphones back on and returned his attention to the in-flight movie. The kiss had sobered her up a little, enough for her to feel all the sting of his rejection.

He remembered her dumping him for Bill? Well, what about him cheating on her with Vivian? *What about that shit, huh?*

She angrily turned around in her seat and lowered the armrest back into place between them. They both sat in silence for almost an hour, pretending to ignore one another.

"You know," she began, jabbing his shoulder, wanting to pick a fight with him when she couldn't stand the silence any longer. He took off his headphones again. "I'm still not convinced that Clarissa and Jared are doing it."

"Why are we back to this? Cindy, how naïve are you? It's pretty damn obvious that they're doing it! I told you, half of the condoms are gone, and he sure as hell isn't making water balloons with them!"

"Just because he's using condoms, doesn't mean he's been using them with Clarissa! Maybe he's having sex with someone else."

Korey paused. "Are you calling my boy a man whore?"

She haughtily raised her chin into the air. "Like father, like son."

"What's that supposed to mean?"

"You know what it means! You cheated on me! I see no reason why your son wouldn't cheat on Clarissa."

"What? When the hell did I ever cheat on you?"

"Oh, please. Don't insult my intelligence, Korey! Less than two months after we broke up, you were engaged to Vivian and she was already pregnant. Are you honestly trying to tell me that was some kind of a sixty-day whirlwind romance, that you weren't seeing her behind my back the whole time?"

His jaw tightened. "I didn't date Viv until you broke

up with me to become the trophy wife of some rich man almost twice our age!"

She waved away his denial. "Sure, you didn't. Everyone in school knew she was after you. I did too. I saw the way she looked at you. I just trusted you when you said there was nothing going on between you two."

"Because there was nothing going on between us!"

"Yeah, right," she murmured, gazing out the window. "I was gullible back then, Korey, but I'm not anymore. So you can just save it!"

"Fine, believe whatever the hell you want, but I know the truth! I married Viv because she picked my heart up off the ground after you *ran over it!* She offered me a warm embrace and, yes, a warm bed while she was at it. But what did I know? I was eighteen years old! I didn't know any better! So when she came to me in tears and said she was pregnant, what was I supposed to do? I asked her to marry me. I wasn't in love with her, but I thought I owed it to her to marry her after what she did for me!"

Cynthia bit down on her lower lip as she glared at the clouds outside her window. Was he telling the truth?

"And I don't regret my decision," Korey continued. "My marriage to Viv wasn't the greatest, but we produced a great kid. I love Jared. I'd do anything for him! That's why I'm here."

She slowly turned to face him. "I love Clarissa too. That's . . . that's why I'm here."

"Good, so we both agree that's why we're here, for the kids—and that's all. So let's not muddy the water with bullshit about the past."

She pursed her lips and nodded. He put his headphones back on and glared at the TV screen.

He said not to muddy the water, but it was too late. If he was telling the truth about not cheating on her with Vivian all those years ago, then that changed everything. Cynthia had to see the past in a new light, and she didn't like what she saw.

Chapter 11

"You ready to go in, baby?" Crisanto asked.

Lauren Gibbons-Weaver distractedly looked up at her husband. She forced a smile as she stepped away from their car. "Of course," she said as he shut her door for her. She then linked her arm through Cris's just as he handed the waiting valet his ECU key to his Aston Martin convertible.

The smiling young man, who had to be no more than eighteen, nodded before eagerly climbing behind the wheel and pausing to admire the car's leather interior and the varnish on the dashboard. He looked practically giddy when the engine purred as he pulled off, leaving Cris and Lauren standing at the foot of an asphalt driveway bordered by two stone lion statues.

Lauren was surprised that there was a valet at this party, considering they were parking at a three-story home on a two-acre lot and not some ritzy restaurant downtown. But she should have known their host would make a big production out of tonight. There was even a red carpet on the brick walkway.

Subtle, Marvin, Lauren thought sarcastically.

Like many others in Chesterton, Marvin Payton, the owner of a small chain of lawn-care retail stores, had been trying to get into Cris's good graces since Cris moved into town more than two years ago. Marvin had plenty of rich friends, but none were a former star player for the Dallas Cowboys or a Heisman trophy winner like Cris. To count Cris as one of his pals would definitely earn Marvin plenty of respect in town. So Lauren wasn't surprised that Marvin had immediately stepped forward to host a party to help kick off Cris's mayoral run.

"It would be an *honor,* Cris," Marvin had said a week ago. She thought he might bow or prostrate himself at Cris's feet. "It would be my true honor to host a party for you!"

And it looked like Marvin hadn't spared any expense on the party, judging from the valet, the red carpet, and the live band she could see through the home's bay of windows. She also could see a gaggle of partygoers milling about inside. The place looked packed.

"Are you sure you're okay?" Cris asked. He frowned down at his wife as they made their way up the driveway toward the carpet that led to the colonial's front door.

Lauren nodded. "I'm fine. I'm just . . . you know, a little anxious."

"Anxious?"

"About the party." She laughed awkwardly and patted his arm. "You know I'm not very good at hobnobbing. Never have been."

When he continued to squint down at her, looking incredulous, she pursed her lips.

Lauren had never been very good at hiding things from Cris. He had made it clear early on in their relationship that he didn't want her to ever lie to him, and now that he knew her well enough, he could always see the truth on her face anyway. It was best just to tell him what she was really thinking.

"Okay, maybe I'm more than anxious. I guess I'm closer to worried."

"About Clarissa?" he rightly guessed.

"About Clarissa *and* Cynthia," she clarified. "Cindy's really torn up about this, Cris. I've never seen her so hysterical. Even I don't understand why Clarissa would run off to Las Vegas to get married. *Married!* Can you believe it? Has she lost her damn mind?" She shook her head ruefully. "I mean, I get that Clarissa is upset at her mom. Cindy isn't easy to deal with sometimes . . . okay, *a lot* of times. But this is so extreme! And now Cynthia is on a flight to Vegas to find her and stop the . . ."

When Lauren realized she was ranting, her words faded. She sighed.

"I'm sorry, honey. I'm sorry for talking about the usual family drama. I know this is a big night for you. You don't need to hear about all this crap."

They climbed the short flight of brick stairs. "It's okay. I'm used to it by now. There's never a dull moment in the Gibbons family, is there? You girls like your drama."

"I'm afraid so, but I warned you in the beginning," she said playfully, wagging her finger up at him.

"That you did," he whispered before leaning down to kiss her.

His lips brushed hers just as the colonial's front door swung open.

Lauren had been told that the dress code for tonight was dressy casual, so she had worn a teal eyelet lace sundress and sandals. Cris had on a dress shirt and tan slacks. But the woman standing in the doorway obviously hadn't gotten the dress code memo or had simply ignored it. She had on a slinky black sequined halter gown, garish diamond jewelry, and about two pounds of imported Malaysian weave on her head. She held a wineglass in her hand. A grin was plastered on her red glossy lips.

"And here's the man of the hour!" she gushed. "Mr. Crisanto Weaver himself! Welcome to our home, Cris!"

Lauren fought back a laugh as she watched Judy Payton, their hostess, teeter slightly on her stilettos. Judy stepped back from the door and ushered Cris and Lauren inside her foyer.

The woman had obviously gotten the party started early. She looked like she had had more than just a little to drink.

"Hey, Marv!" she slurred over her shoulder, shouting to be heard over the jazz trio that Lauren had spotted from the driveway. The trio played a Duke Ellington tune on the other side of the room, near the fireplace.

Judy wobbled again as she shut the door behind Cris and Lauren. "Marv! Cris is here, honey bun! Come say hi!"

Cris and *his wife, Lauren*, Lauren corrected silently. But she kept smiling, giving no hint of her irritation.

She knew how it was. Everyone went out of their way to be nice to her husband, but many chose to either be stiffly polite with her or to ignore her completely. She was a happily married mother and chef. She hadn't chased after a rich man in years, not since her nasty breakup with her abusive ex-boyfriend, James Sayers. She had changed her ways, but many still saw her as nothing more than a ruthless gold digger.

"Welcome! *Welcome!*" Marvin bellowed as he strode across the hardwood floors, shoving through the throng of partygoers to make his way toward Cris. When he reached the towering man, he instantly embraced him. Cris awkwardly hugged him back.

"Cris, I'm so glad you're here!" Marvin cried.

"Thanks for inviting us."

"Of course! Of course!" He grabbed Cris's elbow. "Let me introduce you to a few people. Councilman Connelly is here. And of course, I have to introduce you to the Murdochs—George and his son, Evan. If you get their approval and support, you've pretty much won the election," Marvin said, lowering his voice. "I'm sure you know everyone, but just in case you don't, I don't want you to miss the chance to win over potential voters. Am I right?" Marvin loudly laughed, slapped Cris on the back, and attempted to steer him across the foyer toward the living room, but Cris halted and turned toward Lauren instead.

"You're okay on your own?" he whispered into her ear.

She smiled, warmed to know that her husband was so thoughtful and protective of her.

"I'm fine," she whispered back, shooing him away. "Don't worry about me. Go and win those votes, Future Mayor."

He nodded, kissed her cheek, and turned back to Marvin. "Lead the way," he said.

Lauren watched as Marvin guided Cris to a group of men who stood near the living room's entrance.

She turned and found Judy staring at her. The woman's bleary eyes narrowed as she scanned Lauren over the lip of her wineglass. Lauren had seen this stare before. It was usually followed by a sneer, a lip smack, or the mutter of "Can you believe this bitch?"

and it was usually directed at her from an angry wife or girlfriend.

"Thank you for hosting the party for Cris," Lauren said, deciding to play nice. "He's incredibly thankful for the support."

"Well, Marvin wants to help Cris as much as he can." Judy paused to sip from her wineglass. "He wants to make sure Cris connects with the *right* kind of people and not just any ol' trash off the street," she scoffed.

Lauren cocked an eyebrow, wondering if she was the "trash" Judy was referring to. She didn't get the chance to ask. Someone rang the doorbell and Judy turned back toward the door.

"If you'll excuse me," Judy said before abruptly walking away from Lauren, leaving the young woman standing alone in the middle of the foyer.

Lauren looked around uneasily, watching as those around her engaged in animated conversations. She felt like the high school nerd at the popular kids' party. If the evening continued like this, it was going to be a long night.

Despite the rough start, she managed to make it to the end of the party, knowing that it would look bad for Cris if his wife wanted to walk out before the little shindig was over. She even managed to talk to a few people, avoiding the ones who seemed openly hostile.

When the jazz trio started its third rendition of Ellington's "Take the 'A' Train," Lauren glanced at her watch. She saw that it was almost eleven o'clock. She had officially hit her limit of fake smiles and uncomfortable chitchat. It seemed like a good time to leave the party. She tugged her shawl tighter around her shoulders and sauntered over to her husband, who stood in the center of a throng of people, retelling one of his football stories. His audience seemed riveted.

She tapped Cris on his broad shoulder. He turned to look at her quizzically.

"Sorry, honey, but we have to head home now."

"What?" Marvin looked crestfallen. "You're leaving already? But Cris was just—"

"I told our nanny we'd be back by eleven thirty," she explained quickly, hoping that using the baby as an excuse would stop any arguments. "I'd hate to be late getting home. She might worry that something is wrong."

Cris slowly nodded. "She's right. It is getting a little late. We should call it a night."

"If you think this is late, you should come to one of the council meetings!" drawled a baritone voice from behind them. "The longest one dragged on almost until dawn!"

Lauren turned to find a light-skinned man with a pencil-thin mustache and a long, curly gray mane rivaling Al Sharpton's striding toward them. His matronly–looking wife was at his side, holding her purse in front of her like it was a Trojan shield.

When Lauren saw the couple, she grimaced. It was Thurmond Knightly, longtime mayor of Chesterton and Cris's opponent. Lauren knew Thurmond well because he had once been a close friend of her ex, James Sayers. She could understand why Thurmond and James had been such good buddies: Both men had huge egos and liked to intimidate others with their power and position.

"But I guess if you're not too keen on working past bedtime, you're really not cut out for the job as mayor," Thurmond continued with a grin and booming laugh that made Lauren cringe. He slapped Cris on the back. "Might as well throw in the towel now. Go home to your bed and your baby, son!"

At that jibe, Lauren instantly felt her blood boil. She fisted her hands on her hips and glared at Thurmond. To Cris's credit, the warm smile didn't leave his handsome face.

"I've got no problem working late into the night. You, on the other hand, should be careful. A man at *your* age should get his rest," Cris said, thumping Thurmond just as hard between his shoulder blades, making the older man flinch.

Well played, baby, Lauren thought. *Well played.*

"Thurmond," Marvin said uneasily. Several conversations in the room fell silent as they watched the two men squaring off. Marvin made a furtive glance around him as he nervously cleared his throat. "I-I, uh . . . I didn't know you'd be stopping by."

Thurmond adjusted his suit jacket lapels. "Of course I had come to your little party, Marvin! Had to welcome the competition!" He turned back to Cris. "But I must say, Cris, I'm surprised you've decided to throw your hat into the ring. Big-time football player and businessman like you . . . I'd think you'd be bored being the mayor of a little ol' town like Chesterton."

"Why is it a surprise? I've adopted Chesterton as my home. I care about this town. It's a good place, but it could be even better. I could help Chesterton with my know-how . . . you know, help bring it into the twenty-first century."

Thurmond tilted his head. "You're talking about making changes around here?"

"Why not?" Cris asked. "The town could be modernized a bit. The same businesses have been on Main Street for decades. We could entice some new blood into town. Maybe work with the Chamber of Commerce to start a business incubator here for start-ups.

And while we're at it, some public facilities are in desperate need of improvement. The library on Popular Street doesn't have—"

"Modernization! Change!" Thurmond boomed as he pointed up at Cris. "See, that's where you're wrong, son! That's where you're confused about this town! Chesterton is all about tradition. . . . Traditional *values* . . . community . . . a sense of morality!"

"Praise the Lord," his wife cried beside him, closing her eyes and waving her hand slowly like she was in a pew at church.

Lauren frowned. Up until this point, she'd thought the older woman was mute.

"And we need leadership that represents that," Thurmond continued. "We need a mayor and a mayor's *wife* who represent those values." He then gave a none-too-subtle side glance to Lauren.

Lauren gaped in amazement. *So he was going to go there, huh?*

She wasn't the only one who noticed the little dig. Cris's jovial expression disappeared. He angrily squinted down at Thurmond. "What the hell is that supposed to mean?"

"Calm down, son!" Thurmond barked out another laugh. "No need to get all *puffed* up! I'm just saying that if you're going to run for office, make sure there're no skeletons in that house of yours. Make sure *all* those closets are clean and set right . . . if you get my drift."

"And when it comes, it finds the house swept and put in order," Thurmond's wife said solemnly with a nod. "Luke chapter eleven, verse twenty-five."

So now the woman was quoting Bible verses? *Good Lord,* Lauren thought.

Everyone knew what Thurmond and his wife were

talking about. Lauren's past was far from stellar, and perhaps it wasn't an ideal past for a mayor's wife, but Thurmond was wrong in one regard: She didn't conceal any skeletons. Her past was an open book in the town of Chesterton. It had been gossiped about ad nauseum in every hair salon and cocktail party within a twenty-mile radius. She had nothing to hide!

"Cris, let's head home," Lauren whispered, linking her arm through her husband's. She could tell he was fuming, and though Cris didn't generally have a temper, he didn't back down from a good fight, either. She didn't want him to say or do anything that could make him look bad—or, worse, hurt his chances of winning the election. She tugged him gently. "Let's just go."

"You go on home, son! Give a kiss to that baby of yours for me!"

When Lauren saw Cris grit his teeth and the vein pulse along his temple, she immediately stepped forward to intercede again.

"Thank you for the party," Lauren said politely to Marvin. She then began to walk toward the foyer, but stopped when she realized her husband wasn't walking with her. Cris didn't budge an inch, at first. Instead he continued to glare at Thurmond. Fury positively radiated from him.

"Cris," she said yet again. "Honey . . ."

She finally seemed to get through to him then. Cris started to walk toward the front door with her. Most of the partygoers had fallen silent as they made their exit. Even the jazz trio had stopped playing—finally! She didn't think she could hear "Take the 'A' Train" *yet again*.

"Thank you for coming!" Judy Payton gushed drunkenly from the other side of the room.

Neither Lauren nor Cris responded. Instead they silently walked out the front door and toward the driveway. The sound of whirring cicadas and crickets greeted them.

Lauren glanced up at her husband, finding him still staring stoically ahead. As they walked down the driveway, she sighed.

She wanted to do nothing more than to help Cris, to see him succeed, but now she worried she would be his biggest liability.

Chapter 12

Korey glared out the taxicab passenger window at the Las Vegas Strip, not giving so much as a glance at his female companion sitting on the cracked leather seat beside him. It wasn't that he was fascinated by the twinkling cyclone of lights, the scantily clad women on the sidewalks, or the crazy swarm of people piling out of the casinos and hotels. He just didn't want to deal with Cynthia right now. He was still pissed at her for what she had said on the plane.

Did she really believe all these years that *she* was the one who had been wronged? She thought *she* was the one who had been betrayed? No wonder she had acted so cold and self-righteous toward him! Well, he was glad he had rid her of that little "poor me" fantasy: Pitiful Cindy Gibbons has her heart broken by her big, bad teenage boyfriend and is driven into the arms of her sugar-daddy millionaire.

No, you don't get to play the victim here, Cindy, Korey thought vehemently as they rode in silence toward the hotel where the kids were staying. *Not with the way you treated me, you heartless bitch!*

She was the one who had betrayed *him* by calling him up one night to say she wanted to see him again, having sex with him one last time, then dumping him unceremoniously before she ran back to her new fiancé. Korey was the one who had been left shell-shocked and feeling deceived and heartbroken.

He was glad he had finally set her ass straight! He was owed an apology—a big one—and he didn't want to listen to anything else she had to say until he got that apology.

Korey pulled out his cell phone and scrolled through his contact list.

Cynthia turned to him and frowned. "Who are you calling?"

He didn't respond. Instead, he continued to search for the name of his ex-wife, Vivian, hoping that he wouldn't regret calling her. He had just remembered something, something that was very important that could aid them in their search for the kids, and only Vivian had access to it.

Vivian didn't give him much of a chance to second-guess his decision to call her. She picked up on the first ring despite the fact that it was well past midnight back East.

"Oh, Lord, what happened?" Vivian yelled in a panic. "You better not tell me my baby was in a car crash! Is he all right? Damn it, Korey! I told you about letting him drive that—"

"He's fine, Viv," Korey said, cutting her off before she started a full-on tirade. "Jared is fine."

At the mention of Vivian's name, Cynthia's lips instantly puckered, as though she had just sucked on a lemon. She snapped her head around and glowered out the car window at the Strip.

"Well, if nothing is wrong with my baby, then why the hell are you calling me this late at night?" Vivian squawked.

"Because I need your spyware password."

She went quiet on the other end of the line. "What . . . What spyware? I don't know what you're talking about."

"Come on, Viv! Don't play stupid with me! You put spyware on Jared's cell phone to track him and his phone calls. I know you did! Just give me the site and the password."

"If you know about the spyware, then you know that I took it off! Jared found out about it and got mad at me for spying on him!"

"And you didn't put it back on after that?"

She fell silent again.

"Yeah, I thought so. Just give me the password."

"Why do *you* want to track him, though? You said he was okay. What's wrong?"

"Nothing's wrong! He . . . he just . . ." Korey thought quickly, trying to come up with an answer that wouldn't alarm Vivian and send her racing to Vegas too. "He, uh . . . he lost it. His phone, I mean. Or he thinks someone might have stolen it." Korey shrugged. "Hell, he doesn't know. He's always misplacing that damn thing. I'm hoping we can track it down. I bet he left it at a friend's house."

"*Track down his phone?* Wouldn't it just be easier to buy him a new one?"

"Do you have money for a new one?" Korey asked, turning the question on her.

Five minutes later, he had the Web address, the

username, and the password for the cell phone tracking software. He folded the receipt where he had written the information and tucked it into his jean pocket.

"So how's Vivian?" Cynthia asked. She continued to stare out the taxi window.

Korey slumped back against the leather headrest, ignoring her. With weary eyes, he watched the weather forecast on the television screen embedded in the seat in front of him.

"You two seem to be on good terms," she continued. "Rather chummy."

"Don't start, Cindy," he warned.

It had been a long flight, and thanks to Cynthia's antics and their argument, he hadn't gotten a lick of sleep while on the plane. He wouldn't get any rest once they arrived at the hotel either because they had to immediately start looking for the kids. In short, he was exhausted and not in the mood for Cynthia's crap right now.

"I'm *just* saying that you two get along well," she replied a little too loudly. "I mean, I wish I could call my ex at one o'clock in the morning and say 'hey' and have him—"

"I didn't call her at one o'clock in the morning to say 'hey'!" he snarled, reaching the end of his rope. "If you're going to eavesdrop, make sure you do it right! I called her to find a way to help track down Jared and Clarissa. It's another tool we can use." He shook his head in bewilderment. "I wish you would get the hell over whatever grudge you have against Vivian. It's getting pretty old!"

"Whatever grudge? *Whatever grudge?* You know damn well she insulted my mother and we got into a fistfight once! How could I *not* hold a grudge against her, Korey?"

"You two were teenagers when all that happened. Not to mention that you won the fight!"

"You're damn right I did! *No one* disrespects me or my family, and I let that bitch know it!"

From anyone else, a statement like that would have been empty bravado, but from Cynthia Gibbons it was totally the truth. That day back in 1994 she *did* let Vivian know she wouldn't be disrespected—and she did it with her fists . . .

Korey remembered that day vividly. In fact, it was how the two lovers finally got acquainted.

He had known Cynthia Gibbons most of his life, but they were never friends. She was the aloof, almost bitchy pretty girl he had secretly lusted after, like most of the boys in town. Outside of the occasional flirting, Cynthia wouldn't date or take any of the guys at school seriously. She played with them like a cat would a ball of yarn. She was much more interested in older men who drove nice cars, could take her out to fancy restaurants in the city, and buy her whatever her young gold-digging heart desired.

One fall day, Korey and his boys stumbled upon Cynthia and Vivian battling it out in the school parking lot in the center of a circle of screaming and jeering girls. Vivian had a fistful of Cynthia's hair twined around her fingers and was whaling on her with her purse, swinging the leather clutch like a billy club. But Cynthia delivered a one-two punch to Vivian's stomach, sending her opponent careening backward. The girls landed on the cracked asphalt with a thud. That's when Cynthia got the better of Vivian. She climbed astride Vivian like she was a Shetland pony and started pummeling her. Korey stared, slack-jawed. He had never

seen a girl that fine fight so hard. He had expected
someone like Cynthia to fight with fussy slaps and
wild, windmill-like swings. Instead, she battled with
the focused intensity of a prizefighter.

But her victory was short-lived. Vivian's friends
started to pull at and hit Cynthia. That's when Korey
knew he had to intervene. He had no idea how the fight
had started, but it was one thing for the two girls to
duke it out and settle their dispute among themselves.
It was another thing for all of Vivian's friends to suddenly decide to fight Cynthia simply because their
buddy was losing.

He took a fortifying deep breath and stepped into
the fray—braving the swinging purses and clawing
nails—and his boys reluctantly followed. They pulled
the girls apart, and Korey dragged Cynthia away, kick-
ing and screaming.

She was still cursing when he opened his car door
and shoved her inside. They pulled off seconds later.

"What the hell do you think you're doing?" Cynthia
shouted as they turned left and sped away from the
school parking lot just as the aging security guard hobbled through the front doors onto the school's concrete
steps to see what all the ruckus was about. "I didn't
need anyone to pull me out of that! I didn't need any
help!"

"What do you mean you didn't need any help? You
were about to get your ass whupped!" He glanced at
her as he drove. "Those girls were about to jump you!"

"I could've taken them!" She glared at him as she
tried to finger-comb her hair back into place.

"Yeah, right," he muttered. "About a half dozen
girls? You could've taken them all? Who the hell do
you think you are? *Bruce Lee?*"

"I could've done it! Damn it, if need be, I can take you too!"

He drew to a stop and turned to face her. Her hazel eyes were blazing. Her ponytail was undone, and tufts of hair were sticking up around her head. Her shirt was askew and ripped at the collar. She looked like a deranged woman. At the sight of her, he burst into laughter.

"What's so funny?" she asked.

"*You!* You're so funny." He laughed again and took off when the light turned green. "I'm trying to rescue you, and here you are threatening to kick my ass. I bet you would do it too. Wouldn't you?"

Her face softened. She returned to finger-combing her hair back into place. A wry smile tugged at her lips. "Probably."

Korey shoved his hand into his jean pocket and pulled out a wad of napkins he had taken from the school cafeteria earlier that day. "Here. Your mouth is bleeding a little."

She hesitated before taking it. "Thank you." She then lowered the passenger-side visor and gazed at herself in the mirror as she wiped her face. "So where are we going anyway?"

"Your house. I figured that's where you'd want to go."

"You know where I live?"

"*Everyone* knows where you live, Cindy."

"Really?" She cocked an eyebrow. "Am I that famous?"

"Your family is."

She eyed him warily. "Oh, so you're about to talk about my family now too, huh?"

"No! No! It's just . . . well . . . everyone in town knows you guys. That's all."

She sucked her teeth. "Yeah, I bet they do. And I can only guess what they say about us."

"A lot," he answered honestly, "but I never put much into what other people say."

"Is that so?"

This time a genuine smile appeared, making his stomach clench and his palms sweat as he clutched the steering wheel.

For a few minutes he had forgotten that he was alone in a car with Cynthia—*the* Cynthia Gibbons, whom he had fantasized about for years, trying his best not to ogle her in the school halls or from the back of geometry class. But now that she was smiling at him, he was unnervingly aware of her—her warmth, her smell, and that alarmingly sexy mouth of hers. He could feel a budding hard-on nudging against his jean zipper.

Cynthia turned and flipped up the visor. "Man, I look like shit!"

"No, you don't. You couldn't look like shit even if you tried," he blurted out, then wanted to kick himself as soon as he said it. She laughed at the alarmed expression on his face, and he felt his cheeks grow warm. "I mean . . . I mean, you look—"

"I can't let my mama see me like this," she continued, cutting him off. "She'd want to call the police or sue somebody. Is there anywhere else you can take me besides my house? I wanna clean myself up before I go home, and I'd prefer a place with not a lot of people," she added. "I don't want anyone to stare at me . . . with me looking the way I do." She fingered her ripped shirt.

If someone had told him that he had won a million dollars, Korey wouldn't have been any more happy or shocked as he was at that moment. Cynthia wanted to go somewhere alone—*with him?*

"Uh . . . uh, yeah," he uttered, putting some bass in his voice, trying his best to sound smooth and casual though he was bursting at the seams on the inside. "Yeah, umm, I-I know a place."

He drove her to a creek near Chesterton that only the old-timers and die-hard fishermen frequented. He waited patiently on the dock as Cynthia sat in his car and fixed her hair and makeup, but even after she tidied herself, she didn't seem ready to go home. They walked along the waterfront and talked until dusk about school, Chesterton, the football season, and what they wanted to do after they graduated.

For the first time, Korey realized that Cynthia wasn't as aloof as he once thought. She was funny too, another thing that pleasantly surprised him. He had always had a crush on her, but that day he started to fall for the *real* Cynthia, not some untouchable girl he mooned over from afar.

When he dropped her off at her house that night, she leaned across the seat and kissed him. She did it so quickly that he didn't realize until after she pulled away that she had done it. He could only remember the ghostly sensation of her lips: warm and honey sweet. He watched in awe as she threw open the car door and climbed out of his mom's beat-up Cavalier.

"Thanks for the ride," she said nonchalantly before slamming the door shut and racing up the slate driveway to the Gibbons mansion's French doors.

She didn't look back.

Korey drove home, not knowing what to think. He lay awake in bed later that night, replaying that day, wondering if what happened between them held any potential.

No, he resolved before turning off his television and lights and closing his eyes. A girl like Cynthia would never be interested in him. He had been a passing amusement, and it was best for him to forget what had happened.

By the time he arrived at school the next morning, he had prepared himself to once again be ignored by Cynthia, and she proved him right. He saw her near her locker, and she looked past him as though he were a pane of glass. He saw her in line at the cafeteria, and she continued to chatter and laugh with her sister Dawn, like he wasn't there.

"Told you so," a voice in his head chided as she walked by his lunch table, completely oblivious to him.

So when the school day ended and he walked back to his car, he was shocked to find—of all people—Cynthia leaning against his car hood, waiting for him.

"Wanna go for another ride?" she asked with a grin.

What was he supposed to say? *No?*

He eagerly nodded and stepped forward to unlock his car doors.

That's how it all started . . .

"That bitch Vivian knew she couldn't win in a fight with me, so she got back at me the one way she knew how—by fucking *you!*" Cynthia screeched as she pointed at him, making the cabdriver lean over to stare at her in the rearview mirror, then slowly shake his turbaned head.

Korey rolled his eyes. It was obvious that she hadn't paid much attention to his suggestion of letting go of her grudge against Vivian.

"She knew we were together! She knew you were—"

"I don't know how she would have known that," he

replied, deciding if Cynthia wanted an argument, then damn it, he would give her one. "How would anyone have known we were together with all the cloak-and-dagger bull you made me do! 'No one can know we're together, Korey! It can't get back to my mom,'" he said in a high-pitched voice, mimicking her. "For seven months, I kept making up stuff and sneaking around like a criminal so no one would figure out we were a couple. It got so bad my mama thought I was on drugs! She was about to send me off to rehab until I told her about you!"

"Well, Vivian sure as hell figured it out! She wanted you all along and she got you!"

"And you got everything else! So what's your point?"

"What?" She stilled. "What does that mean?"

What did she think he meant? If you considered how the two women's lives had turned out, Cynthia definitely was the victor. She was wealthy and beautiful—basically a more mature version of the knockout she had been in high school. Meanwhile, the years hadn't been as kind to Vivian. She was about sixty pounds heavier, had a lot more wrinkles, and was far from wealthy. In fact, she and her second husband were up to their eyeballs in debt thanks to Vivian's crazy spending habits. She had even swallowed her pride and borrowed money from Korey a few times to pay overdue bills.

"You won, Cindy. You won, all right?" he said. "You got the big house. You got the millionaire. You got everything your little heart desired. Why can't—"

"No, I didn't," she blurted out, making him frown.

"No, you didn't what?"

"I didn't get everything my heart desired," she answered softly.

Their eyes locked, and Korey saw longing and regret in those irises that unnerved him.

Not possible, he told himself. There were many things he knew Cynthia was capable of, and remorse wasn't one of them. She was probably still drunk from what she'd swallowed on the plane, and he remembered that sometimes alcohol made her maudlin and moody. She'd turn back into the old Cynthia as soon as she sobered up.

The cab pulled to a stop in the semicircular driveway in front of their hotel. Korey broke his and Cynthia's mutual gaze, ending the charged moment. He reached into his pocket to pull out his wallet. "When we get to the reservation desk let me do the talking, okay?"

Her brows furrowed. "Why do you get to do—" She then snapped her mouth shut. Her nostrils flared. "Fine," she murmured, surprising him.

He had definitely expected an argument.

Thank God for small favors, he thought.

Korey handed several bills to the driver as Cynthia threw open the taxi door, stepping out of the AC and into the dry desert heat. He climbed out after her. Each had a carry-on case in their hands when they made their way to the hotel's gold revolving doors: his was a cheap pleather case that he had picked up at JCPenney four years ago; Cynthia's was a brown Louis Vuitton luggage bag.

Probably given to her by one of her ex-boyfriends, he thought.

Korey hoped he wouldn't have to wear any of the clothes he had hastily packed. He wanted to find the kids as quickly as possible, before they had the chance to do anything stupid that could impact the rest of their lives. But time wasn't on his side. He glanced down at his watch. It was already 10:13 p.m. Pacific time.

Korey and Cynthia stepped through the glass revolving doors and were hit by a rippling wave of sound. They entered a maze of gift shops that sold a menagerie of shot glasses, liquor bottles, T-shirts, baseball hats, and every overpriced tchotchke one could imagine emblazoned with the words "Las Vegas" or "What Happens in Vegas . . ."

They then passed rows upon rows of slot machines. In front of each machine was someone on a stool pulling a lever—men and women, young and old, some chain-smoking and others sipping their drinks with tiny red straws. Several had giant plastic tubs filled with coins perched beside them.

Korey and Cynthia finally reached the opulently decorated lobby, with its three-story Corinthian columns and cheesy six-foot Roman statues. They dodged a group of rowdy drunken men who were laughing and high-fiving one another and then a bellhop who was struggling to load more than a half dozen suitcases onto a luggage cart.

Korey walked up to the reservation desk with a smile. The petite brunette at the counter smiled back, showing the dimples in her plump cheeks.

"Hello, sir, welcome to Pompeii Hotel and Casino! How may I help you today?" she asked warmly.

"I'd like to get a room if you have any available." He glanced at her name tag. "Judy."

"Well, if you had tried to book one last week when we had that big convention, probably not. But this week, you've got a good chance." She winked. "Just let me check to confirm." She punched a few buttons on the computer touch screen. She squinted. "I was right. You're in luck! We have a king and a few doubles available. Can I have your name, sir?"

He gave it to her and she nodded, inputting the information into the computer. "Looks like this is your first time as a guest at our hotel. Is this your first time in Vegas too, Mr. Walker?"

"No, I've been here before . . . back in the late nineties. Came here with a group of buddies."

"Bachelor party?" the young woman asked, scanning the screen again.

Cynthia grumbled behind him. He had forgotten she was there for a second. He turned to find her with her arms crossed over her chest, impatiently tapping her foot.

"Something like that," he said, turning back to the woman at the reservation desk. "We were trying to convince him not to get married. None of us liked his girlfriend very much. We figured a weekend in Vegas at strip clubs and getting him drunk would bring him to our way of thinking."

The young woman giggled. "Well, that's an interesting tactic."

He shrugged. "What can I say? We were twenty-something dudes. It made sense to us at the time. It didn't work, though. They got married anyway."

"Really? Did you guys—"

"Ask her about Clarissa," Cynthia interrupted, whispering from behind him. "Ask her!"

The young woman frowned.

"Excuse me, Judy," Korey said, holding up a finger. He then turned to Cynthia. "I am going to ask her," he whispered back slowly, leaning toward her. "Calm down, woman. I told you to let me handle this."

"You're not handling it! You're shooting the breeze

like you're sitting on someone's front porch, drinking lemonade. You're wasting time!"

"You ever heard the saying 'You catch more flies with honey than with vinegar?'"

"Yeah! And?"

"Okay, then let me do this *my* way—with honey. Just calm the hell down."

Cynthia's eyes narrowed. Her lips tightened. Korey turned back to the woman at the desk.

"Sorry about that. You were saying?"

The young woman laughed nervously. "I was going to ask you if you guys eventually warmed up to his wife. But that's all right. You're probably eager to just get to your hotel room."

Korey grinned. "No, I'm fine. And no, we didn't warm up to his wife. But as it turns out, we didn't need to. They got divorced three years later."

They chitchatted for a few more minutes as she finished checking him in. Korey turned on the charm, making her laugh several times, and making her blush at his bawdy humor. Meanwhile, Cynthia seemed to grow more and more annoyed. He could sense the tension emanating from her like a stink cloud. She wasn't being very subtle with her loud sighs, which sounded more like moans, and restless foot tapping.

The young woman handed Korey a small envelope. "In there you'll find two keys to your room, Mr. Walker. You're in room ten-sixteen, in the second tower. You want to go through the lobby," she said pointing over his shoulder, "make a left at the Aphrodite statue, then another left at the giant seashell, and you'll find the bank of elevators that will take you to your floor."

"Thank you." He tucked the magnetic cards into the back pocket of his jeans. "Hey, would you happen to know what restaurants I can—"

"Oh, for chrissake, Korey!" Cynthia threw up her hands, making the woman at the reservation desk jump in surprise. "I can't take any more of this crap! Would you just ask her already?" She then barged forward, shoving him aside.

The young woman at the desk looked aghast. Korey merely shook his head in exasperation. He should have known Cynthia wouldn't stay quiet and leave this up to him.

"Look, we're looking for a girl and a boy, okay?" Cynthia said, dropping her hands to her hips. "Two black kids in their late teens. The girl kind of looks like me—but darker. They probably checked in earlier today. The girl's name is Clarissa Simpson. The boy's name is Jared Walker. They would have booked the room under her name, more likely."

"I'm . . . I'm sorry. I don't remember anyone like that checking in today," the young woman said uneasily.

"Well, can you check your database to see if they checked in?" Cynthia asked, pointing down at the reservation screen. "I *gave* you their names!"

"Ma'am, we have to respect the privacy of our guests. We can't reveal if they—"

"Are you telling me," Cynthia said between clenched teeth, "that child can steal my credit card, use it to get a hotel room where she could be doing God knows what with that boy, and you have to respect her privacy?" she bellowed, making several people who were lounging on the lobby's plush chairs stop their conversations to look at her. Even the koi in the nearby oversized fish tank seemed to do a double take. "Are you kidding me?" Cynthia screeched. "She got that privacy with my credit card! She's not even twenty years old!"

Out of the corner of his eye, Korey could see an officious-looking older white man in a suit with a gold nameplate near his lapel walking toward the reservation counter. A deep frown marred his wrinkled face. A security guard trailed after him. Korey suspected Cynthia's little meltdown was about to get them politely escorted out of the Pompeii Hotel and Casino only fifteen minutes after arriving there.

He instantly stepped forward, grabbed Cynthia's arm, and pulled her away from the counter.

"Uh, thank you for your help," he said to the woman behind the desk. "We'll just head to our room now."

"I'm not going anywhere until I find out what room Clarissa's staying in!" Cynthia shouted. "Do you hear me?"

Korey forced a grin. "It was nice talking to you, Judy." He then yanked Cynthia across the lobby.

"If my daughter ends up pregnant," she yelled as she was dragged toward the elevators, "I'm suing all of you!"

Chapter 13

"Have you lost your damn mind?" Korey asked as the elevator doors opened.

He shoved Cynthia inside the circular elevator car, catching her off guard. She almost stumbled in her heels on the Berber carpet.

"That was some crazy shit! Crazy even for you! Were you trying to get us kicked out of here?"

His mouth was tense. His dark eyes were set in a steely glare. Cynthia had never seen Korey so angry. She would have told him he looked damned sexy if he didn't also look like he wanted to murder her at that moment.

"I wouldn't have flipped out if you'd handled it like you said you would! What was with all the conversation? Were you trying to find out where the kids are or get her phone number?"

He slipped his magnetic card key into the elevator wall-panel slot, then punched in the number ten. The elevator instantly shot into motion, zipping up its glass tube, emitting a soft beep as they ascended from floor to floor.

"How could you even ask that question? Of course, I was trying to find out about the kids . . . and I would have if you would've just shut the hell up!" He fell back onto the glass wall and gripped the metal wall bar so tightly it looked like he was trying to rip it out of the glass.

While he continued to grouse as they shot to the tenth floor, she fell silent—feeling her first pangs of guilt.

"Would it have killed you to just let me handle it? Huh?" he asked. "Would it have killed you?"

She didn't answer him. Instead, she stubbornly crossed her arms over her chest again, refusing to look at him and gazing at the view of the Las Vegas Strip outside the elevator compartment instead. Cynthia couldn't explain to Korey that the whole time he was charming Chatty Cathy, she was envisioning what Clarissa and Jared were doing in their hotel room, and it made her sick to her stomach. What if they were already married and the newlyweds were enjoying their wedding night? What if they were long past kissing? Long past fondling? Dear God, what if they were—like Korey had said—having sex on the regular?

They can't! They just can't, she thought desperately. And she wasn't speaking from the perspective of an overprotective mother, concerned about her daughter's virtue. Nope. There was a lot more at stake here than Clarissa's virginity.

Cynthia couldn't tell Korey her real worry about the kids getting married. If she did, he would definitely lose it. Her worry was rooted in something that had lingered in the back of her mind for more than a decade.

It had eaten at her like an insidious disease, lying in wait until it came bursting to the forefront when Keith first mentioned the name Jared Walker and Cynthia realized Jared was Korey's son.

Congratulations, Cynthia Gibbons! You could have a catastrophe on your hands!

Her worry started *years* ago, soon after she discovered she was pregnant with Clarissa. It came as surprise to both her and Bill. He had been married twice before, and none of his previous wives had gotten pregnant, even after fertility treatments. Bill was eventually diagnosed with a low sperm count and weak swimmers. But, wonder of wonders, he had managed to knock up Cynthia within a month and half of them sharing a bed together.

"It's a miracle!" the jubilant father-to-be had proclaimed when she told him the news.

Bill had taken the pregnancy as a definite sign that he and Cynthia were meant to be. But what Cynthia didn't tell him is that it was less likely a miracle—and more likely a case of her horrifically bad luck. She had slept with Korey the last time only days before she had slept with Bill. She hadn't had any pregnancy scares with Korey before, but there was a first time for everything. She just hoped that this wasn't the first time.

Korey, by then, had already hooked up with Vivian. It would be a waste of time to run back to him, Cynthia had thought. No, it was better to stick with what she had, to stay with Bill and hope for the best, that the baby was his child.

But after Clarissa was born and Cynthia marveled at her beautiful baby girl, her suspicions returned. She counted Clarissa's fingers and toes. She played with her black curls and her button nose. Everything seemed in order on her little girl, but as Cynthia gazed into her daughter's big brown eyes, something seemed . . . off.

Everyone remarked about how Clarissa was the spitting image of Cynthia, but few paid Bill a similar compliment. That's because Clarissa didn't look a damn thing like him! She didn't have his beady little eyes or his pale complexion. She didn't have his stubby fingers or his proud brow. As Clarissa grew older, you couldn't find two people who looked more different than Clarissa and her dad. Cynthia started to wonder if, over time, Bill started to notice it too since he became colder and colder to this daughter over the years. But Cynthia tried diligently to brush it off.

So she doesn't look like him, Cynthia had convinced herself. *So what? Lots of children don't look like their fathers!*

But the worry stayed there in the back closet of her mind, under the piles of day-to-day concerns like picking up the dry cleaning and getting her oil changed. The worry got wrinkled, dirty, and dusty, but it didn't disappear.

And now that Clarissa had met Jared and the two had fallen in love, all those old suspicions and worries became brand-spanking-new! Cynthia couldn't say for sure that Korey was Clarissa's father—not without a DNA test. But part of her knew, deep down, that he probably was. And if he was, what the hell did that mean for Clarissa and Jared? A brother and sister couldn't get married or have sex! What would Korey do if he found out about Cynthia's long-held suspicions regarding his paternity? He'd probably be furious! He'd never forgive her.

"Those are a lot of 'what-ifs.' Don't lose it just quite yet," a voice in her head urged soothingly. "You don't know any of this for sure. Korey might not be her father."

But what if you're wrong, Cynthia thought frantically in reply. *What if you're WRONG?*

The elevator slid to a smooth stop and the metal doors opened, revealing a small lobby on the hotel's tenth floor. Korey strode out, then paused and turned when he saw Cynthia wasn't following him. He raised his brows expectantly.

"You coming?"

She looked around her. She had been so lost in thought she hadn't realized they'd arrived at his floor. She hesitated.

"But I thought . . . I thought we weren't staying in a room together," she said.

Mild irritation crossed across his face. "We're not. Believe me. But I don't think you want to go back down there and try to book a room right now. Do you?"

He had a point.

"Look, I'm going to my room to drop off my things and then try to find a business center with a computer. I need to try to track down Jared's phone since now we have no chance in hell of finding their room from anyone who works at this hotel," Korey muttered. "You can either come with me or keep riding up and down these elevators."

He then turned away from her, glanced up at the fake marble plaques on the wall, and followed one of the arrows in search of his hotel room.

The elevator doors slowly began to close. Cynthia grimaced as she shoved the doors back open, causing a loud buzzing sound to fill the compartment. She then ran onto the landing and followed Korey down the hall. She reached him just as he inserted his key card into the door of his room.

"You don't need to find a computer!" she shouted after him, making him pause. "We can . . . we can use my phone. I can get the tracking Web site on it."

He turned the door handle and shoved it open. He then stepped inside, beckoning her to follow him. "Then let's drop off our stuff and get started."

"Are you sure this is right?" Cynthia asked as they waited for the doorman to hail them a cab.

"That's the address the Web site gave us," Korey replied. "I don't see why it wouldn't be right."

When a white taxi pulled up to the curb, Korey opened the door for her, letting her climb in first. He jumped in after her and gave the address to the driver.

Cynthia grimaced as the car lurched forward on squeaking tires. She gazed down at her phone screen, looking at the little red pin on the digital map. Their destination was somewhere on South Las Vegas Boulevard, but they had no idea what the place was since the map wasn't accurate to that level of detail.

"What if this damn thing is sending us on a wild goose chase?" she mumbled, tossing her phone back into her purse.

"It's legit. Say what you want about Viv, but she knows how to keep tabs on her son. She wouldn't invest her husband's hard-earned money in software that was crap. Believe me."

Cynthia pursed her lips, deciding to keep quiet on that one. If all of this was based on her confidence in Vivian, then Cynthia knew they were definitely screwed. She glared at the bumper-to-bumper traffic outside the cab window. Even if the spyware was right and Clarissa and Jared were at that address, she wondered if she and Korey could make it there before the kids left.

"Hey! How long before we get there?" she shouted to the cabby.

"In this traffic?" The older white man with salt-and-pepper beard stubble tilted his head and shrugged. "Maybe twenty . . . twenty-five minutes."

Twenty-five minutes? She slumped back into her seat and closed her eyes. This was going to take for-damn-ever!

The older man laughed a grainy smoker's laugh, then coughed. "Hey, at least you've got time to hop out and grab yourself some flowers if you need 'em."

Korey frowned. "Why would she need flowers?"

"For your wedding." The cabdriver gazed at their reflection. Cynthia could see his watery gray eyes in the rearview mirror. "That's where you're headed, right? To get hitched?"

"Why do you think we're getting married?" Korey asked.

"Because that's the address you gave me . . . you know, to the wedding chapel."

Cynthia's blood ran cold. She gulped for air. "Wait! *What?* We're headed to *a wedding chapel?*" she squeaked, her throat tightening.

"Yeah," the driver said. "It's one of the most famous chapels around here! You guys didn't know that?"

Cynthia instantly scooted forward. She slapped her hands flat against the bulletproof glass and almost climbed through the small opening between the back and front seat. "I don't care what you have to do," she said in a low, menacing voice, "but you get us to that wedding chapel in ten minutes or less! Do you hear me?"

"I can't get you there in ten minutes!" The driver's bushy eyebrows bunched together as he pointed a gnarled finger at the windshield. "You blind, lady? You can't see all those cars?" He slowly shook his head. "Crazy damn tourists," he muttered, digging the same gnarled finger into his hairy ear. "Act like you're supposed to work a friggin' miracle."

Cynthia's face contorted with rage. She was just about to spew a few choice four-letter words at the curmudgeon driving their cab when Korey clapped a hand on her shoulder. She turned and found him shaking his head at her.

"What?" she snapped.

"Remember . . . think honey, not vinegar," he whispered. "Just try it for once."

Oh, to hell with that! She reserved her honey for rich men who drove sports cars and kept summer homes. The rest of the world would just have to accept what she gave it.

"But Korey's right," the logical voice in her head urged. "You want to find the kids. Just be nice for once."

Cynthia slowly released air through her clenched teeth and flared nostrils. When she turned back around to face the cabdriver, she had a smile so sweet it gave her a toothache.

"Sir," she began calmly, "we would greatly, *greatly* appreciate it if you can do everything humanly possible to get us to that wedding chapel in the next ten minutes—please," she added as an afterthought. "You see, it's very important that we get there, and we don't have a lot of time."

"What do you want me to do? Sprinkle fairy dust on the car so I can *float* above traffic? I told you how long it'll take, and nothing is—"

"I'll give you an extra hundred if you get us there in less than ten, all right?" Korey said from behind her, catching her by surprise.

"A hundred?" The cabdriver paused and squinted into the rearview mirror again. "Let me see it first."

"No, he's not letting you see it!" Cynthia slapped an open palm against the glass, making the driver jump in alarm. "You better just—"

"Here! Here's the hundred!" Korey said after opening his wallet. He held the Benjamin in plain view of the rearview mirror. He glanced at his watch. "I've got three minutes past eleven. If you want this hundred, you find a way to get us through this traffic so that we're pulling up in front of that chapel at eleven thirteen. No later! You got me?"

"All right, but you're ponying up more cash if I get a ticket, buddy." He then put on his turn signal and suddenly veered to the left, almost taking out a group of drunken pedestrians who were stumbling their way through a crosswalk. The driver punched down on the gas pedal and threw Korey and Cynthia back against their seats. She gripped the door handle so hard that her fingernails dug into the door's grubby upholstery. She tried more than once to put on her seat belt, but it was broken. She had a hard time steadying herself as the driver made a series of wild turns. More than once she landed face-first in Korey's lap.

They arrived at the wedding chapel nine minutes later, in *less* time than the cabdriver had said was possible. After Korey handed him the money, they strode toward the chapel's entrance.

"I can't believe you gave him a hundred bucks! Aren't you the same guy who rather than give a bum a whole dollar asked him if he could give you back fifty cents in change?"

"That was then. This is now. I'm older. Maybe I've changed."

"Uh-huh." She stared at him warily. "Well, don't get too crazy with your generosity, big spender. You're gonna go broke out here if you keep doing that."

"I'm not worried. We made it here, didn't we?"

They had indeed, and the Las Vegas wedding chapel was just as Cynthia had envisioned—or, more accurately, what she had feared.

A giant, flashing, heart-shaped neon sign was out front, two stories above the roadway, advertising complimentary Vegas show tickets with each wedding ceremony. Dancing cherubs were positioned over the archway entrance, and when Cynthia and Korey stepped through the double doors, an organ rendition of Elvis Presley's "Love Me Tender" greeted them, courtesy of hidden speakers.

Cynthia looked around the semicircular lobby—at the dusty plastic flowers and ivy, the glass-paneled walls, the fire-engine-red carpet, and the sundry photos on the walls of couples throughout the ages who had gotten married at the chapel—and she felt almost faint. She wasn't sure if she was more alarmed at the idea that Clarissa could be behind one of those doors fifteen feet away, exchanging wedding vows with Jared, her possible brother—or that Clarissa, her own flesh and blood, could get married in a place this cheap and tacky!

"Welcome to the Blue Moon Wedding Chapel!" the woman behind the counter drawled. She looked like she hadn't changed her hairstyle and makeup since 1984; she had frosted, teased bangs and a puffy ponytail held back by a neon pink scrunchie. She wore heavy purple eye shadow, blue eyeliner, and enough rouge that she vaguely resembled Bozo the Clown. She adjusted her butterfly-shaped glasses. "How may I help you? If you'd like to look at our list of wedding packages, I can—"

Korey held up his hand to stop her. "We're not getting married. We're here looking for a couple who might be."

The woman gazed at them in confusion. "Excuse me."

"Two teenagers," Cynthia said, stepping forward. "A girl named Clarissa and a boy named Jared. Did they get married here?"

Cynthia's mouth went dry and her heart raced as she waited for the answer.

"Teenagers?" the woman squinted behind her tinted lenses. "Well, we had a young black fellow and his fiancée come in about twenty minutes ago."

"You did?" Cynthia didn't think it was possible, but her heart raced even faster. "Where'd they go?"

The woman pointed over Cynthia's shoulder. "To the . . . well, to th-the Blue Hawaii room," she stuttered. "They were fired up to get married, so we gave them the first opening we had, but—"

"Clarissa!" Cynthia shouted as she raced toward the door.

"Ma'am, what are you doin'?"

"Clarissa!" Cynthia yelled again as she threw the door open. Korey reluctantly followed her after mumbling his apologies to the woman behind the desk.

"Ma'am, you cannot interrupt our ceremonies!"

Cynthia ran down the grass-mat aisle of the tiki bar-themed room, just in time to hear the minister utter the words, "I now pronounce you man and wife."

The minister wore a lei and a Hawaiian shirt to match the room décor. The two smiling witnesses were dressed as hula dancers with grass skirts and bikini tops.

Jared and Clarissa turned to each other to seal their wedding vows with a kiss.

"No, you can't!" Cynthia bellowed. "You can't! Stop! Don't kiss him!"

The bride and groom paused as their mouths hovered inches apart. They turned to Cynthia.

That's when Cynthia skidded to a halt. That's when she finally realized that she wasn't looking at Clarissa and Jared, but at a petite Hispanic woman who looked to be in her early twenties and an older black man. Both stared at her, slack-jawed.

Oh, damn, she thought.

She had barged into the wrong wedding.

"Why the hell can't I kiss him?" the woman asked, dropping her hand to her hip.

"Uh." Cynthia flapped her arms helplessly. "Uh . . . well, umm . . . I . . ."

"Sorry!" Korey stepped forward. "Sorry to interrupt, folks! She thought you were . . . someone else."

"What?" the groom barked.

Cynthia whipped around to Miss Frost and Tease. "What the hell is this? You said Clarissa and Jared were in here!"

"I said we showed them to the room," the woman argued, her face now bright red, "but if you would've let me finish, I could've told you they didn't make it to the ceremony part! They signed the license and the girl rushed out a few minutes later!"

Cynthia's shoulders slumped. "Oh."

"'Oh?'" the woman shouted with widened eyes. "You just ran through this establishment screamin' at the top of your lungs! You just ruined someone's wedding, and all you have to say for yourself, lady, is 'Oh?'"

"It was an honest mistake!" Cynthia argued stubbornly.

Miss Frost and Tease pointed to the opened door. "Leave! You two better leave right now before I call the cops and have you escorted out!"

Korey wrapped a hand around Cynthia's arm. "Come on," he mumbled as he tugged her toward the door. "Let's get the hell out of here."

Chapter 14

"At the rate you're going, we're gonna end up getting arrested long before we manage to find the kids," Korey muttered as he sat in the leather seat of the taxi.

They had hailed a cab not too far the Blue Moon Wedding Chapel. They were heading back to their hotel.

"How the hell was I supposed to know that Clarissa and Jared had walked out already?" Cynthia glared down at her phone screen. She pulled up the app to track Jared's cell phone. "That Cyndi Lauper reject said they were getting married! I was trying to stop it! That's what we came here to do, right?"

Korey slowly exhaled, telling himself to stay patient with her, though dealing with Cynthia was sometimes like being locked in a room with a raging lunatic. Still, it was best not to choke her—or throw her over his knee and spank her.

Hmmm, he thought. A faint smile crossed his lips. That second option might not be such a bad idea. In fact, it could be rather enjoyable. He could imagine her plump, golden rear end in a red lace thong, bent over his knee. He could imagine caressing it, maybe smacking it playfully. That could be fun.

Korey snapped out of his reverie. His smile faded. *Damn.* Where had that come from?

"Where do you think it came from?" the voice in his head mocked. "The longer you're around her, the more likely you are to be attracted to her. You always were in the past!"

But he was on his guard now. He wasn't a lovesick eighteen-year-old chump anymore. He was a grown man, and he wouldn't get sucked into her crap. He knew what pain came with sleeping with and falling for Cynthia Gibbons. There was no way he was going back down that treacherous road.

"I'm just saying that I ain't eager to see the inside of a Las Vegas jail tonight, that's all." He turned away from her and peered out the window. "So if you could keep the crazy to a minimum, I'd appreciate it."

. "Korey, if you call me crazy one more time, I swear I will . . . Wait! *Wait!* I found Jared!" She sat forward in her seat as the light turned red and the cab drew to a stop. "Sir, we have a slight detour. Can you take us to this address?" She held the phone up to the driver's face.

He nodded. "Sure."

She looked almost giddy when she sat back beside Korey.

"Where are we headed?" he asked.

"No idea! I just gave him the address. I guess we'll find out when we get there."

"Hopefully it's not another wedding chapel."

"I highly doubt that. Based on what that lady said, they're not going back into any wedding chapels tonight—maybe not ever!"

"Why do you say that?"

"You heard her! She said they got the marriage license, but Clarissa ran out before they could start the ceremony. Obviously, my little girl is coming to her senses! And it's about damn time she did!"

Korey grimaced. He didn't want the kids to get married any more than Cynthia did, but hearing that Clarissa had rushed out of the wedding chapel before she and Jared had a chance to exchange vows didn't make him want to jump for joy either. The kids were in love. He still wished them all the happiness in the world; he just wished they would take things slower.

"If we're lucky," Cynthia continued, now grinning, "they've already broken up."

"I don't want them to break up," he began slowly. "I just don't want them to get married. They're too young for it now. Maybe in the future, they could—"

"They will *never* get married. To suggest they should get married, even in the future, is just"—she curled her lip in disgust and gazed out the cab window—"a horrible idea. Let's just put it that way."

"Why is it a horrible idea?"

"It just is. Okay?"

"Are you saying that because of that Gibbons family rules bullshit?"

"It's not bullshit!" She turned around to glare at him. "They are . . . are important, time-honored rules in my family that—"

"They're bullshit! Bullshit! Bullshit," he repeated, drowning her out. "It's all bullshit, Cindy! I know you drank the Kool-Aid back then, but I'd hoped you weren't still gulping it down now that you're tappin' on middle age. You should know better!"

"I don't need to be reminded of how old I am, Korey Walker," she countered tightly.

He could tell he had hit her Achilles heel with that one. A vain woman like Cynthia was bound to feel self-conscious about her age.

"And I wasn't drinking any Kool-Aid back then!" she shouted. "I was being logical and practical. I considered all the alternatives presented to me and decided what was best."

"Which is why you called me up in the middle of the night, asked to meet, fucked me in the backseat of my car, and then announced you were gonna marry someone else?"

She pursed her lips and closed her eyes. "That is not how it happened."

"No, that's *exactly* how it happened!"

He should remember. He had been replaying that night in his mind over and over again for almost twenty years, wondering how he had allowed Cynthia to set him up like that. How did she make him hope they were going to be reunited, only to crush him in the end? It must have been amusing for her—one last "ride" on Big Korey before she walked down the aisle with her sugar daddy. It had taken Korey years to finally let go of his anger toward her, to finally move on from what she had done that night, but now the anger and hurt came bubbling back to the surface.

"What you did was . . . was . . ." He struggled to find the right words. "It was cold-blooded . . . heartless . . . downright—"

"Oh, for God's sake, Korey! I wasn't trying to—"

"Here you go!" the cabdriver announced. "That'll be twenty dollars and fifty cents."

Korey momentarily shoved aside his anger, opened his wallet, and handed the fare plus tip to the driver. He climbed out, not looking back to see if Cynthia followed him. He didn't want to think about her right now. Instead, he wanted to focus on the task at hand, which was finding the kids. He gazed at the sign above him and squinted in disbelief.

"The Big Lizard?" he murmured.

It was an apt name. A ten-foot-tall plastic lizard stood near the entrance. The doorway looked like it was cut out of craggy rock. Several drunken partygoers carrying giant drinks shaped like didgeridoos stumbled through the door. Behind them, loud music played, and voices and laughter could be heard.

Korey glanced over his shoulder at Cynthia, who had just stepped out of the cab.

"Are you sure that *this* is the right place?" he asked her.

She nodded even though she seemed every bit as doubtful. "That's . . . that's what the app said."

He looked up at the sign again, shrugged, then tugged open the door. They both walked inside, where they were greeted by a perky blond hostess wearing a safari hat and a stuffed koala draped around her shoulders, making them halt in surprise.

"G'day, mates!" she gushed in a bad Aussie accent, shouting to be heard over the clamor. "Welcome to the Big Lizard! Is it just the two of you?" She picked up two plastic-encased menus from a small shelf behind her. "Would you like a seat at a table or at the bar?"

"Uh, actually, we're here to look for . . . I mean to meet . . . *meet* someone," Korey immediately corrected himself and grinned. "They're probably waiting for us, so we'll just . . . you know . . . head back there."

"Sure! Go right ahead," the hostess said before turning her attention to another group who had just stepped into the restaurant.

"Let's split up!" Korey called to Cynthia as they pushed their way through the rowdy crowd that was yelling at the game on the flat-screen TV near the bar. "Keep an eye out for the kids, and text me the moment that you see them!"

Cynthia nodded, then turned to walk in the opposite direction.

Korey gazed around him, staring at the patrons who stood at the bar, danced on the dance floor in a small pit several feet below, and sat at the small dining tables. The place was filled wall-to-wall with people, so finding Jared and Clarissa would be a challenge. Not to mention the fact that the lights were turned low and fake fauna hung from the ceilings and along the walls, creating even more visual obstacles.

Korey eased through the crowd, excusing his way past tray-laden waiters and waitresses. When he neared the bathrooms, he paused. He spotted a couple standing several feet away, talking to one of the waitresses. The waitress pointed them toward the bathrooms and walked off. When the couple turned, Korey's heart skidded to a halt. He blinked in amazement. He instantly recognized Jared and Clarissa.

The two looked resigned, almost sad, which made sense considering that they had allegedly walked out of their own wedding little more than an hour ago. Jared leaned down and whispered something into Clarissa's ear. Clarissa nodded. Jared wrapped an arm around her shoulder, gave it a squeeze, then began to walk toward the bathrooms.

"Jared!" Korey yelled, making his way to the bathroom doors, no longer saying "Excuse me" as he bumped into people. "Jared!"

"All right, party people, you know what time it is!" a loud voice simultaneously blared on the overhead speakers, drowning out Korey's shouts. "It's midnight and we're about to get—"

"Messed uuuuuuup!" the crowd in the dance pit shouted.

The music then spiked so loud that the walls seemed to vibrate.

"Jared!" Korey barked. "Jared, damn it, boy!"

But his son didn't hear him. Instead, Jared continued on his path to the bathroom and pushed open the door with a metal kangaroo on the front that said MATES in bright orange letters underneath.

Korey raced after him, almost knocking over a waiter who carried a tray covered with drinks, a side of ribs, and skewered grilled shrimp. Korey hastily murmured an apology before rushing to the bathroom. When he pushed the door open, he saw several men standing in front of the urinals. One man opened a door to one of the stalls. A few more stood near the sinks, but nowhere did Korey see Jared.

Damn it, he thought with frustration, clenching his fists. It had only been a matter of seconds between the time that Jared had walked into the bathroom and Korey had followed him. How had he lost him already?

He stood awkwardly near the entrance, stepping aside so other men could walk around him and use the bathroom.

"Well, don't just stand here!" a voice in his head urged. "If you just hang around staring at everybody, they're going to think something's wrong with you."

Korey wavered only a few more seconds before walking toward the stalls, trying to inconspicuously lean down and gaze at the shoes underneath. Maybe he could spot Jared that way. As he passed one stall, the door swung open and he jumped back to keep from getting hit. A towering Hulk Hogan type in a ripped T-shirt stepped out and glanced at Korey quizzically.

"You waiting for this one?" he asked, pointing over his shoulder to the empty stall.

Korey paused, then nodded and stepped inside. He glanced at the toilet. He stood awkwardly for nearly a minute.

I'm in here, might as well use the bathroom, I guess, he thought. He had just lowered his pants to his ankles and sat down when he heard a familiar voice.

"Yeah! Yeah, it's cool, I guess," Jared said. "I'll hit you up when I get back. All right? . . . Whatever, man! I got this! . . . Yeah, talk to you later. Okay, bye."

Korey frantically jumped to his feet and raised his jeans back to his waist. He was zippering his fly just as he shoved the door open and rushed outside the stall. He looked toward the sinks and saw Jared standing with his back toward him, washing his hands.

"Boy!" he exclaimed, as he ran toward Jared. He grabbed his son by the elbow and roughly turned him around. "What did you think you were doing? I've been running all over this damn town looking for—"

When the young man turned from the sink with soaking-wet, soapy hands and glared at Korey, Korey knew instantly that it wasn't his son.

"What the hell is your problem!" the younger man shouted, yanking his arm out of Korey's grasp. "Do you mind?"

Korey gaped. "Sorry, I thought you were . . ."

Korey's words faded as he turned back to the stall doors. He could have sworn it had been Jared he had just heard.

"Hey, did somebody lose their phone?" a voice shouted at the other end of the line of sinks, near the bathroom entrance.

Korey looked up to find a skinny white man with a

goatee waving a cell phone in the air. The plastic blue casing looked eerily like his son's phone.

"Uh, that's . . . it's mine, I think," he said, walking toward the man.

The guy frowned. "*You think?* Either it is or it isn't, pal."

"It's mine," Korey said firmly before snatching the phone out of the man's grasp, making the stranger grumble.

He scanned the phone and saw that it was indeed Jared's. He could tell from the Batman sticker on the back and the crack on the edge of the screen.

"Shit," he muttered. So it had been Jared who had walked into the bathroom, after all, but Korey had missed him—again. Worse, Korey's son had left the phone behind, making it impossible to track him. Dejected, Korey dropped the phone in his jean pocket and walked out of the men's room.

"You didn't find them either?" Cynthia asked as she neared the hostess desk where Korey stood, waiting for her.

He held Jared's phone aloft, showing it to her. "No, but I found this. It's Jared's."

Cynthia grabbed the phone out of his hand. She glared at it. "So they *were* here?"

He nodded as her face fell.

"But if we have his phone, how the hell are we going to use the tracking app?"

Korey released a long, slow breath. "We can't."

"So how are we going to find them, Korey?" she cried.

"We'll find them." He tried, but he didn't sound very

convincing. He was starting to lose hope himself, but he didn't want to reveal that to Cynthia. She looked like she was near tears. "We just . . . we just have to find a different way to do it."

"And that would be . . ."

"I have no clue," he answered honestly.

She dropped her face into her hands.

"Come on," he muttered, steering her to the restaurant door and rubbing her shoulders consolingly. He kneaded the knots in her muscles and she moaned. He instantly pulled his hands away, not liking the sound of that. It reminded him too much of other moments long ago when Cynthia had moaned like that, and he didn't need those carnal images in his head right now.

"Let's head back to the hotel and get some sleep," he said. "We'll try again in the morning."

Chapter 15

Cynthia opened her eyes in the darkened hotel room that she had checked into only nine hours ago and stared at the glowing orange numbers of the alarm clock on her night table, feeling more exhausted now than she had when she laid her head on her pillow to sleep.

Damn, its eleven o'clock already, she thought. The day was already almost half over!

She turned, rolled onto her back, and stared at the faux fresco relief on her ceiling.

It was hard to believe that little more than twenty-four hours ago she had been making bacon and eggs in her own kitchen back in Chesterton, Virginia, preparing herself to have a heart-to-heart with her daughter. Now she was thousands of miles away in some ancient Rome–themed Las Vegas hotel suite, and she had absolutely no idea where the hell Clarissa could be. Had her daughter found another chapel and married Jared after all? Was she still at the hotel now? Was she even still in Vegas?

Cynthia grumbled as she threw an arm over her tired eyes.

She was no closer to finding her daughter, stopping the wedding, and averting disaster than she had been when her flight touched down at McCarran International last night. She and Korey still didn't know the kids' room number at the hotel, and now that Jared had lost his cell phone, they couldn't use the software to track him that way either. But there *had* to be a way to find Clarissa and Jared, short of wandering up and down the Strip, shouting their names. There had to be a way to avoid Clarissa marrying her brother!

"You still don't know for sure if he *is* her brother," a voice in Cynthia's head countered.

No, she didn't. But as long as she allowed herself to consider the possibility, she felt a sense of urgency. It was the kick in the ass that told her she couldn't give up.

Think! Think! There has to be a way to solve this, damn it!

Suddenly, an idea came to mind. Cynthia lowered her arm from her face and opened her eyes.

Oh, my God! That's it!

Almost frantic, she turned onto her stomach and reached for the night table, knocking a notepad to the floor and tipping over a glass. Water dribbled onto the plush carpet. She grabbed her cell phone and accessed the Internet.

Keith had figured out the kids were heading to Las Vegas after checking Cynthia's credit card charges. Maybe she could use that same credit card information to figure out where the kids were now or what the kids would do next. Maybe they had charged a meal at a restaurant or tickets to a dinner show. *Who knows?*

She typed in the password for her credit card account and went to the Web page that listed current and pending charges. She scanned the screen. Then she found it—a new charge! She typed in the name of the vendor in Google and squinted when she saw the service they provided. The Web site showed a photo of a grinning couple on a romantic gondola ride.

"A gondola?" she whispered, then shrugged.

Well, it looks like Korey and I are about to take a boat ride, she thought before dialing Korey's cell phone number.

"Hello?" he answered; he sounded out of breath, making her frown.

"Why the hell are you breathing so hard?"

"I'm at the gym!" he shouted over the sound of thumping feet. "I'm on the treadmill. What's up?"

He was at the gym, huh? She had never envisioned Korey as a gym rat. Working out certainly hadn't been high on his list of things to do in high school, but she supposed his muscular physique would be all dough by now if he didn't step into a gym every once in a while.

"I think I know where the kids are headed," she said.

The sound of thumping feet slowed. "Okay, I'm listening."

"They're going to take a gondola ride."

"What the hell's a gondola ride?"

"Come on, you know what a gondola is!" She slung her legs over the side of the bed and climbed to her feet. "You know . . . those little banana-shaped boats on canals."

"Oh, okay, I got you now." He was still huffing. She guessed he was still on the treadmill.

"Anyway, the Venetian offers gondola rides, and it looks like the kids bought one for eighty bucks. If we head there, we might catch them." She raced into her bathroom and turned on the lights, squinting at the sudden brightness. She grabbed the makeup bag on the granite counter and tucked her cell phone underneath her chin as she fished out her toothbrush. "I'm getting ready now so we can—"

"So we're just supposed to stand on a dock all day *hoping* that we run into Jared and Clarissa. That's the big plan? What if the boats leave from more than one dock?"

Cynthia had turned on the faucet and just started to brush her teeth. When Korey posed his question, she stopped.

"Shit," she garbled, spitting frothy mint toothpaste onto the bathroom mirror.

Why did Korey have to keep pointing out the gaping holes in her plans?

"Do we at least know the time of their gondola ride?" he asked.

There he goes again with those questions, she thought, now annoyed. They were very practical and logical questions. *Damn him!*

She wiped the toothpaste away from her mouth with a washcloth. "No, we don't," she answered softly.

She heard him sigh gruffly on the other end. Her annoyance quickly morphed into anger.

"Hey, don't knock it if you can't come up with a better idea!"

"You're right. I apologize. At least it's a start, I guess." The thumping sound finally ceased. She supposed he had finished his run. "Look, how about we do this? How about we think about this a bit more and meet for lunch at the buffet downstairs? We'll talk it over and figure out what to do next. I'll meet you there at noon, okay?"

"See you at noon." She then hung up and stared at

her reflection in the bathroom mirror, feeling a lot less excited now than she had when she'd made her online discovery.

"It's not the end of the world," the voice in her head reassured. "Maybe you guys can still use the info."

Cynthia grabbed her toothbrush and started to brush her teeth again. The odds weren't in their favor, but she wouldn't give up. She couldn't.

Cynthia arrived at the restaurant a little before noon and was gobsmacked by how massive it was. It was like someone took about a dozen small-town buffets and decided to dump them all into one place, except the space wasn't filled with cheap Formica tabletops and seating booths covered in plastic and pleather. Instead, there were glass chandeliers, coffered ceilings, ice sculptures, and expensive artwork. The buffet stations weren't what she was used to seeing either. They didn't feature runny eggs, congealed chicken and mushroom casserole, and biscuits that had hardened under heat lamps. Instead, she saw snow crab legs, Kobe beef, rack of lamb, and caviar.

Cynthia wandered around the restaurant, zigzagging through tables in search of Korey. After ten minutes, she still hadn't found him. The room was teeming with people and seemed to be the size of a high school gym, making her wonder how she was going to find Korey in all this mess. She'd have better luck finding him at a football stadium.

Cynthia threw up her hands in defeat. She pulled out her cell phone and dialed his number.

"Korey, where the hell are you?" she snapped when he finally picked up.

"Over by the soup station."

She rolled her eyes and hung up. A few minutes later, she found him sitting at a table near a topiary display. A smiling Asian woman with tanned skinned, high cheekbones, and big boobs was sitting at the table with him. When Cynthia saw her, she frowned.

Who the hell is she?

Korey and the woman were huddled so close that it looked like the woman was whispering in his ear. She said something, making him burst into laughter. The couple was so engrossed with their conversation that Korey didn't seem to notice Cynthia walking toward them. She loudly cleared her throat, making Korey finally look up at her.

"Oh, hey, Cindy," he greeted, the smile never leaving his face. "Guess you finally found me."

"Guess so," she said dryly.

He turned to the woman sitting beside him, who now stared up at Cynthia.

"Shino, meet Cynthia. She's a . . . an old friend of mine."

Cynthia's frown deepened. *An old friend? That's what I am to him?*

"Well, what was he supposed to say, girl? Meet Cynthia, my ex-lover who dumped me soon after high school graduation," the voice in her head mocked. "Oh, and we're on a mission to stop our kids from getting married."

No! Not that! But why did he have to refer to her as his "old friend?" It made her sound like an old couch or an old shoe.

"The woman standing in front of you is old news," his words seemed to imply. *"You don't have to worry about her."*

"Uh, pleasure to meet you," Shino said uneasily.

"Yeah, same here," Cynthia answered flatly.

"Shino and I met at the gym this morning."

Shino tossed her long, jet-black hair over her shoulder and leaned toward Korey. "He was showing me the proper way to bench-press."

"The way you were doing it, you might've hurt yourself."

"Well, then, thank God you were there! You're my hero," she cooed, making Cynthia cringe.

"Yeah, well, sorry to interrupt you guys, but, Korey, you and I have something to discuss." She glared at him. "That's why we're both here, right? Or did I wander around this restaurant for fifteen minutes just for the exercise?"

Shino sat back in her chair, removing the arm she had linked through his. "Oh, I didn't mean to . . . I mean I didn't know that—"

"It's okay," Korey reassured, patting her hand soothingly. "Look, why don't we meet up later. How about seven o'clock? We can finally have that meal together. Next time, I'll make sure not to eat before you get here."

Shino rose from her chair. "Sure, meet you at seven."

Cynthia waited impatiently as they exchanged numbers and flirted a few minutes longer. When Shino finally left, Cynthia flopped down in the now vacant chair beside Korey and slammed her python purse on the table, making the utensils and his plate rattle.

"Good afternoon to you too," he replied with a smirk before drinking some of his iced tea.

She crossed her arms over her chest. "Here I was thinking we were in Las Vegas to find Clarissa and Jared. I had no idea you were here in search of out-of-town booty!"

"*Out-of-town booty?* Cindy, just because I was talking to a woman and we're supposed to meet for dinner doesn't mean I'm trying to get some ass."

"Yeah, right! I'm sure you're going out with Shamu because of her witty conversation."

"It's *She*-no. Shamu is a killer whale."

She shooed away his correction. "Shamu. Shinu. Whatever!"

He chuckled and shook his head. "Same ol' same ol', huh?"

"Excuse me?"

"Twenty years have passed and it's still the same ol' stuff with you. You never liked me talking to other women. You always assumed I was going to cheat on you, to the point that you even created this lie in your head about a secret affair I was having with Viv. I never knew why you were like that." He sat down his glass and gazed at her. "You're an attractive woman, Cindy. You shouldn't be so insecure."

She stared at him, absolutely stunned. "*Insecure?* You think I'm insecure?"

"Hell, I don't think you are; I *know* you are! That's probably the reason why you were always so jealous."

"I was *not* jealous!" she shouted, slapping her hands on the table, making several visor-wearing old women nearby turn to look at her. "And I'm damn sure not insecure!"

He lowered his fork, took a deep breath, and looked at her wearily. "Are you going to make a scene here too? Are you trying to cover every venue in Vegas?"

She shot up from the table. "To hell with you! I don't have to sit here and be insulted! I don't need this . . . this bullshit!"

Korey watched as she stormed off. Instead of looking alarmed by her outburst, he seemed bored. He returned his attention to his lunch after waving at the table of women sitting beside them.

"Sorry. She's off her meds," he lied.

One of the old women nodded solemnly then made a *tsk, tsk* sound. "My daughter gets like that. Mental illness is a horrible thing."

Meanwhile, Cynthia was still mumbling to herself as she stomped across the restaurant, looking every bit as crazy as Korey claimed her to be.

"Jealous," she muttered between clenched teeth. "I'm not jealous . . . and I never have been!"

And if she ever did anything that *seemed* like jealousy in the old days, it wasn't her fault, she insisted. It was *his!* She had told him that they had to keep their relationship on the "down low," and he had hated the idea and had been vocal about it. So to rub it in, he had gone out of his way to seem like the single guy. He had flirted with the girls in class and in the lunchroom right in front of her. He had refused to skip the senior prom with her and instead went with a small caravan of his boys. The whole night Cynthia had sat home alone, envisioning Korey getting busy on the dance floor with some ho in a tight, low-cut dress—and then getting busy again with that same ho later that night in the back of his Chevy.

All those times Cynthia had wondered if Korey would finally decide he was tired of keeping up the farce. Maybe one day he would conclude that all the sneaking around and secrecy wasn't worth it anymore, dump her, and move on to a girl whom he could date in the open.

Cynthia slowed as she approached the dining room's exit.

"Admit it. That does sound a bit insecure," the voice in her head argued.

Maybe, she thought, glancing over her shoulder to look back across the restaurant. *But that doesn't mean I'm still that way.*

"So prove it," the voice in her head insisted. "Don't storm out and let Korey think seeing him with that woman got to you. Don't prove him right!"

Cynthia groaned. She clenched her fists. It looked like she would have to go back.

Muttering again, she walked back across the restaurant, feeling as if her shoes were made of lead or concrete. When she approached his table, Korey looked up at her, sucking up a string of linguini that was hanging out of his mouth.

"Forget something?" he asked mockingly between chews, raising his brows.

She lowered herself into her chair, primly crossed her legs, and adjusted the hem of her skirt over her knees. "I went to the bathroom. Now I'm back."

"Uh-huh," he uttered, obviously not believing her.

"So can we finally discuss what we came here for? I told you about the gondola ride. What do you propose we do about it?"

"We still don't know where or when they're taking this boat ride though, right?"

She rolled her eyes. "We know it's at the Venetian Hotel. That's about it."

"Well, how about we find out more?"

"And we would do that by . . ."

He lowered his fork and thought for a second. "Can you pretend to be Clarissa and call the company? Tell them you want to confirm the time of your ride."

Cynthia's scowl immediately morphed into a grin. "I knew I kept you around for a reason."

"My sexy good looks?"

"Not likely," she said dryly. She lowered her sunglasses from her crown to eyes. She then ran her fingers through her blond tresses. "All right, I'll find out the time and place and let you know. We'll meet around there about a half an hour before that."

"Okay." He started to eat again. "But if I'm late from my date with Shino, go ahead without me."

She did a double take. "You're joking, right?"

"Why would I be joking?"

"Korey, you're not seriously going to miss the one last possible opportunity we have to find the kids because you have a date with Shiba Inu?"

"That's the name of a dog."

"Whatever!" She pushed back her chair and stood. "Look, enough of this! I'm done arguing with you! I didn't take a nail-biting flight and endure only eight hours of sleep in two days for you to play the love connection in Vegas. I'll meet you by the dock at the time we're both supposed to be there. And if you're not there, Korey Walker, so help me God . . ." She furiously shook her head. "You don't want to see what will happen!"

She then turned and strode away, not giving him a chance to reply.

Chapter 16

Lauren took the pan of beef tenderloin out of her Wolf convection oven just as she heard her husband, Crisanto, shut the front door behind him.

Good, she thought as she placed the pan on a wooden block on the kitchen's granite countertop and closed the oven door. Cris's timing was perfect. The meat only needed to rest for another five to ten minutes before it would be ready to cut and serve.

"Hey!" he called out. His keys jingled. She could hear the sound of his heavy footsteps as he walked across the travertine tile in their foyer and headed toward the kitchen. "Is that dinner I smell?"

She stirred the pureed potatoes. "It is, indeed, baby!"

Lauren then turned and glanced at her fuzzy reflection in their stainless steel refrigerator door. She hoped she looked just as delectable as the entrées she was preparing. To surprise her husband, she had made him a home-cooked meal and decided to serve that meal in nothing but an apron, oven mitts, a lace thong, and four-and-a-half-inch heels.

Lauren was a chef, but she had to admit that she rarely cooked for her husband nowadays. She was often too busy at the restaurant. Even tonight it had been a challenge to do this. When she had told her sous-chef she was skipping the dinner rush for yet another night with Cris, the young man looked like he was about to bust a coronary. But she had to, especially with how badly things had gone at the Paytons' party yesterday. Lauren felt like she had to make it up to Cris somehow. After all, a large part of the grief that he was now enduring had to do with her and her family drama.

Speaking of family drama, there would be no talk of any of it tonight. She wouldn't tell him about the hour-long phone conversation she had had with Stephanie about Steph's weight gain and whether Keith still found her sexy despite her "double-wide behind." She wouldn't tell Cris about her mother's ongoing hunt for yet another rich husband. Yolanda was currently in Nantucket with her new boyfriend. He was a particularly good prospect since he seemed to be near death's door. (He was on oxygen and spent most of his days in a wheelchair.) Lauren would skip over mentioning that Cynthia had officially left Chesterton twenty-four hours ago and had yet to find Clarissa. In Lauren's opinion, it was almost certain that her niece was now Mrs. Jared Walker, whether the family liked it or not.

No, tonight the focus would be solely on Cris.

When Cris stepped through their expansive kitchen's entrance, she greeted him with a flourish. "Ta-da!" she sang, throwing out her arms.

He stopped in his tracks. His eyeballs nearly popped out of his head.

"Did I surprise you, honey?" she asked as she walked around the kitchen island toward him.

Cris nodded as he slowly looked her up and down. "You . . . you certainly did."

"I'm making you beef tenderloin with garlic mashed potatoes . . . *your favorite!*"

He didn't respond. Instead he seemed riveted by her current ensemble—or lack thereof. He hungrily licked his lips. Judging from how he was staring at her, she suspected the mashed potatoes on the oventop weren't the only thing he was hungry for.

"And I'm *finally* wearing the apron your mom sent!" She fluffed the lace edging. The words "Mrs. Weaver" were stenciled on the apron's pink and white damask front.

Her mother-in-law had given it to her as a birthday gift, along with a set of matching oven mitts. Lauren had told her that she loved cooking. Somehow Cris's mom had misinterpreted that as her being a home-maker who wore God-awful aprons like this one. Whenever she put it on, she felt like the black Donna Reed. She had decided, this time, that if she was going to wear the ugly thing, it would look so much better if she was topless underneath.

"So what do you think?" she asked.

"You look good. Damn good!"

"Why, thank you, kind sir." She held the edges of the apron as she did a little curtsy.

He walked toward her with his arms extended, like he was about to wrap her in an embrace, but he suddenly paused, then glanced over his shoulder. "Wait! You're not dressed like that while the nanny is here, are you?"

Lauren rolled her eyes. "Of course not! I gave her and the rest of the staff the night off."

"So where's Cris Jr.?"

"With my sister Dawn."

"With *Dawn?*" he choked.

Lauren slapped his shoulder. "Don't say it like that! Dawn's a responsible woman. Besides, Xavier is helping her out. I think he talked her into offering to babysit tonight. He thought watching Little Cris overnight might help convince her they should have a baby. She's hoping that it'll convince him of the opposite." Lauren laughed.

"Well, I . . . I guess it's okay then," Cris said, though he still looked a bit uncertain.

"Our baby will be fine, honey. Trust me! I've got a nice evening planned for you, and I'd hate to have to change things by bringing Cris Jr. back home. There's beef tenderloin and mashed potatoes for dinner, strawberry shortcake for dessert, and uh . . ." She stood on the balls of her feet, wrapped her arms around his neck, and pulled him close. "There's a little surprise after that."

"Why don't we skip the dinner and dessert and go straight to the surprise?" he whispered against her lips.

"Why did I have a feeling you were going to say that?"

They kissed, and Lauren felt the same heady thrill now that she had felt the first night Cris had kissed her and the same tingle that had made her heartbeat quicken and her knees weak. She opened her mouth and Cris languidly slid his tongue inside. Dual waves of heat and pleasure surged all over her body. He pulled her even closer. It was a struggle of willpower, but she tugged her mouth away, making him grumble with disappointment. She grinned.

"Oh, stop! You still get your surprise. I just want to give it to you upstairs."

"I'm just as happy to have it down here," he said, pushing her back against the kitchen island and easing aside the front of her apron to fondle one of her breasts.

Lauren laughed again, before tugging his hands away. "*Upstairs*, Big Boy."

He waited as she turned down the temperature in the oven and put the tenderloin back inside to stay warm. She led him to their winding staircase and then to their bedroom.

Lauren had turned off the overhead lights and lit candles all around the room—tea lights, pillar candles, and scented candles. Red and pink rose petals were strewn along their off-white bedspread. Candles were also placed in the bathroom, where a warm bubble bath waited for them. Two champagne glasses sat on the tiled edge of the whirlpool tub.

He slowly looked around him. "You've been busy."

"I aim to please," she said seductively.

"You're not about to lay some bad news on me, are you? You didn't total the car? I don't have to bail one of your sisters out of jail?" He paused. "Did Cindy start a small war in Las Vegas?"

"O, ye of so little faith!" she exclaimed, pushing his suit jacket off his shoulders. "The only surprise you're about to get tonight, sweetheart, is what's about to happen in that bathtub—as soon as you get out of those clothes."

Cris cocked an eyebrow. It didn't take him long to accept her challenge. He quickly loosened his tie, then tugged the garment over his head before tossing it to the hardwood floor. He unbuttoned his shirt and discarded that too. He took off his slacks. Within seconds, he was tugging at his boxer briefs.

He may have been retired from the NFL, but that didn't mean Crisanto Weaver's body was any less sculpted than it had been when he played on the football field. His nutmeg-brown skin glowed in the flickering candlelight, and Lauren's eyes were instantly drawn to his tattoos: the winding Chinese dragon on his right forearm and the jersey number on his left pec. When he took off his boxers, her gaze dropped to his burgeoning arousal. He went from half-mast to full attention in ten seconds flat.

He stood naked in front of her, eagerly rubbing his hands together. He gestured toward her apron.

"Your turn."

She turned her back toward him.

"Can you help me with the strings?" she asked, brushing her hair over her shoulder. "The knots are hard to undo."

Cris instantly stepped forward and undid the apron strings for her. But he couldn't take the teasing way she slowly let the apron slide down her chest and then to the floor. He lowered his mouth to her neck and began to nibble and kiss her before descending to her shoulder. She felt him rub and grind against her backside, and she closed her eyes, arched her spine, and tilted back her head to give him more access. While one of his hands roughly pulled down her underwear, the other reached for one of her breasts and held it. He caressed her nipple between his fingers.

She pulled his hands away again and turned to face him. "You're not going to make it to that bathtub, are you?"

His hands instantly dropped to her bottom, cupping the cheeks as he pulled her against him. "Not with all this temptation."

"Well, let me put you out of your misery." She playfully tapped his nose then stepped out of his grasp. She kicked off her heels and walked into the bathroom.

She climbed into the bathwater first, turned on the whirlpool jets, and instantly moaned. The hot water and massaging currents felt delicious. Cris climbed in after her.

"Bring your foot over here, baby," Cris ordered from the other side of the deep-sunken tub.

Lauren raised her right foot from the hot, soapy water and languidly dangled it in front of him. He took her foot into his strong hands and started to rub it, kneading the ball of her sore foot and heel, making her moan again.

Lauren closed her eyes and sank farther into the vanilla-scented bubbles, not even caring if her hair got wet. She rested her head back against the edge of the tub, letting the whirlpool jets and Cris's hands soothe her. She could feel herself drifting off to sleep.

"Oh, no, you don't! You made some big promises about all that I was supposed to get tonight, Mrs. Weaver. You better wake up!"

She slowly opened her eyes. A smile crossed her pink lips. "If you don't want me to fall asleep, then you shouldn't rub my feet like that."

"Fine. I'll switch ends then," he said with an impish grin.

He lowered her foot back into the water, came to her side of the tub, and lay beside her. The instant he did, he was all hands and all mouth. Lauren knew she certainly wouldn't be falling asleep now.

He toyed with her and she toyed with him—until they were both panting and groaning. Finally, *she* couldn't take anymore. She straddled him and braced her hands on his shoulders. He adjusted her hips and himself before plunging inside her. Her grip on his shoulders tightened as she threw back her head and shouted out into the bathroom. Their hips moved rhythmically as they kissed and ground against each other. The pace of their lovemaking gradually increased, making the water lap over the edges of the tub and pool on the bathroom floor, taking out a few candles with it.

Lauren could feel herself getting close. She tore her mouth from his and buried her head into his shoulder. Her body clenched when the tremors started to overtake her, making her whole body quiver and her toes curl. To stifle the shouts of her climax, she nipped his shoulder and dug her fingernails into his back.

His arms tightened around her. She heard a low guttural growl and felt him jerk. His arms then went slack and fell into the water with a loud splash.

When Lauren finally regained her breath, she lifted her head and dazedly looked down at her husband.

"Thank you for my surprise," he said, making her chuckle.

"You're welcome." She kissed him again.

An hour and half later, they lay naked in bed together. The rose petals had been tossed aside and now lay crumpled and shredded on the hardwood floor. Many of the candles had either dissolved into a puddle of wax or were smoldering, filling the room with the faint smell of smoke and vanilla.

The now-empty champagne glasses and empty plate of beef tenderloin and pureed garlic potatoes sat on one of the night tables. The half-eaten strawberry shortcake sat on the bed beside them.

"Oh, damn," Cris moaned as she fed him another forkful of whipped cream, strawberries, and angel food cake. "Good God, Lauren! It's like I've died and gone to heaven, baby!"

She grinned. "Is the cake that good?"

"It's not just the cake!" She licked traces of whipped cream from the side of his mouth, making him moan. "Do you know how many men's fantasies it is to be fed a home-cooked meal in bed by a beautiful naked woman who just fucked them six ways from Sunday?"

She shook her head. "I have no idea."

"Too many to count!" He ate another forkful, then slumped back against the satin pillows behind his head. He closed his eyes. "Goddamn, that's good."

"Well, I'm glad you liked it. I wanted to make up for what happened yesterday," she confessed, making his smile disappear.

"You mean what happened at the party? None of that was your fault, baby."

"Yes, it was!" She put the cake plate next to the champagne glasses on the night table. "Mayor Knightly was giving you crap because of me, because of what I've done in the past, and I just . . ." She cringed. "I just hate that."

Cris shook his head. "No, that asshole was giving me shit because he was trying to embarrass me in front of a room full of potential voters. It wasn't about you, Lauren."

"But I'm the chink in your armor. You're married to a former gold digger who's been around the block more than just a few times. It's bound to—"

Cris held up his hand to stop her. "Can we not talk about this right now?"

"But, Cris, you're running for mayor, baby. You have to realize that—"

"I don't want to talk about it!" he boomed, making her jump. She stared at him, dumbfounded, as he shoved her aside, pushed back the sheets, and climbed to his feet. "Look, I'm . . . I'm sorry for yelling like that.

But"—he balled then unclenched his fists—"I know who you are, who your family is, and what you've done, Lauren. I don't need to be reminded of it again. Like I told Marvin, if it's such a big issue, then damn it, those people don't have to vote for me! Vote for that hypocritical, self-righteous asshole Mayor Knightly."

She squinted. "Wait, you and Marvin were discussing me?"

It was bad enough that Marvin had been sucking up to Cris. She didn't want Cris to really become friends with the man. Why was Cris discussing their personal life with him?

Cris sighed tiredly, looked away from her, and nodded. "We got into it a little during the meeting we had this afternoon."

"You had a meeting with Marvin? *Why?*"

"It was just a lunch date with him and his wife. That's all, Lauren."

A lunch date to which I wasn't invited, she silently noted.

"Cris, why are you so chummy-chummy with Marvin Payton now, anyway?"

"He asked to be my campaign manager."

She gaped at her husband. "What? When the hell did that happen? Why didn't you tell me? I didn't even know you wanted a campaign manager!"

"I didn't—at first. It was Marvin's suggestion. He made it last night, and we met for lunch today to discuss it in more detail. He thought my campaign could use some organization. I agreed with him, but I told him that I had to think about it."

She sucked her teeth. "Well, Marvin is just *full* of suggestions, isn't he?"

"He's only trying to help, baby. He wants me to win."

"I bet he does, which is why he was discussing with you how having a whore for a wife can look bad! What else did helpful Marvin suggest? Dropping me and getting another wife before the election?" she asked sarcastically.

"You know damn well that's not what he said!"

"Yeah, I can only imagine what he said," she muttered. She then crawled to the other side of the bed and climbed to her feet.

Didn't Cris realize what a kiss-ass Marvin was? In some ways, he was worse than Mayor Knightly. A man like Marvin could be the wolf in sheep's clothing. Couldn't Cris see how someone like Marvin could have an insidious influence on them and their marriage?

She walked toward their bedroom door.

"Where are you going?" he shouted after her.

"To sleep somewhere else!" she shouted back at him as she strode naked into their second-floor hallway. "Don't forget to put the dirty dishes in the dishwasher. Good night!"

She then slammed the door closed behind her.

Chapter 17

"Have you made your selection, sir?" the waiter asked eagerly as he leaned over their table.

"Just a sec," Korey said.

His eyes tap danced over the wine list, shifting between the two oversized pages. He flinched a little at the prices he saw listed next to each bottle of Pinot Grigio, Merlot, and Dom Pérignon.

What the hell are they sellin' . . . liquid gold?

But he told himself that it really wasn't *that* much money—considering how nice of a restaurant it was. They gave out complimentary caviar like it was nothing, like it was the garlic cheese biscuits at Red Lobster! And it's not like he was destitute. His longtime financial planner, Dan, often argued that a guy like Korey—the owner of two auto repair shops—could stand to take a hit.

"I encourage my clients to behave conservatively with their money, Korey, but honestly, you give new meaning to the word 'cheapskate!'" Dan once barked at him over the phone.

And Korey kept reminding himself that he was in Las Vegas—the land of fast times and fast cash. Plus, he was on a date with a very beautiful and desirable woman, and he wanted to impress her. He couldn't exactly do that if he asked her if she wouldn't mind eating at TGIFriday's instead.

"Splurge a little," the voice in his head urged yet again.

He glanced up from his leatherbound menu to find Shino smiling at him. He shifted the menu toward her.

"Does anything on here interest you?"

Her seductive smile widened as she leaned closer. "As long as it's bubbly," she whispered, looping one of her arms through his, "it doesn't matter to me."

"We'll have the Moët then," he said promptly before the tightwad in him screamed hysterically for him to stop.

"Very good choice, sir. I'll be right back with your champagne." The waiter then took the menu from Korey and disappeared.

"He's right. That was a good choice." Shino inched closer to Korey, pressing her breasts against his forearm and elbow. She traced a finger over his knuckles. "And you know what they say about champagne?"

"No, what do they say?"

The pink tip of her tongue darted over her glossy bottom lip. Her lashes lowered as her hand dropped from his arm to his thigh. "They say that it's an *amazing* aphrodisiac."

He chuckled. "Yeah, I guess I've heard that."

"Care to test the theory later?"

Korey did a double take.

"Here you are," the waiter suddenly interrupted, making the couple jump in surprise.

A busboy removed their red and white wineglasses and replaced them with champagne flutes.

The waiter grinned. "Your bottle of Moët, sir." He held the chilled bottle toward Korey for inspection.

Korey absently nodded while he felt Shino sliding her hand up and down his inner thigh underneath the table. She was making it hard to concentrate on the bottle label—let alone anything else in the room.

"So," she whispered as the waiter poured champagne into their glasses, "you own your own business, huh?"

"Yeah." He cleared his throat as her hand wandered an inch higher, sending his pulse into overdrive. "A couple of auto body and repair shops back home."

"So you're a gearhead *and* industrious? You know, that's pretty sexy. In fact, everything about you I find sexy, Korey."

She then leaned forward and kissed him, lightly kneading her warm, plump lips over his before playfully darting that pink tongue inside his mouth. Korey was caught off guard at first, but he only hesitated a few seconds before kissing her back. She moaned softly and pressed against his chest. The kiss deepened as she linked her arms around his neck.

"I'll, uh . . . I'll be back with your entrées," the waiter mumbled before backing away from their table. He bumped into the busboy, who was gaping behind him with a pitcher of water in his hands. The two men openly ogled the kissing couple. The busboy was so engrossed that he was almost spilling water onto the floor. The waiter grabbed the pitcher, muttered something in Spanish, and shooed the busboy away from the table.

A few seconds later, Korey tore his mouth away

from Shino's, coming up for a gasp of badly needed air.

"Damn," he murmured between breaths, making her grin again.

"Mmm-hmm." She bit down on her bottom lip. "My sentiments exactly!"

She then leaned forward and kissed him again.

Korey had assured Cynthia that he wasn't on a date with Shino tonight to get some out-of-town booty, but that pretty much seemed to be where Shino was heading. She was definitely sending out "Anyway you want it, honey" vibes.

"To hell with Cindy," the voice in his head argued. "If this woman is offering you some ass, then you get some ass, brothah!"

And how long had it been since he had had sex anyway?

Months, he thought. *Hell, almost a year!* He hadn't done it since he went out with the recently divorced hairdresser who wanted a revenge fuck against her cheating ex-husband. A man like Korey didn't have the luxury of turning down a woman like Shino. He didn't know when an opportunity like this would come around again.

But despite the fact that he had this gorgeous woman's tongue in his mouth and her breast against his chest, Korey could not get Cynthia out of his damn mind. And it wasn't just Cindy, whom he could practically hear psychically nagging him to get up from the table and get his ass to the Venetian Hotel. No, he was thinking about Jared too.

Jared.

Though his son may be nineteen years old and put on a bravado like he was ten years older, in some ways

Korey knew Jared was still the little boy who proudly showed off a slam dunk on his Playskool basketball hoop in their driveway, who stumbled around the stage in his tap-dancing shoes and Christmas tree costume during his second-grade play. That Jared could be easily saddened and hurt.

Even after all these years, Korey's urge to protect his son hadn't waned. It wasn't that Korey was a "helicopter parent." He knew that messing up and disappointments were part of growing up, but Jared was millimeters close to making one of the biggest mistakes of his life by marrying Clarissa Simpson. And despite all his best efforts, Korey probably couldn't stop it from happening.

He had once thought the couple might have a chance at happiness, but now he knew Jared was only in for pain and suffering if Jared entangled himself in the ongoing soap opera known as the Gibbons family. Clarissa wasn't a bad girl; she was rather sweet, to be honest. She couldn't help the family that she had been born into, but Clarissa had the unfortunate luck to be born to a Gibbons girl. Now that Korey had spent the day with Cynthia and was reminded of their family's bizarre rules, rituals, and mercenary ways, he didn't want his son to have anything to do with Clarissa. It would only lead to heartbreak.

"If he's in love with her, Jared is not going to avoid heartbreak," the voice in his head insisted. "He won't be able to avoid it any more than you did."

And knowing that fact broke Korey's heart all over again.

"Are you not into this?" Shino whispered against his lips.

Korey opened his eyes and blinked. "Huh?"

"I asked if you weren't into this," Shino repeated, shifting back slightly. "This doesn't seem to be working for you."

"Why do you say that?"

"Well, considering where my hand is, I thought I'd have your undivided attention by now—and I don't seem to."

Korey looked down and saw that underneath the tablecloth, Shino's hand had wandered from his thigh to his crotch. She was almost cupping his balls. How the hell had he missed that?

"Sorry. Guess I . . . I guess I was focused somewhere else."

"Obviously." She removed her hand and sat back in her seat.

Korey reached for her champagne. They fell into an uncomfortable silence, and Korey frantically grappled for a way to salvage their date. He'd be damned if he let Cynthia ruin this from afar.

"I'm . . . I'm just worried about my son," he mumbled, deciding to be honest with her. "That's all."

"You have a son?"

"Yeah, his name is Jared. He's nineteen years old."

"Nineteen, huh?" Shino lowered her glass. "So I guess you're worried he's raising holy hell back home? I wouldn't be too concerned, Korey. I used to do the same thing when I was a teenager and I could—"

"Jared's not back at home. He's here in Vegas."

"Well, if he's here, then that's even less of a reason to be worried about him." She placed a warm hand on his again. She gave it a squeeze. "Do you need to step away and make a quick phone call to see what he's up to? I don't mind. Go ahead."

"It's not that. Look, it's . . ." He took a deep breath. "Jared is here in Vegas to get married, all right?"

Shino looked as if she was about to spit out her champagne. She squinted at Korey. "Come again?"

"My son ran away to Las Vegas to elope with his girlfriend. That's why I'm here to . . . to stop them. I hopped on a plane as soon as I found out what he was up to. I came here so that I could talk some sense into him. We both came."

"Who's we?"

Korey hesitated again, wondering if introducing the topic of Cynthia right now was a bad idea. "'We' is Cindy and me. We made the trip together."

"Cindy?" Confusion marred Shino's pretty face. "Who the hell is Cindy?"

"You met her earlier today. Remember? At the hotel buffet?"

She squinted, then suddenly realized who he was talking about. "Whoa! That woman from this morning? *That's* who you came with?"

Korey nodded. "The girl my son is marrying is her daughter."

"So *that's* why she was so bitchy." Shino slumped back into the plush leather booth. "It was like she was trying to melt me with her eyes! Now I know why! For a second there, I thought you two had something romantic going on."

He looked at her as if that was the most absurd thing he had ever heard. "*Me and Cindy?* Oh, hell no! We haven't been together in *years.* I'm just with her now because I'm trying to find Jared. That's it! The woman is insane . . . unstable! I would never get with her."

"Never get with her *now*, you mean. But you were together before?"

"Yeah . . . about twenty years ago! We were together back when we were teenagers. We were . . . I guess you could say we were first loves."

"First loves?" With that, Shino scrutinized him more carefully. "Did you guys run away to get married too?"

"No. Cindy would never do that. She was terrified of defying her mom, and her mother would never, *ever* have approved of her being with a guy like me. It's all about money with them, and I certainly didn't have any of it back then."

"But you wanted to marry her. I mean you would have?"

How had the topic shifted from his search to find Jared to whether he wanted to marry Cindy?

"Really, that's all in the past. Why are we talking about this?"

"If it's in the past, then you shouldn't mind answering the question." She searched his eyes. "Did you want to marry her . . . back then, I mean?"

Korey sat and thought for a minute, going back to the mind-set of the young man he was in 1994. "Yes," he finally answered. "I would have married her. But all that's so long ago that it's not even worth talking about. Trust me. There's nothing going on between us now."

Shino cocked an eyebrow. "Are you sure about that, Korey? You know what they say about first loves."

"I told you. She's crazy, and I'm not a boy anymore with his head in the clouds . . . who doesn't know his ass from a hole in the ground. That was then, this is now. I know better. I would never get mixed up with her again. We're done."

But even as he said it, he knew that wasn't totally true. If he was really completely over Cynthia, he wouldn't keep obsessing over the "who, what, when, and why" of their breakup all those years ago. He wouldn't still be holding out for an apology.

Shino assessed Korey again with her dark eyes. She

didn't look like she believed him. He could see the incredulity plainly on her face—the way the corner of her lips tightened, the furrow between her brows—but at least she was polite enough to pretend she believed him.

"Well," she said holding her half-filled champagne glass aloft, "here's to leaving behind crazy exes."

He forced a smile and held his glass toward her. They clinked the rims of their glasses together. "Here's to leaving behind crazy exes."

They drank and fell into another awkward silence. The waiter brought their entrées, placing the dishes on their table. As they began to eat, Shino gazed at him again.

"So . . ." She grinned. "Back to what we were discussing before."

"Which was?" he asked between bites.

He honestly didn't remember since he had become so preoccupied with Cynthia and Jared.

Focus, Korey, he told himself. *Focus. Remember? Prime piece of ass right next to you!*

"Which was what plans you have for us tonight." The pink tongue darted out again. "What exactly did you have in mind?"

"Well, I—"

Korey paused when he heard his phone ring in his suit jacket pocket. He knew instinctively who was calling him at that moment. It could only be Cynthia, and she was probably wondering where he was.

"To hell with Cynthia!" the voice in his head argued.

"I . . . well, I—"

His phone rang again.

He could envision her waiting for him at the dock, gritting her teeth and tapping her foot impatiently, despite him urging her to go on without him. It was so typical of her. If Cynthia wanted something, she expected him to drop everything and come running. She hadn't changed in all these years. But he wasn't doing it this time! If Cynthia thought he was about to end this date and give up the chance to sample a piece of Shino pie in his hotel room later that night, she had another thing coming!

"You *what,* Korey?" Shino asked expectantly. "Are you going to answer that, by the way?"

His phone was ringing a third time, and instead of thinking about Cynthia, he remembered Jared in his Christmas Tree costume . . . Jared, who was probably boarding a gondola to sail away with his future teenaged wife, only to collide with disaster.

Korey's shoulders slumped as his phone rang yet again. "I'm sorry, Shino, but I think I'm going to have to cut our dinner short."

Chapter 18

I'm going to kill him, Cynthia thought as she listened to the line ring. She finally pressed the button on her phone screen to end the call. *I swear to God that I am going to kill him!*

She didn't think it was possible, but her anxiety went up another notch as she looked at the people who streamed past her on the vaulted bridge overlooking the hotel's manmade canal. Clarissa and Jared could appear at any second, and here she was scoping out the crowd, searching for Korey. It was now more than fifteen minutes after the time she told him to meet her here. She had called him three times already, but each time the call went to his voicemail.

"Asshole," she muttered under her breath.

She glared down at her wristwatch, squinting under the street lamp at the watch's glass face as dusk descended into night. The orange, reds, and purples from the sky above that had reflected off the canal water were now blending into a deep navy that was quickly becoming ink black. More lights started to turn on along the bridge, the dock, and the front of the restaurants lining the canal.

Korey had said that if he didn't make it back from his date in enough time to go ahead with the search without him. But she didn't think he would actually *do* it. He had to realize how important this was! But now they were probably going to miss the kids because Korey was more interested in having a candlelit dinner with some chick he met at the hotel gym than he was in finding their children.

And he thinks my priorities are out of whack, she thought flippantly as she impatiently tapped her Tory Burch leather slipper. Cynthia scanned the crowd one last time and shook her head, finally giving up on him. She stomped across the bridge and along the sidewalk to the spot on the canal where a row of gondolas were docked. A short line of people waited there on the cobblestone. She fell in line behind them, standing on the balls of her feet to see if Clarissa and Jared were in line in front of her or in one of the boats drifting away from the dock. But they were nowhere to be found.

"So I guess you didn't run into them?" Korey asked from behind her seconds later, making her jump in surprise at the sound of his voice.

Cynthia whipped around to face him. At the sight of Korey, the tirade she was prepared to unleash died on her lips. She blinked in amazement.

It was like someone had waved a magic wand and transformed the gruff mechanic with grease under his nails into a debonair businessman. Korey had suddenly morphed into the black Adonis she had spotted in the shopping center parking lot almost a week ago, except Korey was three times as sexy.

He had finally gotten rid of his five o'clock shadow and was clean-shaven. He was wearing an expensive-looking, European-cut, charcoal-gray suit and a simple, silk black tie, something she presumed he hadn't packed when they decided to take their impromptu trip to Vegas. Instead of Korey's usual understated aftershave, the scent of a very familiar and expensive cologne wafted toward her. She knew the scent because one of her boyfriends had worn the same cologne on several occasions.

Korey better be wearing a knockoff, Cynthia thought angrily. She knew the real version cost about sixty bucks an ounce. That meant between the cologne and the suit, he had probably spent almost a grand for his date with Shamu, and that didn't even count the dinner itself!

"It's Shino," a voice in her head corrected.

Whatever!

This is the same man who once balked in high school at paying an extra twenty-five cents when she asked for the medium instead of the small popcorn at the movies. And judging from where he lived and what he drove, Korey was still as much of a penny-pincher as she remembered. Now he was tossing around money in Vegas like he had a bottomless wallet. What the hell had gotten into him?

"Why didn't you answer my calls?" she asked through clenched teeth, crossing her arms over her chest.

"I didn't need to. I already knew what you were going to say."

"That your ass should be here! That I can't believe you'd—"

"Look, I don't need a lecture from you, all right? I told you to—"

"Go ahead without you. Yeah, I remembered!"

"And you didn't, which was your choice. I just don't understand why the hell you're pissed at me."

Oh, where do I begin, Korey?

She was pissed at him for blowing off the search for the kids like it wasn't of the upmost importance and the sole reason they had traveled all these miles. She was pissed at him because he had acted as if he wasn't remotely interested in her romantically despite their steamy history, yet he had just wined and dined a woman whom he had only met hours ago. She was pissed at him for marrying Vivian and making Cynthia believe that her best chance at happiness was to stick with Bill and hope that he was Clarissa's father. In short, Cynthia was pissed at Korey because everything about him at that moment made her absolutely furious.

She opened her mouth to say as much when a voice suddenly called out behind them, "We've just had a last-minute cancellation, folks! If anyone is interested in a ride, we'd be happy to grant you one. One hundred bucks!"

Cynthia and Korey looked at the young man with freckles and slicked-back red hair who stood near the dock.

"A cancellation?" Cynthia asked.

The young man nodded. "Yeah, you guys interested?"

"If Jared and Clarissa aren't the ones who canceled, then maybe they're already out there on the canal," Korey said, leaning toward her. The warmth of his breath along her ear combined with the tantalizing smell of his cologne sent chills up her spine. "We'd have a better chance of finding them out there."

"I know that," she snapped, not liking how her body was reacting to him. She was supposed to be angry. She preferred anger to the other emotion that was roiling inside her: desire. She turned to the guy in the polo shirt near the dock, who waited for their answer. "We'll take it."

Minutes later, Cynthia and Korey were climbing onto one of the gondolas. Korey offered his hand to her as she boarded, but she shoved it away and instead decided to wobble along on her own before finally falling onto the velvet-cushioned seat. Korey took the spot beside her.

"Good evening, *signor* and *signorina*," the gondolier in the too-tight, black-and-white T-shirt said after they finished boarding. Though he tried his best to tug it down over his hairy belly, the shirt made him vaguely resemble Baby Huey. He grinned down at Cynthia and Korey. "Prepare for a romantic evening."

I wouldn't be too sure about that, honey, Cynthia thought dryly.

The boat started to glide away from the dock.

"Ooooooooooo, soooooooloooo meeeeeeoooooo!" the gondolier began to bellow seconds later, making Cynthia cringe and Korey wince. *"Oooooooooo—"*

"Could you please not do that?" Cynthia shouted.

The gondolier instantly fell silent.

"It's his job," Korey whispered as they passed underneath another bridge. "Just let him sing the damn song."

"His job is to steer the boat, not to murder our eardrums!"

Korey tiredly ran his hand over his face. "Okay, I get that you plan to be a bitch to me the whole night, but do you really need to torture this man too?"

"Well, I wouldn't be such a bitch if you had shown up at eight thirty like I asked!"

"Again . . . did I or did I not tell you to go ahead without me?"

She didn't respond, but instead turned her back to him and glared obstinately at the buildings along the canal.

"Fine," he muttered, adjusting his suit jacket as he turned his back to her too. "Let's just keep an eye out for the kids. Maybe it's better if we don't talk anyway."

The two fell into silence. The gondolier glanced down at them apprehensively.

"Umm, perhaps you two would like another song selection," he ventured.

Neither of them answered. He must have taken their silence as a "yes" because he loudly cleared his throat and took a deep breath.

"Wheeeeeeeen theeeeeee . . ."

Cynthia sank lower in her seat, slapped her purse on her lap, and rolled her eyes.

For the next twenty minutes, she and Korey sat in the gondola, staring in opposite directions, refusing to look at or talk to one another as they were serenaded with horrible renditions from the 1950s Hit Parade.

Cynthia perked up when a couple approached them in an almost identical gondola. She got excited not just because the guy singing on that other boat had a much better voice. She hoped Clarissa and Jared might be on board. She stared as the gondola drew near. To her disappointment, it wasn't the kids. Instead, a black woman, who looked to be in her late twenties, was riding in the boat. She had her head on a young black man's shoulder and gazed up at him adoringly. The young man had an arm slung around her. He leaned down, and they shared a kiss that was both deep and passionate. In the movies, that would have been the moment when fireworks blasted overhead, when violins began to play.

I think I'm gonna be sick, Cynthia thought flippantly. Everything—from the boat ride in the middle of a fake canal trailing around a Las Vegas hotel, to the dewy-eyed couple who would probably break up in a day or two—screamed cheese, more cheese than could *ever* be manufactured by Velveeta. However, twenty years ago she would have found this whole setting and moment very romantic. Twenty years ago it would have been Korey and her in the other gondola gazing into each other's eyes.

She took a furtive glance at Korey, who continued to ignore her.

But I'm a grown-up now, she reminded herself. *We both are, and we know better.*

Yet, at that moment, she didn't feel any more grown-up than she had when she made the fateful decision to see Korey one last time to say good-bye before she married Bill. She didn't feel any more self-assured either . . .

Cynthia tiptoed in the dark through the hallway and down the staircase, feeling like a cat burglar. The house was eerily quiet. Everyone was asleep upstairs and the staff had gone home for the day hours ago. Only the groundskeeper was still around, probably getting drunk in one of the sheds out back. She hoped he was drunk enough not to notice the car at the far end of the driveway. Cynthia had warned Korey to turn off his headlights when he drew near the house so he could stay hidden in the dark.

When Cynthia reached the second-to-last riser on the staircase, she tripped slightly on the runner and almost plunged face-first onto the marble tile below. But she grabbed the banister in just enough time to catch herself.

"Damn! That was close," she whispered.

If she had fallen, who knows how much noise she could have made. She could have woken up one of her sisters—or, worse, her mother! She took a deep breath and tiptoed to the French doors. She gave one last furtive glance over her shoulder before unlocking the front door and stepping into the night.

She looked around her, squinting as she peered at the end of the driveway, searching for Korey's Chevy Cavalier. The kelly-green lawn now had a dewy scent thanks to the rain that had stopped more than an hour ago. Fireflies twinkled faintly. The incessant melody of crickets played in the distance, but everything else was silent. Like her family, it seemed that the rest of the world was fast asleep—well, everyone except her and Korey.

Cynthia soon spotted his car. She ran toward the Cavalier, which waited fifteen feet away, feeling her heart race and her palms sweat. She was almost beside herself with anticipation. She pulled open the passenger-side door and climbed inside.

"Hey," she said as she shut the door behind her.

He didn't return the greeting. Instead, he silently shifted the car into drive and did a slow U-turn, steering out of the driveway and onto the gravel road leading off the Gibbons property, using the light of the full moon to guide his way. When they were almost a quarter of a mile from her house, he turned on his headlights and picked up speed.

They drove in silence for several minutes. Meanwhile, Cynthia kept glancing nervously at Korey. She couldn't see him well in the dim moonlight, but from what she could see, he looked angry.

"Thanks for doing this. I know . . . I know it was probably a surprise."

"Yeah, you could say that," he mumbled, still staring at the windshield.

"How have you been?"

"How have I been?" He shook his head with disbelief. "Cindy, why the hell am I here? We haven't spoken in weeks, then suddenly you call me out of the blue and—"

"Because I had to see you," she answered honestly.

He turned to her, searching her face. "Why?"

Because she knew now that she couldn't move on with her life with Bill until she closed this final chapter with Korey, and the quick phone call she made last month hadn't cut it. But she couldn't tell Korey that. If she did, he'd probably do another U-turn, take her back to her home, bid her a "Fuck you, *adieu*," and pull off. So instead she turned the question on him.

"You didn't want to see me?"

He slowly exhaled, looking more tired than angry now. "Of course, I wanted to see you. But I figured that was out of the question based on the last conversation we had. Remember?"

Their last conversation hadn't been pretty. She had kept it short and sweet that night after the fight with her mother, calling Korey and telling him that she was breaking up with him, that they would never work out. When he asked her why, she had stayed vague. She didn't want to tell him she was breaking up with him not only because her mother had found out about them, but also because things with Bill were starting to get serious and her mother warned her she was putting her chances with Bill at risk by continuing to see Korey.

Cynthia had been dating Bill off and on for months, based on her mother's urgings. She did it to keep her mother off her back. Needless to say, Korey hadn't been too happy with the arrangement despite Cynthia's explanation. He said it was cheating.

"What if I up and decided to date someone else too, huh? Just to 'keep up appearances,'" he had said, quoting her words back to her.

The idea of him going on a date with another girl made her jealous and furious, and he knew it. They had had many arguments about that.

And we're about to have another one because I have to tell him I'm engaged to Bill, she thought sadly.

"I remember what I said," she finally answered, "which is why I asked to see you again. I regret how I handled it. I owe you more than that. We need . . . we need to talk, Korey."

"Fine. So talk."

"Not here. Please, let's go to our spot. To the spot where you took me the first time we went on a car ride."

He sighed and nodded.

They arrived at the creek fifteen minutes later. It was, of course, deserted at this late hour. The fishermen who sometimes sat at the dock with rod in hand were at home. The crabgrass-covered shoulder along the waterfront that usually served as a makeshift parking lot was now empty.

When Korey parked the car and turned off the lights and engine, Cynthia stared out the window at the creek's undisturbed, moonlit surface. The fireflies were here too, like they had been back on the Gibbons property, along with the crickets. Frogs croaked steadily, creating a wall of sound. She committed the scene to memory, hoping she would remember this moment for the rest of her life.

"So what did you want to talk about?" Korey asked softly.

"Remember . . . remember you told me once that you had been watching me for years," Cynthia began, still gazing at the creek. "You said that you used to sit in the back of geometry class, trying not to stare at me. I thought it was . . . so . . . so sweet, that you were . . . that you were so scared to approach me, to even say hi."

"I was intimidated by you. Most of the guys in school were."

"I know. But you're the only one who talked to me anyway." She turned to him. "Why?"

He unbuckled his seat belt and leaned his head back against the headrest. "Because that day you looked like you needed help, that you needed rescuing. It's not like I planned it."

"Well, I'm glad you did it. I'm glad you finally talked to me. I never would have done it myself, even though I . . . even though I had been watching you too," she confessed, making him widen his eyes in surprise. "It's true, Korey," she said with a nod. "I had been watching you just as much as you were watching me. I'd been doing it since junior high, but . . . but I knew it was pointless. You don't come from a family with money. You don't drive a nice car. You're a small-town guy who will probably always *be* small-town. I'd just be wasting my time with you."

"Oh, thanks," he said flatly, clenching his jaw, sounding wounded.

"But none of that was true," she added quickly, grabbing his arm. "*None of it.* You weren't a waste of time. Being with you . . ." Tears pricked her eyes. "Being with you, Korey, has been the best thing in my whole entire life. I'm not going to get this again. I know that. I'm never going to love anyone or be loved like this again."

"So why end it?" he asked, placing his hand over

her hand that held his arm. "If we love each other so much and it's so perfect, why throw it away?"

The tears were spilling now. "Korey, don't you get it? Don't you get what I'm trying to say? I don't want to, but—"

"Then don't." He cupped her face. "Who the hell cares what your mother thinks! I don't, and you shouldn't either. If you don't want to break up, then we don't have to. It's that simple!"

No, it's not, she thought fiercely, her heart crumbling. She was already engaged to another man. They were supposed to get married in a couple of months and had planned to go on a romantic getaway to New York in a matter of days, a getaway that would more than likely include she and Bill having sex for the first time. She had put off getting intimate with Bill for months, but she knew that now that he had given her a four-carat engagement ring, he wouldn't wait to get into her pants any longer. But how was she supposed to tell Korey all of this?

"Korey, I—"

She didn't get to finish. He leaned forward and kissed her before she could.

I should push him away, she thought as he coaxed her mouth open and their tongues danced. *I should tell him to stop.*

But she didn't want to. The sensation felt too good, and she had missed this. She missed his kisses and the feel of his hands on her body. She missed the passion they shared and the delicious thrill it gave her. Why not enjoy it? Why not savor it for one last time?

He lowered his hand to her breast, making her nipples go rigid. He nuzzled her neck, licking at the peach-scented skin. His hands shifted from her breast and descended lower. He pulled up the hem of her ruffled jean skirt and rested his hand between her legs, teasing her through the cotton fabric of her panties. Cynthia spread her legs wider in invitation. She moaned just as his mouth returned to hers.

The kisses were getting heavier now, more fervent, and the steering wheel and emergency brake were getting in the way of them getting at each other. Cynthia shoved Korey back, catching him by surprise. She gave an impish smile before climbing into the more spacious backseat of the sedan. Within seconds, she was pulling her pink T-shirt over her head. She tossed it aside, revealing the black lace bra underneath. She then hooked her finger, beckoning him to follow her.

Cynthia didn't have to tell him twice! He dove into the backseat after her, landing face-first on the cushion, making her laugh. As he tried to sit upright, she was tugging at his shirt, pulling it off of him. Those tight quarters became a whirlwind of flailing limbs and flying clothes. The two snorted and cackled with laughter as they undressed each other.

When she was down to just a skirt and panties and he was only in his boxers, they started kissing again. But then Korey suddenly wrenched his mouth away.

"Cindy, I didn't bring anything," he confessed. "I wasn't exactly expecting this."

She shook her head. "It's okay. Don't worry about it. I'm still on the pill," she assured him before cupping his face and kissing him again.

They hadn't had sex without a condom before. She had always been too terrified of getting pregnant to not use one, but there was no way she was stopping this.

Not now, she thought.

The pace became less frantic and Korey did what he did best: made her toes curl, made her whimper and moan. She didn't mind the rug burn she was getting from the seat upholstery or the window handle that kept grinding into her back. He fondled her breasts again, toying with the nipples, licking and squeezing them until she cried out in ecstasy. He showed just as much attention to the moist spot between her legs. He finally just took off her panties and tossed them over his shoulder. They landed on the dashboard. She squirmed and bucked. She moaned and groaned.

"Oh, God," she whimpered. "Oh, my . . . my God! Oh, God! Don't you dare stop, Korey!"

And he didn't. He coaxed her to orgasm with his expert fingers, and when the tremors started undulating all over her body, she let her legs fall akimbo and cried out again. She returned the favor by taking "Big Korey" in her hands and stroking him. Korey groaned when she leaned down in the backseat and took him whole in her mouth. He threw back his head and closed his eyes almost reverently as she sucked him.

Minutes later, he eased her back against the seat so that her head rested near the window. Cynthia spread her legs again, as far as space would allow, letting Korey lie between them. He hoisted one of her legs higher so that the heel rested on the back of the driver's seat. He then kissed her again and plunged forward. She took an audible breath as he entered her.

She told herself to remember this, to remember the sensation of him swelling inside her, of feeling his hips grind against hers, of hearing his heavy breaths and moans against her ear. But instead of committing it to memory, she got lost in the moment. Her hips rose up to meet him stroke for stroke. She dug her nails into his shoulders and his back. She felt her legs trembling under the strain of spreading so wide to accommodate him and yet another impending orgasm.

When she came, she cried out one last time. He did

also, soon after, crumbling against her with a satisfied grunt.

By the time they finished, the windows of the Chevy were so fogged up that neither of them could see the creek outside. Only the hazy glow of the moon reflecting off the water came through the window.

They lay holding each other, not talking, listening to the steady *creek, creek, creek* of the frogs and *chirp, chirp, chirp* of the crickets nearby. She wished the moment could last forever, but, of course, it couldn't. It was time to do what she really came here to do.

Time to say good-bye, she thought.

"I should be getting back," Cynthia whispered.

Korey raised his head and looked down at her. "Yeah, I know. It's getting late, isn't it? Everyone will be waking up in a couple of hours, and the fishermen around here get an early start." He chuckled. "I'd hate for them to find us this way."

"I would too." They sat upright. "I don't exactly look my best right now."

She was topless. Her hair was standing all over her head. Her mascara had run, and her lipstick had smeared.

"What do you mean? You look beautiful," he whispered as he handed her her shirt.

And with those words, it was like a dagger had been driven into her heart.

"So when can I see you again?" He pulled his T-shirt over his head and stuck his arms through the sleeves. "Next week? Are you free Saturday? Should I pick you up at the house or meet you at—"

"Korey, we can't . . . we can't see one another again."

He paused from dressing and squinted at her.

"What do you mean we can't see each other again?"

"That's what all this was about. That's why I wanted to see you one last time. I was saying good-bye."

"*Good-bye?*"

"Yes, good-bye. I'm . . . I'm getting married."

His mouth fell open. He stared at her, dumbstruck. "*You're getting married?* What the hell do you mean you're getting married? Getting married to *who?*" he shouted.

"To Bill Simpson," she explained. "To that . . . to that guy I was dating. I told you about him."

She watched as Korey closed his eyes and dropped his head into his hands.

"He proposed last week. We're supposed to get married in August. That's what I came here to tell you."

"So you . . . you let me think . . . you let me think this whole time that we . . . that we were . . ." His voice trailed off.

She became alarmed when he started to chuckle. It was a small laugh at first, then it went into full-on guffaws that filled up the car with the loud noise. His shoulders were shaking because he was laughing so hard.

Cynthia frowned. She didn't see what was so funny and asked him as much.

Korey finally pulled his hands away from his face and looked at her, shaking his head. "What's so goddamn funny, Cindy, is that I let you do this." His laughter finally trickled off. "I let you pull the same shit you always pull, and I let you do this to me. I let you set me up like this even though I should have known better!" He shook his head again. "I'm so stupid. I'm so gullible and so . . . so stupid!"

"Korey, I wasn't setting you up. I meant everything I—"

"Bullshit!" he spat. "Bullshit." He then tore his gaze from hers, as though he couldn't stand to look at her any longer. "Put your clothes back on. I'm taking you home."

They rode back to her house in silence. This time he didn't bother to turn off the headlights when they drew closer to the Gibbons property and she didn't ask him to. When they reached her driveway, he pulled to a stop and she climbed out.

"Korey," she whispered, feeling her heart break.

He didn't respond. He didn't even turn to look at her.

She'd barely shut the door before he pulled off with tires screeching. She stood there and watched until his taillights disappeared around the bend.

She didn't see Korey again for several months after that. Though they lived in the same town, she went out of her way to avoid him, and he seemed to do the same. When she finally did see him, he was squiring Vivian Brady around town.

Korey and Vivian were in line at the post office on Main Street, and a very pregnant Vivian was showing off her new engagement ring to a group of ogling women in front of her. The proud papa-to-be was answering questions about the impending nuptials and the baby boy they had on the way.

When Cynthia stumbled upon that scene, she immediately turned around and left the post office, the package she had wanted delivered now forgotten. Cynthia had heard about Korey and Vivian getting together, but it was something completely different to have the fact that he had moved on staring her plainly in the face.

Cynthia, pregnant with her own little girl, waddled with tears in her eyes back to her car—a new silver Jag that Bill had given her as a wedding gift. All she could

think about was that night at the creek with Korey and
how she had walked away from the only man she
would probably ever love.

Cynthia now gazed down at the fake canal, looking
at the quivering reflection of the moon on the water's
surface, remembering that last night with Korey. She
glanced up at him now. He was making a poor show of
pretending to be looking for Jared and Clarissa. It was
pretty obvious that he was trying more to not acknowledge the woman sitting beside him.

How had they gotten to this? How had they gone
from being madly in love to total loathing?

"He doesn't loathe you," a voice in her head corrected. "You don't loathe him either. You're both just
angry. That's all."

But why was she so angry at him? What had he done
to earn this much venom? And it wasn't only Korey
who could get her fired up nowadays. It seemed like
she was *always* angry.

*"I don't want to be rich and divorced and alone and
pissed off all the time like you!"* she remembered
Clarissa screaming at her that night before the young
woman stormed up the stairs and later ran away with
Jared.

Cynthia grimaced. *I'm not like that, am I? I'm not
pissed off and alone.* She quickly shook her head at the
thought. *Of course not!*

What did Clarissa know anyway? She was a naïve
teenager. She wasn't one to give out love or life advice! But still, Cynthia was starting to question why
she had so much fury bottled up inside of her. Where
did it all come from?

"Bitterness, maybe," the little voice in her head ventured.

But why should she be bitter? So what if she didn't marry Korey and they didn't end up happily ever after. She still had a wonderful life! She had her health and still looked pretty damn good for a woman pushing forty, if she did say so herself. She had plenty of money, a beautiful daughter, and men who fell at her feet and were willing to buy her anything and everything she wanted. Life may not have turned out exactly as she had expected or hoped, but she still made out well in the end. She was still happy—*right?*

She glanced at Korey again, trying to ignore the longing that stirred inside her when she looked at him.

Of course, I'm happy, she told herself as she crossed her legs and fluffed her hair. *Why wouldn't I be?*

"Is that Jared?" Korey suddenly murmured. He leaned forward in his seat and squinted.

Cynthia did a double take. "What? You see Jared?"

"I think I see him over there." Korey pointed off in the distance.

Cynthia looked toward where Korey was pointing. Several people streamed along the sidewalk near the wrought-iron railing in front of some outdoor restaurant seating. She saw more than one black young man sitting at a table under one of the red cloth umbrellas, standing near the railing, and walking along the sidewalk. She couldn't tell at this distance if one of them was Jared, though, truth be told, she had only seen Jared for a few fleeting seconds back in Chesterton. She might not recognize him even if he was standing in front of her.

"Do you really think it's him?"

Korey turned and glared at her as if she had just

asked the dumbest question in the world. "Cindy, I think I would know my own damn son."

She looked up at the gondolier, who had started the first bars of yet another tune.

"Excuse me!" Cynthia shouted. "Can you sing less and row faster, please?" Her brows furrowed as she searched the crowd. "Where do you see him, Korey?"

"Standing over there . . . by the lamppost." Korey then cupped his hands around his mouth. "Hey, Jared! Jar—"

"Sheesh!" Cynthia cried hysterically, slapping his arm. "Damn it, stop yelling!"

"I was trying to get his attention."

"Get his attention? Are you crazy? We don't want to let him know we see him! We don't want them to know we're here."

Korey frowned at her in bewilderment. "What the hell sense does that make? I thought the whole point was to come here, find them, and then stop them. How are they going to do that if don't talk to them?"

"Yes, we want to find them, Korey, but we don't want to scare him off and make him run away." She patted his hand gently and spoke slowly, like he was a not-too-bright child. "So let's just keep it quiet for now. Wait until we get closer to see if it's him."

Korey pursed his lips, looking irritated. He yanked his hand away from her. "Fine, but if we lose him this time around, it's not my fault. I don't want to hear anything from you!"

The time that it took for the boat to finish its circuit around the canal and make it back to the dock was probably only three minutes—five minutes, tops—but it felt like an eternity for Cynthia. When they finally docked, she and Korey quickly climbed out of the boat and raced to the spot where Korey claimed to have seen Jared. As they drew closer, nearly twenty yards away, the young man who was leaning against the lamp-post suddenly waved his hand in acknowledgment to someone in the distance, pushed away from the lamp-post, and strode down the sidewalk.

"Damn, where is he going now?" she cried.

Korey didn't answer her but gave chase instead.

Chapter 19

I can't believe this! Korey thought as he felt his heart thud wildly in his chest. His lungs felt like they were on fire as he raced from the dock and over the cobblestone bridge, dodging between tourists and random vendor carts to catch up with his son.

He could still be on a date right now with Shino. They would have finished their meal and probably would be sampling one of those expensive desserts. Maybe they would even be in a cab heading back to their hotel. She'd be taking him to her room to show him just how good of an aphrodisiac champagne could be into the wee hours of the morning. But *no!* Instead he was running along the sidewalk like a crazy person. Instead he had let Cynthia guilt him into cutting the date short and heading back here to continue what was looking more and more like a quixotic quest to stop the kids from getting married.

"Korey!" Cynthia shouted behind him. "Damn it, Korey! Wait up!"

He glanced over his shoulder at her but didn't stop

or slow down. If Cynthia couldn't catch up with him, then to hell with her!

He could still recall the look on Shino's face when he told her he had to leave their dinner date early.

"It's about my son," he had tried to explain as he wrenched his cell phone out of his suit pocket and turned the phone to vibrate to stop its insistent chiming. He tossed the phone on the table. "I have to—"

"Is that who's calling you?" Shino had asked.

She glanced down at his phone and could clearly see the name of the last caller on the screen. When she did, she angrily pursed her lips.

"No. It's . . . it's Cindy."

Shino looked up at him. "I noticed."

"But it isn't want you think. You see, we were . . . we were supposed to meet later to—"

"Don't bother, Korey," she said, waving him off. She removed her dinner napkin from her lap and slapped it on the table. She began to scoot out of the other side of the booth.

"Shino, wait! Let me explain! Cindy's just calling to tell me that—"

"You know, you say things are over between you two. You say that you haven't been together in twenty damn years, but she certainly has a hold on you tonight. I can't and I'm *not* going to compete with that." She then turned and walked away from the table.

"Shino, come on! I—"

"Thanks for the drink," she had called halfheartedly over her shoulder.

As he watched her walk out of the restaurant, he slumped against the table and grumbled to himself while his phone started buzzing again.

Needless to say, he had pretty much blown any chance he had with Shino that night. Now all he had to look forward to was Cynthia's shrill yelling and continual coldness. Now he was chasing after Jared so that he could finally grab his son, drag him onto a plane, fly the hell home, and end this Las Vegas nightmare.

"Korey!" Cynthia shouted again.

They were back on the Strip, and Korey could see his son striding to a line of cabs waiting by the curb. If Jared jumped into one of those cars, Korey would likely lose him—*again!* He couldn't let that happen.

"To hell with this," he muttered, ignoring Cynthia's warning to not let the kids know that they were in Las Vegas tracking them down. He cupped his hands around his mouth. "Jared! Jared!"

Korey thought he saw Jared pause like he heard someone call his name before abruptly opening one of the cab doors and climbing inside.

"Oh, no! Korey, he's getting away!" Cynthia screamed as she raced toward him.

"I can see that," Korey snapped before running toward one of the other cabs. "Can you follow that white cab up there?" Korey asked the driver. Korey pointed at the cab that had just pulled away from the curb and was merging into traffic.

The driver tilted his head and gazed up at Korey through the lowered window with a comical expression on his face. He chuckled. "You're kidding, right?"

Korey sighed, dug into his pocket, and pulled out his wallet. "Here's a hundred bucks that says that I'm not kidding. You get that hundred extra and your fare if you follow that cab."

The cabdriver jabbed his thumb over his shoulder. "Get in."

Korey climbed inside, and Cynthia scrambled in after him.

"Ma'am, I already have a fare," the cabdriver called to her. "You're gonna have to—"

"Its fine," Korey said before glancing at Cynthia. "She's with me. Just drive."

Luckily for them, a car accident farther down Las Vegas Boulevard had slowed traffic on the Strip to a near crawl. It wasn't hard to tail Jared's cab. They stayed at least two car lengths behind him during most of the ride.

"I still don't see how you're so sure that's Jared, Korey," Cynthia murmured anxiously, wringing her purse straps in her hands as she sat forward in her seat, trying to keep an eye on the cab ahead of them.

"I'm sure because I know what my son looks like. It's him!"

Though, truth be told, even Korey was starting to question that assertion. Why hadn't Jared turned to look at him when he'd shouted Jared's name? Why hadn't Jared turned when he heard his father's voice? Maybe Korey was getting so eager to find his son that he was starting to see Jared everywhere, in the face of every young black man he saw wandering along the Strip.

No, it's him, he stubbornly insisted. *It's my son in that cab. I'm going to catch up with him and we're going the hell home.*

"Then why isn't he with Clarissa?" Cynthia asked. "Why is he riding around Las Vegas by himself?"

"How the hell should I know? Maybe they had a fight. Maybe she got sick and decided to stay behind at the hotel. Who knows! All I know is that we came here to find them, and that's what I'm trying to do!"

Cynthia tiredly slumped back in her seat. "Fine, I just hope you're right."

A few minutes later, the cab in front of them suddenly turned off Las Vegas Boulevard, and made a right and then a left onto a road that looked a lot less glamorous. Gone were the dazzling light displays and streets teeming with people. Instead they were in a deserted area with industrial-looking buildings, cracked sidewalks, and strip malls. A few prostitutes and homeless people stood near street lamps and in the shadows of doorways. Korey looked up and saw a few signs, but instead of names like the Luxor, Bellagio, and MGM Grand, he saw Diamonds, Mavis Showgirls, and The Erotic Lounge.

The white cab pulled into a dimly lit parking lot, and their cab pulled in after it. Above the two-story building was a sign with the glowing orange cursive letters.

"The Saddled Pony Gentleman's Club," Korey read aloud.

Korey and Cynthia watched at a distance as the young man climbed out, leaned over to hand something to the driver, then showed an ID—more than likely a fake one—to a bouncer in a black T-shirt who stood near the doors, looking bored. The bouncer nodded before waving Jared inside. He then slumped back against the wall and pulled out a cigarette as Jared disappeared behind the black doors.

"A strip club?" Cynthia exclaimed. "He came to a strip club?"

"Looks like it," Korey murmured. Though seeing this, Korey was starting to doubt even more that the person they were tailing was his son. But they had chased him all the way here. They couldn't stop now.

"So he ditched my baby to tuck dollar bills into some slut's sweaty G-string?" She sucked her teeth.

"That's it! I swear when I get my hands on that boy, I will—"

"You won't do a damn thing, because you're not getting your hands on him. I'm going in there. You stay out here."

Cynthia scrunched up her face with outrage. "Who . . . who the . . . the hell do you think you are, Korey Walker? Don't you dare tell me what to do! If you're going inside that club, so am I!" She pointed at her chest. "There's no way that I'm just—"

"Look, he's *my* son! I want to talk to him, and I can't do that if you start bitching him out in front of everybody in there!"

"I'm not going to 'bitch him out!' I was simply going to—"

"Yeah, right. We both know that's exactly what you were going to do. No, you stay in the cab! I'll go inside." He then handed the money to the driver and offered him another fifty to wait for them. He climbed out of the taxi before slamming the door behind him just as Cynthia started to scoot across the seat to follow him.

"Korey!" she shouted, slapping her hand on the glass. "Korey, don't you dare go in there without me!"

"Stay in the car!" he barked over his shoulder before striding to the club's doors, leaving her behind, fuming.

An hour later, a very pissed-off Cynthia shoved open the velvet curtains to The Saddled Pony Gentleman's Club main room. She scowled as she looked around her, squinting and letting her eyes adjust to the darkened room. Only the phallic-shaped stage was illuminated with soft blue spotlights and up-lighting along the edge. The rest of the club was mostly in shadow.

A few men lingered on stools around the perimeter of the stage, looking almost lost in a collective trance as they watched the topless dancers gyrate and hump the poles above them. One balding man in a Hawaiian shirt wearing bifocals even smiled dumbly and applauded as the stripper in front of him climbed up her pole and did a split in midair that was worthy of any Cirque du Soleil performance. Another man did his own little shimmy near the stage as he tossed dollar bills into the air while a stripper wiggled her ass cheeks in front of his face.

Cynthia scanned the room in search of Korey. He had disappeared in here almost an hour ago. He had actually had the audacity to order her to stay in the car, like she was some errant five-year-old. She had obeyed him and waited, but when ten minutes stretched into thirty minutes and then a full hour, she'd lost it. Cynthia would be damned if she'd just sit patiently with her hands in her lap like a good little girl while Korey did whatever the hell he wanted. She decided to go searching for him and Jared herself.

She soon spotted Korey sitting at a highboy table about five feet away from the stage. When she saw that he was nursing a drink while getting a lap dance from a busty blonde in a hot-pink thong, Cynthia gritted her teeth so hard she could hear them grinding.

Seriously? Again? It was like every time she turned away there was some slut smiling in his face.

"You've got to be kidding me," she muttered as she stormed across the room. She zigzagged through tables and patrons, mumbling to herself. She stopped when she felt someone grab her wrist.

Cynthia turned and stared into the glazed eyes of a big-muscled type. The seams of his white T-shirt sleeves seemed to strain across his tattooed biceps. His short dark hair was spiked with gel. He grinned at her drunkenly.

"Hey, baby," he slurred. "You are hot *as hell!* Give you a hundred bucks if you show your tits!"

She yanked her wrist out of his grasp. "For a hundred bucks, I wouldn't let you see my damn ankle," she sneered before walking away.

"*Two* hundred?" he shouted after her, making her roll her eyes.

She finally drew near Korey, who had just raised his glass back to his lips. The glitter-covered nipples of the stripper's saline-filled double Ds hovered dangerously close to his face, but he didn't seem to mind. In fact, he was so firmly focused on them that he didn't notice Cynthia walking toward him.

"So I guess it wasn't Jared then!" she shouted, crossing her arms over her chest.

She had yelled at him both because she was royally pissed off, and because she had to shout to be heard over the heavy thud of the rock music playing on the overhead speakers. The sound was almost deafening.

Korey lowered his drink to the tabletop and turned toward her, looking like a guilty kid caught with his hand in the cookie jar.

"Oh, hey, Cindy!" A goofy grin crossed his handsome face. "Sorry. The time got away from me."

God damn it, he's drunk, she thought.

"I was looking for Jared and ran into Tiffany here." He gestured toward the blonde, who rose from his lap and took a step away from him on her clear platform high heels. She turned toward Cynthia and waved.

"Hey! Pleased to meet you!" Tiffany drawled.

"Uh-huh," Cynthia answered flatly, not returning the greeting.

"I asked Tiffany if she had seen anyone who looked like Jared come through here. She said no."

"Is that right? And I suppose asking her that question and getting the answer took a whole hour?"

"Well, no," he demurred. "But I had to pay the lady for her time."

Tiffany playfully tapped his button nose. "Oh, don't be hard on him! He's been down in the dumps. He said he's had a rough couple of days."

"I sure have," he replied, taking a drink and smiling up at her.

Tiffany wrapped her arms around Korey's neck and straddled his lap again. She pressed her bare breasts against his chest. "But like I told you, honey, it's gonna get better. Things always do. Don't worry!"

"Yeah, well, thanks for the pep talk," Cynthia interrupted, resisting the urge to punch both Korey and Tiffany in their throats. "We have to go." She turned to Korey and stared at him menacingly. "We have to find our kids . . . *Remember?*"

Tiffany's smile widened as she dropped a hand to her hip. "Kids? Are you guys here in Vegas on a family vacation?"

"No," Korey explained quickly, shaking his head, "we are *not* together."

Cynthia's face settled into a scowl again. Why did he always have to clarify that so quickly? What objection did he have to people thinking they were together?

"My son and her daughter are a couple, though," he continued. "They ran away to Las Vegas to get married." He glanced at Cynthia. "I think her daughter was just desperate to get away from her, if you wanna know the truth."

He then laughed, long and loud, and the glare Cynthia gave him spoke volumes.

"Awww! Your kids are getting married?" Tiffany brought a hand to her ample chest. Her false eyelashes fluttered as she grew misty-eyed. "That's so romantic!"

I really am going to punch her in the throat, Cynthia thought.

"Korey, let's go! Now!" Cynthia ordered through clenched teeth.

"Ooooo, the bitch is back," Korey sang, then chuckled. He gently eased Tiffany off his lap and stood. "But she's right. We should head out and try to find them. It was nice meeting you, Tiffany."

"You too, cutie. Good luck finding your kids." She then turned to Cynthia. "Hey, have you ever thought of dancing professionally?"

Cynthia cocked an eyebrow. "You better mean dancing for the Rockettes."

"No, silly!" Tiffany gushed with a giggle. "I mean . . . you know . . . exotic dancing. You've got a nice little body on you." She looked Cynthia up and down. "You could make some good money, honey! You should check with Ricky if you're interested." She pointed in some far-off distance. "He's the club owner. He's looking for a bitchy dominatrix type, and you *definitely* fit the bill."

"Bitchy dominatrix type," Korey murmured as their taxi drove them back to their hotel. He laughed and slapped his knee. "Damn, Tiffany had your number!"

"Shut up!" Cynthia barked, making the cabdriver cringe in the front seat. "I seriously don't want to hear anything from you right now!"

"If I disobey you and keep talking, will you break out the whips and chains?" he asked with a smirk.

She ignored his joke. "I am so . . . so furious at you! You said you were going in there to find Jared, and instead you're in there getting drunk!"

"I'm not drunk! I had one . . . okay, maybe two drinks. That's all! I needed to let off some steam. I had a—"

"Rough day," she finished for him. "Yeah, I heard. So was the lap dance supposed to be some kind of morale booster?"

"Why do you care? Are you jealous again?"

"For the last time, I am *not* jealous!"

"Come on! Admit it! You were a little jealous," the voice in her head mocked.

"Look, I'm a grown-ass man, and the last I checked, I wasn't married to anybody," Korey argued. "If I want to get a lap dance, I'll damn well get a lap dance!"

"Not while you're wasting time that could have been spent looking for the kids! You keep acting like time isn't of the essence here! We're trying to stop them before they get married. So man up, pull your shit together, and help me out for once, or is that too much for you?"

Korey fell silent. He then shook his head. "Fuck this," he muttered. He reached into his back pocket and tossed another fifty dollars to the driver through the glass partition. "Take her back to the hotel. I'll find another ride."

"What?" Cynthia watched, utterly shocked, as Korey threw open the cab door when they reached a stoplight.

He saluted her before shutting the door and walking away, falling into the maze of people along the Strip.

She jumped out of the cab and ran to catch up with him, almost getting hit by a stretch limo as she darted along the crosswalk. She tripped on the storm drain, losing one of her shoes in its murky depths.

"Damn it," Cynthia grumbled. That had been one of her favorite, not to mention most comfortable, slippers.

She hopped on one foot as she trailed Korey and dodged between pedestrians simultaneously.

"Korey!" she shouted after him, waving away an old man who shoved a flyer into her face. "Korey!"

"Would you stop shouting my damn name? I'm tired of it!" he bellowed back at her. "I'm tired of your nitpicking and lecturing me like I'm some child! You want to pull that Ice Queen stuff, do it with someone else! I'm out!"

"Out? Out *where?* Where do you think you're going? What about the kids?"

"Kids?" He stopped and turned to look at her. His shoulders slumped. He seemed worn down and tired. "For all we know, the kids are already married."

"No, they aren't! Don't say that! They only had a few hours' lead on us. We got here in enough time. You heard what the lady at the wedding chapel said! Clarissa ran out! She didn't go through with it. They—"

"None of which means they couldn't have made up and gone to *another* quickie chapel to get married."

"But it's only been two days! Why are you giving up so easily?" she shouted, stomping her foot and wincing at the pain. She had forgotten she was barefoot.

"Why are you pushing so hard?" he yelled back.

"What do you mean, 'Why am I pushing so hard?' I'm trying to protect my daughter, just like I thought you were trying to protect your son! I don't want Clarissa to make a huge mistake!"

"You mean making a huge mistake by following her heart . . . something you weren't brave enough to do?"

"*Are you serious?* Are you sure all you had in that strip club was two drinks?"

"Yes, I'm serious, and for the last time, I'm not drunk! You're just mad that your daughter has more balls than you did!" He jabbed his finger at her. "She's willing to tell her mother to go to hell! She's willing to take a risk that you wouldn't take!"

Cynthia looked at Korey as if he had just lost his mind, but she could tell, even in the flickering, kaleidoscope of lights, that he had his full capabilities about him.

"I cannot believe you would bring up what went on between us twenty years ago right now! That has no relevance to this!"

"It has *every* relevance to this! You dumped me because you were brainwashed by your mother and all that crazy shit about the Gibbons family rules!"

She closed her eyes and dropped her face into her hands. *Why did they keep coming back to this?*

"You're trying to brainwash Clarissa just like your mother brainwashed you! You're trying to break them up just like your mother broke us up!"

"Korey!" She opened her eyes and threw back her head. "We've already talked about this. It happened so long—"

"I don't care how long ago it happened! I know when it happened because I've been lugging around the memory of it ever since! You . . . *ripped* . . . my heart out!" he yelled, making several people passing by stare at him and do double takes. "Do you realize that? You keep acting like it never happened, like what you did wasn't that big of a deal!"

She stared at him.

He looked absolutely ridiculous, raving at her in his wrinkled and sweat-stained suit while an Asian family standing beside him snapped pictures of themselves in front of the MGM Grand. She was sure she had to look equally absurd standing there in her disheveled clothes with one missing shoe. Is this what they had come to after all of this chasing and searching for two days, after all of these years of misunderstandings, heartbreak, anger, and recriminations—their final confrontation was culminating to *this?*

She didn't know why, but she couldn't help but laugh. She started to giggle, and then her laughter grew louder to the point that she had to cover her mouth to stop people from looking at her uneasily, like they were brushing shoulders with someone who had just escaped the psych ward.

Korey glared at her in disbelief. "You think . . . you think this is funny?"

She tried to answer him, but the only thing that came out was more giggles. She was laughing so hard that her stomach hurt.

As she continued to hoot and snort, the expression on his face suddenly hardened. "You are one cold, heartless bitch, you know that?"

Cynthia's laughter tapered off. She watched him turn and walk away again.

"Oh, come on, Korey! I wasn't laughing at . . ."

He ignored her and kept walking, making her grumble in frustration.

Okay, maybe when a man tells you that you crushed him and ripped out his heart, laughter wasn't the best response. But how did he expect her to react with him being so melodramatic?

Fine, I broke his heart! So what the hell does he want me to do? Drop to my knees and grovel for his forgiveness? I was just a kid back then! He can't forever hold me to what I did as a confused eighteen-year-old!

"No," the nagging voice in her head answered. "But you could apologize. It might make him feel better."

Well, to hell with that! Cynthia Gibbons didn't apologize, *especially* to a man. Hell would freeze over first.

She turned to walk back toward their hotel but stopped.

What am I thinking?

She didn't stand a chance of finding the kids alone. Korey was the one who had tracked down Jared's phone. Korey was the one who had suggested pretending to be Clarissa so that they could find out more details about the gondola ride. If it wasn't for him, she'd be wandering around the Strip, showing a picture of Clarissa to every passerby and hoping they could point her in the right direction. She'd be at a total loss.

God damn it, she thought. She was going to have to do some groveling, after all.

"Korey!" she yelled as she walked swiftly after him. "Korey, wait up! Korey!"

"I told you to stop calling my damn name," he said between clenched teeth.

"At least tell me where you're going!"

"Back to The Saddled Pony!"

At that, she flinched. "Why? So some dumb blonde can shake her fake titties in your face?"

"*Why not?* She had nice titties!"

She picked up the pace and had to run to catch up

with him. It wasn't easy. The sidewalk was teeming with people, and he was taking long, angry strides. Plus, she still had just one shoe. "Korey, come on! Look, I can't do this on my own! Please, I need your help!"

"No, you don't! Cynthia Gibbons has been and will always be a one-woman show! She doesn't need anyone—definitely not me!"

"But I *do* need you!" She grabbed his arm, stopping him in his tracks. She took a deep breath. She couldn't believe she was about to say this. "Look, Korey, I'm ... I'm sorry. Okay?"

He pulled his arm out of her grasp. "Sorry for what?"

Her lips tightened. "You know what I'm sorry for."

"No, I don't. Say it," he ordered, still glaring at her.

She swallowed and could feel saliva clog her throat. She had never done this before in her life: humbled herself before a man. It was the hardest thing she had ever done.

"I'm sorry ... I'm sorry for breaking your heart. I'm sorry for what I did to you, okay? It was a mistake. I know that—*now*. But I was eighteen years old back then and confused. It's not an excuse," she rushed, holding up her hands when it looked like he was about to argue with her. "It's just an ... an explanation. I'm explaining where my mind was back then."

"I was confused too. My mom wasn't fond of your ass either, but I went to the wall for you. And then I found out later it was all just a joke ... just a waste of my time!"

"It wasn't a joke! It meant something to me too! *We* meant something! It's not like I set out to hurt you, like our relationship was some big setup! Breaking up with you hurt me too! But I thought ..." She shrugged helplessly and looked away from him. No longer able to meet his gaze, she stared at the twinkling lights of the Eiffel Tower replica in the distance. "I thought I was doing the right thing."

Korey pursed his lips and nodded. "I know," he said coolly, making her stare at him again. Her face morphed from surprise to exasperation.

"If you knew, then why'd the hell you make me go through all this?"

"Because I wanted to hear you *say* it. I wanted you to finally acknowledge what you did."

She crossed her arms over her chest. "Well, I said it." Her expression softened. "So can we move on now? Can we finally put this behind us?"

Korey continued to gaze at her, not uttering a word. She held her breath until he nodded.

"Yeah, okay, fine," he said, but he didn't sound very convincing.

"You mean it? You're really going to let this go?"

"Yes, I mean it." He nodded again and ran a hand over his face. "Look, I'm exhausted. I think these past few days are finally catching up with me. I want to go to my room, take a shower, climb into the bed, and go the hell to sleep. So let's just call it a night. All right?"

Cynthia was half tempted to argue that it wasn't even ten o'clock yet and they had a few more hours available to brainstorm and continue their search, but she could see from the weary look on Korey's face, his reddened eyes, and the slump in his shoulders that he wasn't lying when he said he was exhausted. She was tired herself. Maybe they should just wait until tomorrow.

"Sure, let's . . . let's go back," she said quietly.

Chapter 20

Cynthia and Korey drew a few curious stares as they tiredly walked through the Pompeii Hotel and Casino lobby to the elevators. Cynthia hobbled in one Tory Burch slipper, dragging her crocodile-skinned hobo bag behind her. Korey had long ago removed his suit jacket and tie, slinging both over his arm, revealing his T-shirt and the sweat stains under his arms and along his chest.

Cynthia sucked her teeth and rolled her eyes at the few hotel staff and patrons that openly stared at them. She knew she and Korey looked like a hot mess, like they had just come off a weekend bender. They didn't need to be reminded of it!

She sneaked a glance at Korey again as they passed the giant seashell statue near the elevators. She was definitely worse for the wear, more so than he was. Even exhausted and disheveled, he was still handsome and unbelievably sexy.

She wondered if maybe, just maybe, the fact that he had forgiven her meant they could finally start anew.

She certainly had been fighting the attraction she felt toward him because of the resentment he had radiated. Now that his resentment was gone, would he be willing to give her a second chance?

Not romantically, of course, she thought quickly.

She had no interest in falling in love again with Korey or starting a relationship, she told herself. She still wanted her big fish with enough wealth to buy a small island, but reigniting the passion she and Korey had once shared was something she was more than willing to consider too.

It didn't sound like Korey was in a serious relationship now. Neither was she. Maybe they could come to a mutual agreement. Sex could be something they could both enjoy on the side whenever they got an itch.

"Could you honestly see Korey agreeing to that, though?" a voice in her head asked.

Probably not, she thought. But it was worth a try!

Her eyes drifted to his mouth again.

It had been so long since a man had made her toes curl, since she had thrown back her head and shouted in ecstasy. She bet Korey could make her do that. She bet if he—

"All right, I'm taking my ass upstairs, ordering room service, taking a shower, and going to bed," Korey said as he pressed the UP elevator button, snapping her out of her carnal thoughts. "I'll see you in the morning."

"In . . . in the morning?"

She watched as the elevator doors opened and Korey stepped inside the compartment. She shuffled in after him. After he inserted his key card into the wall panel and punched in their floor numbers, Korey turned to her and nodded.

"Yeah, maybe nine a.m. or so," he said as the elevator shot into motion. "I'll call you and let you know after I wake up."

That was it?

He wasn't going to invite her to his room?

The elevator chimed, and the doors slowly opened.

"See you later." Korey stepped into the hall and waved absently. "Try to get some sleep."

"Wait! Wait!" she shouted, making him stop in his tracks.

He turned to her with raised brows. "What?"

With Korey gazing at her, her resolve faltered. There was no way she could ask him to be what amounted to no more than her fuck buddy. She had tried to seduce him while she was drunk and hopped-up on sedatives on the plane, but she couldn't work up the nerve to do the same thing now—sober. What if he rejected her again?

"N-nothing. Good . . . good night," she replied weakly just as the elevator doors closed.

Back in her room, Cynthia dropped her purse onto her night table and flopped onto the bed face-first. She kicked off her remaining shoe and closed her eyes.

Today had been mixed. They still hadn't found the kids, but at least Korey didn't openly hate her anymore.

Should have asked him to come to my room, she thought, remembering his tempting mouth.

"No, you shouldn't have," the voice in her head countered. "You just would have embarrassed yourself—*again.*"

Maybe, but there could be worse things—like wondering for the next twenty years whether she should have taken a chance with Korey like she had been wondering for the *past* twenty years. Could she really spend half a century wrangling over this stuff?

Cynthia sighed, envisioning a bleak future filled with money, luxury, and flights to exotic places, but devoid of passion and delight. The only thing she'd have to turn to was her vibrator and her hot tub until menopause set in and her sex drive withered away.

"God, that sounds depressing," she murmured against her comforter.

Cynthia slowly raised her head. She knew what she had to do if she could just work up the courage to do it.

She slung her legs over the edge of the bed and stood up. She strode to the small refrigerator nestled in a cabinet underneath her flat-screen television. She swung it open and quickly scanned the half dozen or so mini-bottles inside. She finally settled on a bottle of Jim Beam, twisted off the cap, and took a swig. After a few more gulps, she finished the bottle.

"Okay," she said, clapping her hands, feeling the hot sensation of the alcohol make its way down her throat, "let's do this!"

Half an hour later, Cynthia stepped off the elevator car before she could lose her nerve and strode down the hotel hallway to Korey's room. She had changed into a sexy red wrap dress and even sexier bra and thong. She had thrown on some makeup, liberally sprayed herself with perfume, and downed half of another mini-bottle—this time, Smirnoff vodka.

But despite her sexy clothes, alluring scent, and liquid courage, her legs still felt like taffy. Her heart thudded wildly in her chest. Shallow pools of sweat were forming under her armpits. She glanced down at her palms. Even *they* were sweating. But she wasn't going back to her room. She wasn't going to let this moment slip by. In the past, she had let immaturity and self-doubt shape the choices she made when it came to Korey—all of which she now regretted. A quirk of fate had brought them back together. She wasn't going to let this second chance pass her by.

After all, it wasn't like she was asking him to fall in love with her again. She wasn't asking for anything permanent here. She just wanted to spend the night together. That's all! Any red-blooded man would be amenable to that—*right?*

When she reached his door, she took a deep breath, then knocked. She paused when she heard a murmur and then a burst of female laughter coming from inside.

Who the hell is that? Did he have someone in the room with him?

Cynthia pressed her ear to the door and squinted with concentration, trying desperately to determine if she recognized the woman's voice. She wondered if it was that chick Shino or that silicone-laden stripper, Tiffany, from earlier that night. She heard more murmuring and more laughter, but the voice was unrecognizable.

You son of a bitch! You son of a bitch, she thought. He had said he was tired! If that was the case, then why the hell did he have a damn woman in his room? Here she was about to throw herself at him—to give him booty on a platter—and he had the audacity to be getting down with someone else!

Just then, the door swung open. She yelped as she stumbled inside, landing face-first against Korey's chest, getting her face full of terrycloth and her nose full of zesty body wash.

"What are you doing?" he asked. Laughter was in his voice.

She jumped back and quickly regained her composure, pretending like she hadn't been caught red-handed eavesdropping. She adjusted the front of her dress and smoothed her hair. She glared at him. "I was just about to ask you the same thing!"

"I just got out of the shower." He gestured to the hotel's complimentary bathrobe he was wearing.

"You mean '*We* just got out of the shower'!" she barked. "Isn't that more accurate?"

He looked confused. "What are you talking about?"

"I'm talking about the fact that you have someone in here with you, Korey! Some woman!"

He shook his head. "There's no one in here with me."

"Oh, bullshit! You're a grown-ass man, as you keep reminding me! You have some chick in here! Just own up to it!"

"Not that I have to explain myself to you," he said tightly, "but I'm telling you the truth. There is no one . . . I repeat, *no one* in my room, Cindy, but you and me."

When she continued to stare at him, the image of incredulity, he waved over his shoulder.

"Fine, then! Have a look yourself if you don't believe me."

She hesitated for only a second before barging past him. She marched through the suite's living room and into the bedroom. It had the same layout as her suite four floors above.

She came into the bedroom, expecting to find a half-naked woman lounging on his bedspread, maybe eating strawberries or holding a paddle, for all she knew! Instead, she found an opened suitcase on the footstool and a discarded wet bath towel spread out on crumpled bed sheets. She walked toward the bathroom and saw it was also empty. Another bath towel was on the marble floor tiles, near the open glass shower door.

But I could have sworn I heard someone.

The television was blaring. Cynthia turned to look at it. The commercial on the screen ended, and suddenly a redhead appeared, giving a throaty laugh just before she stuck a cigarette into her mouth. She said something to someone off camera. Cynthia instantly recognized the woman's voice. She had heard it on the other side of the hotel door.

Damn, Cynthia thought. That same old jealousy had crept up again, despite her best efforts. What was it about Korey that made her feel so irrational, so insecure?

"Told you so," he said from behind her.

Cynthia turned to find Korey leaning against the bedroom doorjamb, looking smug.

"Honest mistake," she muttered.

"Uh-huh." He walked toward her. "Look, why did you come down here, anyway? It wasn't just to check on me to see if I was sleeping alone, I hope."

She stared at the carpet, unable to meet his gaze. She felt ridiculous. This isn't at all how she'd envisioned this moment going down.

"So why'd you come?" he persisted.

She started to wring her hands. She pivoted anxiously from one heel to the other. She closed her eyes and pursed her lips.

"I wanted to have sex," she blurted out, opening her eyes.

He gaped.

"I wanted to . . . to have sex . . . with you. There's no . . ." She flapped her arms helplessly. "There's no other way to put it. That's what I came here for." She nervously gnawed on her bottom lip. "The chemistry is still there. I can feel it, and I'm tired of denying it." She took a deep breath. "I . . . I want you, Korey."

She waited for his response.

"What if I don't want you?" he asked, making her mouth drop open.

She had prepared herself for rejection but not for him to be quite that blunt. That wasn't like Korey at all. That was definitely more her style.

"You don't want me?"

He cocked an eyebrow. "Cindy, did you ever consider that maybe getting a piece of your ass is not as enticing as *you* think it is? Or maybe, even if I was attracted to you, there's no way in hell I'd have sex with you again since the last time we did, you up and disappeared and married someone else!"

"But you know why I did that! I explained it to you a hundred times already!"

"That you did," he agreed dryly with a nod.

"And you said you understood and forgave me."

"Yep, I did." He shrugged. "Okay, then maybe it's just because I don't want to have sex with you—period. Maybe it's as simple as that."

She cringed. She had thrown herself at him twice—once on the plane and now in his hotel room—and he had said no. And not just no, but he had made it clear he wasn't remotely interested in her. She couldn't recall any man ever turning her down, definitely not this coldly. He said he had forgiven her, but obviously he hadn't.

"Told you this was a bad idea," the voice in her head chastised.

She didn't want to show Korey how much his rejection had hurt her. She pushed back her shoulders, raised her nose into the air, and strode toward the doorway. "Fine. Good night, then."

He groaned in frustration, reached out, and grabbed her arm as she passed. "Wait, Cindy."

"I'm not waiting! Get off me," she said through clenched teeth, yanking her arm out of his grasp.

"Look, I'm sorry! I was trying to be an asshole to you the way you were a bitch to me all those years ago."

"Well, you succeeded! You got your little jab in. You don't want to fuck me! Fine! Accepted. I won't ask again. Now leave me the hell alone!" she yelled, striding to the door.

"Look, it was petty and uncalled for. I know that! I said I was sorry, all right?"

She finally stilled.

"Do you know what it's like to have these . . . I don't know what you call them . . . revenge fantasies, I guess . . . all these years, to wait for the moment to get back at the woman who broke your heart two decades ago? I couldn't resist—and now I feel like shit for doing it."

They both fell silent. Only the sound of the television filled the room.

"You were . . . you were never very good at being mean," she finally whispered.

"And I paid the price for it. I should have been more of an asshole back then and not worn my heart on my sleeve."

"But if you were an asshole, I never would have fallen in love with you. A bitch and an asshole are a bad match. We balanced each other out."

He nodded. "That we did."

They gazed into each other's eyes. The air around them seemed charged again, like an arc of electricity could shoot between them at any second.

Cynthia hesitated. She didn't know if her ego could take him rejecting her a *third* time, but she took a chance. She leaned forward and kissed Korey lightly on the lips. Despite his protests earlier that he didn't want her, he didn't back away. She leaned forward and kissed him again, deeper this time, savoring the texture and taste of her former lover's mouth.

This time, not only did he not back away, but he also kissed her back. She felt his lips move against her own. His tongue slid inside her mouth. He wrapped a hand around the base of her neck and tilted back her head. She opened her mouth wider and met his tongue with her own. He looped his arm around her waist and pulled her tighter against him. She murmured with delight against his lips as they continued to kiss. He growled back hungrily from the base of his throat.

The sound of the television seemed to dim. All Cynthia could hear was the thud of her heart, the steady *whoosh* of blood in her ears, and their breathing. She wrapped her arms around his neck, pulling him even closer, drowning in him. His hand shifted from her back to her bottom, cupping the cheeks, pressing his pelvis against her own. She felt the hardness of arousal there, nudging urgently against the terrycloth of his robe and her groin. She answered it with her own arousal. A budding wetness formed between her thighs, and her nipples hardened. Those little round nubs pushed against the fabric of her dress and his chest.

The fervor of their kisses only intensified, and the next thing Cynthia knew, they were panting as they fell back against the bed and began stripping off each other's clothes. Korey didn't have far to go to get undressed. In five seconds flat, he removed his bathrobe and stood before her, stark naked.

She sat back on her shins and gazed down at him in all his naked glory. His body was still slightly damp from his shower, so it glistened in the dim light of the night table lamp and the glow of the television. Thick cords of muscle showed in his arms and along his shoulders. He still had washboard abs. Her eyes drifted lower. A smile crossed Cynthia's kiss-chapped lips. Something else hadn't changed. "Big Korey" was just as long and thick as she remembered, all eight inches of sexual delight.

"*Damn,* I missed you," she whispered, referring more to the appendage than its owner. She leaned down and greedily kissed Korey again.

Unfortunately, getting Cynthia undressed took much longer, and Korey didn't seem to have the patience for the whole process, torn as he was between removing her clothes and devouring her body. He'd try to untie the knot on her wrap dress, only to pause to pull aside the fabric and lick and nip her neck and shoulders, making her tremble with pleasure. He'd start to remove her bra, only to get distracted by her breasts and start fondling them, giving her goose bumps and making her whimper.

Don't get her wrong—Cynthia wasn't complaining! Her body loved the attention he gave it! She was getting wetter by the second. But at this rate, getting undressed was going to take forever, and he was practically taunting her with all those kisses and nips, fondling and caressing. She finally undressed herself, tossing her clothes and underwear onto the hotel floor. She climbed on top of him and let herself explore him just as eagerly as he had explored her.

God, he's a beautiful man, she marveled as she trailed her hands over the length of him. She remembered a few tricks that had made him moan back in the day: licking his nipples and navel, pressing her breasts against his thighs while she teased him by running her lips and tongue over Big Korey.

He remembered a few tricks of his own, cupping

her breasts in each hand, making the skin tingle. He ran his thumb over the brown nipples, flicking them back and forth and then in a circular movement. When he finally lowered his mouth to one, she breathed in audibly. She closed her eyes. When he tugged the nipple between his teeth, she moaned.

He cupped her bottom and showed equal attention to each breast, suckling them and licking them until she arched her back, dug her nails into his shoulders, and bit down hard on her bottom lip to stifle her moans.

When she felt his fingers tickle the slick wetness between her thighs, she cried out. Her hips started to meet the tantalizing stroke of his fingers. The tingle that had started along her skin now sank deeper, all the way to the bone, and it coasted like undulating waves over her body.

She slowly rode his fingers until the tremors started. When he picked up the pace, so did she. She tossed back her head and bucked her hips, grinding against him. The whimpers turned into moans and back again. Finally, when she was about to shout out his name, he abruptly stopped, pulling his hand away. The explosion that had been building up inside her swiftly dissipated.

What . . . the . . . Seriously, Korey?

She opened her eyes. "Why'd . . . why'd you stop?"

"Would you rather have caviar or fast-food sex?" he asked.

She pushed her hair out of her face. "Huh? What the hell are you talking about?"

She had been so close! *So close!*

"It's been twenty years since we've done this. We've got all night, Cindy," he said, running his tongue over her breasts again, making her quiver. "We don't have to rush. Savor it," he urged, before closing his mouth over her nipple.

He wasn't lying about not rushing it. He toyed with her body, paying attention to every part of her with painstaking detail, dragging her to edge and then stopping just before she came. After he did that the third time, she almost punched him.

"Remember when I said you weren't good at being mean?" she asked breathlessly while lying spread-eagled on the bedroom floor.

They had taken a tumble off the bed and onto the carpet a while ago. Neither of them had wanted to stop their foreplay to make their way back onto a mattress.

He nodded as he climbed on top of her. "I remember."

"Well, I lied!" She shifted from underneath him and tried to crawl to her knees.

"Hey, where do you think you're going?" he asked, pinning her down.

"To the bathroom! I'm going to use the massage setting on that showerhead in there to finish what you refuse to!"

He grinned. "I thought you women liked a man who took his time."

"Korey, do you realize how damn long it's been since I had an orgasm? There was a Republican in the Oval Office! Okay? That's how long it's been!"

His grin disappeared. "That long, huh?" He leaned down and kissed her. "I guess we better take care of that then." He reached for the night table drawer.

A few seconds later, Korey had a condom on, and she squirmed eagerly with anticipation. She was going to have an orgasm tonight if it killed her!

He kissed her languidly, and she looped her arms

around his neck, kissing him back. She felt the hotel room carpet dig into her shoulder blades as he pressed against her. She felt Big Korey nudge against the inside of her thighs. It looked like she wasn't the only one getting impatient.

Korey raised her hips, centered himself between her legs, and eased forward. Their bodies joined with one thrust and this time she did cry out—in pain.

What's happening, she thought frantically. *What's happening?*

This certainly wasn't what she expected. It was a tight fit—a lot tighter than she remembered.

Damn, had Big Korey always felt like this? Maybe Big Korey was *too* big.

Oh, you have got to be kidding me!

Korey squinted down at her with concern. "You all right?"

She nodded and winced, taking short, quick breaths to ease her way through the discomfort. "Just . . . just don't move yet. Okay? Give me . . . give me a sec."

She spread her legs wider, giving him more room.

"Cindy?"

Inhale, exhale. Inhale, exhale. She lay there, letting her body reacquaint itself with someone it had once known very well.

"Cindy?"

After a minute, she felt the pain ease to a dull throb, then disappear almost completely.

He sighed. "Maybe we should stop."

"No! No, I'm . . . I'm all right now."

She didn't wait twenty years for this opportunity to come around and then wimp out this soon. If she had conquered Big Korey before—then damn it, she could do it again!

"You sure?"

"I'm all right—really." She did a tantalizing swivel of the hips to demonstrate. "Come on. Don't stop now."

She felt him ease himself farther inside her, and she felt a twinge again, but it was nothing like before. She gazed into his dark eyes as she and Korey slowly rocked and ground. She raised her mouth to his, and they hungrily kissed again. He held her breast and trailed his hand along her thigh as they made love on the hotel floor with their bodies tangled in the bed sheets. Their moans and whispers broke the silence. It was like the rest of the world outside of the room had disappeared.

Cynthia's heart pounded like the pistons of a steam engine. The tingle she had felt earlier was now a raging fire that sent her nerve endings into overdrive so that his every touch sent her purring. She could tell from the pressure that was building up inside her that her body would get its release soon, and when it did, she knew she wouldn't be able to hold back her shouts.

The deliciously slow rocking suddenly picked up in tempo. Korey's hands shifted back to her hips and bottom, as he thrust harder between her thighs. He bit down hard on his bottom lip—so hard that the pink skin now was virtually white. He closed his eyes.

Cynthia started to tremble. She gripped his broad back to steady herself, but it was of little use. She was quaking all over, feeling her legs and her arms rapidly turn into putty. When the shock wave finally crested over her, she closed her eyes and shouted his name. Her back arched. The muscles in her legs and arms clenched. She bucked her hips with each spasm, still shouting.

Korey came soon after. She felt him swell inside her, then he cried out. He tightened his hold around her hips. He dropped his head against her shoulder and gulped for air. He shuddered, and his body shook with each tremor. Cynthia cradled him in her arms until the shudders subsided.

He raised his head a minute later and gazed down at her.

"So did we end your losing streak?" he asked, grinning.

"What do you think?" she whispered groggily.

"I think we should make up for lost time and see if we can get you there again."

"I'm game." She tiredly thumped his shoulder. "Just let me catch my breath first."

"Well, do it quick." He licked his lips. "We're far from finished."

She certainly hoped so.

Chapter 21

Cynthia woke to the sound of a knocking. She opened her eyes and winced at the bright morning light that came through the cracked bedroom blinds.

"Korey?" she croaked, smacking her lips. She lifted her head and looked to her left. Korey's side of the bed was empty. Only the indentation of his head was still on the down pillow. She wondered if he had gone to get the door.

The knocking was insistent now, even though they had put the "Do Not Disturb" sign on the outside door handle hours ago.

Cynthia pushed herself to her elbows and looked over her shoulder. Couldn't they read the damn sign? She hoped nothing was wrong. It wasn't hotel management, was it? She frowned. She and Korey hadn't been *that* loud, had they?

Their lovemaking had dragged on until dawn and had gotten a bit rowdy as the night progressed. Okay, maybe *she* was the one who had gotten rowdy, but it was hard to keep quiet when she was having that much fun. A long line of bad lovers had left her without an orgasm in *years,* but last night Korey had made up for that. Her orgasm dry spell was officially over.

She heard the sound of a deadbolt being unlocked and a door opening.

"Good morning," someone said in a thick Spanish accent. "Your breakfast order, sir."

Breakfast? Good! Cynthia was hungry enough to eat the complimentary magazine in the night table.

Korey appeared a few minutes later while she was trying frantically to fix herself so that she was a bit more presentable. It was a Gibbons family rule that a woman should look as gorgeous in the morning when she woke up beside a man as she had been when she fell asleep beside him. Cynthia glanced at herself in the dresser mirror one final time. She wasn't wearing makeup, and her hair was slightly disheveled, but at least she didn't have drool on her face. By the time Korey nudged the bedroom door open with his shoulder, carrying a tray of silver platters, Cynthia was as close to flawless as one could get under the circumstances.

"Stay where you are," he said as she started to toss back the covers and walk toward the little desk in the corner where she thought he was about to place the tray. "No need to get up. I can serve you there."

She smiled. He was bringing her breakfast in bed? How sweet! In the old days, Korey had been full of romantic gestures like these, leaving freshly picked flowers at her locker, drunkenly serenading her from underneath her bedroom window on her birthday. She remembered shouting at him to quiet down before her mother heard him, even as her heart warmed at the fact that he had done something so reckless, ridiculous, and charming. And now he was doing it all over again, making her heart flutter a little.

"Don't start," the blunt voice in her head warned. "You guys just spent the night together. So he's bringing you breakfast! Big deal! This isn't a love thing, girl!"

She watched as he removed the metal lids, revealing a plate of toast, scrambled eggs, and bacon, and another plate of fat sausage links and Belgian waffles sprinkled with powdered sugar. A bowl sat beside it. It was filled with fresh fruit and covered with Saran Wrap.

"Thanks for the food, Korey, but why didn't you wake me?" She would have liked to pick her own order.

"I tried!" He walked toward her and sat the tray on the edge of the bed. "You shoved me away and told me, 'Go away! I'm sleeping.'"

She laughed. That sounded like something she would say.

Cynthia sat up in bed, piling pillows behind her, and reached for a slice of toast. Korey removed the lid from a small glass jar and began to pour syrup on his waffles.

"I guess we'd better eat fast if we're going to head to the lobby to see if we can catch the kids there," she said, breaking her toast in half. "They're teenagers, so I don't expect to see them down there before noon. That'll give me enough time to go to my room to change clothes."

She also wanted to head back to her room to refocus. The longer she stayed here, the more nostalgic she got. It made her forget the reason she had come to his room last night: for sex only. She had no other expectations. It was best to leave now with a slightly sore vajayjay and a full belly.

Korey stopped chewing. "Cindy, maybe at this point we should focus less on stopping the wedding and more on how to deal with the aftermath."

She stiffened. "Why do you say that?"

"Because it's probably time to accept that they're already married. Maybe we should—"

She furiously shook her head. "They're not married."

"—just wait until they come back to Virginia, and push that they get an annulment or something. It can't be—"

"They're not married, Korey! They can't be!" she insisted, making him pause.

"Why can't they be?" He furrowed his brows. "Look, Cindy, why are you so hell-bent on stopping this? I know you're upset about it. So am I! But I've come to accept it. Why not you? You aren't *that* stubborn, are you?" He narrowed his eyes at her. "Why are you fighting this so hard? What aren't you telling me? Do you know something I don't?"

She looked away from him guiltily and stared at the breakfast tray instead. She wanted to tell him the truth. She was so tired of carrying around the burden of her secret, but she knew she couldn't share it with him. They had shared a wonderful night together. She didn't want to ruin the moment with her little bombshell. Not this soon.

"I just don't want her to get married, Korey," she lied, before eating her toast. "It's as simple as that. Look, let's change the subject. Let's instead focus on the fact that you're eating all the damn bacon!" She jabbed her finger at the slices he had piled on his plate.

"Since when do you like bacon?"

"Since now," she said, taking a slice away from him and popping it into her mouth.

"You never liked it before!"

She shrugged. "That was twenty years ago. Things change."

He smirked. "Not everything."

She grabbed another slice.

"I remember something you really used to like then," he began slowly, "and I bet you still do."

"Like what?"

"Do you remember the game we used to play?" Korey asked with a wicked smile as he pushed the breakfast tray to the other side of the bed and stretched beside her.

Cynthia paused mid-chew. She adjusted the bed sheets over her breasts. "A game we used to play?"

Korey nodded and leaned across her legs. He slowly rubbed her thighs, not taking his penetrating gaze off of her. She could feel the heat of his touch even through the sheets. "Yeah, it was a game you liked *a lot,* if that rings any bells."

The memory of what game Korey was referring to suddenly dawned on her. Cynthia lowered her bacon back to her plate. Her face reddened as she licked the remaining grease from her lips. "I remember."

"Uh-huh. I bet you do."

"It was another one of *your* ideas. You had a kinky imagination back then."

"And I still do."

She pursed her lips, ignoring his saucy retort. "The game was whether or not you could spell my full name before—"

"You came. Yeah, I got so good at it that I could get you to do it before I finished the 'a' in Cynthia."

She snorted. "Only because you cheated! I bet you were spelling some letters twice."

"*Really?* That sounds like a challenge to me."

Her eyes widened as he began to tug at the bed sheets. She started to tingle all over as the cotton slid over her breasts, then her stomach and then her thighs before he tossed the sheets aside. She sat naked before him.

"Lie back for me, baby," he whispered.

Her throat went dry.

"Lie down." He laid his hands on her shoulders and gently but firmly pressed her back against the pillows behind her.

She stared at the fluffy cloud-and-angel relief painted on the hotel ceiling. Her heart was starting to race a mile a minute. Her nipples hardened. She was getting wet again just thinking about what he was about to do to her.

"Spread your legs."

Cynthia closed her eyes and slowly did as he ordered.

"A little wider, sweetheart."

She could remember him whispering those same words twenty years ago. His magic spell was working again. This was all too much, just too much. She had come here for sex—that's all! Not for butterflies in her stomach, not for all these emotions. She was starting not to feel like herself anymore. She wasn't the plain-spoken, coldly rational Cynthia who saw men as easy prey and didn't believe in love. She had regressed back to a love-struck eighteen-year-old girl who was full of hope and passion and all that other nonsense that now made her adult self roll her eyes in disgust. She didn't want to be that girl again. That Cynthia was too vulnerable and too easily disappointed.

She opened her eyes and started to sit up from the bed.

"Korey, I should—"

"Oh, no, you don't." He chuckled. "*You* threw down the gauntlet by saying I cheated. Give me a chance to defend my honor, woman."

She hesitated before she lay back again. She held her breath and felt the mattress dip slightly underneath his weight as he shifted to the bottom of the bed and nestled between her legs. She shivered when she felt him leave a trail of butterfly kisses along her inner thighs.

"I'll say the letters out loud," he whispered, gently coaxing open her moist womanly folds with his fingers, making her tremble. "That way you'll know I'm not cheating this time." He gave her one last kiss—this time between her legs. "Are you ready, Cindy?"

Cynthia murmured something in response, though it wasn't any recognizable word, because she immediately felt his mouth and his tongue and all intelligible thought disappeared. She closed her eyes and bit down hard on her bottom lip, loving the sensation and the thrill he was giving her.

"C," he whispered seconds later.

She felt his warm, wet mouth again, and she balled the bed sheets in her fists. Her legs fell akimbo and she moaned.

"Y."

Her hips arched to meet his tongue. Her toes curled. If she felt like she was wet for him before, that was nothing compared to now.

"N."

Each slow, deliberate stroke was better than the last. Her eyes flew open. Her moaning only increased. She was starting to throb now.

"T."

The throbbing was spreading. It started from her core and was vibrating down her legs and up her stomach. Her breathing became shallower. She turned her head so that half of her face was buried into her pillow.

"H."

Oh, God! She bit down hard on the feathers inside the pillowcase. Her legs were starting to tremble. Her hips were squirming so much that Korey had to steady them with his hands.

"I."

Cynthia closed her eyes again. She could feel it coming over her. There was no fighting it. Damn Korey and his magic mouth! She could feel all her muscles tighten into an intolerable knot, then unwind even faster, sending electric currents up and down her limbs, giving her chills. She twisted and arched her back. She pounded her fists against the mattress and called out his name.

He sat back on his elbows and watched as she trembled and writhed in ecstasy, as the waves of pleasure crashed over her.

A minute later, Cynthia's eyelids fluttered open. She took another deep breath and swept her hair out of her face. Dazedly, she pushed herself to the sitting position and looked down at Korey, who lay on his side now, wiping his mouth and licking his lips. He was smiling from ear to ear.

"And that was 'a,'" he said proudly. "So my record still stands."

"Oh, you . . ." She slowly shook her head. "You are so full of your damn self, you little—"

"Baby, there is *nothing* little about me." He cocked an eyebrow. "You know that . . . or do I have to demonstrate that to you again too."

She was struck speechless. *You cocky bastard!*

She suddenly grabbed one of the pillows from behind her and hit Korey over the head with it, knocking the arrogant smile off his face. He wrestled the pillow out of her hands, grabbed her arm, and tugged her toward him. She laughed and shrieked when they went crashing back to the mattress. They rolled around naked for a few seconds, and he climbed on top of her, pinning her to the bed. Cynthia giggled and squirmed underneath him. But her laughter died on her lips when she gazed up at him and saw the look in his eyes.

"What? What's wrong?"

He didn't say a word for a long time and just traced a finger along her lips. "I forgot what this feels like . . . how good we used to be together."

She fell silent.

"I know we fought sometimes. I pissed you off. Hell, you pissed me off too. But I still loved you, Cindy, and I think after being with you these past few days, after all these years"—he paused—"I still love you."

Korey, damn it! Don't do this to me. Not now!

She turned away from him, choosing to stare at the grotesquely tacky headboard instead. What was with this hotel and its cheesy décor?

He held her chin and turned her around to face him again.

"And if I'm reading you right, I think you still feel the same way about me too. Or is that just my ego talking?"

"We're here for the kids," she answered softly. Her eyes began to water. "Remember? Remember what you said on the plane?"

"To hell with what I said! I was lying. I was lying to protect myself, but I'm not lying anymore. I'm putting it all out there. So do the same and answer the question. Do you still love me, Cindy, like I love you?"

Cynthia closed her eyes, feeling her lashes dampen with tears.

Shit, she thought. *Shit! Shit! Shit!*

He was pressing down on her, pressing his weight on her body so that she couldn't move. On the inside, she could feel the same weight on her heart. Korey was squeezing it at all sides to the point that she couldn't think and could barely breathe. He just wouldn't let it go.

Cynthia kept insisting that she wasn't the same girl she had been twenty years ago, but deep down she knew she was. She had just built a brick wall around the girl, locked her away in a tower, and threw away the key. But that girl, who was still innocent and open-hearted, had returned, and she still loved Korey. She always would.

Cynthia slowly nodded.

"Don't nod your head. Say it to me like I said it to you."

Korey loosened his grip on her arms. He shifted in between her legs, coaxing them open again. She could feel the wet tip of him pressing urgently between her thighs, begging to be inside her.

She wrapped her arms around him and gazed into eyes. "I love you, Korey," she whispered and kissed him again. Less than a minute later, he put on another condom and entered her. She cried out into the silent hotel room. Her grip around his back tightened.

Cynthia met each stroke with the rise of her hips. She spread her legs wider so that he could fill her completely. Their bodies moved in a steady rhythm—slow and deliberate at first, then gradually picking up the pace. Like she had twenty years ago, she locked this moment in her memory. She wanted to remember every sensation: the warmth of his perspiring skin against hers, the feel of his lips against her mouth and neck, and the swell of him inside her. When her orgasm rocked her body, she cried out again and twisted underneath him. Her toes curled. Her back arched. Her nails dug into his skin.

He came soon after, shouting out her name into the silent room before collapsing on top of her.

They lay quietly for several minutes—she, staring at the bedroom ceiling, and he with his head nestled on her shoulder and buried in the covers. Cynthia suspected that, like her, Korey was deep in thought.

She had just admitted to him that she loved him and he had admitted the same to her. What did that mean for them both? What about her plans to focus on meeting and marrying her next rich husband—the one who had enough wealth to buy a small island? Korey didn't meet those standards by a long shot. He lived in a tiny bungalow, drove a crappy car, and was a mechanic. If she ended up with him, then, just like her sisters, she would be settling for less.

But he's not less, she corrected herself.

Twenty years ago, he had been everything to her, and she had let him slip away.

No, I pushed *him away.*

But she wasn't going to do that again. Life had thrown her more than just a second chance to roll around in the sheets with Korey Walker. It had given her a second chance at happiness, and damn it, she wasn't pushing it away this time!

She trailed her fingers along his spine. "That was perfect," she whispered.

He raised his head and pushed himself to his elbows. "Well, perfect—almost," he said, making her frown and knocking her off her cloud of bliss.

"*Almost?* What do you mean almost? What was wrong with it?"

"Well"—he leaned down and lightly kissed her cheek, then her neck, making her tingle again—"you haven't brushed your teeth yet, baby."

The tingling instantly stopped. Her mouth fell open in shock.

"I mean"—he shrugged—"hell, I love you! I'll make love to you even with morning breath and sleep in your eyes. I was going to say we could take a break so you can get minty fresh, but I didn't want to ruin the—"

He didn't get to finish. His words were cut short by a pillow to the head.

"Did you just tell me I have morning breath? You . . . cocky . . . asshole!" she yelled as she hit him again and again.

He wrenched the pillow out of her hands, leading to another tussle on the bed. They lost their balance and fell to the hotel floor as Cynthia shrieked with laughter.

Chapter 22

Lauren gazed out the window, watching as her sister Dawn's cobalt blue Mercedes-Benz convertible pulled to a stop in her driveway. She glanced at her blurry reflection in the stained-glass windowpane, quickly wiped away the last of the tears from the corners of her eyes, and sniffed, not wanting to give a hint to her sister about the emotions that were waging a little battle inside her.

She had slept in one of the guest rooms last night after her argument with Cris and awoke this morning to find her husband had left the house without saying good-bye to her. She was disappointed but not surprised. After all, *she* was the one who had stormed out of their bedroom last night and refused to come back. Maybe he thought she wasn't interested in talking to him, but the truth was that she had lain awake for most of the night, waiting to hear Cris's soft knock at the guest bedroom door. But it never came.

She just wished she could make Cris understand

why she had reacted the way she did. It was bad enough
that so many people in town whispered about her and
seemed to pity him for being married to a woman like
her. Why did he have to ally himself with one of those
people? He didn't need Marvin Payton to win this
election. Cris could easily go against Mayor Knightly
on his own, she insisted. All Marvin would do was
make Cris second-guess his confidence in his judgment and his confidence in her.

Lauren politely shooed away the housekeeper, who
was walking toward the front door. Lauren answered it
instead, pulling open one of the French doors just as
Dawn's driver-side door flew open. Even from such a
great distance, Lauren could hear her infant son bawl-
ing. She instantly bounded down the steps toward the
parked car.

"Laurie!" Dawn shouted as she hopped out of the
convertible. The usually impeccably dressed woman
looked absolutely frazzled in her jeans and wrinkled
T-shirt. She rounded the car and swung open the back
passenger door, where Crisanto Jr. was crying and flailing in his car seat. "I have no idea what's wrong! He's
just been crying and crying, the poor thing!"

Lauren rushed toward the car and removed her son
from his car seat. She held him in her arms and gently
rocked and shushed him. "What's wrong, honey? Tell
mommy what's wrong."

She then patted his back a few times, and he let out
a tremendous burp that made both women's eyes
widen in amazement. Suddenly, his tears ceased.

"Oh, that was a big one, buddy!" Lauren gushed.
"Do you feel better?"

He looked up at his mother and gave her a gummy
grin.

Dawn whipped off her sunglasses. "You have *got* to be kidding me! That's all it was . . . *gas?*"

Lauren laughed. "I'm afraid so."

Dawn's shoulders slumped. "Oh, to hell with it!" She reached inside the backseat of her car and grabbed the diaper bag that Lauren had loaned her. She slammed the car door shut. "I give up. I'm just not cut out for this mommy thing, Laurie, and I told Xavier as much."

The two women walked toward the mansion's front door.

"But he's still gung ho about having a baby," Dawn moaned. "We're not even married yet. I told him he'd have to put a ring on my finger before I would even *think* about getting knocked up. He told me no problem, give him my ring size, and he'll have the ring by tomorrow."

Lauren burst into laughter again as they mounted the stone steps.

"It's not funny, girl! Doesn't he realize I'm an old woman? My body probably couldn't even take a pregnancy right now!"

"Dawn, you're thirty-seven years old! You are not, by any estimation, an 'old woman.'"

"Tell that to my gynecologist," Dawn muttered as they entered the foyer. Dawn closed the door behind them. "She told me that the clock is definitely ticking." Dawn tapped the invisible watch on her wrist for illustration. "I asked her if I could just freeze my eggs and try in a few years. She said—and I quote—'Most of your eggs aren't really that viable to begin with.'" Dawn continued in a snippy voice. "'I would advise any woman at *your* age to start trying to have a baby as soon as possible.'"

Lauren shook her head. "I'm sorry that you have pressure coming at you from all sides."

Dawn shrugged as she followed her sister into the great room. She looked around the yawning space, designed to resemble a Viking hall with its timber-beam ceiling and massive stone fireplace. "It's okay. It's hard to explain to Xavier that it's not that I don't *ever* want to have kids. I just never envisioned myself being a mom. You know? It's still a concept I'm trying to get used to. I never thought I'd fall in love! I never thought having a family was a possibility! I'd thought I'd get married and divorce, and live off my big alimony settlement. That's what the women in our family are supposed to do! But now it's all"—she took a deep breath and fell onto one of the love seat cushions—"complicated."

Lauren nodded as she felt her son drift to sleep in her arms. "I can understand that."

Like Dawn, she had been raised to have certain expectations from life. She never thought she'd now be in a situation where she loved her husband so much that it ripped her apart that they weren't speaking to each other.

"But enough about me and my *old* womb!" Dawn turned to her sister, fluffing a pillow behind her as she adjusted on the sofa. "Have you had any updates from Cindy?"

"Nope. Not one. She hasn't even responded to the text messages I sent today." Lauren bit down on her bottom lip. Her brows furrowed. "I hope everything is all right."

"I'm sure she's fine," Dawn said with a wave of the hand. "She's just too preoccupied with finding Clarissa right now to give us a call. So how are things with you? Did you guys enjoy being a childless couple for one night?"

"Oh, things are good." Lauren sat down on the facing leather sofa. She laid Crisanto Jr. on the baby blanket resting on the cushion beside her. She gently patted her son's back as he slept. "We . . . uh . . . we enjoyed ourselves. We had a good time. It was . . ." She grappled for the right word, the right lie. "It was nice."

"Nice?" Dawn eyed her sister. She cocked a finely arched eyebrow. "Okay. What's wrong?"

"Why do you think something is wrong?"

"You're being vague and evasive. That's not a good sign. Plus your nose is puffy and your eyes are a little red." Dawn squinted. "Have you been crying?"

Lauren sighed and looked away.

Damn it, she thought. Was she that transparent?

"Come on. Tell me what's wrong! You and Cris didn't have a fight, did you?"

Lauren hesitated then finally, nodded.

"Why? What happened? Most of the time the two of you are so perfect together it's sickening."

"It's about the election. Cris is hiring a campaign manager and didn't tell me."

"I didn't know you were involved enough in his election campaign that you would care. You guys really fought over that?"

"It wasn't just that! It's not just that he wants to hire someone to be his campaign manager; it's *who* he wants to hire. Dawn, the guy he's considering is such a kiss-ass, and it's obvious he doesn't respect me. His wife acted like she wanted to toss me out of their house."

Dawn held up her hand. "Wait, Cris hired that guy anyway after you told him about that?"

"Well, no. I didn't tell him."

Dawn frowned in confusion.

"And he hasn't hired him—yet," Lauren further explained. "He said he was only thinking about it."

"Well, if you didn't tell him what happened and he hasn't hired the guy, then what's the issue?"

Lauren stopped patting her son's back. "I'm just . . . I'm just tired of being treated like a side piece and not a wife. I'm tired of being seen as a liability. For better or for worse, I'm Mrs. Crisanto Weaver." She gritted her teeth. "No, I may not be the ideal wife, but I'm *his* wife. I deserve some respect!"

Dawn sat in silence as she listened to her sister. Finally, she asked, "Has Cris ever treated you like you were a side piece? Has he ever called you a liability?"

Lauren paused. "Well, no . . . but I know everyone else sees me that way."

"So who cares what everyone else thinks? Look, Laurie, I know you're not a fan of everything Mama says, but she's right about one thing: You can't base your life on other people's opinions or expectations. You certainly can't build a marriage on it."

"I'm not basing my life or my marriage on their opinions!"

"Then why are you angry at Cris for what other people say or think? Why did you have a fight with him when it sounds like your beef is really with these people whispering about you?"

Lauren's mouth clamped shut. She had no response to that one. She thought she had long ago given up proving herself to the people of Chesterton, that she had been at peace with knowing she was a woman with a tainted past but a brighter future. Unfortunately, Cris's mayoral run seemed to be bringing back all those old feelings of inadequacy, shame, and self-doubt. And she had taken out those feelings on Cris.

"Damn," she muttered, dropping her face into her hands.

Dawn nodded. "Damn indeed. I don't know where your man is, but you need to find him and go apologize."

Lauren grudgingly nodded just as her phone rang. She rose to her feet and walked to the cordless that sat on one of the end tables.

"Weaver residence. Lauren speaking," she answered as Dawn walked to the other couch to sit beside Cris Jr.

"Are you near a computer?" Stephanie yelled, making Lauren cringe and pull the phone away from her ear for a second.

"Huh? Why do I need to be near a computer?"

"Who's that?" Dawn asked.

"Steph," Lauren said over her shoulder.

"Oh!" Dawn grinned. "Tell her I said hi. And I will remind the both of you that we still need to settle on a menu for her engagement party."

"I know. I know. I've just been a little . . . preoccupied lately." Lauren held the phone back to her mouth. "Dawn said hi and that we still need to settle on a—"

"Wait! Dawn's there? Tell her to get to a computer too! She's on there with the rest of us."

Lauren paused. "On where, Steph?"

"The Web site!" Stephanie shouted, making Lauren pull the phone away from her ear again. "Girl, here I was thinking that I was going to have a tranquil day and just take one of my clients to look at a few houses and I had to see this on my phone screen! I am three months pregnant and the sleep-deprived mother of an infant. I don't need this today!"

Lauren inwardly groaned. *Oh, Lord, what now?* She turned to Dawn again.

"Hey, do you have your cell or iPad on you?"

Dawn looked taken aback. She nodded. "Yeah, in my purse. Why?"

"Steph wants us to see some Web site."

A few minutes later, Dawn and Lauren were huddled in front of the coffee table. Dawn's new iPad sat in the center of its wooden surface and she had pulled up the Web site in question on the screen. As she did, her and Lauren's jaws dropped simultaneously.

"What the hell is this?" Dawn said breathlessly.

"My thoughts exactly," Stephanie muttered on the other end of the phone line. She was now on speakerphone.

Cris Jr. had already woken up from his nap and preoccupied himself by idly playing with his feet while his mother and aunts commiserated.

The Web site they were staring at was low budget, with stark fonts and minimal pictures. It looked like someone's teenaged son could have built it over the weekend. But the poor quality wasn't the issue. What had Dawn and Lauren's eyes practically bugging out of their heads was the site's subject. Under the heading "Chesterton Scandals" were a series of blurbs about the exploits—both real and fictional—of all the women in the Gibbons family. It talked about past husbands, boyfriends, and affairs. It named names and put on the screen the gory details about the family that had been gossiped about in Chesterton for decades.

"Xavier and I are on here!" Dawn exclaimed. She scrolled down the screen and scanned a few words. "According to this, I seduced him away from my halfsister, Constance. I also secretly drugged my father and talked him into adding me to his will." She balled her fists in her lap. "*None* of that is true! None of it!"

"You're not the only one being lied about," Stephanie said. "The site says that I cheated on my ex-husband, which is a damn lie! That asshole cheated on me with that twenty-year-old bimbo at his dealership! That's the chick he married after he treated me like last season's Manolos and handed me off to Goodwill."

As Lauren read the Web site, her heart rate increased. The site alleged that she had gotten her position as head chef of Le Bayou Bleu only because she'd slept with the former head chef, Phillip Rochon. It also said she was playing Cris for a fool by having affairs with numerous men around town. It even speculated whether her son, Crisanto Jr., was really Cris's son at all.

When she read that line, she almost saw red. She understood what Dawn had said earlier about not letting other people's opinions have such an impact on her, but how was she possibly supposed to ignore an allegation like that? She wanted to find the person who made the Web site and beat them to a pulp!

"I want to sue the ass off of whoever wrote this stuff, but there's no name or contact info on the site. I can't figure out who the hell did this!" Stephanie yelled. "Do either of you know who it might be?"

Lauren nodded. "I think I do."

"Who?" her sisters asked in unison.

"Mayor Knightly . . . or one of his lackeys."

"Why do you think it's him?" Dawn asked.

"Because everyone has been gossiping about this crap for years, and no one bothered to make a Web site about it before. Now that Cris is running for election, the site *just happens* to pop up. It's too much of a coincidence. Knightly did this to humiliate me"—she paused to suck her teeth—"and to embarrass Cris by association."

"So how do we prove it?" Dawn asked.

"I doubt that we can," Lauren replied.

"Well, damn," Stephanie said.

Lauren wondered if Cris had seen the site already and shuddered at what the fallout would be.

Chapter 23

"You won again," Cynthia muttered with a dejected sigh. She then gathered up the cards to deal their next game of gin rummy.

Korey smiled before glancing up at the bank of elevators several feet away. One of the elevator doors opened. He leaned forward eagerly to see who would step out, then sat back when a group of guys in swim trunks with towels draped around their necks slowly strolled into the lobby.

"Do you know where the pools are?" one of them shouted to Korey.

Korey pointed over his shoulder. "Down the hall, then make two lefts."

"Thanks," one said with a smile and a wave.

Korey and Cynthia had been sitting in the lobby for the past three hours, hoping to spot the kids. It was their last option; they had exhausted all other alternatives. So far they were having no success finding Clarissa and Jared, but Korey seemed to be on a winning streak with the game of gin rummy they had been playing with the complimentary pack of cards from the hotel. They had been dealing out cards to each other for the last hour to pass the time while they waited for the kids.

"Are you kidding me?" Cynthia exclaimed ten minutes later when Korey won yet another game, then tossed down her cards on the couch pad between them. He laughed, making her look up at him.

"Ah-*hee-hee-hee*," she mocked, then rolled her eyes.

"We can go back to playing spades again if you want. You were the one who said we had to play this old lady game."

"You were winning when we were playing that too!" She squinted one eye at him. "You better not be cheating!"

He laughed even harder. "I'm not cheating!"

"You've won nine out of ten games, Korey. What are the chances? I know you aren't that damn good of a player," she argued, pretending to be mad, though he could tell she wasn't. A smile tugged at the corner of her mouth.

He leaned forward. "Maybe I've just had a change in luck," he whispered against her lips, gazing into her hazel eyes, where flecks of gold now danced.

"Maybe," she whispered back, meeting his gaze. "But maybe n—"

He kissed her before she could finish, letting the deck of cards tumble from his hands. She held his cheeks and eagerly kissed him back.

Korey's change in luck definitely had been for the better. Who would have thought when he and Cynthia boarded the plane back in Virginia two days ago that they would be so happy now? The incredible sex was a given. They had always been good at tearing up the sheets. But he never would have believed, after all these years, that Cynthia Gibbons would not only admit that she had been wrong for what she had done to him back then, but also admit that she was still in love with him. The cold, conniving money-hungry Cynthia he had thought she had become wasn't capable of that, but the charming and warm Cindy that he remembered had been capable of such vulnerability. He was glad to discover that the old Cindy was still in there.

Even though they couldn't rewrite the past, now they had a chance for a future together. As soon as they got back to Chesterton and settled things with the kids, he wanted to take her out on a proper date. He wanted to know more about her. What had gone on in her life in the past twenty years? What was her daughter Clarissa like? There were so many things that—

"You don't think you're jumping the gun?" a voice in his head asked. "It's not like she hasn't done this before. She's gotten your hopes up in the past only to disappoint you later."

Korey furrowed his brows at that thought.

No, she's changed, he insisted. *I can feel it! I know it!*

And frankly, if this was going to work between them, he had to change too. He couldn't continue to keep up his guard around her. He couldn't keep anticipating the moment when she would let him down or when she would drop some bombshell on him. He had told her that he had forgiven her and that he loved her. He *had* to trust her.

"Yeah, good luck with that," the voice in his head mocked.

All I've had lately is good luck, he thought as he won yet another game of gin rummy. *Looks like the odds are in my favor.*

"That's it," Cynthia said, tossing down her cards yet again fifteen minutes later. "I'm not playing you anymore. You've got some weird hoodoo going on."

He chuckled. "You're just a sore loser."

"Eh, maybe." She shrugged before looking up again when one of the elevators opened. He watched as her shoulders slumped as an old woman in a velveteen tracksuit stepped out of the elevator and shuffled into the lobby.

"Why don't we take a break?" he asked.

"A break? *Now?* But what if the kids—"

"We've been here for three and a half hours, and neither Jared nor Clarissa has shown up," he said, gathering the cards into a deck. "If we disappear for a half an hour, I doubt that'll be the moment when they suddenly decide to do cartwheels and go screaming through the lobby."

Cynthia leaned her head back against the stucco wall. She stared at the elevators again. Disappointment clouded her face.

"You don't think we're going to find them, do you?"

"Honestly?" He tucked the deck into his jean pocket and shook his head. "At this point, no, but I'm willing to sit here and wait if that's what you want to do. I know how much it means to you."

"It's not just me! I thought it meant a lot to you too!"

"It does, but I've accepted that they're probably already married, Cindy. It's just something we'll handle when we all get back home. You should just accept it too." He put a hand on her thigh and rubbed it soothingly. "You'll feel a lot a better."

"No, I won't," she whimpered, closing her eyes. "I'd rather throw myself off the Woodrow Wilson Bridge than see those two married, Korey!"

Korey frowned. That was a bit melodramatic, wasn't it? The idea of their kids getting married wasn't *that* bad.

He had always remembered Cynthia being stubborn, but she was being particularly stubborn about this, even though the likelihood of stopping the wedding after all this time was remote. He didn't know why she was digging in her heels about it. Maybe he could find a way to distract her, to keep her from obsessing.

"Come on." He stood up from the sofa, grabbed her hand, and dragged her to her feet.

"What?" she asked as they walked toward the elevators. "Where are we going?"

"To one of the casinos," he answered as they walked down a corridor.

"Why the casino?" Her eyes widened. "You think the kids are there?"

"No, but we're in Vegas, and we haven't been to a casino once. Plus, I'm finally going to use all this good luck to my advantage."

"Seriously, Korey? You want to gamble?" she exclaimed in exasperation as he dragged her along.

"Don't look at me like that. If I win big, I'll buy you dinner . . . or a Maserati." He winked.

Fifteen minutes later, they walked past the craps and poker tables. Korey scanned the vast casino, looking for the perfect game.

"I cannot believe you plan to bet that much money," Cynthia said, shaking her head at the two thousand dollars' worth of chips in his hand. She folded her arms over her chest. "You couldn't start at one hundred or even two hundred? Huh? I'm really starting to worry that Las Vegas is making you lose your damn mind."

He held up the stack of chips and shrugged. "It's really not that much."

"Not that much compared to what? That's a month's worth of income for some people!"

"Not for me," he said as they passed another set of tables.

At one table a crowd of people were gathered and screaming with delight. At another nearby blackjack table, a man in a suit that was so wrinkled and stained that he had to have been wearing it for several days loudly swore as the dealer called out the last card. He took off his cowboy hat and slapped it on the floor, startling the waitress who had just walked past him with a tray of drinks.

"What do you mean not for you? Why do you keep acting like you're rich?" she asked.

"Because I am rich," he replied nonchalantly.

"Wait!" She grabbed his arm, halting him in his tracks. "What do you mean you're rich? You . . . you aren't rich—are you?"

He sighed. He hadn't wanted to talk about this. The fact that he had money wasn't something he liked to advertise and particularly wasn't something he wanted to discuss with Cynthia—a woman who was proudly a gold digger.

When some of the women Korey had dated figured out his secret, their eyes would light up as if they had just discovered Shangri-la. Those were usually the women whose phone numbers he lost. He had learned to be wary of being taken advantage of. Hell, even his ex-wife, Vivian, had no problem begging him for cash because she knew how much money he had! He could only imagine how Cynthia would react once he told her he was wealthy.

But she did say she loved me without knowing about my money, he thought. And if they were going to start anew and going to be in a relationship, she would find out about his wealth soon enough. He couldn't continue to keep this secret from her.

"I'm no Bill Gates, but my net worth is a couple of million or so," he confessed, then paused. "I haven't checked with my accountant lately, though. It could be up to three by now."

She blinked in amazement. "*Maybe three million? B-but you're a mechanic!*"

"I also own two businesses, started investing in properties and renting them out ten years ago, and I own blue-chip stock. Did you really think I was poor?"

"Not poor, b-but . . . but definitely not . . . you know, rich. I saw your house and your car." She glanced at his outfit, which was a plain, no-name brand T-shirt and jeans he could have purchased at any big-box store. "I mean, the way you usually dress . . . none of it exactly screams, 'He's a baller or a big fish!'"

"Maybe not, but"—he shrugged—"I am." He then continued to walk down the aisle. "I'm just a baller who also happens to be frugal."

"You mean cheap."

"Well, I'm not going to be cheap today."

When she continued to gape at him, he slapped her on the ass, making her jump in surprise. He suddenly spotted a roulette table and beelined for it.

The minimum bet was one-hundred dollars. Korey placed his chips on the table, trading them all in for roulette chips.

"Korey," Cynthia cautioned a minute later as Korey took half of his new chips and bet on black, making a bet of one thousand dollars, "do you really think you should bet that much?"

"Don't worry," he whispered to her as the dealer released the ball and the roulette wheel began to spin. "It's just money."

She closed her eyes and grumbled.

Thankfully, his good luck held. The ball landed on black twenty-eight.

And with each bet after that, Korey upped the stakes. He went from making the safer outside bets to the riskier inside bets, and each time he won. Even he was shocked as the dealer called out each number.

A crowd started to gather around the table. It was small at first, then more and more people joined the throng. The waitress started to bring him free drinks. The dealer and floor manager started to watch him more carefully to make sure everything was on the up and up. A few of the other players started to follow Korey's bets, putting their chips on whatever bet he made. As the chips in front of him started to stack higher and higher, Korey felt higher than a kite, and it wasn't the whiskey the casino was plying him with. He was high on adrenaline.

He was rich, in love, and he seemed to have the golden touch. He felt invincible!

When the stack in front of him climbed up to almost twenty thousand dollars in chips, he turned to Cynthia, expecting to see the same expression of ecstasy and joy on her face. Instead, she looked ill. Her face was pale. Her mouth was tense.

"What's wrong?" he asked.

She took a deep breath and slowly shook her head. "I can't believe you're doing this."

"*Doing what?* Having fun?" He kissed her and grinned. "Come on, Cindy, we're in Vegas. Lighten up!"

"Please, just quit while you're ahead."

"Oh, hell, no! Don't quit!" a fat man on the other side of him urged. "Make another bet!" He slapped Korey's shoulder and turned to the woman beside him. "I made five hundred bucks off this guy! I'm hoping to make a thousand before it's all over!"

Korey scanned the table. His eyes closed in on red eighteen.

Eighteen . . . the age that he fell in love for the first time. *Eighteen* . . . the age that he lost the woman he loved forever—or so he thought. But now they had a second chance, and life was full of chances to be taken, right?

He pushed all his chips onto red eighteen, drawing a few claps and gasps of awe from those crowded around him.

"Look at the size of the balls on this guy right here!" the fat man yelled. "They gotta be made outta brass!"

"Korey," Cynthia whispered, "why did you do that?"

"No more bets!" the dealer shouted before tossing the ball onto the spinning roulette wheel.

Korey and the rest of the table leaned forward eagerly, while Cynthia closed her eyes and turned away, refusing to look. A hush fell over the table. They all watched as the ball bounced and the wheel spun around and around. Most of the people looked anxious as they watched, but a blissful calm fell over Korey. He had every confidence in this moment. He was as sure about this win as he was about his love for Cynthia and her love for him. The ball bounced, landed on red eighteen— then it bounced again.

"Black seventeen!" the dealer shouted before placing the marker on the winning number.

Korey's face fell. The crowd groaned.

That couldn't be right. He blinked in shock. His stomach plummeted.

"So I guess that's the end of your winning streak," a voice in his head mocked. "Let's hope you have better luck with Cindy than you have at the tables."

"Let's go," she whispered, making him turn to her. "Let's go back home now, Korey. I think we're done with Vegas and Vegas is done with us."

He slowly nodded.

Korey and Cynthia stepped off the elevator with bags in hand. They had both packed and already booked their flight back home. They were in a somber mood not only because they had finally given up their quixotic quest of finding the kids, but also because of the beating Korey had taken at the casino.

He still couldn't believe it. How had a cheapskate like him, who usually debated whether to supersize his meal because he wasn't sure if the larger size was worth the extra fifty cents, lost two thousand dollars and blown almost twenty thousand dollars in just a matter of hours? What had gotten into him?

"Cynthia Gibbons," the voice in his head said. "Or better yet, you got into her . . . and it made you stupid—as usual."

Well, maybe the euphoria of being in love again had made him dumb with his money, but it didn't mean he was also being dumb with his heart. He still believed they stood a good chance of making this work.

"Ready to check out?" he asked her.

"After I use the bathroom. You go ahead. I'll meet you at the desk."

Korey nodded and watched her disappear into the

ladies' room. He then tiredly walked to the reservation desk, distracted as he dug through his wallet looking for the key card to his room so that he could return it.

"Where did I put that thing," he muttered as he flipped through the wallet folds.

"Mr. Walker?"

Korey looked up to see a familiar face smiling at him. The woman behind the reservation desk waved.

"I thought it was you! How are you, Mr. Walker? It's good to see you again."

"Judy," he said, remembering the name of the hotel staffer who had checked him in the first night he arrived in Vegas. "It's good to see you again too."

"How can I help you?" she asked eagerly.

"Well, I was planning to check out."

She frowned. "You're leaving us already? That was such a brief stay!" She started to type into her touch screen.

"Not brief enough. I just lost my shirt down in the casino."

"Oh, I'm sure it wasn't *that* bad! You can make it back!"

"I doubt it. I blew almost twenty grand down there."

Her fingers paused over the glass screen. She breathed in audibly, then bit her pouty lower lip. "Twenty . . . *twenty thousand?*"

"Yeah, I don't think I'm willing to keep betting to try to make it back. Better just to quit now or you guys will own my house."

"I'm so sorry, Mr. Walker."

"Why are you apologizing? It's fine," he said, waving her condolence away. "It was my stupidity."

She hesitated, then leaned across the counter toward him. "Did you at least find your son?"

Korey shook his head. "Nope, no luck with that either . . . which is why I figured at this point, I'm pretty much done with Vegas. Better just to head home."

Her frown deepened. She looked down at her touch screen again, then looked over her shoulder. A white-haired gentleman Korey presumed was the hotel manager had been hovering nearby. One of the other staffers tapped him on his shoulder. He nodded then walked off. When he did, Judy turned back to Korey.

"Give me his name," she whispered.

"Huh? Whose name?"

"Your son . . . and the name of his guest. I can try to find him that way too."

Korey grinned. "Really? I thought you couldn't—"

"Shsssh!" She raised a finger to her lips. She took another furtive glance over her shoulder. "Just don't tell anyone I did this. Okay? I could lose my job!"

He eagerly nodded. "Don't worry. Believe me, I won't tell."

Chapter 24

Cynthia stepped through the bathroom door and watched as Korey went from a swift gate to a near run as he crossed the lobby and headed to her. He was grinning from ear to ear.

What's he so happy about?

He seemed awfully jubilant for a man who had just blown twenty-thousand dollars with the turn of a roulette wheel. Just thinking about it made Cynthia inwardly cringe. The thought of him blowing away that much money at the casino downstairs still made her sick to her stomach.

"Why?" a voice in her head chided. "You've never cared about a rich man's money before—unless he was spending it on *you!*"

But this was different. This was Korey. She didn't care how rich he was, though finding out he had that much money had been quite a surprise.

I told him I loved him, damn it, and I meant it, she thought.

And God help her, she did!

"Why are you smiling?" she asked him.

He swept her up in his arms, lifted her about a foot off the ground, and spun her around, catching her off guard. When he finally stopped, she stared at him, even more confused.

"Korey, *what* are you doing?"

"Kissing you," he whispered before bringing his mouth to hers.

Her eyelids fluttered closed, and she draped her arms around his neck, sinking into him as they kissed. Every limb of her body seemed to transform from hard bone and taut muscle to almost liquid. All thoughts momentarily left her.

Then, after what seemed like forever, he pulled his mouth away and slowly lowered her back to the floor. She gazed up at him dazedly.

He has to stop doing that or I won't be able to think straight!

"I found them," he whispered after licking his lips. "I found the kids!"

She suddenly stood ramrod straight. Her eyes bulged as she gaped at him.

"*You found them? Are you serious?*" she asked frantically, grabbing his shirt collar. "Where are they? How'd you find them? What—"

He gently tugged her hands away. "The woman at the check-in desk who I tried to butter up the first night we came here decided to show me some mercy. She gave me their room number."

Cynthia grinned and looked across the lobby at the receptionist, who was now handing key cards to a family of four.

"Remind me to send her a fruit basket and flowers in thanks!" Cynthia said.

"Hell, before you say thanks, we've got to get the

kids first. Come on!" Korey steered her toward the elevator doors and pressed the UP button. "They're in Room 1276." He glanced down at his wristwatch. "It's getting late. Maybe they're still upstairs. If we're lucky, we can catch them."

The elevator doors slowly opened, and Korey stepped forward, tugging her along with him.

"Wait! Wait! We're going up there *now?*" she asked, pulling back.

He stepped inside the elevator. "Of course we're going up there now. We don't want to miss them!"

"B-b-but what . . . what are we going to say if we find them?" She pulled him back into the hallway again. "We need to have some kind of a game plan. We can't just barge up there!"

"*Game plan?* What do you mean 'game plan?' What the hell are you talking about?"

"I mean we need to come up with a plan on how to do this? W-w-we need to, umm . . . we need to figure out how to, umm, how to . . ." She struggled to find the right words, and as she did, Korey narrowed his eyes at her.

"Cindy, what's wrong?"

"Nothing's wrong! I just . . . I just—"

"You're just what?" He looked exasperated. "We finally found the kids after all this time and after all this running around! This is what you wanted!" He paused to step aside as a formally dressed, older couple walked onto the elevator. "Or at least I thought it was. Now you want to stand here and talk about what to do next? Come up with a game plan? What sense does that make? Why are you stalling?"

Why was she stalling? Maybe because she had finally settled into the idea of giving up stopping the wedding and heading home, and now she had to suddenly shift gears again. Or maybe it was because she knew that if they went to the twelfth floor and managed to find the children, things would change between her and Korey. She'd have to confront not only Clarissa and Jared, but also her biggest fear—that Korey was Clarissa's father. Korey would have to finally know the secret Cynthia had been harboring all this time.

No, he doesn't! I don't have to say a damn thing about any of that, she thought.

"You can't keep this secret forever, girl," the voice in her head argued. "It's not fair to him or Clarissa."

"Pardon me, but are you getting on?" asked an older gentleman, making Cynthia blink in surprise. The gentleman leaned out of the elevator car, held open the door, and gazed at Cynthia and Korey expectantly.

Korey turned to him and nodded. "Uh, yeah . . . yeah, we are. Thanks for waiting." He turned back to Cynthia and inclined his head toward the elevator. "Come on."

Cynthia sighed, then stepped in front of him, easing into the space beside the couple, who waited patiently. Korey followed her.

The four rode in silence. With each ascending floor, Cynthia felt a growing sense of dread. She glanced anxiously at Korey's profile as he stared up at the digital screen that ticked away the numbers.

When all of this is over, she thought, *please don't hate me, baby.*

The doors slowly opened and Korey stepped out. Cynthia slowly followed him, feeling a lump form in her throat.

He glanced up at the plaques on the wall, looking at the arrows and the lists of room numbers. "This way," he said, pointing to his right.

They walked down the hall, passing a man in uniform who was pushing a room service cart laden with trays and dirty linen. He nodded at them in greeting.

As they drew close to Room 1276, Cynthia grabbed Korey's arm, making him halt and turn to her in puzzlement.

"What?" He frowned. "What now?"

She had to tell him! She couldn't let him find out this way.

"Korey, I . . . I have . . . I want to . . ."

But she couldn't say the words. No matter how hard she tried, they wouldn't come out.

"Cindy, seriously, what is wrong? You're starting to worry me."

"I . . . I love you, Korey," she whispered. "I always have. But I have to te—"

"And I love you too," he said, cutting her off. He leaned down and lightly brushed her lips. "Now let's go get the kids so we can finally fly the hell home." He abruptly turned and knocked on the door, standing back from the peephole.

"Room service!" he said in a high-pitched, nasal voice that was almost comical.

Cynthia would have laughed if she didn't feel as if she was going to vomit at any moment. Why hadn't he let her finish saying what she needed to say?

"Oh, man, right on time!" someone on the other side of the door shouted. "I hope you brought more towels!"

Cynthia heard a lock click. The door opened. A young man stood in the doorway in a white terrycloth bathrobe, smiling. He was pulling a ten-dollar bill out of the bathrobe's pocket, presumably a tip that he had intended to hand to room service. But when the young man saw who was standing in front of him, his smile instantly disappeared. He gaped, and the ten-dollar bill fell from his hand and fluttered to the carpeted floor.

"Pops?" he squeaked.

Korey's jaw clenched as he glared at his son. "Jared."

Jared blinked. His Adam's apple bobbed up and down as he swallowed. "What are you . . . I-I mean . . . How did you . . . I-I-I mean . . . What—"

"Did they bring more towels?" Clarissa called.

At the sound of her daughter's voice, Cynthia snapped out of her malaise.

"Get out of my way!" Cynthia shouted, stopping Jared mid-stutter. She shoved the young man aside and rushed into the hotel room, with Korey trailing behind her.

"Clarissa, baby, where are you?" Cynthia yelled.

"Ma?"

Cynthia followed the sound of her daughter's voice. She rounded a corner into the hotel suite's small living room. When she walked through another door and saw Clarissa sitting on the satin bedspread, which was covered with red rose petals, and that the young woman was also wearing a bathrobe, Cynthia almost fainted.

Oh, my God, she thought frantically. *I'm too late! I'm too late!*

She then made the mistake of turning to look at what Clarissa had been watching on the bedroom's television. When she saw the leather-clad male and female trio going at it on the television screen, her eyes almost bulged out of her head.

"Oh, my God!" Cynthia cried.

"What?" Korey shouted, running into the bedroom. "What's wrong?" When he stood beside her, he followed Cynthia's gaze and almost choked with laughter at the movie Clarissa was watching. When Cynthia turned her glare on him, he stopped laughing, then shrugged.

"Sorry, but I warned you," he whispered.

"Ma? Mr. Walker? What . . . what are you guys doing here?" Clarissa asked, quickly turning off the television. She set her half-filled champagne glass on the night table and rose from the bed. She held the lapels of her bathrobe together and tightened the belt around her waist. "How . . . how did you find us?"

"How did I find you?" Cynthia yelled. "How did I find you? You run away like a thief in the night and I don't know if you're dead or alive and that's all you have to say is, 'How did I find you?' What the hell were you thinking, Clarissa, running away to Las Vegas with this boy?"

"I'm not a boy," Jared said indignantly. He stepped into the bedroom and walked toward Clarissa. He then wrapped an arm protectively around Clarissa's shoulder and puffed out his chest. "I'm a man."

"A man?" Korey snorted. "Jared, I can barely get you to take out the trash most days, and doesn't your mama still pack your lunch for you at home?"

"None of that matters!" Jared argued. "I'm a man and . . . and Clarissa and I are in love. We came here to get married!"

Cynthia was starting to feel faint again. She grabbed the bedroom door handle to steady herself. "Did you get married?" she asked quietly, terrified to hear the answer.

Clarissa slowly shook her head. She stared down at the floor. "No, I chickened out at the last minute."

"But we're going to try again tomorrow!" Jared said. "We said we'd give it a few days and try again. And you can't stop us!" He glared at both parents. "Legally, we can get married. We don't need your permission."

Cynthia fought down the bile that was rising in her throat. She took another step toward her daughter. "Baby, just answer one question . . . did you or did you not have sex with Jared?"

"*Ugh,* Ma!" Clarissa exclaimed in disgust, with a curl in her lip. She rolled her eyes again.

Korey loudly released a breath. "Cindy, come on . . ."

"Just answer the question, Clarissa!" Cynthia screamed.

Clarissa stomped her foot. "Why do you care if Jared and I had sex? It's not like I'm a virgin!"

Jared frowned. He dropped his hand from Clarissa's shoulder. "Wait, you weren't a virgin? I thought you said you were! Damn it, I knew you were lying!"

"Honey, can we not talk about this right now?" Clarissa asked.

Jared crossed his arms over his chest and silently fumed.

"Ma, you're just going to have to get over it, okay?" Clarissa said, putting her hands on her hips. "Stop trying to run my life! I know what I'm doing! What difference does it make if Jared and I have sex? We're getting married . . . at the same age that you got married, I might add! I know how to—"

"It makes a big damn difference!" Cynthia screeched tearfully. "It makes a big damn difference because you can't have sex with your brother! You can't marry your brother!"

The room fell silent. Korey, Clarissa, and Jared stared at Cynthia, absolutely speechless.

"*What?*" Korey asked. His voice was barely above a whisper. "What did you just say?"

Cynthia couldn't answer him. She was sobbing too much. She raised her fist to her mouth and bit down on her knuckle to stifle the sobs, but it didn't matter. They were coming out anyway. He grabbed her shoulders and whipped her around to face him. His grip around her arms tightened as he gazed into her watery eyes.

"Cindy, did you just say Jared was Clarissa's *brother?*"

She continued to weep helplessly.

"Nod yes or no, damn it!" he ordered, shaking her like a rag doll.

"I don't know!" she cried. Her mascara ran in muddy streaks down her cheeks and over her chin. "I don't know! He might be!"

"*He might be?* What the hell does that mean?"

"Oh, God, I think I'm going to throw up!" Clarissa garbled as she rushed to the hotel's bathroom. While she retched over the bathroom toilet, Jared slowly sat down on the edge of the hotel bed, looking more than just a little dazed.

"I don't know if he's her brother . . . I mean her half brother," Cynthia said as Korey finally released her. "The last time you and I slept together was . . . was about a week before the first time I slept with Bill. When I found out a month later that I was pregnant, I didn't know which one of you was the father!"

"I thought when we were together you were on the pill!"

"I was"—Cynthia paused—"kinda. I was never very good at taking it all the time, though."

Korey closed his eyes. His hands fell to his sides.

"I wanted to tell you, Korey! I did! But then I found out that you were going to marry Vivian and I thought I had lost you anyway, s-so . . ."

"So?"

"So I thought I might as well stick with Bill."

His shoulders sank.

"Korey, please see it my way. I thought you had cheated on me with Vivian! I couldn't go crawling back to you. I was already engaged to Bill. I didn't know what else to do! I thought I would . . . I would just have to get over it and move on."

He finally opened his eyes. When he did, she could see so much fury in them that it scared her. "Move on with my child, you mean."

"But we don't know that for sure! Clarissa might not be yours, and I didn't want to open a can of worms unless I knew for sure. Plus, you were away. You had your own life and I had mine! I didn't know you didn't cheat on me! I didn't know you'd get a divorce and move back to Chesterton! How was I supposed to know you would come back?" she cried hysterically. "How was I supposed to know Clarissa and Jared would meet each other and fall in love? I had no idea this would happen, Korey!"

His nostrils flared as he balled his fists at his sides. For a split second, she thought he was going to hit her, but he didn't. He unclenched his fists, took a deep, steadying breath, and faced his son.

"Jared, I want you to pack up all your stuff and meet me down in the lobby in thirty minutes."

"I've committed incest," Jared muttered dully. "I'm going to *hell!*"

"Jared, did you hear me?" Korey snapped.

Jared blinked and looked up at his father. "Huh?"

"Pack your things and meet me downstairs in thirty minutes."

Jared frowned. "But—"

"No buts! If I don't see you downstairs in half an hour, I'm coming back up here to get you myself. And heaven help you if I have to do that."

Korey's tone and face must have shown how serious he was about following up on that threat. Jared hastily nodded and stood up from the bed. He walked to the corner of the bedroom and grabbed a black suitcase.

Cynthia watched as Korey turned and walked out of the bedroom. She trailed behind him, following him into the suite's living room.

"Korey!"

He didn't stop his angry strides. She sniffed, reached out, and touched his shoulder.

"Korey, please wait. I know you're—"

"Don't touch me," he said menacingly as he whipped around to face her. "Don't you *ever* touch me again, you selfish . . . manipulative . . . psychotic bitch! Or I swear I'll . . ." His jaw tightened. "I should have known hooking up with you again would only lead to this shit! You're fucking toxic!"

"I didn't mean to hurt you," she said as she wept. "Please, believe me! Really, I didn't."

"Oh, bullshit! That song is so tired! You suspected *all* these years that I was Clarissa's father and you didn't say a damn thing! Not one damn word! No wonder you were so freaked out about her and Jared hooking up! Well, you didn't stop it! They had sex! Now all of us will have to go to therapy!" He turned back around. "Stay the hell away from me!"

He then stalked out the room and slammed the door behind him.

Cynthia slowly walked to the suite's sofa and sat down. She stared bleakly at the wall. Honesty was the best policy—or so the saying goes. So why had things blown up in her face when she finally told the truth? Why had she fallen in love only to have her heart broken all over again?

Chapter 25

It was a warm, luminous day outside the glass walls of Yolanda Gibbons's sunroom, but the mood inside was far from sunny. The room was relatively quiet, with the exception of the sound of cutlery clinking against porcelain, the soft tinkling of glasses, and the occasional clearing of someone's throat. No one talked. Most rarely looked up from their meals to gaze at one another and instead seemed totally engrossed with their bacon, eggs, and cups of coffee.

Yolanda glanced around the table at her guests, sat back in her rattan chair, and folded her arms over her chest. She slowly shook her coiffed, curly head.

"Well, is this a Saturday brunch or a funeral, I ask you?" she murmured, her voice echoing in the quiet room.

No one responded.

"So is this what I have to look forward to from now on?" Yolanda persisted. "Just the sound of my own voice?"

"We're all dealing with a lot right now, Mama,"

Lauren explained, taking a hesitant glance at her husband, who seemed to be avoiding her gaze. "None of us are . . . well, none of us are really in a talkative mood."

Particularly Cris . . . He hadn't spoken to and barely looked at Lauren for the past couple of weeks. She supposed she deserved it. She had picked a fight with him, and now it looked like she was the cause of all his troubles. She and her family probably would be the reason Cris would lose the mayoral election.

They still didn't know who had created the "Chesterton Scandals" Web site, though Lauren had her suspicions that Mayor Knightly was the mastermind behind it. But who had done it was irrelevant. Whoever had created the Web site had achieved their purpose. The gossip mill was churning full throttle in Chesterton thanks to the site's debut. Old rumors were being whispered again, and the focus seemed to be less on how great a guy Cris was and how great a town leader he would be, and more on the unsavory exploits of Lauren and her sisters. Mayor Knightly had said that Chesterton needed a mayor *and* a mayor's wife who represented traditional values, community, and a sense of morality. Someone had made it abundantly clear that Lauren didn't fit the bill.

Meanwhile, Cynthia and Clarissa were dealing with their own fallout from their disastrous trip to Las Vegas a few weeks ago. Mother and daughter were barely on speaking terms, Clarissa was no longer returning Jared's phone calls, and Cynthia had received a terse letter from Korey Walker's lawyer requesting a blood test to prove paternity. They were currently awaiting test results.

The family was still stunned and confused at the news that Korey could be Clarissa's father. No one had heard of the man before a few weeks ago, though Dawn vaguely remembered hearing Cynthia mention a boy of that name a few times back when they were teenagers.

"But I don't remember her saying anything about seriously dating him," Dawn had said over the phone a couple days ago. "I certainly had no idea he was her baby daddy!"

Lauren gazed across the table at Cynthia, who was making a poor show of pretending to eat her brunch. Lauren shook her head in bewilderment. How had Cynthia managed to keep such a big secret for this long? Doing something similar would have eaten up Lauren from the inside out.

"Like you've never kept secrets," a voice in her head ridiculed. "You keep secrets from Cris all the time! He still doesn't know why you're really angry at him."

She lowered her eyes at the Chenille tablecloth. No, he didn't, and that made her feel even worse. She promised him that she would always be honest with him, and once again, she was breaking that promise.

"Well, I hope everyone's mood improves soon," Yolanda proclaimed as she tossed aside her linen napkin and pushed back her chair. She rose from the table. "Because I swear I've gotten more laughs and conversation at a wake!"

With that, the brunch had ended. The maids collected the last of the half-eaten plates of food and tepid cups of coffee. Stephanie, Dawn, Cynthia, and their respective families mumbled their good-byes before shuffling out of the sunroom. Lauren, Cris, and Crisanto Jr. were the last to leave. When they did, Lauren paused at the corridor leading out of the sunroom to speak with her mother.

"I'm sorry today's brunch was such a bust," Lauren said as she cradled her slumbering son to her chest.

Yolanda adoringly ran her hand over Cris Jr.'s head, then shrugged. "Oh, it's fine. I know how it goes. You and your sisters worry too much about things that'll be taken care of with time. You must get it from your fathers, because you certainly didn't get that worry-wart gene from me."

"But things won't just be 'taken care of,' Mama. It's not like any of us can wave some magic wand to fix all this stuff. Cris could lose the election! Cindy doesn't even know who's the father of her child, and—"

Yolanda held up a hand, closed her eyes, and nodded. "All these things will be settled with time, Laurie. Trust me. I've been through enough paternity suits to know not to get in a tizzy over it. And as far as the election, well . . ." She opened her eyes, inclined her head, and smiled. "Everyone will get their justice due. You'll see. Don't worry." She patted Lauren on the shoulder. "Now you two drive carefully. Don't forget to take some leftovers with you."

Lauren walked away from her mother, sighing in exasperation. Of course Yolanda didn't think any of this was that big of a deal! Whenever she had a problem, she simply had one of her men write a check or make a phone call to fix it. But none of the fixes would be that simple this time.

Ten minutes later, Lauren and Cris drove in their Aston Martin in silence back to their home a few miles away. Lauren glanced in the rearview mirror to find Cris Jr. still slumbering quietly in his car seat in the back. She then glanced at her husband. He looked tired.

On impulse, she reached out and placed a hand on his knee to comfort him. To her surprise, he reached down and placed a hand over hers and squeezed it.

"I'm sorry," she whispered, feeling as if those words were long overdue, feeling as if a massive weight had been lifted off her shoulders.

"Sorry about what?"

"About storming out of the bedroom a few weeks ago. About making you think that I was angry at you for meeting with Marvin and his wife when I was really just being insecure and frustrated with the same ol' . . . the same ol' small-town nonsense." She let her head fall back against the leather headrest. "I'm sorry I wasn't honest with you—and honest with myself. I'm so, *so* sorry, Cris."

"I just don't understand how you could ever think I would put Marvin Payton's opinion—or anyone else's, for that matter—above my love for you. I mean . . . damn, baby—"

"Say 'doody'," she whispered, glancing over her shoulder at Cris Jr. "Remember, we said we would watch our language in front of him."

"He's asleep," Cris said tightly. "I'm not going to say 'doody' when I mean 'damn,' because 'damn' is what I mean. What else do we have to go through for me to prove myself to you?"

"You don't have to prove anything!"

"So why are you still questioning me?"

"I'm not, Cris! I swear I'm not!"

He pulled his hand away. She watched him gnaw the inside of his cheek. He didn't look convinced.

"I'm . . . I'm questioning myself, like I always have." She released a long, slow breath. "And it's getting so goddamn old."

Great, now even *she* was cursing.

The car turned onto the gravel road leading to their mansion.

"I don't know what to tell you, Lauren. We've been through this before. You're not going to change people's minds. You're just going to have to accept that."

"But it holds you back! They're turning against you because of me and—"

"And it's their loss! I knew that coming in, before I even agreed to run for mayor." He glanced at her and then returned his attention to the road. "Look, you're my wife. We're a package deal. If they can't accept you, then they can't accept me. That's it!"

"Even if it means you lose the election?"

"Even if it means I lose! I don't give a fuck, Lauren!" he shouted, making her bring her finger to her lips. She pointed over her shoulder at their son.

"There are worse things," he said in a lower voice, ". . . like finding out you're the father to a kid who you didn't even know existed."

Lauren winced. She knew he was referring to Cynthia. "That's a low blow, Cris. Cindy didn't—"

"Didn't what? Didn't know she had been lying to the man all this time?" He curled his lip in disgust. "Come on, baby, I know you want to defend your sister, but even you have to admit that was some shady shit she pulled."

"And she feels bad about it."

"Yeah, I bet she does. Now that her ass got caught!"

"She didn't get caught! She doesn't even know for sure if he's Clarissa's dad! Besides, either way, she and Clarissa need our support. This is a very—" Lauren paused midsentence as her cell phone began to ring. She frowned, reached inside her purse, and pulled out her iPhone. She stared down at the name and number on the screen. "Speak of the devil. It's Cindy."

"Satan herself, you mean," Cris mumbled.

Lauren gave him the side eye, then pressed the green button to answer the call. "Hey, Cindy, what's up?"

"It's here," Cindy answered. Her voice was tense.

"What's here?"

"The paternity test result!" Cindy cried shrilly. "We just got it in the mail!"

"Uh-oh," Lauren whispered, making Cris frown at her in confusion.

"What's wrong?" he mouthed. She quickly shook her head.

"Oh, God, Laurie, what if the results show that Korey's the father?" Cynthia sniffed on the other end of the line. "Girl, I am terrified to open this thing!"

"Give me a half an hour," Lauren said. "I'm coming over there."

Chapter 26

"**O**kay," Lauren said as she dropped her purse onto the foyer table and Cynthia closed the front door behind her. "Where is it?"

"In here," Cynthia whispered as they walked into her French county kitchen, where Clarissa sat on one of the stools, staring at the certified envelope on the butcher block as though it contained some unknown explosive that could go off at any second.

Just looking at the envelope made Cynthia ill. How had things gotten this bad? Why was Korey putting them through this?

"Because he has the right to know if he's Clarissa's father," a voice in her head reminded her.

"Hi, honey," Lauren said before resting her hand on Clarissa's arm.

Clarissa jumped in surprise as if she hadn't noticed her aunt come up behind her. "Hi, Aunt Lauren," she mumbled.

"So . . ." Lauren's eyes shifted between the two women. "You guys ready to do this?"

"I guess," Clarissa said. She then reached for the manila envelope, turning it around and around.

Cynthia bit down hard on her bottom lip, waiting for her daughter to open it. She watched, dejected, as Clarissa sat the envelope back down on the kitchen island and slowly slid it toward her. "You open it, Ma."

"You want me to do it? W-w-why?"

"Because I can't," Clarissa answered softly. "I'm too scared to read it."

Cynthia stared at her daughter, then the envelope. The kitchen fell silent again.

"Well? Are you going to open it?" Lauren asked.

Cynthia picked up the envelope. She took a deep breath, deciding to just bite the bullet. She ripped open the side.

What if it's true? What if Korey really is her father? It's going to devastate Clarissa. It's gonna break her heart!

Cynthia paused just before she slid out the papers inside. Her hands began to shake. She sat the envelope back on the counter and shook her blond head.

"I can't do it, Laurie. I can't read that thing! You do it."

"*What?* But it's not my test!"

"What affects one of us, affects all of us, right?" Cynthia asked. "Hasn't that always been the case? All for one, and one for all. That's how we do things in this family."

Lauren's lips formed into a grim line. After some time, she nodded. "Okay. I'll do it."

Cynthia held her breath again, and Clarissa closed her eyes as Lauren slid out the papers, letting them fall to the butcher block. Silently, Cynthia prayed for it to say that Korey wasn't a match. She apologized for past mistakes and rash decisions. She promised God that if

He got her out of this jam she would change her ways. No more man-hunting. No more lies. She'd become a chaste woman, and she would focus on being the best mother she could be and making amends to Korey for keeping her secret fears from him for so long.

Cynthia watched as Lauren scanned a few lines of text. She couldn't read her sister's facial expression, adding to her frustration.

"*Well?* What does it say, Laurie?" Cynthia asked.

Lauren slowly lowered the sheet of paper back to the island. "Ninety-nine point five percent match."

Clarissa's eyelashes fluttered open. Her brows furrowed in confusion. "So what . . . what does that mean? Are they saying that Mr. Walker is my dad?"

Lauren paused, then nodded.

Clarissa clutched the edge of the counter. She lowered her eyes.

"Oh, baby . . . honey." Cynthia walked around the island with her arms outstretched, wanting to comfort Clarissa. "I'm so sorry. I didn't—"

Clarissa's face hardened. She stepped out of her mother's grasp. Cynthia watched, feeling the acute sting of rejection as her daughter ran for the staircase. Her hands fell to her sides while she watched Clarissa race up the stairs to the second floor.

"Just give her some time," Lauren said softly from behind her when they heard Clarissa's door slam. "It's a lot to take in."

"No shit!" Cynthia snapped. When she saw Lauren frown, she shook her head. "I'm sorry. I didn't mean that. I'm just . . ." She dropped her head into her hands. "God, Laurie, why is this happening? Why was I so . . . so *stupid?* I should have known Korey would be her father! Of course, he would be!" she shouted as she paced back and forth in front of the kitchen's bay window. "It seems like if there's a worst-case scenario, then it's going to happen to me!"

"It's not just happening to you, Cindy. It's affecting a lot of other people too. What about Clarissa . . . or Korey, for that matter? He's about to find out that he has a daughter he didn't even know existed until a few months ago. Not to mention poor Jared." She made a *tsk, tsk* sound. "He had the crappy luck to fall in love with his own sister!"

Cynthia stopped pacing. "Yeah, I get it. It's all my fault. Thank you very much for pointing that out!"

"I'm not saying it's all your fault." Lauren wavered. "Well, okay, maybe it is *a little*. I mean . . . if you had just come clean in the beginning when you found out you were pregnant and let Korey know he might be the father, you could have—"

"Laurie, I know I messed up! Okay? You're supposed to be making me feel better, damn it! Not worse!"

"Okay, okay." Lauren held up her hands. "I'm just saying you could have handled it better, but I know you were eighteen years old back then. You did what you thought was best at the time, I guess. You can't beat yourself up over mistakes you made in the past. What's done is done. You guys just have to move forward from this."

"But how can I? Clarissa's had her heart broken, and I have too!"

"What do you mean? Why is your heart broken?"

"Because I've been in love with the same man for the past twenty damn years, and now he's dumped me! Because I thought I finally had a chance to experience something legitimate, long-lasting, and real with him, and now it's over! And it's all my damn fault! It's all my fault! That's what I mean!"

"Wait! Wait, back up! You were *in love* with him . . . with Korey, you mean?"

"Yes, Korey! Who the hell else would I be talking about?"

Lauren gazed at her in shock.

"Why are you looking at me like that? Is it so hard to believe that I fell for someone?"

Lauren paused. "Well, frankly . . . yeah."

"Oh, thanks a lot." Cynthia glanced at the staircase. "I'm going to check on Clarissa."

"Okay," Lauren muttered, still looking stunned, "I'll be down here if you need me."

Seconds later, Cynthia knocked on Clarissa's bedroom door. "Baby, can I come in?"

Clarissa didn't respond, but the door was unlocked, so Cynthia went inside the bedroom anyway. She found Clarissa splayed across her satin bedspread with her head buried in one of her lace-edged decorative pillows. The young woman was sobbing.

"Oh, honey," she said, rushing across the room. She sat on the edge of the bed and instantly noticed that Clarissa clutched a cordless phone in her hand. It was beeping, as though Clarissa had left it off the hook. Cynthia took the phone away and hung it up before putting it back in its charger on Clarissa's night table. She then rubbed Clarissa's back. "Baby, please don't cry." She sniffed and felt tears well in her own eyes. "If you keep crying, I'm gonna lose it too."

Clarissa mumbled something into her pillow, making Cynthia frown.

"What did you say, honey? I didn't hear you."

Clarissa slowly raised her head. "I said I broke up with him. I called Jared, and I broke up with him." She wiped at her runny nose. "I told him we got the results today, and I said I couldn't be with him anymore."

"I'm sorry to hear that, sweetheart."

"No, you're not!" Clarissa shouted, pushing herself away from her pillow. "You're not sorry! You've wanted us to break up all along—and now you finally got what you wanted!"

"But I didn't want to see you hurt. I wanted to avoid this. Really, I did. Why would I want something like this to happen?"

Clarissa stilled. She started to pick at one of the loose strings on her pillowcase. "Jared didn't want to break up. He said . . . he said he didn't care that I'm his sister. I told him he would care if we had mutant babies," she muttered. "I said I would always love him. I'd just have to love him . . . like a sister. He didn't like that. He . . . he hung up on me." Her shoulders trembled. She turned her face away and started to cry again. Cynthia wrapped Clarissa in her arms and let her sob on her shoulder. "But I don't love him like a sister! I still want to be with him, and now it's sick and it's gross and I . . . I . . ."

Cynthia shushed her and rubbed her head as she wept.

"Please, Ma, can you leave me alone?" Clarissa asked, pushing Cynthia away. "Just . . . just leave me alone, okay?"

Cynthia hesitated then nodded. She rose from the bed. "All right, honey. If that's what you want."

She walked across the bedroom and closed the door behind her, shutting out the sound of her daughter's sobs. She stood in the hallway, feeling a profound sense of loss descend over her. Cynthia hadn't felt this helpless in quite a long time.

Chapter 27

With a heavy heart, Korey watched as his son loaded a collection of video games into a cardboard box. Jared unrolled a strip of masking tape and taped the lid shut, running his hand over the seam. He then climbed to his feet, carrying the heavy box in his arms.

"I can take that for you," Korey said softly, stepping forward.

"I got it," Jared snapped, pulling the box out of his father's reach. Jared walked around Korey and into the hallway. He then sat the box next to the others that were stacked already in the living room, creating a mini-tower of cardboard.

Jared had been snapping at Korey a lot lately. Harsh words were the only thing he seemed to have for his father now that they had gotten the paternity test results and discovered that Clarissa was indeed Korey's daughter. Korey found out that Clarissa had broken up with Jared as soon as she heard the news. He could understand why. Siblings couldn't date—no matter what the mitigating circumstances were. But that didn't mean Jared's heart understood.

This is a big mess, Korey thought with frustration as he looked around him at the bare walls and half-empty floor of his son's bedroom. And he couldn't fix any of it.

Jared was moving out. He said there was no reason to come back to Chesterton now that this had happened. He had no desire to run into Clarissa again, though the fact was, now that they were brother and sister, it would be nearly impossible to avoid each other completely. But Korey respected his son's decision, even if it hurt him to see Jared go.

"I think that's the last of it," Jared mumbled, just as his mother threw open Korey's front door.

"Where's my baby?" Vivian shouted. "Where is he?" She opened her arms and ran toward Jared, making Korey roll his eyes heavenward and Jared cringe.

Vivian was wearing one of her colorful ensembles today, an orange and red dress that hugged her body like Saran Wrap. In her younger days, it may have been flattering, even sexy. But Vivian had put on quite a few pounds in the last two decades, and the dress did nothing for her now ample frame. Korey supposed she tried to deflect attention from her expanding waistline with the teased wigs she always seemed to wear now. He was surprised she made it through the front door with the big curls she wore today.

"Hey, Viv," he muttered halfheartedly.

She glared at him. "I'll deal with you later." She then returned her attention to their son. "Don't worry, honey! Mama will take care of everything!"

She wrapped Jared in her arms like a swaddled babe and planted a kiss on his cheek, leaving a smear of red lipstick near his chin. Jared instantly shrugged out of his mother's grasp.

"I'm fine, Mom."

"You don't look fine!" she exclaimed. "And you didn't sound fine on the phone either! What the hell happened?" She turned and faced Korey with her hands on her hips. "What did you do to my baby? I knew it was a mistake having him stay here all the—"

"He didn't do anything," Jared said tightly. "I just . . . I just wanna go home. That's all."

"Uh-huh," she murmured, sounding far from convinced. "Well, you are coming home—*permanently*. Harvey's here," she said, referring to her husband. She gestured toward the front door. "He brought the van so we can load all of your things and make just one trip."

Jared nodded and began to pick up one of his boxes.

"Please don't do this, son," Korey pled, taking a step toward Jared and feeling his heart break. "I know you're hurt by how all this has gone down, but we can work it out somehow. Don't just—"

"Work it out how, Pops? Just how are we supposed to work this out, huh?"

Korey fell silent.

"I told you I can't stay in Chesterton! If Clarissa's going to be anywhere around here, I damn sure don't wanna be here too."

Vivian frowned at the mention of a girl's name. "Who's Clarissa?"

"She's nobody," Korey answered hastily, not wanting to get Vivian further involved in the drama.

"No one, huh? I bet! Is she one of your hussies, Korey? Are you throwing my son over for some woman?" She crossed her arms over her bountiful chest. "Is *that* what this is all about?"

"Viv, you know damn well—"

"Korey Walker, I should have known you—"

"She's Pops's daughter, all right?" Jared shouted, cutting them both off.

"What?" Vivian squawked, now resembling a barnyard rooster in both colors and sound.

Korey closed his eyes. "Jared . . ."

"She's his daughter and . . . and . . ." Jared took a deep breath. "She and I were going to get married, Mom."

"What?"

"Look, I didn't know she was Pops's daughter when we first started going out. No one did. But now we do, and Clarissa doesn't want to be engaged anymore. She said we can't."

"You're damn right you can't! Not if I have anything to say about it!" Vivian shouted, pointing her finger at Jared. "You're too young to be tied down to some fast-tailed hussy anyway, baby!"

"Tied down to some fast-tailed hussy? Viv, did you just hear what the boy said? Don't you get it? They're brother and sister! They can't date anymore or get married because it would be incest. *That's* why they broke up!"

She paused and looked at both men. "So that's what this is about? Jared wants to leave because he thinks what he and this girl did was incest."

"I don't *think* it, Mom. I did it. Multiple times," he mumbled. "Look, can I just take my stuff to the car now?"

Vivian grimaced. "You're really upset by this, aren't you, baby?" she asked softly, staring at his face.

He hesitated, then finally nodded. "I really liked her, Mom."

"All packed and ready to go?" Harvey asked. The squat, balding man walked through the front door. He rubbed his hands eagerly and looked around the room. "What do you need me to—"

"Hold on," Viv said softly, holding up a hand. "Give us a few more minutes, honey."

Harvey's round face creased into a frown as he watched his wife walk across the living room. "What's the matter?"

"Nothing. Nothing. Just wait for us in the van, will you?"

"Wait in the van?" Harvey paused. "Why?"

"'Cuz I just need you to," Vivian said firmly.

Harvey glanced at Korey and Jared, silently seeking an answer from them. Korey shrugged. He was just as confused as Harvey was. But Harvey knew there was a limit to how much he could question Vivian. She wore the size forty pants in their house.

"All right then," Harvey mumbled. "I'll wait for you outside."

After Harvey left, Vivian lowered herself onto Korey's plaid love seat. "I have to sit down. Both of you should sit down too."

Korey furrowed his brows. "Why do we need to sit down?"

"Because I have to tell you both something."

Korey didn't like the sound of that. "If it's all right with you, Viv, I think I'll stand."

"I think I'll stand too," Jared echoed, after lowering his cardboard box back to the floor.

"Fine. Have it your way." She started to wring her plump hands. "Well, you see . . . you see, the thing is, Jared, baby. Well—"

"Damn it, Viv, just spit it out! What is it?"

She puffed out her chest and glared at Korey. "Fine, I'll just come out with it. Jared couldn't have done any incest with that girl, because she's not his sister."

"Of course she's his sister! She's his half sister because they both have the same father!" He pointed at his chest. "Me!"

"No, they don't," she said through clenched teeth.

"Mom, what are you saying?"

She shifted forward on the love seat and gazed up at her son. "Jared, honey, Korey isn't your father."

At those words, Korey felt the blood drain from his head. He grabbed the wall behind him to steady himself.

"I wanted him to be," she continued. "That's why I chose him. I knew he would be a good daddy to you and take care of us." She curled her lip. "He was much better than your real father—Dustin Graves."

"Dustin Graves?" Korey shouted. "You mean *Boogie?"*

Jared cringed. "My father's name was Boogie?"

"Viv, that guy was the biggest damn pothead in our high school!"

She sucked her teeth. "He wasn't always high! When he wasn't smoking, he was actually pretty nice." She shrugged. "But he was too irresponsible. He couldn't take care of himself, let alone a wife and child. I knew when I got pregnant by him that I had made a mistake—a *big* mistake." She turned to Korey. "So a few days later, when I heard that you and Cynthia had broken up, I knew you were back on the market. I figured that was my chance."

Korey closed his eyes and ran his hand over his face, fighting to hold back his burgeoning anger. First, Cynthia had lied to him about having his baby, then Vivian had lied about having someone else's! Did these women know something about him that he didn't? Did he walk around with the word "sucker" printed on a sign clipped to his shirt?

"So you lied to me. You seduced me and made me have sex with you so I'd think Jared was my child?"

"I didn't *make* you do anything! I don't remember you fighting me off, honey! You were just as eager to get into my pants as I was to get to that big dick of yours!"

"Mom!" Jared shouted, cringing in disgust. "Come on! I don't wanna hear that!"

Viv sheepishly glanced at her son. "Well, it's true. I was just defending myself."

"What is *wrong* with you people? Have you ever heard of condoms?" Jared ranted. "And how is this story supposed to make me feel better? You're telling me that Pops isn't my dad! You telling me that my real father is some dude named Boogie?"

"No, I *am* your dad, Jared." He walked toward his son and placed his hands on the young man's shoulders. "I don't care what the hell your mother says. You have my last name. I raised you and I love you. You are my son."

"But not by blood," Vivian said quietly. "So you see, it wasn't incest. You don't have to worry about that anymore." She grunted as she pushed herself up from the love seat. She fluffed the curls in her wig as she walked toward the front door. "Now when we head home, I'll tell you whatever else you wanna know, baby. Whatever questions you have, I'll—"

"I'm not going home," Jared said, slowly shaking his head.

Vivian stopped in her tracks and turned around to face her son. "Huh?"

"I said I'm not going home with you. I'm . . . I'm staying here—with Pops."

The weight in Korey's chest suddenly lightened. For the first time in days, he smiled.

Vivian dropped her hands to her hips. "But I told you that Korey isn't your daddy! He's not—"

"Yes, he is. He's the only father I've ever known, and I bet he's a better dad than some pothead." Jared turned to Korey. "Can you help me carry my stuff back in my room, Pops?"

Korey's smile widened. "I'd be happy to."

Vivian's mouth fell open. She began to sputter.

"I'll give you a call later, Mom." Jared picked up one of the boxes and began to walk back down the hall to his bedroom. "It probably won't be until late to-night. I've got a few things I've gotta do."

"B-but . . . what about . . . I thought you—"

"Well, it was nice seeing you, Viv," Korey said. He leaned down, grabbed one of the boxes, and winked at her. "You and Harvey have a safe drive home."

He then turned around, still grinning as his ex-wife stammered and fumed.

Chapter 28

Cynthia was working in her flower garden and kneeling in potting soil when she heard her doorbell ring. She laid down her spade, waved away an annoying fruit fly, and lifted the front of her wide-brimmed straw hat. She turned to look at the glass door on her sundeck.

"Clarissa, can you get that, honey?" Cynthia shouted. She then returned her attention to her small pots of geraniums.

The doorbell rang again, making her frown. "Clarissa? Honey, can you get the door?"

When it rang a third time, Cynthia sighed. She should have known Clarissa wouldn't answer. Her daughter had been holed up in her room for the past few days. She had only left to eat or use the bathroom. Cynthia was starting to seriously worry about her.

Cynthia tugged off her gardening gloves and, with a grunt, climbed to her feet. She rubbed her sore back, adjusted the straps of her gingham halter top and the hem of her jean shorts before wiping off the dirt from her knees and shins. She climbed the steps of her sundeck and opened the glass door leading to the sunroom. The doorbell was still ringing when she swung open the front door seconds later.

She found her sister Dawn standing on her welcome mat in a canary-yellow, one-shoulder silk top, tight-fitting navy sailor shorts, and platform canvas sandals. The beautiful vision, who looked like she had just stepped out of a fashion magazine, was smiling.

"Well, it's about time!" Dawn exclaimed, pushing her gold-rimmed aviator sunglasses to the crown of her head. "I thought you were going to leave me standing out here forever!"

Cynthia dropped a hand to her hip as her sister walked past her and into the foyer. "Come in, why don't you?" she muttered sarcastically, shutting the door behind her.

"I don't mind if I do!" Dawn strode through the foyer and into Cynthia's living room. "I've come to rescue you. You two have been stuck in this house *way* too long. It's like you're sitting shivah or something. Your hearts have been broken. I get that. But no one died. Life goes on!"

Cynthia cocked an eyebrow as she watched her sister plop down in the leather armchair and cross her long, ebony legs.

"Funny," Cynthia muttered, "I can remember giving you the same damn advice when you and Xavier had *your* little dustup."

Dawn had stopped talking to Xavier when she thought he couldn't choose between her and her half-sister, Constance. Before they reunited, getting Dawn out of her funk had been a trial.

Dawn waved her off. "That was then, this is now.

Come on, girl! What better way for both of you to as-
sert life than to get mani-pedis and have a fabulous
lunch with *moi?*"

"Mani-pedis?" Cynthia took off her straw hat and
tossed it on the coffee table. "I was in the middle of
gardening when you just barged in, and I can assure
you that Clarissa is in no mood for a spa day."

"But you'll need a manicure and pedicure if you
want to look nice for the party next weekend." She
glanced at Cynthia's nails and curled her lip. "Your
hands are looking rather rough, my dear."

Cynthia frowned again. "Party? What party?"

"Steph's engagement party! The one that you still
haven't RSVP'd for. Remember?"

"Ah, hell!" Cynthia slapped her forehead. "It *is*
next weekend, isn't it?"

"It is indeed. So . . ." Dawn grabbed the arms of her
chair and pushed herself to her feet. "I suggest that you
change into something that makes you look a little less
like Daisy Duke."

Cynthia narrowed her eyes.

"And you and Clarissa meet me downstairs in thirty
minutes," Dawn said.

Cynthia opened her mouth to argue, but stopped
when she heard Clarissa shriek upstairs. Both of their
gazes darted to the ceiling.

"Lord, what's happened now?" she muttered, rushing to the staircase. Dawn was right at her heels. When
Cynthia skidded to a halt at the bottom of the stairs,
Dawn ran into the back of her, and they both had to
grab the newel post to keep from falling down.

They heard Clarissa's thudding footsteps a second
later as she raced down the hall. The nineteen-year-old
was in a tank top and pink yoga pants and was jumping

up and down, flapping her hands wildly in front of her face. She was crying.

"What's wrong?" Cynthia asked. "Baby, what's the matter?"

"Jared and I are back together!" Clarissa shouted, then ran down the stairs.

Cynthia's mouth fell open in shock, while Dawn cringed.

"Wait, isn't he her brother?" Dawn whispered loudly as she nudged Cynthia's shoulder. "Cindy, you need to have a talk with that girl and set her straight, or we've got a Greek tragedy on our hands!"

Cynthia cleared her throat. She took a step forward. "Now, Clarissa . . . honey, we talked about this. I know you're upset that you had to break up with Jared. Believe me, I understand. But you and Jared can't go out anymore because of—"

"Yes, we can!" Clarissa grinned. "All of that is fixed now, Ma! He explained everything! He asked me to take him back and I said yes . . . and he's on his way here!"

"On his way here?" Cynthia pointed down at the floor. "You mean to our house? You mean *now?*"

Clarissa nodded.

The doorbell rang again, and Clarissa resumed her crazed hopping on the foyer's ceramic tile. She skipped to the front door and threw it open. Jared stood in the doorway with his eyes downcast. When he saw Clarissa, he gave a nervous smile and started to open his mouth to say something, but he didn't get the chance. Clarissa immediately jumped into his arms and wrapped her legs around his waist like she hadn't seen him for months, like he was a soldier who had just returned from overseas deployment. Jared immediately grabbed

her bottom and her back to brace her weight and keep
them both from tumbling to the brick walkway. He
looked dazed and a little confused when Clarissa started
to kiss him on his cheeks, mouth, nose, and even his
eyes. After a minute or two, he finally kissed her back.

Despite her initial misgivings, Cynthia's heart melted
a little as she watched the reunited couple. And Clarissa was happy again. What mother wouldn't love
that? She was still baffled as to how this whole disaster
was "fixed," according to Clarissa, but she'd keep her
thoughts to herself for now. She'd give them their moment.

"Are you ready to be a grandmother, Cindy?" Dawn
asked, gazing wide-eyed at Clarissa and Jared.

"I most certainly am not!"

Dawn crossed her arms over her chest. "Well, honey,
you might have to be, with those two. Either that, or
start hosing them down now."

Cynthia started to laugh, but her laughter died when
she saw someone else standing in her doorway. Korey
glanced at the kissing couple, laughed, and shook his
head. He then turned his gaze to Cynthia.

"Well, hello," Dawn said with a low purr. She
leaned toward Cynthia's ear. "Is this the baby daddy?"

"Yes, it is . . . and remember that you're with
Xavier."

Dawn giggled before gliding toward him with her
hand extended. "Hello, I'm Dawn . . . Cindy's sister
and aunt to the lip-locker over there. You must be
Korey Walker."

Cynthia stood back and watched, feeling too unsure
of herself to say anything to Korey. They hadn't spoken since that night in the Las Vegas hotel room, since
he had told her to stay out of his life for good. Those
damning words still stung her.

"Yes, I am," Korey said, shaking Dawn's hand. "And I already know who you are."

"I guess my reputation precedes me." She proudly feathered her asymmetrical bob.

"That and we were only two years apart in high school. Plus"—he shrugged—"I was at your house a few times when we were younger, and I saw you and your other sisters while I was there."

She wrinkled her nose. "Were you the guy I saw dangling out the second-floor balcony window back in April 1994?"

He chuckled. "Maybe."

"That would explain it." She clapped her hands. "So, Korey, please tell me why my sister should be okay with Clarissa kissing that young man over there." She inclined her head in Clarissa and Jared's direction. "It was my understanding that they're blood relatives. I'll admit that we're a nontraditional family, but brother-and-sister love isn't really our thing."

"It isn't my thing either. But I'm okay with it because Jared found out today that they're not brother and sister. I'm not . . ." He paused for a beat then took a deep breath. "I'm not Jared's father."

"Wait! *What?*" Cynthia finally broke her silence and walked toward him. "What do you mean you're not his father?"

His warm gaze instantly went cold as he looked at Cynthia. "I guess Viv felt the same way about being honest with me as you did."

Cynthia lowered her eyes to stare at her dirt-stained canvas sneakers. She guessed she deserved that.

"Well, Korey," Dawn said, loudly clearing her throat, "you're still Clarissa's father though, right?"

His eyes stayed fixed on Cynthia. "Looks like it."

"Then that means you're part of the family now."

She grinned. "So I'm extending an invitation to you and Jared for our sister Stephanie's fabulous engagement party at Le Bayou Bleu this weekend. I'll also drop an official invite in the mail if you give me your address."

"You want me to come to your party?"

She shrugged her slender shoulders. "Sure, why not? If you're worried about whether you being there will bring drama—please don't. Our family practically manufactures it by the truckload! You'll just add spice."

"Jared said he'll come," Clarissa called out as she walked toward them. She had finally managed to pry her lips from her boyfriend, though they were still holding hands. She was smiling from ear-to-ear as she turned to Korey. "I hope you'll come too, Mr. Walker." She blinked. "I mean Dad . . . I mean . . ." She grimaced. "I'm not sure what to call you now."

Korey's eyes instantly softened as he looked at his daughter. "Call me whatever you feel comfortable calling me. If it helps, you can just call me Korey for now."

She gave a small smile. "Okay . . . Korey."

He turned back to Dawn. "Thank you for inviting me to the party."

"No problem! Thank you for making this cutie over here." She nudged Clarissa's chin, making the young woman laugh. "Even if you did it accidentally. We like having her around."

He chuckled again. "Well, on that note. I think Jared and I are going to head back home. I promised him I would drive him here to see Clarissa. I didn't think he was calm enough to get here without running into a tree."

"Pops!" Jared said, rolling his eyes and looking embarrassed.

"It was nice seeing you, Dawn. And I know I will definitely see you again, Clarissa." He turned to Jared. "Let's leave the ladies to their afternoon. We should head back home now."

Cynthia noticed that he had addressed everyone but her. She bit down hard on her bottom lip and balled her fists at her sides.

"Thank you for coming," she blurted out as Korey walked back to her front door.

Korey's jaw visibly tightened. He didn't respond, but instead silently ushered Jared through the doorway in front of him.

Chapter 29

When the ringing started at six a.m., Lauren and her husband let out a collective groan. They had been snuggled under the covers, wrapped in each other's arms, and slumbering contentedly when the silence in their bedroom was pierced by the ringtone of Lauren's cell phone.

"Who the hell is that?" Cris asked groggily.

"I don't know," Lauren said as she turned onto her side and reached for the iPhone on her night table.

"Whoever it is, it better be damn important. Who the hell calls this early on a Sunday?"

"Hello?" Lauren mumbled, pushing her hair out of her eyes.

"Oh, my God, Laurie! Did you hear about what happened last night?" Stephanie cried into the phone.

Lauren pushed herself up to her elbows and turned on the night table lamp. She squinted in confusion. "What?"

"The mayor's house was raided!" Stephanie shouted.

"What?" Lauren screamed, making Cris jump up in alarm. *"When?"*

"What's wrong?" he asked. "What happened?"

"Steph says the mayor's house was raided!" she repeated over her shoulder.

He instantly sat upright and threw back the bed sheets. *"What?"*

"It happened last night! The Sheriff's Office was there. So was the damn FBI! Something about Knightly defrauding the city. Sounds like he's been doing it for *years!*" Stephanie explained. "When the cops came in, his wife was flushing money down the toilet! Can you believe that? Miss Sanctified herself! I heard they had to kick the damn bathroom door in."

"Are you sure, Steph? I mean . . . This sounds so crazy and far-fetched that it can't—"

"I'm sure! One of my former clients is Knightly's next-door neighbor. They saw it all from their living room window, Laurie! They got more details from one of the deputies on site. Her husband is one of his drinking buddies. Seems like the deputy had loose lips or thought the gossip was too good to keep it to himself! Can you believe it? Mayor Knightly is in jail!"

Lauren sat on the edge of the bed, completely stunned. This news had come out of left field. She still couldn't believe it, but the neighbors had seen it happen. Why would they lie?

"Look, it sounds like Zoe's waking up," Stephanie said. Her infant daughter could be heard wailing in the background. "I'll talk to you later. Just give my congrats to Cris, okay?"

"Congrats? Congrats for what?"

"On winning the election, girl! With Mayor Knightly in jail and accused of embezzlement, there goes the competition, honey. Cris is *definitely* a shoo-in for the mayor job now! Gotta go!"

Stephanie hung up, and so did Lauren. Lauren slowly sat her phone on the night table and turned to her husband.

"Was that a joke?" Cris asked.

Lauren shook her head. "I don't think so. Steph said it sounds like Knightly embezzled money from city funds. Even his 'holier than thou' wife knew about it."

"I'll be damned," Cris whispered, flopping back against their headboard, dazed.

"My thoughts exactly. Steph said it sounds like he's been doing this for a long time."

"*A long time?* Well, if he's been doing this for so long, why is it all coming to light now?"

"No clue." She thought for a second. "Maybe it has to do with the election. Do you have any supporters who would dig up dirt on him—like Knightly had people dig up stuff on us? Would Marvin—"

"Marvin ain't capable of something like this. Trust me! He's willing to help me out, but he isn't going to go toe-to-toe with the mayor. He doesn't have that type of backbone."

"But it's an odd coincidence that this happened now, don't you think? Who did Knightly piss off who is powerful enough or has the connections to . . ."

Lauren's voice faded. She suddenly remembered something. As she did, she raised her hand to her mouth and gasped. "Oh, my God! *That's* what she meant!" she exclaimed.

"That's what *who* meant?" Cris paused. "Lauren, do you think you know who's behind this?"

Lauren gently patted his hand and nodded. "I think I do . . . but I have to talk to her first before I can say for sure."

* * *

Lauren walked down the corridor and found her mother sitting in the library at a Queen Anne writing desk. Yolanda had a gilded pen in hand and was scribbling something on a piece of paper. When she heard Lauren walk into the room, she looked up.

"Well, hello, Laurie! I wasn't expecting to see you today, sweetheart! What are you doing here?"

Lauren walked across the library, leaned down, and kissed her mother's cheek. She instantly caught a whiff of Yolanda's signature citrusy fragrance.

"I came here to talk to you about something." She glanced at the desk where her mother was still writing. "I'm not interrupting anything, am I?"

"No." Yolanda sat down her pen and folded the paper. "I was writing a thank-you note to a friend and had just finished up. Everyone sends e-mails or texts nowadays. Call me old-fashioned, but I still believe in writing things on paper. It seems so much more civilized, in my opinion."

Lauren crossed her arms over her chest. "Were you thanking your friend for what happened last night?"

"What happened last night?" Yolanda asked innocently, tucking the paper into an envelope. "I don't know what you mean."

"Mama, you know *exactly* what I mean. 'Everyone will get their justice due,' you said."

Her mother went still.

"That's what you meant, right?" Lauren continued. "You knew the mayor was being investigated. Did you know his house would get raided?"

Yolanda looked up from her desk. She turned to face her daughter and shrugged. "I didn't know when it would happen, but I figured it would happen eventually. I made sure to get assurances that it would happen before election day. I guess they worked faster than I thought." She smirked. "The wheels of justice can turn swiftly, after all."

Lauren dropped her hands to her sides and shook her head in astonishment. She knew her mother knew people in high places, but even this seemed like a major feat for her.

"Mama, how . . . how did you pull this off?"

"Oh, I just called in a favor from an old friend, shall we say."

"You mean one of your lovers?"

"Lauren," Yolanda said, sounding annoyed as she rose from her chair, "don't be *crude.* But yes, if you must know, he has been one of my . . . well, companions over the years."

"Do I know him?"

Yolanda sighed. "George Murdoch. He has contacts in city hall and knows a few things that many people in Chesterton don't know. He had wanted to impress me in the past and had let a few secrets about the mayor slip out, one of which was that the mayor had a secret bank account that he had been funneling city funds into for the past decade or so. Knightly used the money to buy cars, fund vacations, and get his wife those horrendously ugly hats and coats she likes to wear." Yolanda inclined her head and clasped her hands. "I simply reminded George that I knew these secrets and that if he didn't do anything about it, I would do it, or better yet, I would let everyone in town know about our long-standing . . . well, friendship. He took care of the rest for me."

Lauren wasn't surprised to hear that. Murdoch was a very powerful man in town but also very conscious of his image, and he wouldn't want his name associated with Yolanda's.

"But why did you do all this, Mama? You don't even *like* Cris and—"

"I accept that Cris is your husband, and I know how much you love that man, Laurie. By helping him, I was helping *you,*" her mother answered firmly. "Besides, this wasn't just about Cris. I could see how much all of this nonsense was upsetting you, how it was upsetting *all* of my girls! And one of the biggest rules in our family is that we take care of each other, correct?"

Lauren blankly nodded. "I don't know what to say, Mama."

When other moms wanted to do you a favor or cheer you up, they made your favorite meal or would take you for a girl's day out of shopping. Instead, Yolanda had blackmailed one of her lovers into turning in the mayor of Chesterton for embezzlement! It was so outlandish that if anyone but Yolanda had admitted to it, it would be utterly unbelievable. Lauren would say they were lying. But she knew her mother. Yolanda was totally capable of something so warped. But despite how warped her actions were, Yolanda had come from a good place. *This* was how she showed her daughters her love.

"I guess all I can say is . . . thank you," Lauren whispered.

"Don't mention it." Yolanda patted her on the shoulder. She then snapped her fingers. "Oh, and don't forget to give that thing to Dawn for Stephanie's engagement party that I asked you to last week. She's been bothering me about it for a while now, and I keep forgetting."

"Miss Gibbons," one of the maids interrupted from the doorway, "there is someone on the phone for you."

"I'll take it in here, Rita!" She then turned to Lauren. "You'll have to excuse me, Laurie. I have to take this call."

Lauren nodded. "Sure, I was . . . I was heading back home anyway."

"All right. Bye, sweetheart. Enjoy your day." Yolanda brushed her red lips on Lauren's cheek, then walked toward the vintage rotary phone on her desk and picked up the receiver.

"Hello?" Yolanda asked, not missing a beat. "Milton, how are you?" her voice suddenly became sultry. Milton was probably one of her boyfriends. "Thank you for calling me back, honey!"

Yolanda waved to her daughter as Lauren absently shuffled toward the doorway. When she reached the library's entrance, she looked back. Yolanda was still on the phone, laughing and twirling the cord around her finger as she talked. Lauren gazed at her mother in awe.

For years Lauren and her sisters had blindly adhered to her mother's philosophy of life: using men for their money, seeing love as something to be ridiculed and scorned. Gradually, they had each moved away from those beliefs. Lauren had found and married her true love, Crisanto. Stephanie had fallen for Keith and was now well on her way to building a family with him. Dawn had fallen in love with Xavier, despite her best efforts not to, and now Lauren wondered if even Cynthia, who always had been the stalwart gold digger in the family, was even starting to lose faith in the Gibbons family rules. But despite the girls drifting away, there was still a core that held them together. That core wasn't gold digging, but a sense of family and responsibility that Yolanda had engrained in them since they were in diapers. That would never change, no matter how many times they fell in love, no matter how many of the other family rules they ignored. Thanks to Yolanda, they were still family.

Lauren smiled before giving one last wave and walking out of the library.

Chapter 30

Korey reclined in his suede lounger with his feet up, his remote control in one hand, and a beer in the other, preparing himself for a quiet Saturday evening at home. He raised the remote and pressed a button, randomly flipping channels on his flat screen. He glanced over his shoulder when he heard Jared walk into the living room.

"What are you doing?" Jared asked while he concentrated on tying his paisley necktie.

Jared was wearing one of Korey's charcoal gray suits tonight. The young man hadn't owned a suit since he was fourteen years old, and Vivian had packed up that one and sent it off to Goodwill years ago.

Korey's suit was a little too big for Jared, but Korey had figured with a good belt and the pants hems rolled up that it would work for tonight's party. As he now gazed at Jared, he nodded with approval. Korey had been right; you could barely tell that the suit wasn't Jared's.

"What does it look like I'm doing?" Korey asked.

"It looks like you're watching ESPN when you should be getting ready for Clarissa's aunt's engagement party," Jared muttered, adjusting his necktie.

Korey took a sip from his beer. "Why would I go to the party?"

"Why not, Pops? They invited you too. Damn it, *why can't I get this?*"

Korey put his bottle aside on the scuffed end table and stood up from his lounger. "Boy, how many times have I showed you how to tie one of these things? Let me see it."

Jared dropped his hands to his sides and stood with his shoulders slumped as Korey undid the askew knot in Jared's tie.

"So why aren't you going to the party?"

"Because I don't want to," Korey answered bluntly. "Because it'd just be too . . . too awkward." He adjusted the tie around Jared's neck. "Raise your chin."

"No more awkward than me going! Clarissa and I just broke up a week and half ago because we thought we were related."

"But now you know you're not related."

"Yeah, but that doesn't mean everything is perfect! Because it ain't! Everything is different now. It's . . ." Jared hesitated. "It's weird. Clarissa doesn't know how to act around you now that she knows you're her . . . you know, her dad."

Korey stilled. "Yeah, I would imagine it's uncomfortable for her. I know it's uncomfortable for the both of you." He returned to adjusting Jared's tie. "But we'll all work it out. Don't worry. It'll just take time."

"Clarissa says it's hard too because you hate her mom now."

At that, Korey flinched. "I don't *hate* Cindy."

And the *last* person he wanted to think he hated

Cynthia was Clarissa. He would love to take on more of a fatherly role with his daughter in the future—if she would allow it. He had missed so many years and milestones. He didn't want more of them to slip away. But his relationship with Clarissa was complicated at best, and he didn't want anything making it even more complicated—like her believing he hated her mother.

"But you're mad at her mom, though?"

"Of course I'm mad, Jared! The woman dumped me to marry some rich guy, then lied for almost twenty damn years about who was the father of her baby!" He tightened the tie knot, making Jared wince. "She dragged me around Las Vegas for two days and didn't say a damn thing about the fact that she thought you guys were brother and sister! I mean, who does that? She lies as a reflex! Cindy is a lying, manipulative, money-hungry, cold-hearted b—"

"Pops, you're choking me," Jared squeaked, reaching for his throat.

"Oh, I'm sorry!" Korey exclaimed, dropping his hands as Jared tugged the knot open and gasped for air. He reached for Jared's collar again. "I can fix—"

"No!" Jared held up his hand and stepped back with widened eyes. "No, I got it, Pops! Thanks."

Korey grimaced.

After Jared finally regained his breath, he eyed Korey. "I don't know, Pops. You said you don't hate her, but that all sounds like hate to me."

"I *don't* hate her, Jared!"

"Hate" wasn't the right word. He was furious at Cynthia. He was disappointed that every time he lowered his guard and bothered to trust her, it inevitably came back to bite him in the ass. He was hurt that she could take his love and squander it so casually, even after all these years.

Hurt—yes! *That* was the right four-letter word in this instance. Cynthia Gibbons knew how to hurt a man, how to rip his heart and his ego to shreds. Korey felt like the world's biggest fool for letting her do it to him again, even though he should have known better. Twenty years had passed, but he still was none the wiser.

She was just the wrong bet, he told himself, like that twenty-thousand-dollar spin on the roulette wheel back in Vegas. *She always has been.*

Korey shook his head. "You don't understand, son. You'll see what I mean one day when—"

"I get older?" Jared sucked his teeth. "I hate it when old folks say stuff like that! Trust me, Pops. I'm old enough to know what I'm talking about. You hate Miss Gibbons, but she doesn't hate you. Clarissa said her mom is strung out over you, and Miss Gibbons doesn't get strung out over just *any* dude!"

Korey flopped back into his lounger. *"Strung out?* Uh-huh. When pigs fly," he muttered before raising his beer bottle back to his lips.

"I'm serious, Pops!" Jared adjusted his jacket collar and sat in the chair facing Korey. "Clarissa said the lady cries every night! Miss Gibbons tries to mask the sound with Sade and tired jazz music, but Clarissa can still hear her. She said it goes on for hours. It's really depressing."

Korey stopped mid-sip and frowned. *Crying for hours?*

"It's really messed up," Jared continued absently as he stared at the television screen. "Clarissa said she's never liked any of her mom's boyfriends, but she hopes her mom finds one soon so she'll lighten up, so it will distract Miss Gibbons." Jared sucked his teeth again, this time at the game replay on the screen. "Oh, snap! How'd he miss that shot?"

Korey slowly lowered his bottle back to the end table, his beer now forgotten. Cynthia wasn't really that torn up, was she? She certainly wasn't that torn up over him!

"But you heard Jared," the annoying voice in his head insisted. "Why would Clarissa lie? She said she heard Cindy crying, didn't she?"

Korey furiously shook his head.

No, he told himself, *no, I'm not falling for this again!*

There was no way that Cynthia Gibbons was shedding any tears over him. Maybe she was crying over the years of child support she'd have to pay back her ex once he discovered he wasn't Clarissa's father. *That's probably it,* Korey thought with a snort. If Cynthia had to take a hit to her wallet, it would certainly make her start weeping. But she wouldn't shed any tears over a man. That wasn't her style.

"Tell Clarissa not to worry about Cindy," Korey said. "Her mother knows how to bounce back. Nothing keeps that woman down. And tell her that I don't hate Cindy. I don't ever want Clarissa to think that."

Jared stood from the couch. "Tell her yourself. Tell her at the party tonight."

"An engagement party isn't the time or the place for a conversation like that, son."

"Then when *is* the time and place, Pops?"

Korey opened his mouth to reply, but clamped it shut. It was pointless. He wasn't going to any party, especially one Cynthia would attend. He didn't care how much Jared argued with him.

He watched as Jared walked toward the front door.

The young man grabbed a set of car keys from a hook on the wall.

"All right, I'm out, Pops," Jared proclaimed. "And I'm taking the Taurus."

"Fine," Korey said, returning his attention to the television screen. "Make sure you don't leave the tank empty this time. The damn thing was on E after the last time you took it! And don't lose your cell phone again, either. Oh, and be back by—"

"Midnight." Jared rolled his eyes and opened the front door. "I know. Clarissa said she has to be back by then too."

She better be back by then, Korey thought. No daughter of his would be out into the wee hours of the morning.

At least Korey didn't have to play the role of the protective dad and give Jared a lecture about treating Clarissa respectfully. That was the one perk of this whole debacle. He had raised Clarissa's boyfriend and taught Jared everything he knew. Jared was a good kid, a kid that Korey had no qualms about dating his daughter.

"You guys have fun tonight!" he called after Jared.

"Bye, Pops!" Jared then shut the door behind him, leaving Korey to the soft murmur of the television and relative quiet of the empty house.

For the next thirty minutes, Korey tried to return his attention to ESPN and tried to enjoy his beer, but he could do neither. Instead, Jared's words kept nagging at him.

Was Clarissa really that worried about her mother? Did Clarissa believe his feelings toward Cynthia were affecting his relationship with his daughter?

"Well, you haven't really talked to Clarissa since

this whole thing came to light," the voice in his head argued. "Why wouldn't she think that you aren't talking to her because you hate her mother?"

But that couldn't be any further from the truth! He wasn't avoiding Clarissa. He was just as confused about how to handle this as the kids were. He wanted to reach out to Clarissa, to tell her that he was here for her to talk to if she wanted, but he wasn't sure how to approach her. They had been virtual strangers a few months ago. Now they were father and daughter and, to make matters even more thorny, Clarissa was dating the boy Korey had raised as his son. There was no road map on how to handle any of this, but Korey was willing to try. He was willing to come as close as he possibly could to making things right for all of them.

"Then tell her all of that, Pops," he could hear Jared urge in his head.

Korey grimaced again and glanced at the clock on the living room wall, wondering if he still had a copy of the invitation to the engagement party.

"Where are they having this damn thing anyway?" he grumbled.

An hour later, Korey stepped into Le Bayou Bleu, feeling like he had unwittingly parachuted behind enemy lines. The restaurant was filled with people, and among the crowd he spotted a few of the Gibbons girls. They were hard not to notice. The sisters were some of the most attractive women in the room. One Gibbons girl in particular strode toward him with a wineglass in her hand. She wore a gold silk, one-shoulder cocktail dress and turquoise-and-diamond bracelet and earrings that gleamed off her dark skin, making the tall, regal beauty look like a modern-day Somali queen. When she saw Korey, a grin spread across her face.

"Oh, my God!" Dawn exclaimed. "You actually came!"

He frowned. "You guys didn't want me to come?"

"No, it's just . . ." She waved her hand and shook her head. "Never mind. I'm just surprised, that's all! Cindy was sure you wouldn't show up. She is *definitely* gonna pee her pants when she sees that you're here!" Dawn looped her arm through his and turned to guide him toward the onyx bar, where more than a dozen people stood. "Let me take you to her. She's holding court by—"

"I didn't come to see Cindy." He tugged his arm out of Dawn's grasp. "I was going to find Clarissa and maybe give my congrats to the happy couple. That's it."

"Oh." Dawn's smile faded. "Well, uh, Clarissa is around here . . . somewhere. I think I saw her and Jared over there a while ago." She pointed off into the distance. Her brows furrowed as she leaned toward him. "Are you sure you don't want me to take you to Cindy?" she whispered. "I know she'd really, *really* love to see you, Korey."

Korey clenched his jaw. "No disrespect, Dawn, but I think I'll pass on that one."

Dawn released a slow, deflating breath, then nodded. "Sure, I understand. Like I said, Clarissa and Jared are around here somewhere. Can I get you a drink, though? Would you like some wine or champagne?"

He shook his head. "No, thanks. I'll just look for the kids, if you don't mind."

He could feel Dawn's eyes on him as he walked away and crossed the restaurant, easing his way through the throng of well-wishers. Dawn had looked disappointed when he had said he had no interest in talking to her sister, but he was just being honest. If he managed not to cross paths with Cynthia the entire night, that would suit him fine. Clarissa was his objective—not her mother.

Korey looked around him, searching for his daughter while admiring the restaurant where Stephanie Gibbons and her fiancé were holding their engagement party. He knew Lauren, the youngest Gibbons sibling, was the head chef here, though he had never eaten at the restaurant.

It was an impressive space, with its rich mahogany wood paneling and sumptuous semicircular booths decorated with cream-colored fabric embellished with a navy blue damask pattern. In addition to the small pendant chandelier over each booth, an oversized chandelier cascading with crystal hung over the onyx bar. Across from the bar was a live band that played soul music, though, to be honest, Korey could barely hear the band above the banter and laughter around him.

Korey squinted and peered at the crowd again. He finally spotted Clarissa and Jared several feet away, dancing near a group of dining tables. Korey walked toward them and lightly tapped Jared on the shoulder, making Jared turn around. The young man's eyes widened when he realized who was standing behind him.

"Pops?" Jared shouted over the music. "What are you doing here?"

"Mr. Walker!" Clarissa cried, looking at that moment like her mother and every bit as beautiful. She cringed when she realized what she had called him. "I-I mean, Dad . . . I-I-I mean, Korey . . . I-I . . ." Her shoulders slumped as her words faded. "I'm so sorry. I'm still not used to this."

Korey chuckled. "Don't worry about it. Can I cut in for sec, son?"

"Oh, yeah! Sure!" Jared nodded, stepping away from Clarissa. "I'm gonna get something to eat. I'll be right back."

Clarissa nodded.

As Jared walked away, disappearing to the buffet table, Korey and Clarissa stood awkwardly on the make-shift dance floor, staring at each other. Korey finally held out his hand to her as the band began a few bars of another song—a slow one. It sounded vaguely like a Smokey Robinson tune.

"I don't know if I have the same skills as Jared, but I'm a decent dancer, if you want to give it a try," he said to Clarissa, making her smile.

"I'd love to. Thanks for asking."

She took his hand and placed her other hand on his shoulder. They began their first father/daughter dance under the low lights of the restaurant. After a few minutes, Clarissa leaned back to look up at him.

"I'm surprised you're here. Jared said you weren't coming."

"He was right. I wasn't—at first. I changed my mind, though. I wanted to have the chance to talk to you."

She raised her brows. "Talk to me about what?"

"About everything that's happened, about finding out I'm your . . . well, you know, your father. I haven't done a great job of communicating with you, and I'm sorry about that."

"You don't have to apologize." Clarissa shrugged. "It's okay. I know it's complicated, especially considering how you feel about my mom and—"

"Let me stop you right there. How I feel about your mother has nothing to do with my relationship with you, and I want you to know that." He stepped back from her. "Look, I'm here for you in any way you want me to be. If you want me just to be Jared's dad to you like before, I'll do that. If you want me to be that wise-cracking old man down the street who you go to for advice, I'll do that too. But if you really want me to be a father to you, I'd be honored and more than happy to do that." He held up his hands. "I'm not trying to re-place your real dad, the one that raised you, but—"

"There isn't much to replace." Clarissa's eyes drifted to the hardwood floor. "My dad has been doing his own thing in Chicago with his other family for years. We barely talk. I see him every once in a while. That's about it."

Korey's face fell. "I'm sorry to hear that."

She shrugged again and finally raised her dark eyes. "It's okay. I'm used to it. It hurt my feelings when I was younger, but not so much anymore. You get over it."

"But you shouldn't have to 'get over it.' I won't do that to you, Clarissa. If you want me to be there for you, I always will be."

"Thank you."

"I mean it," he said emphatically. "I'm always here."

"I believe you, Korey . . . and I appreciate it."

"And maybe someday next week I could stop by. We could have lunch or something."

"That would be nice."

"What? You aren't dancing anymore?" Jared asked between bites of deviled egg and caviar.

Korey turned to Jared, shaking his head at the young man, who was smacking his lips. "No, I think we're done. You can have your lady back now."

"That's good," Jared said as he licked his fingers and focused on Clarissa," because your mom told me to come and get you. They're about to do the toast to your aunt."

"Oh, okay, I'll be right there." Clarissa looked as if she was going to walk away, but then she stopped. She suddenly turned, grabbed Korey's hand, and squeezed it affectionately. "You're going to stay, right?"

Korey paused. He hadn't planned to stay. He had already done what he came here to do.

"At least stay for the toast," she said, noticing his uncertainty. "Please?"

Korey gradually nodded. "Sure."

He followed the young couple back across the restaurant to the bar. As they neared it, Korey spotted Stephanie Gibbons—the bride to be—talking with another woman. Cynthia's sister Stephanie was still as pretty as Korey remembered—though a little plumper. Stephanie's arm was wrapped around a tall, dark-skinned man, and she was beaming as she broke away from her conversation and gazed up at him. Korey assumed the man was Stephanie's fiancé. Beside Stephanie stood Yolanda Gibbons. Shockingly, the older woman's smile seemed genuine. Jared had mentioned that Clarissa's grandmother hadn't been too happy with Stephanie marrying a man like Keith, one the older woman felt was beneath her, which didn't surprise Korey in the slightest. If a guy wasn't a millionaire, then Yolanda would never consider him good enough for any of her daughters. But he was surprised to see Yolanda happy today.

I wonder if someone slipped something into her drink, he thought sarcastically.

Next to Yolanda were Lauren and a muscular guy who nearly towered over her. Korey recognized that guy instantly. That was Crisanto Weaver, the former football star and likely future mayor of Chesterton. Korey had heard good things about him.

He scanned the crowd again, wondering where Cynthia was. Finally, he spotted her. She walked hand in hand with Clarissa toward the rest of the family. When he saw her, he felt a sharp stab to the chest that was all too familiar.

Damn, he thought. Of course, she looked gorgeous. *Would it have been too much to ask for her to look bad tonight—just a little?*

She probably had half the single men in the room salivating.

Cynthia wore a simple black cocktail dress that was cut low in the front and flowed around her hips. The hem stopped just a few inches above the knees. She was wearing her hair down today, letting her blond curls cascade around her shoulders. Her makeup and jewelry were understated, but she still shone like a lighthouse beacon in the room.

"Hello! Hi, everyone!" Dawn's voice said over the loudspeaker as the band finished its last few notes. A tall, light-skinned man stood behind her, motioning for the band to stop playing. He then whispered something into Dawn's ear and kissed her cheek. She nodded and tapped the cordless mike in her hand. "Hey, everyone! Over here! If I could have your attention, please?"

The clamor in the room died down as Dawn waved frantically from where she stood near the band.

"Thank you, everyone, for coming tonight to celebrate the engagement of my sister, the indomitable, sexy, and oh-so-fabulous Stephanie Gibbons—"

Stephanie did a little hip wiggle and blew a kiss to everyone in the room, causing uproarious laughter from the crowd.

"—and her handsome and ever-so-patient fiancé, Keith Hendricks!"

Keith pumped his fist into the air, making the audience break into applause.

"We're here tonight to celebrate the fact that after one baby, a lot of drama, and several designer shoe purchases, Keith has decided to stick around. He's taken on the brave task known as falling in love and making a life with my dear sister Stephanie Gibbons, and decided to put a ring on it, ladies and gentlemen!" Dawn said.

After that intro, several people, including Stephanie and Keith, walked to the stage and shared heartfelt speeches honoring the engagement, drawing more applause and a few tears from those in the room.

Korey was shocked at all the warmth he felt radiating from the couple and the Gibbons clan in general. Considering their well-earned reputation as merciless man-eaters, he didn't expect all this love and bliss. It made him uneasy, seeing the girls like this. Where was the ruthlessness? Why didn't they seem colder? Had the Gibbons family finally changed after all these years? Did that mean Cynthia could change too?

No, he told himself. It was all an illusion. Fast forward a year or two and Lauren would probably be divorced from her millionaire husband Crisanto, and still wrangling with him in court over alimony and child-support payments. Stephanie would have dumped Keith for a geezer who owned several mansions. Dawn would be zeroing in on her next husband.

And Cynthia?

Cynthia will be doing the same shit she always does, he told himself.

After the fifth and what seemed like the final speech,

Korey glanced at his watch, wondering if he could inconspicuously make his way to the doors. After all, Clarissa seemed engrossed with her family and Jared at the moment, and the crowd around the bar seemed to be dispersing. Korey could probably sneak out without Clarissa noticing.

He turned and started to head toward the exit, but he paused when he heard a familiar voice.

"Excuse me! Excuse me, everyone!" Cynthia said into the microphone, making Korey instantly turn back to the stage. "Wait! We're not finished yet. It's my turn!"

The crowd fell silent again.

"Yes, I know. I know everyone is shocked that I'm going to give a toast to Steph and Keith too, but I swear, everything I have to say is good."

"Girl, it better be or I am yanking that mike out of your hand!" Stephanie barked, making several in the audience laugh.

"Look, I know that I haven't been the most supportive of you and Keith," Cynthia began. "Maybe I've even, shall we say, disparaged your relationship a few times. Okay, maybe more than just a few times . . . maybe *a lot*. But"—she held up a finger—"I can be the first to admit when I'm wrong."

"Since when?" Lauren asked, making her other sisters and even their mother burst into laughter.

"And," Cynthia said loudly, before giving her youngest sister a withering glance, "even I can't deny, Keith, how happy you make our Steph. Being in love with you has definitely . . ." She cleared her throat. "It has definitely changed her." Cynthia slowly scanned the room. Her eyes stopped, and she locked gazes with Korey.

Several people in the crowd turned to see whom she

was staring at. Korey gritted his teeth when he became the focus of *their* stares.

If this was supposed to be some type of apology from Cynthia, it was falling on deaf ears.

I said I'm not getting sucked back in and I meant it, he thought. He didn't care how many damn speeches she made.

"It's changed her a lot, b-but in a good way," Cynthia quickly clarified. "It's made her a better person, Ko-... I mean, Keith. So please, cherish what you two have. Be honest with one another. Be dedicated to each other. Don't ... don't let anyone or anything take that away from you."

Cynthia lowered the mike, and an awkward silence fell over the room.

"Uh, to ... umm ... to Stephanie and Keith!" Dawn suddenly shouted, holding up her wineglass.

"To Stephanie and Keith," the audience echoed just as Korey turned around again.

To hell with this, he thought. He had heard enough.

"Korey?" Cynthia shouted from behind him as he walked through the restaurant doors. "Korey, wait up! *Please!*"

For five seconds, he contemplated ignoring her and continuing walking down the sidewalk to his car, but that wasn't his style. Plus, he wouldn't give her the satisfaction of him fleeing as if *he* had done something wrong.

Korey slowly turned to face Cynthia. When his eyes settled on her as she emerged from the shadows and into the glow of the overhead street lamp, he was slightly irritated at the fact that he was still awed by her. He couldn't deny that. Even after all she had put him through and their painful history, he still wanted her. No, he was more than slightly irritated by that fact. It really pissed him off. That woman had an unholy hold on him, but he wouldn't let it rule him anymore.

"What do you want?" he asked tersely.

She took another hesitant step toward him. "I-I saw you talking to Clarissa earlier. I just wanted to . . . I wanted to say thank you for doing that."

His mouth fell open in shock. That wasn't the answer he had expected. It caught him off guard, but he quickly recovered. "You don't have to thank me. I didn't do it for thanks. I wanted to see her."

"Is that why you came tonight? To see her?"

He nodded.

"I was hoping you two would get the chance to talk."

"Well, it was long overdue."

She pivoted from one stiletto heel to the other. "I was . . . I was hoping we would get the chance to talk too, but you didn't seem to want to talk to me. I thought you were avoiding me."

He opened his mouth to argue, but she quickly held up a hand.

"And you're right to avoid me! If I were you, I'd be . . . I'd be avoiding me too. What I did was wrong. I know that."

"Wrong?" he asked, raising his brows comically and taking a step toward her. "You think what you did was wrong? No, wrong is putting it lightly. What you did, Cindy, was so fucked up it can't even be put into words how fucked up it was! What you did was—"

"I had my reasons, Korey."

"And none of them were justified! So don't even try that 'see my side of this' bullshit with me!"

"I wasn't going to . . ." She closed her eyes. "I wasn't going to ask you to see my side. I just wanted to apologize."

"Yeah, well, frankly, your apologies don't mean much. I've heard them before."

She winced. "I figured you'd say that. Look, either way, Korey, I wanted to apologize to you. I know you will probably never forgive me—"

"Because I won't," he answered bluntly.

"Look, you don't have to like me, but we have a daughter together. We're . . . we're co-parents now, and it would be . . . it would be good if we were on speaking terms, at least, for Clarissa's sake."

Who was this woman standing in front of him, making valid, mature arguments? Who was this woman who was apologizing and taking responsibility for her actions like a grown-up? Was it a trick, more subterfuge on Cynthia's part?

"Can we at least be on speaking terms?" she asked.

He nodded. "I guess I can do that." A polite hello every now and then wouldn't kill him. He glanced at his car in the distance. "Is that it? Is that why you followed me out here, to ask if we could be on speaking terms?"

"No." She hesitated again. "I also wanted to ask for your forgiveness, but I figured it was pointless to ask."

He gave a cynical smile. "It is."

"Korey, everything that I said in there, I meant. And I wasn't just talking about Steph; I was talking about me too. I *have* changed. I have!"

"Cindy . . ."

"I've changed for the better—"

"Cindy . . ."

"—and I owe that to you! I don't—"

"Stop!" he said, grabbing her shoulders. He shook her, making her blink in surprise. "Stop! I don't want to hear this!"

"But I don't know what else to do! I can't make—"

"Let it go! You can let it go and move on! That's what you can do. That's what *I'm* going to do."

She stared at him blankly.

"It's over. Okay? This has dragged on for almost twenty damn years, and I'm not doing it anymore."

"But what about what happened between us? Everything that we've been through? What about—"

"What happens in Vegas stays in Vegas, right?" he answered weakly. "Let it stay there."

"What?" Her eyes filled with tears. "There's no way I could . . . There is no damn way it's that simple, Korey!"

"It can be if we let it be." He dropped his hands from her shoulders and took a painful swallow, dislodging the lump that had formed in his throat. Despite his best efforts, his emotions were overwhelming him. He had tried to put up a wall, but he wasn't succeeding.

"We're Clarissa's parents. We're on speaking terms—but that's it," he said. "That's all we are. All right?"

She looked shell-shocked, and frankly, he was a little startled himself by the words that were coming out of his mouth. Cynthia would always be more than a fellow "co-parent" to him. He knew that in his heart. But he couldn't cave on this one. She had put him through too much.

She took a deep breath. "All right," she whispered.

But she didn't seem all right. She looked so hurt and downtrodden that it crushed him.

"At least we're better off now than the last time we did this," he ventured, trying to make them both feel better. "At least there's that."

She gave a sad smile. "You mean you aren't driving off angry, leaving me on the side of the road?"

"Hold up! I didn't leave you on the side of the road. I left you at your driveway."

She shrugged. "It was all the same to me."

"The details are important, though."

"They are . . . like the fact that I never appreciated you and realized what we had," she said forlornly.

Korey pursed his lips. He wasn't getting sucked into that whirlpool of emotion again. He'd never get out of it. He started to turn to walk back toward his car but paused. "Look, I've gotta go. Maybe I'll see you next week."

She frowned. "Next week?"

"Yeah, I'm supposed to meet Clarissa for lunch."

"*Lunch?* Oh, I-I can make something for you guys," Cynthia volunteered eagerly, wiping her eyes with the back of her hands. "Sandwiches or . . . or something nicer than that. Just let me know when you want to stop by. Just . . . just let me know. I'll . . . I'll . . ." Her words tapered off.

"I will." He waved. "See you around. Give your sister my congratulations."

"See . . . see you around," she whispered.

It took a great deal of effort, but he turned and walked away, putting one foot in front of the other, forcing himself not to look back.

Epilogue

"What are you doing in there?" Lauren asked as she frantically knocked on the bathroom door.

Dawn rushed into the bridal suite, lifting the hem of her pale-gray silk bridesmaid gown. "She's *still* in the bathroom? The ceremony was supposed to start thirty minutes ago!"

Lauren rolled her eyes. "I know that! I can read the clock on the wall. I've been trying to get her out of the bathroom forever!"

"Is she sick . . . I mean, nauseous or something?"

"I don't know! I have no idea what's wrong! She isn't answering me!"

"Damn it, we don't have time for this!" Dawn lamented. She tossed her bouquet of peonies and lilies of the valley onto the nearby king-size bed and stomped in her high heels over the plush carpet to the bathroom door. She stood beside her little sister and also started knocking. They banged their fists simultaneously, making it impossible to ignore them.

"I know you hear us!" Dawn shouted. "Answer the damn door!"

"What?" a voice inside the bathroom finally snapped.

"It's Dawn! Open up!"

"Give me a few minutes! I'm . . . I'm getting myself together."

"Honey, we don't have a few minutes," Lauren said. "You're already late. We have to put on your dress and get you downstairs *now!* Everyone's waiting!"

"Mama's starting to get antsy, and you know how she gets!" Dawn said.

Both sisters pressed their ears against the door, waiting for a reply, but heard nothing.

"Are you coming out?" Dawn asked.

They waited again. Still nothing. Dawn and Lauren turned to each other and slumped against the door in defeat.

The vows hadn't even been exchanged yet, and it looked like today's spring nuptials were off to an inauspicious start. The outdoor wedding had to be moved inside because of rain, though the forecast had predicted perfect blue skies. The buttercream icing on the tiered wedding cake was melting faster than the makeup on half of the attendees' faces in the humidity and heat. And the minister was now squawking that he had another wedding later that afternoon and he would have to leave if the ceremony didn't start in the next hour.

Considering how long the bride had waited to finally get her man, none of the sisters could understand her sudden cold feet.

"Cindy, *please* come out!" Lauren pleaded.

"What the hell is going on?" Stephanie yelled as she strode into the room, dragging the flower girl, Zoe, behind her. Flower petals trailed behind them down the hall and onto the bridal suite carpet. A wreath of rose-buds fell into the toddler's eyes. "The string quartet has played the same four songs five times now. There's only but so much stalling we can do down there!"

"Cindy won't come out of the bathroom," Dawn explained, pointing to the door.

"What?" Stephanie crossed her arms over her chest. "Enough of this! I'm going to take care of her."

Lauren and Dawn's eyes widened.

"Come over here and stand next to your auntie, sweetheart," Lauren said, taking Zoe's little hand and steering her to her side as Stephanie stalked across the room.

"Better cover those little ears," Dawn warned out of the side of her mouth.

"Cynthia Nicole Gibbons, if you don't get your yellow ass out of that bathroom right now," Stephanie said through clenched teeth, "put on the gown you've got hanging up out here, and come downstairs, I'm going to tell Korey not to bother with your loopy ass anymore! He should just save himself the time and frustration. You obviously don't want to marry him!"

The three sisters breathed in audibly when they finally heard the door unlock. It swung open, revealing Cynthia, who stood in the doorway in her underwear and champagne-colored satin heels.

"You better not say a damn thing to him or it's me and you, Steph!" she threatened, pointing her finger into Stephanie's face.

"What difference does it make? If you're so eager to marry him, then why the hell are you barricaded in the damn bathroom?" Stephanie shouted, shoving Cynthia's hand away.

Cynthia winced. "Because . . . because what if . . . what if Korey doesn't want to marry me?"

"What?" the sisters all cried in unison.

Stephanie groaned. "Seriously, we don't have time for this, Cindy!"

"What do you mean what if he doesn't want to marry you?" Dawn asked in exasperation. "The man has been downstairs for the past half an hour staring at his watch, wondering why you're taking so long!"

"But what if he doesn't want to *stay* married?" Cynthia walked across the room and sat down on the bed. She dropped her head into her hands. "What if he walks away again? I've messed up with him so many times. And you all know I'm not perfect!"

"That's for sure," Stephanie muttered.

"What if I do it again? God, what if he leaves me again?" She closed her eyes and threw back her head. "I don't think I can take it a third time!"

Cynthia's sisters sat on the bed beside her. Stephanie tugged Zoe onto her lap while Dawn rubbed Cynthia's back soothingly.

It had taken almost a year to earn back Korey's love and even longer to earn his trust, but Cynthia had managed to do it. They had started off slow with their "strictly co-parenting" routine. Korey and Jared had come to Cynthia and Clarissa's house once every couple of weeks for dinner, and the four sat through what were initially strained conversations over meat loaf and mashed potatoes that eventually became fun nights filled with food and joking. One evening Clarissa and Jared accidentally forgot to mention that they couldn't make it to dinner (though Cynthia still wondered whether it was really an accident and if the kids were trying to set them up). Korey and Cynthia ended up eating alone. They had such a good time that night that they started to enjoy more and more dinners alone when neither of them had a date and the kids were busy. Then they started to take a few evening walks, much like they had when they were teenagers. During those strolls, Korey got to know the new and improved Cynthia Gibbons, and the coldness that had set into his heart gradually thawed. After a dinner and late-night movie on the couch last August, one thing led to another and Korey and Cynthia ended up spending the night together. A few months later, Korey popped the question—to Cynthia's great shock. Now it looked like that shock had morphed into paranoia that he was going to change his mind and dump her.

"Look, Cindy," Lauren began, "there are no guarantees in any of this, but that doesn't mean you shouldn't take a chance, honey. You've wanted this man for . . . for basically . . . *forever,* right? Together you've been through three marriages and twenty years between you to get to this point. You keep being drawn back to one another. *Why?* Because you love each other! So—"

"So just put on the damn dress, grab your bouquet, and let's do this! Come on!" Stephanie said, scooting Zoe off her lap and rising to her feet. "We're late!"

Cynthia ignored her sister and continued to shake her head. "When he left me the first time, I became a cold, heartless bitch. When he left me the second time, I was devastated and didn't know how I would make it through it. What if—"

"Then don't mess up," Dawn said firmly. "Finally be the girl you always wanted to be. Be the woman *he's* always wanted you to be! Leave that cold, heartless bitch behind for good."

But it had been her armor for so long: Cynthia Gibbons—the Ice Queen, the cold-blooded seductress who stole your heart and emptied your wallet. Could she really leave that persona behind forever?

Cynthia gazed at her engagement ring. Korey hadn't

given it to her on bended knee in front of a saxophone player like Bill had twenty years ago. Nor had he proudly slid the velvet box across the table at a high-end restaurant like her second husband, Richard. No, that wasn't Korey's style. Instead, Korey had done it in the car after pulling into the makeshift parking lot near a creek, near the old-timer's favorite fishing spot in Chesterton, where they had gone so many times when they were younger. When he killed the engine and turned to her, she wondered why he had driven her to the empty lot.

"Why are we here?" she had asked, scrunching up her face in confusion as she peered out the windshield. "I thought we were going to—"

"I brought you here to give you this," he had said, cutting her off, holding out the ring to her. A lump had instantly formed in her throat. "I wanted to do this right here twenty years ago but . . . well, I didn't get to. I had planned it in my mind. Practiced what I was going to say." He had grinned. "Of course, I can't remember any of the words now, but . . . better late than never, right?"

Her eyes had welled up with so many tears that everything went blurry.

"Cynthia Gibbons, will you fuss, fight, make love, and laugh through the next fifty years with me?"

She had been so overwhelmed with emotion that instead of immediately saying yes, she had sat in the passenger seat blubbering instead. All she could do was emphatically nod as he put the ring on her finger.

Ice queens definitely don't weep like that, she now told herself.

Who was she kidding? She wasn't the same old girl anymore and never would be. She had Korey to thank (or blame) for that. And it was true. She wouldn't mind spending the next fifty years fussing, fighting, making love, and laughing with him. Hell, she'd like to spend a lot more!

"Okay," Cynthia finally muttered, opening her eyes.

"Okay, what?" Lauren asked.

Cynthia rose to her feet. "Okay, help me get into my wedding gown."

When her sisters started to clap their hands with joy and even started dancing, Cynthia rolled her eyes.

"Save the damn cheers for some other time. We're late," she said, making them burst into laughter.

She was new and improved—but that didn't mean she had to stop being bitchy entirely.

Thirty minutes later, Cynthia officially and *finally* became Mrs. Korey Walker. When the bride and groom kissed, Lauren, Dawn, and Stephanie breathed a sigh of relief.

"Girl, I didn't know if she was going to make it," Dawn whispered into Lauren's ear as the string quartet began "Pomp and Circumstance" while the happy couple walked back down the aisle.

Lauren nodded in agreement. "Me neither!"

By the time Cynthia and Korey made it to the reception, Cynthia's little bridal suite meltdown was all but forgotten. She and the groom gazed into each other's eyes during their first dance and couldn't keep their hands off each other for the rest of the night.

"All right now," Stephanie said as she tapped Cynthia on the shoulder. "Come up for air, you two!"

The bride pulled her mouth away from the groom long enough for him to be dragged off by one of the groomsmen and a few of the mechanics from his garage.

"You better watch it or you'll be next in line for a baby," Stephanie said as she gently patted baby Danica's back. The infant was slumbering on her shoulder while her older sister Zoe was being twirled on the dance floor by her father, Keith.

Cynthia emphatically shook her head. "Oh, no! This shop is closed! My daughter turned twenty last month, and I'm about to turn forty years old in a few weeks! There's no way in hell I'm getting pregnant again."

Stephanie turned to Lauren.

"Uh-uh! Don't look at me!" Lauren exclaimed. "I'm not even thinking about having another baby anytime soon. Things are starting to pick up at the restaurant. Little Cris takes up enough of whatever energy I have left." She then turned to Dawn. "So I guess the only one left is you."

Cynthia snorted. "Dawn isn't going to have any baby! Right, girl? You're not crazy. Your shop is closed too."

Dawn hesitated. "I don't . . . I don't think it's crazy, per se. I have room for a couple of last-minute sales before my 'shop' goes out of business."

"Last-minute sales?" Cynthia frowned. "What does that mean?"

Lauren smiled. "It means Xavier finally won you over to the idea of having a baby?"

"I guess you could say that."

"Wait!" Stephanie squinted at her. "You aren't pregnant now, are you?"

Dawn lowered her champagne glass from her lips. "What makes you think that?"

Stephanie grabbed Dawn's glass and sniffed. "Because you're drinking ginger ale, *not* champagne! You big faker! I *knew* it!"

"Maybe I wanted ginger ale!" Dawn argued.

"Oh, please, girl! I don't think I've ever seen you at a party without a glass of chardonnay in your hand," Cynthia said.

Dawn winced. "You guys are making me sound like an alcoholic."

"Not an alcoholic—just a really bad liar," Lauren said. She then squinted at her sister, examining her more closely. "*Are* you pregnant, Dawn?"

"The rate of miscarriage for women my age is a lot higher," she began, staring into her drink, evading their gazes. "My doc advises his higher-risk patients to hold off telling people at least until the second trimester but . . ." She suddenly looked up and grinned. "Yes, I'm pregnant!"

Lauren, Cynthia, and Stephanie all started screaming and jumping up and down, drawing a few stares.

"Please! Please keep it quiet for now," Dawn begged. "It's hard enough making Xavier keep his mouth shut. He'd tell the world if he found out I told you guys."

"When are you due?" Lauren asked.

"In December . . . if I make it that far."

"What do you mean if you make it that far?" Stephanie cried. "Of course, you will, girl! Stop being so pessimistic!"

"Well, when you're pregnant with twins, you don't always deliver at full term, so I—"

"*Twins?*" Cynthia gasped, wide-eyed.

Dawn nodded. "I know. I was shocked too. Oh, my God!" At that moment, Dawn looked almost faint. "What was I thinking letting Xavier talk me into this? *Twins!* And they'll be twenty-one when I'm like . . . what? Sixty!" She stared at her sisters. "I'm insane, aren't I? I'm completely insane."

Cynthia threw her arm around her sister's shoulder. "Nope, just dumb—and in love."

* * *

The party wound down just after midnight. Though the rain had stopped hours earlier, humidity still hung in the air as the bride and groom made their grand exit. Everyone assembled outside on opposite sides of the brick walkway with sparklers in their hands as Korey and Cynthia ran smiling to the waiting Rolls Royce that Crisanto had loaned them for their wedding. After Cynthia and Korey pulled off under the glow of the full moon and the sound of cheers, the rest of the throng started to depart.

Lauren found her husband, who was surrounded by several town residents who wanted to grab the ear of the new mayor of Chesterton.

"Sorry, folks," she said as she grabbed his hand and began to tug him away. "It's well past the little one's bedtime. We have to head home, but I'm sure he'll be more than happy to talk to all of you tomorrow morning at city hall."

Stephanie and Keith left soon after with Zoe slumbering on his shoulder and their youngest, Danica, passed out on hers. They absently waved good-bye before loading the kids into the car and driving back to their town house, which they had put on the market just last week. They were looking for a four- or five-bedroom house this time around.

"It'll give us room to grow," Keith had argued.

"Grow?" Stephanie had frowned. "Oh, no! I'm not getting pregnant again until I lose fifteen . . . no, twenty pounds! You're not making me into the Goodyear Blimp!"

"You're never gonna be the Goodyear Blimp, baby. And even if you were, you're a gorgeous, intelligent woman. I wouldn't care."

"Awww, thank you, honey!" she had whispered before kissing him.

Dawn and Xavier were the last stragglers, though, truth be told, she was exhausted by the time they left. The pregnancy was already taking its toll. Her energy level was at an all-time low, and she tired so easily now. Xavier could see how worn-out she was and actually tried to carry her out of the tent—to her great embarrassment. She slapped his shoulder and told him she could make it, but he only let her walk once he had wrapped a protective arm around her waist. He kept patting her stomach absently.

"I told my sisters," she confessed as they drove back to his condo, unable to keep her secret any longer.

"You told them what?"

"About the babies."

"You told them you were pregnant?" he shouted, making her wince. "Oh, now it's on! I'm telling everybody! My mom! The staff at the community center! I'm having a billboard printed!" he exclaimed.

She laughed.

Ten minutes later, Yolanda walked out of the reception alone. It had been one of the few times when the matriarch did not bring a date to a social event, but tonight she hadn't wanted to share her focus on her daughter's wedding with some man. As she waited for the valet to bring around her car, she shook her head. She had tried so hard to teach her daughters the Gibbons family ways, the rules of gold digging. They had followed her guidance for a while. Some of the girls had done it longer than most, but, with time, all had taken their own path.

Even my Cynthia, she thought sadly, which still shocked her.

She had failed with all of them.

But, she thought, *there's still the next generation.*

Clarissa may be with Jared now, but that didn't mean she was entirely a lost cause. There were also little Zoe and Danica, and who knew how many more grand-daughters the girls might have one day. Who knows how many she could one day train!

Or maybe I could take it beyond the family, Yolanda thought, her eyes widening. Maybe she could start her own training program, write a book, or make an instructional DVD!

"Miss Gibbons's Rules of Gold Digging," Yolanda whispered. She liked the sound of that!

"Your car, ma'am," the valet said, handing the keys to her, holding open the door to her Mercedes.

"Why, thank you, young man!" She grinned and climbed inside. The wheels were now turning in her head at full speed.

Secrets and scandals are a way of life for the
Murdochs of Chesterton, Virginia. But the lies that
bind them may end up tearing them apart . . .

Don't miss Shelly Ellis's latest book in the
Chesterton Scandals series,

Bed of Lies

On sale now!

Chapter 1

Terrence

"**Y**eah! That's what I'm talking about, baby!" Terrence Murdoch yelled over the heavy bass before tossing one-hundred-dollar bills into the air and letting them fall like confetti. The cute brunette in front of him showed her appreciation by doing a split on the stage, clad in only a smile and a bright yellow G-string that glowed under the blue-hued stage lights. Two other strippers danced beside her in clear platform stilettos, gyrating and swinging around each pole as Terrence and his friends hooted and yelled with delight in the VIP section of the club.

Terrence didn't know where to look first. It was a delectable sampling of full breasts, round thighs, and pert behinds. He just wanted to dive in and bask in all the womanly beauty.

He raised his beer bottle and toasted the sexy performance. "I've died and gone to heaven!" he cried.

He then turned to his older brother, Evan, who had hung back from the stage and chose to stay at the table behind them. "Ain't they beautiful, man?"

When he saw what Evan was doing, his grin disappeared. He slammed his bottle back to the table in outrage. "Ev, what the . . . what the fuck? Are you kidding me?"

Instead of admiring the strippers, Evan had been peering down at his BlackBerry under the flashing strobe lights. At Terrence's cry of outrage, the company CEO glanced up from his phone screen.

"Huh?" Evan asked absently. "Oh yeah, it's great, Terry." He began to type on the phone keys again.

"Ev, put that damn phone down and look at this, man!"

"I'll be right with you. Just let me finish this e-mail," Evan said, still furiously typing. "Got to get this out tonight. They're in a different time zone."

Terrence reached over and yanked the BlackBerry out of Evan's hand, catching his brother by surprise.

"No, look at it now! How can you be doing business when you have this in front of your face?" he asked, jabbing toward the stage.

One of the women dropped to her knees before turning her ass toward the men huddled around her. She did a twerk that made the men holler for more. Another stripper hopped up on a pole and twirled around and around, letting her blond curls dangle inches above the ground.

"I mean . . . come on!" Terrence turned back to look at his brother with a grin that was so wide it could barely be contained on his face. "Look at this!"

Evan gazed at the two strippers, inclined his head, and nodded. "Nice," he said thoughtfully, like he was considering a new pair of shoes.

"Nice?" Terrence comically looked at the women onstage, whipped his head to glare at his brother, then stared at the women on the stage again. "What the hell do you mean, 'Nice'?" He jabbed his index finger at the strippers. "Those women are fuckin' perfect, Ev!"

Evan emphatically shook his head and smiled as he reached into his jacket pocket and whipped out another cell phone. He dragged his index finger across the screen, scrolling through a series of photos. "No, *this* is perfect."

He held the glass screen toward Terrence. Terrence squinted under the club lighting to see what his brother was showing him. It was a photo of Evan's fiancée, Leila. She was wearing a tank top and yoga pants and rolling her eyes as Evan took the picture, like she had wanted anything but to be photographed at that moment.

Terrence had to admit that his future sister-in-law was one gorgeous woman. And Evan had been pining after her for years—hell, *decades!* He had been secretly in love with her since he was nine years old. In Evan's mind, Leila Hawkins had probably reached almost mythical proportions in beauty, brains, and loveliness.

But still, how could a man ignore what was right in front of his face? It destroyed the whole purpose of Evan being here at the strip club if he sat toward the back of the room, fiddling on his BlackBerry.

Terrence had invited Evan out with his friends for a night of drinking and debauchery to give Evan a long-needed break. His older brother was a consummate workaholic, and now when he wasn't working, he was almost plastered to the side of his new fiancée. Terrence had wanted his big bro to have some fun. But

Evan looked like he would be more entertained if he was sitting at his desk going over contracts and sales figures at Murdoch Conglomerated, where he was CEO. Or maybe he'd rather be sitting beside Leila, staring at tablecloth swatches for their wedding reception.

"Are you telling me you aren't just a *little* bit interested in looking at those titties?" Terrence pleaded. He once again pointed to the stage. "Not just a little?"

Evan burst into laughter. "I'm sorry, Terry, but from here they look like average breasts to me. But you know what? Go ahead and enjoy yourself. Don't let me ruin your fun." He yanked his BlackBerry out of Terrence's hand. "But if you don't mind, I'll take this back."

Terrence slowly shook his head in bemusement as he watched his brother sit down in one of the leather club chairs and start scanning through his e-mails again.

Operation: Get Evan Turnt Up was going down-hill—*fast*.

Terrence glanced at the drink Evan was now sipping: a Shirley Temple. He could try to ply Evan with alcohol to make him loosen up, but he knew that wouldn't work. Evan didn't drink thanks to his alcoholic wife, Charisse. Her drunkenness had been part of the reason they were now getting a divorce—that and the fact that she had been cheating on Evan.

Nope, getting him drunk is out of the question, Terrence thought.

An idea suddenly popped into Terrence's head. A wicked smile crossed his full lips.

"Well, if they just look like average titties from here, I guess you're going to have to see them up close."

Evan frowned quizzically as he lowered his glass back to the marble tabletop and looked up from his e-mail. "I'm sorry . . . what?"

Terrence suddenly turned on his heel, marched toward the stage, and shoved a group of his friends aside so that he was front and center.

"Ladies!" he shouted as he whipped out a series of hundred-dollar bills, spread them into a fan and brandished them in the air. "My brother would like a lap dance. *Now!* A grand to the first woman who does it."

The three strippers paused mid-routine. One almost fell off her pole. Another scrambled off her knees. The three women ran off the stage and came barreling toward Evan, whose mouth was agape. One looked like she nearly twisted her ankle trying to make her way down the short staircase.

"No!" Evan said, holding up his hands in protest and furiously shaking his head. "Really, ladies, I'm fine. I don't . . . I don't want a lap dance!"

Terrence cackled as he watched the strippers shove and elbow-check each other to get to Evan first. The blonde turned out to be the victor and promptly fell onto Evan's lap and started gyrating for all her worth.

"Terry!" Evan yelled, trying his best to rise out of his chair without touching the half-naked women who were huddled around and over him. "Terry!"

"Enjoy it, Ev!" Terrence grabbed his beer and held it up before tossing the hundreds in his hand into the air and taking a swig. "You deserve it!"

"Hey, you forgot this," Terrence said as he handed Evan his suit jacket.

The two men walked out of the strip club almost

two hours later into the chilly February night. A few of Terrence's friends trailed behind them, laughing and joking with one another.

"I didn't forget it," Evan mumbled as he tossed the suit jacket over his forearm. "It was *stolen* from me."

Terrence chuckled.

One of the strippers had ripped off Evan's suit jacket as soon as they had descended on him like a herd of locusts. His necktie had been removed, too, when one of the other strippers used it to bind his hands behind his back when he kept struggling. Another had smothered his verbal protests by shaking her double-Ds in his face.

"Come on! Admit it!" Terrence prodded, looping an arm around Evan's neck in brotherly affection. "You had fun, didn't you?"

"It was . . . interesting," Evan said just as one of the guys behind them leaned over and vomited on the walkway not too far from the club's red carpet.

"Oh, hell no!" the burly bouncer boomed, hopping off of his stool in front of the door. "Y'all better get his ass outta here!" he ordered, making one of the guy's companions nod and grab his sick friend around the shoulders. Another helped guide him toward a car that was parked at the end of the block.

Evan and Terrence shook their heads in disgust as they watched the trio walk off.

"Is your friend gonna make it?" Evan asked.

Terrence waved his hand dismissively. "He'll be fine. One of them will get his sorry ass back home tonight. I don't know what his wife will think when she sees him like that, though, but"—Terrence shrugged— "that's his problem."

Evan narrowed his eyes at Terrence. "You had plenty to drink yourself. Are you going to be okay driving back to your place?"

"Me?" Terrence pointed at his chest and laughed. He had a slight buzz, but that was about it. He could remember being in far worse states than he was now. "Man, please! I am far from drunk. Trust me. I'll be fine."

"You sure about that?" Evan asked again, just as a black Lincoln Town Car pulled up to the curb. Evan's driver climbed out, quickly walked to the rear door, and held it open for him. Evan paused before climbing onto the leather seat. "I could give you a ride, you know."

Terrence waved him away again as he started to walk in the opposite direction in search of his Porsche. "I'll be fine, Miss Daisy. Just give Lee a kiss for me. All right?"

"Oh, I most certainly will," Evan said with a wink before climbing into the sedan. The driver shut the door behind him.

Terrence turned and walked down the block back to his car. He raised the collar of his wool coat to block out the chill and rubbed his hands together to warm them. He bet Evan would give Leila a kiss as soon as he got home. Thanks to the erotic performance the men had witnessed tonight, he bet Evan would give her a lot more than that.

After a few minutes, Terrence spotted his silver Porsche two-seater and he breathed a sigh of relief.

"There's my baby," he whispered, almost with reverence.

The strip club hadn't had valet parking and he had been loath to leave her parallel-parked along the curb in this neighborhood, but he had had no other choice.

Terrence inspected his car with a careful eye and whispered a prayer of thanks when he saw no dents or scratches. The paint on his Porsche still glistened and the rims still sparkled from the wash, waxing, and buffing the car had gotten earlier that day.

If the love of Evan's life was Leila Hawkins, then the love of Terrence's life was certainly his 2015 Porsche 911 S Coupé. A close second was maybe the De'Longhi ESAM6700 Gran Dama Avant Touch-Screen Super-Automatic Espresso Machine on the granite kitchen countertop back at his condo in Chesterton, Virginia. If he could be buried with that thing, he would.

Terrence didn't have a love of the female variety and he had no desire to fall in love with anyone. Oh, he was no monk; he dated often. He had his fair share of girlfriends and one-night stands. But so far, no woman had made him want to "put a ring on it," so to speak. Terrence had seen the ravages married life could have on a person by witnessing his parents' horrendous marriage for decades and the trials Evan had gone through for the five and half years he was married to his soon-to-be ex, Charisse.

Though Evan often encouraged him to finally settle down, Terrence couldn't work up enough optimism about love and relationships to try his hand at anything permanent with a woman. He'd rather live in the moment and collect honeys like they were Pokémon trading cards.

He opened the door of his Porsche and climbed inside. As he drove, he listened to the voice messages on his iPhone. Unlike Evan, he had turned off his cell while inside the club, not wanting to be disturbed.

"Hey, Terry," a female voice cooed over the phone's speaker as Terrence merged onto a roadway, "it's

Asia. I've texted you three times today, baby! Where are you? I was hoping we could meet up this weekend. Give me a call back when you get this. I miss your fine ass. Byeeeeee!"

Asia was a waitress at a Cuban restaurant downtown. She had full lips, big thighs, and a beautiful smile, but lately, she had become kind of clingy. Terrence wondered if he should call her back or cut her loose.

"Bonsoir, mon ami!" Terrence heard next, instantly making him smile. *"Ça va?"*

He knew that throaty purr from anywhere. It was Georgette, a blond Victoria's Secret model based out of Montreal whom he had met back during his modeling days. He loved Georgette because of her good taste in food and wine, her French accent, and because she understood the true definition of "no strings attached" sex. They had been hooking up off and on for the past six years.

"I will be in the city for a few weeks," Georgette continued. "Let me know if you wish to meet, huh? I packed the lace teddy you like and the . . . you know . . . the stuff that you lick . . . *qu'est-ce que c'est?* Ah, who cares! I show you, Terry! *Je te veux!* Can't wait to see you, *mon ami. Au revoir!*" He heard kissing sounds and then the line clicked.

Oh hell, yeah, he thought.

He would call her back as soon as he got home. He would check her schedule and make reservations at their favorite spot. After dinner, he'd take her back to his place and they would try out "the stuff that you lick."

"Terry!" a voice suddenly screeched from his iPhone, snatching him out of his sexual reverie and making him wince. "Terry, you know who this is. Don't play like you don't! I saw you with that chick yesterday. Yeah, she was all up on you. Is she your new girl now? How dare you dump me like I was yesterday's trash, you son of a—"

Terrence reached over the armrest and immediately pressed a button on the phone's glass screen to delete the message.

Oh, Monique, he thought with exasperation.

Now, that was a girl who *definitely* did not understand the definition of "no strings attached" sex. Monique Washington had given off alarm bells the moment he had met her—she had been high-maintenance, constantly had checked her reflection in mirrors, and had wanted to talk endlessly about trips to Europe and trust funds. But he had pushed his misgivings about her aside. So what if she was a little shallow? He wasn't a deep man himself. And besides, she was good in bed and when he had told her that he wasn't ready for a real relationship, she had seemed okay with his revelation. But he should have trusted his first instincts. She had turned out to be a real nutcase. She went past clingy and straight to *Fatal Attraction*, showing up at his condo at all times of the day, threatening other women that he was dating. When he had tried to shake off Monique, she started blowing up his phone, leaving pissed-off and threatening messages.

He wouldn't make that mistake again. If he sensed that a woman wasn't up to staying at a distance, then he wouldn't bother to start anything with her. For now, he would just have to block Monique's number.

"On to the next one," Terrence murmured as he pulled to a stop at a stop sign.

"Hey! Heeeeeeey!"

Terrence frowned and turned to find two women

smiling and waving at him on the sidewalk. Despite the temps being in the low thirties, both women were wearing short skirts and flimsy shawls. One had flowing dark hair. The other looked like she was wearing an auburn wig. They both seemed to be heading home from a hard night of partying.

"Hey, cutie!" the dark-haired one yelled, motioning wildly for him to lower his car window.

Terrence obliged.

"Evening, ladies," he said in his smoothest Billy Dee Williams voice.

They ran toward his Porsche—or more like stumbled—holding onto each other for balance. "Is that your car, baby?" the auburn-haired one slurred, leaning on her friend.

Terrence inclined his head. "I'm driving it, aren't I?"

"Where you headed?" the other asked eagerly, sticking out her chest.

"Home," he answered.

The dark-haired one licked her red lips and smiled. "Well, it looks like we're headed there, too."

"Home with me?" He raised his brows.

The two women nodded in unison. "Yeah! Let us in!" the auburn-wigged one shouted before groping for the passenger door handle and missing it by several inches. She fell back onto the sidewalk instead and landed on her rear, making her wig shift askew. Her friend burst into laughter.

Terrence shook his head. "I'm afraid not, ladies. But get home safely, okay?"

Terrence waved at the comedic duo and floored the accelerator, unaware of the Mitsubishi Galant that was simultaneously plowing through the four-way stop in the opposite direction. It hadn't paused or stopped.

"Hey! Watch out!" one of the girls shouted.

Terrence turned in just enough time to see the bright headlights of the Mitsubishi coming toward him, but not in enough time to brake before the two cars collided.

Tires squealed. Metal crunched. Glass shattered in all directions. That's when the two women began to scream.